CW01668159

THEIR FINAL MOMENTS

An addictive crime thriller full of absolutely breathtaking twists

(Detective Mike Croft Book 3)

JANE ADAMS

Part One first published as "Fade to Grey" in 1998
Part Two first published as "Final Frame" in 1999

JOFFE BOOKS

Revised edition 2019
Joffe Books, London
www.joffebooks.com

Part One first published as "Fade to Grey" in 1998
Part Two first published as "Final Frame" in 1999

We hate typos too but sometimes they slip through.
Please send any errors you find to
corrections@joffebooks.com
We'll get them fixed ASAP. We're very grateful to eagle-eyed readers who take the time to contact us.

ISBN: 978-1-78931-104-4

DEDICATION

For Kerry. Blessings.

PART ONE

1998

town with it, that was elsewhere. Already distributed on the multimedia wave.

No, it wasn't the content that made this little package rare, but the scarcity of the commodity.

There would be no more centrefolds of this little lady. Not unless, of course, you liked your meat well done . . .

CHAPTER ONE

Thursday, 15 December
Norwich 6.05 p.m.

Stacey hesitated before squeezing through the gap next to the park gates. It was dark in there but it was also the quickest way of getting home. Besides, turning around and walking back the way she'd come would mean running into Richard again and she just knew he'd be standing around, waiting for her to come back to him. Well, sod that! Stacey wasn't going to apologize for anything. Let him stew for a while.

Once inside the park she stopped and groped in her bag for the little penlight torch she had attached to her key-ring. The thin beam of light showed her only a few yards of the muddy path before it was swallowed by the thick darkness. She slid her finger through the ring, posting the key in between her fingers the way that guy in the self-defence class had told them to. Nervous now, her mind niggling about those reports in the papers.

Maybe after all she should go back and find Richard. Not apologize exactly, just open the discussion enough for him to give her a ride home.

She glanced back over her shoulder one more time, startled by what sounded like a footstep.

'Richard? Is that you?' No reply. 'Richard. Oh for Christ's sake, if that's you . . .'

She shone the torch back through the wrought-iron gates but could see nothing, no one at all walking along the lonely street.

Stacey moved swiftly down what she could see of the slimy, leaf-covered path. The silence seemed to close in all around her, only the heels of her boots clacking with a reassuringly steady beat as she walked and the jingle of loose change in her pocket breaking the quiet.

Stacey shivered. It had begun to rain and the air was damp and clammy against her skin. Thinking she would be driven home, she had worn her denim jacket and left her umbrella on the table in the hall. She quickened her pace now as the rain fell more heavily.

And then it happened, footsteps, the sound of someone running making her look back. Richard's name half spoken before one hand was clamped around her mouth and a second hand grabbing at her breasts, the man's body pressed tight against her back. Then he shifted sideways and she was on the floor even before she realized that she was falling. The hand gone from her mouth now, Stacey screamed in fear, then in pain as the fist came crashing down at the side of her head.

Only half-conscious, she still tried to wriggle away from him. Felt the sudden chill of air on her legs and stomach as he wrenched her skirt up above her waist. Hard fingers bruising as they grabbed between her legs.

Stacey tried to scream again, but he was on top of her, his body heavy on her chest and his breath hot in her face. He was saying something but Stacey was too stunned to understand the words.

The torch, the keys, somehow she had managed to keep hold of them, the ring still tight around her finger.

She brought her right hand up, striking into the man's face. Her left hand reaching and grabbing at his hair, winding her fingers tight and pulling as hard as she could. Adrenalin and fear had overcome the pain of her bruised and bleeding head and half-closed eye.

The man was yelling now, loosening his grip on her just for an instant. Stacey hit out at him again, fighting for her life as he came back at her, his hands tightening on her throat.

Norwich 7 p.m.

Mike sat uneasily between Maria and her sister Josie, watching as three wise men, bearing gold-wrapped boxes, slow-marched across the stage. Enthusiastic music, played on a slightly off-key piano, helped to keep them in time, left feet, right feet, lifted in unison like an odd, dissociated caterpillar making its way towards the manger.

He tried desperately not to fidget. The hard plastic of the chair was digging into his back and there was no room to stretch out his long legs. A tall man who liked space to move around, Mike felt over-large and over conspicuous wedged in between proud parents and grandparents. His body cramped and his mind overwhelmed by remembrance of another time when his son Stevie had been one of the three kings. Wearing his father's old plaid dressing-gown and holding his gift high as he presented it to the little girl cuddling the baby doll.

'Doesn't she look lovely?'

It was Maria, smiling happily at her niece. Little Essie was grinning so much she almost forgot her words. Her thick black hair, braided tightly and threaded with blue and yellow beads, swung around her face as she strutted forward with her arms outstretched to take the presents from the kings. Mike didn't have to look sideways to know that Josie dabbed at tears watching her little girl up on the stage.

He tried hard to smile, knowing he should feel grateful to be included in such a family time, but it brought back so many morbid thoughts; since Stevie had died, he'd always found it hard to cope with this pre-Christmas rush of emotion.

The angels were just about to break into a new song when the beeping started, breaking into the giggling hush of children too small to be really quiet. Mike grabbed at his pocket to silence it, aware of Maria's glare as he peeked a look at the number on the LCD screen. He unfolded himself awkwardly from the little plastic chair, trying hard not to catch her eye as he headed for the door, apologizing as he went and horribly conscious of every inch of his six-foot-two frame.

Maria caught up with him at the outer door.

'I thought I told you to leave that bloody thing behind.'

'Well, no, actually it was the phone you told me to leave behind . . .' He smiled sheepishly. 'It's work,' he said.

'Isn't it always?'

'Um, I need the car keys, the phone . . .'

She sighed in exasperation and dug into her pocket for the keys. 'You'd better take the car,' she said. 'I'll get a lift back with Josie.'

'Thanks.' He paused, wondering if he should risk a kiss goodbye. He reached out and caught her hand instead.

'I'm really sorry.'

'You're always really sorry.' Maria shook her head. 'God! Never get yourself involved with a policeman.'

He watched her as she stalked away, shoulders set, irritation flowing from every pore. This was the third time in as many already scarce evenings off that he'd been called away. He could understand her getting mad at him. Mike was relieved when she glanced back from the door, not quite smiling, but her expression softening enough to let him know he was off the hook . . . almost.

Then he got into the car, rummaged in the glove compartment for the phone and called the office. 'DI Mike Croft.' He listened in silence as they told him about the latest attack.

'They've taken her to the Royal and District, Mike. Price is interviewing the boyfriend.'

'Is she badly hurt?'

'Bruising, shock. They'll be keeping her overnight though. You'll want to speak to the boyfriend?'

Mike signed off and turned the ignition key, listening to the low purr of the engine for a moment or two before pulling away. His mind already cataloguing the new information, he turned the car towards the hospital.

CHAPTER TWO

West Kennet, Wiltshire 7 p.m.

The light drizzle had begun when the old man left the house, walking the dogs out of Avebury village and across on the straight route to the Devizes road. It was already dark, and the mist and rain cut visibility even further. To his left the ridge of West Kennet long barrow rose from the downs, and the cone of Silbury Hill loomed out of the mist in front of him. He could barely make out either familiar landmark through the dark and rain that fell more determinedly minute by minute. And it was turning uncomfortably cold. He decided that he and the dogs were getting too old to be traipsing about in this kind of weather. That he should cut the evening walk short and head for home.

As he turned, a red glow caught his eye. He peered through the grey murk trying to make sense of it and as he did the redness grew larger flowering more brightly against the backdrop of grey.

'What the . . .' He took a few steps across the road and started along the path that led up the ridge towards the barrow. The blaze had full hold now and as he drew closer he realized that what he was seeing was a car, flames and thick black smoke billowing out of a part-open window.

'Bloody joy-riders.' He watched enough television to know the latest trends in crime.

But he was curious about the car and, thinking about it, more than a little confused. Surely if joy-riders had set the vehicle alight he should have seen them running away. Seen something, even through the filthy rain doing its best to penetrate his topcoat. It would have made most sense for them to have run back towards the road, towards him and the dogs and away from the fire. Go the other way and they'd have to scramble over fences into the fields beyond.

Leaning heavily on his stick, not certain whether he should beat a hasty retreat — who could tell what kind of young hooligan stole cars and then set fire to them? — or go further up the track and see if he could make out which way the miscreants had run, the old man took a few hesitant steps forward. He circled wide of the burning car, knowing that the petrol tank could blow at any time.

'Oh my sweet Lord,' he whispered, 'Oh my Lord,' as the black plumes of smoke parted just for an instant and he could see through the open window a slumped figure in the driver's seat of the blazing car.

CHAPTER THREE

Hoton, Norwich 8.15 p.m.

John Tynan sipped his tea and stared absently at the television set. He often wondered why he watched television police dramas. They were usually so far removed from anything he'd ever been involved with while he was on the force, and their ignorance of procedure often made him cringe. Still, he enjoyed them all the same.

This was better than most, he thought. Good characters, so he could forgive the inaccuracy. And he was pretty certain he knew who'd done it.

Tynan leaned forward to get himself more tea, watching the screen as he eased the blue and yellow knitted cosy from the brown pot, following the two major characters as they poked around in the aftermath of a house fire.

'Damn and blast!' The insistent ringing of the doorbell broke across his concentration. 'Who the hell . . . at this time of night?'

Reluctantly, John Tynan made his way across the overcrowded little room and out into the hall, wrenching the front door open with an impatient tug.

'Hello, John.'

'Maria!' He stared in surprise at the tall black woman standing on his doorstep. 'Come in, come in.'

Maria turned to wave her hand towards a waiting car, then stepped into Tynan's hallway. 'Oh, but it's cold out there. Josie just dropped me off,' she said, explaining the car. 'I had to let Mike take my car, only realized after he'd gone that his flat key was on the ring and it's too far to get back to Oaklands tonight.' She turned to kiss John swiftly on the cheek. 'Hope you don't mind?'

'Mind? No. Welcome as spring, my dear. But hurry in, I'm watching that police thing on TV and he's just about to get it all wrong again.'

Maria laughed and followed John through to the living-room, unbuttoning her coat and unknotting the green silk scarf she wore at her throat.

'Are you cold? Pull the chair close to the fire, that's it.' John took her coat and laid it on the ottoman that stood near the window, then resumed his place on the two-seater sofa. 'I'll make you some tea in a minute.'

'No hurry, John.' She nodded towards the television. 'Know who did it yet?'

'I'll put money on the husband.' He smiled across at her. 'Mike get called in again?'

'That's right. It's getting to be normal. I don't know, but my guess is it's another assault.'

John nodded in agreement, glancing back at the television to keep up with the plot. 'They seem to be getting nowhere about as fast as this lot do,' he said.

Maria stretched, then got up again. 'Mind if I use your phone?' she asked. 'I'd better leave him a message. Tell him where I am or he'll think I'm really mad with him.'

'Well, help yourself, my dear. I'll see about getting some more tea.'

9 p.m.

Mike had spent only a short time at the hospital. Stacey had been able to tell him very little. Concussion and shock, her doctor had said. It would be better to try again in the morning. Mike had agreed. Stacey's mother had arrived by the time he'd left; the parents had been out at a party and it had taken a bit of time to find them. They'd been horrified, devastated that this had happened to their child. At first furious with Stacey's boyfriend, for letting her storm off alone, then, in the same breath, grateful that he'd decided to follow and had saved their daughter.

The front office was empty but for the desk sergeant who buzzed him through. Mike mooched towards his own office, wondering what Maria was doing and if she'd recovered her good mood yet. Used to being on call herself, she was tolerant of the strange hours he often kept but just lately the interruptions had seemed constant.

Sergeant Price was already there, seated behind Mike's desk and sorting through some papers. He looked up with a quick smile as Mike came in.

'Oh, hello there, guv. It's not typed up yet, but I thought you'd want a look first thing. By the way, Maria phoned. Said she's at John Tynan's. Apparently you took her keys.'

'Blast it.' Mike felt in his pocket. 'One more thing wrong tonight.'

He plonked himself down in the chair opposite, eyeing the paperwork Price had been shuffling. 'What's that?'

'Statement of one Richard Mattheson. Boyfriend of Stacey Holmes, the girl who was attacked.'

'Oh. I've just come from the hospital. Big waste of time that was. Too shocked and too well sedated to get anywhere tonight.'

'I've sent the boyfriend back to the hospital.'

'Oh, so he's already gone?' Mike was a little put out. 'I came in intending to talk to him.'

'Sorry, guv, but he'd already made a full statement and he wanted to get back to his girl. We dragged him over here while forensics did their bit, but it didn't seem right to hang on to him longer than we had to.'

Mike sighed. It had been a wasted evening all round, it seemed. He suddenly felt surplus to requirements and bitter about having lost time with Maria to no purpose. 'The boyfriend. What did he have to say?'

'Briefly, that she'd stormed off after a silly argument. He'd let her stew for a while then followed her.' Price smiled tightly. 'Seems she's the fiery type. He generally gives her a bit of cooling off time before he tries to make peace. Anyway, he got concerned and went after her. Followed her and realized when he reached that dead end near the park gates that she must've gone through. Just gets over the gate and he hears her screaming. The bastard's on top of her by the time lover-boy arrives and drags him off, and of course he's too busy comforting the girl to go chasing after her attacker. Just knows he ran off towards the main path.'

'How long before our people were on the scene?'

'Less than seven minutes. We beat the ambulance. The boyfriend had a mobile, called it straight in. No sign though. It's pitch black in the park that time of night.' Mike nodded thoughtfully and skimmed through the written statement. 'She fought back?' he asked, picking up on the one thing Price hadn't mentioned.

'Yeah.' The sergeant sounded chuffed at the thought. 'Like the boyfriend said, she's got a temper. She'd got her keys in her hand and hit the bastard at the side of the face with the sharp end. Pity she didn't take his eye out. As it is, he'll hopefully have nice, visible scratches to remember her by. We've told the press office to make a big thing of that. Might shake a few trees.'

Mike nodded. Anything new would be welcome just now, though it was just as likely to result in the exposure of anyone who'd cut themselves shaving that morning.

'Right then,' he said, getting wearily to his feet once more. 'Nothing more to be done tonight.' He paused at the door. 'Eight thirty at the hospital. They should have breakfast over by then.' He grinned wryly, remembering his own recent stay. He'd returned to full duty only two weeks before and been landed with a serial rapist.

'Sick leave,' Superintendent Flint had told him ironically. 'DI Pike's been handling it but he's off with a hernia. Caseload too heavy for him, no doubt. So I've put it in your in-tray. Time for a fresh eye.'

Making his way down the stairs to the front office, Mike wondered vaguely why he always managed to get landed with the messy ones.

CHAPTER FOUR

Friday, 16 December, 2 a.m.

Jake had been waiting for close on an hour. He was good at waiting, patient that way. What he needed now was a little luck. The right person to come out and to do it soon before the crowd started to leave en masse. It was always a gamble, when Jake was asked to make something to order like this. However much forward planning he did there was also an element of luck in casting the right person for the role and, sometimes, luck wasn't available for hire. Jake figured he had maybe another fifteen minutes of clear time; after that, the game would not be worth the risk. There would be other nights.

The street was off the main drag; there was little passing trade not headed for the club. By two in the morning even the doormen had retreated inside. Usually, by that time, more people had already been crammed inside than would upset the local fire chief. After that, the doors opened at intervals only to let people out.

That suited Jake. Standing in the shadows, he could see with little risk of being seen and those that occasionally emerged were far too drunk or otherwise involved to take notice.

Jake was about to give up when the right one came out. First, two young men, arms thrown about each other, sailing through the door on a raft of music. The one Jake wanted was with them. His blond hair brassy in the street-light, tight shirt and jeans accentuating a lithe body. He stood almost still, pulling on a leather jacket, shivering against the sudden cold.

He was perfect, Jake thought, just perfect.

Jake waited as the three of them went through their farewells, the small ritual, exaggerated by alcohol becoming stumbling pantomime. Jake could hear their laughter from where he stood across the street, invisible and silent until the couple finally helped each other stagger on their way and the one he wanted wandered on alone down the empty street.

Jake waited a little longer, knowing there was no hurry. The sound of the young man's uneven footsteps were audible even when he turned the corner into a side road. Jake followed then, not wanting to be too far from his car. His rubber-soled shoes made little sound on the wet path and he moved without hurrying, not troubling to hide himself now. Anyone looking would just see a man walking as though he had somewhere to go, he wouldn't even get a second look.

Turning the corner, Jake saw the one he wanted right ahead. He was making slow progress, his steps meandering, body swaying slightly as though he had forgotten that he'd left the club and could still hear music. Deliberately, Jake crossed the road, not following now, but seeking to draw level, then a little ahead. His target saw him, glancing his way briefly but seeing only a man who'd stopped and was searching through his pockets to find a cigarette. Glancing across the street, Jake put the cigarette between his lips and patted at his pockets, frowning a little. Then he crossed the road.

'Scuse me, mate, you haven't got a light, have you?'

'Sorry, I don't smoke,' the man shrugged. His words were slightly slurred, then he swayed backwards slightly, taking a step to steady himself. He pointed. 'There's a little shop round there somewhere. Always open. Bet they'd have some.'

'Right, thanks.' Jake took the cigarette from between his lips and put a hand in his coat as though to find the pack. The younger man began to turn away but Jake had fired the Taser before he took another step, and he fell down, gasping, trying to cry out, as 25,000 volts surged through his system, the wire pinned to his body gleaming in the street-light. Then Jake had the hypodermic in his hand and plunged it into his victim's arm.

Bending, he hauled the young man to his feet and pulled a limp arm around his neck. The victim was just about conscious enough to move his feet as Jake half-dragged him along the road. His car was parked only a street away, and Jake didn't hurry; he slurred his footsteps and his speech, falling off the pavement and stumbling along in the gutter, enjoying the role even though there didn't seem to be anyone to hear.

Then he dumped the now unconscious body into the boot of his car and settled himself in the driver's seat. Jake was smiling as he drove away.

Norwich 2.15 a.m.

The silence of the sleeping house was soothing as he sat alone, television on, sound turned right down.

His face was sore where she'd caught him with the keys and his jaw ached from where the man had thumped him in the mouth.

The physical discomforts, though, they were nothing compared to the piercing anger at having been interrupted.

He had hung around the park afterwards, staying in the shadows just feet away from the police searchers storming their big-footed, cocky way down the narrow maze of paths.

One passing so close he could have reached out and tripped him. Watched him break his great fat face falling on to the concrete.

It gave him one hell of a buzz, that. Knowing he was so close and they knew nothing about it. Almost made up for what he'd lost. Almost . . .

Time for another letter, maybe, telling them just what great clumsy fools they'd been.

He'd been disappointed when they hadn't published his letters. Not even mentioned them in any of the reports that he had read or seen on the TV.

It did cause him a moment's worry, that they knew. Knew about him and about the other one. The one who'd started the whole game.

CHAPTER FIVE

5 a.m.

DCI Charlie Morrow sat at his desk in Devizes HQ with his back to the radiator, steaming gently. It was a filthy night. Charlie was soaked through despite his coat and there had been no sleep and bugger all to eat.

He glanced at the pictures in front of him. The first ones, processed in a hurry and rushed through to him only moments before.

The photographs made the crime scene look like a film set. The bright glare of the dragon lamps and the eerie flaring from the lights of the fire tender heightened contrast and detail. Blackness beyond the rough circle of light and activity, though even the darkness was in turn swallowed up by the mist rolling wetly across the downs.

What the photographs could not show was the cold misery of spending the best part of the night waiting for a bloody car to cool down enough for SOCO to get a proper look.

He pulled the photos of the body closer to him and stared hard at the charred remains. Contorted legs and arms, blackened torso. The whole looking more like a lump of burned carpet than what had, a short time before, been a human being.

The growling of his stomach reminded Charlie that he was hungry. He was also dead tired and not in the best of humours. Impatiently he shoved the photographs into the folder and dumped it on top of the pile of telephone statements. Then he heaved his not inconsiderable bulk out of his chair and ambled towards the door.

The car was stolen, that much they knew; it had gone missing from its owner's drive two nights before. The owner had not been best pleased to find his pride and joy was now not only a burned-out wreck but had a badly fried body in the driver's seat. He'd been even less pleased to be woken at three in the morning to be apprised of the fact.

Charlie lifted his coat from the peg and shrugged into it, shivering slightly at the feel of damp clothes beneath. He really ought to go back and change before the morning's briefing. At least that would give Mickey's place a chance to open and he could fit breakfast in before the hired help arrived. Brightened by the fact that he'd solved at least one of the morning's problems, Charlie Morrow switched out the light and headed for home.

CHAPTER SIX

7.50 a.m.

'Will you need a lift back to town?' Maria asked.

Mike shook his head. 'Thanks, but no. Price is coming out to pick me up; the garage should have finished with my car by midday.'

'Why don't you just give in and part-ex it? Get something like mine.' Maria's new Mazda was her pride and joy.

'He wouldn't get part-ex on a roller skate, the state his old wreck's in,' John began.

'There's nothing wrong with my car . . .'

'That a can of petrol and a lighter wouldn't solve,' Maria put in swiftly. 'Seriously, Mike, it's about as reliable as a burnt match. This is the third time in a month you've had problems with it.'

'I know, I know, but it would be like trading in an old friend.'

'I hope when I get that decrepit you'll have sense enough to give me a decent burial,' John told him. 'You're heading straight to the hospital?' he continued, changing tack.

Mike nodded. 'Said we'd get there early to talk to the girl. And the initial forensics reports should be back this morning.'

A car horn sounded from the narrow road outside John's cottage. 'That'll be Price.' Mike bent to kiss Maria. 'I'll give you a ring.'

'I must be off too,' she said. 'I'll just give you a hand to tidy up, John. Then back to it, I guess. You're out tonight, aren't you? Your wife's old friend?'

'Yes, Theo Howard. You've got a busy day?'

She nodded. 'Full case load today and some private stuff tonight.' She grinned. 'Got to pay for the car somehow, you know.'

The cottage seemed very empty after Mike and Maria had gone. Tynan finished putting away the breakfast things and then wondered what to do with the rest of his morning.

A small Christmas tree stood in the hall, ready to be trimmed. First time he had bothered in years, since Grace had died in fact. Mike and Maria would be spending the holiday with him this year. Grace had loved this time of year. John was used to being busy and retirement had not come easily. There had been a time, while his wife Grace was alive, when the prospect of time at home without the pressures of police work had been a very attractive one. But Grace had died. Cancer taking her from him. Nothing had ever quite filled the gap.

Tynan wandered into the living-room and switched on the radio. It was still tuned to her favourite station. Tchaikovsky, one of the few composers he could actually recognize, flooded the room with richness. Impatiently, Tynan wiped the blurring of tears from his eyes.

8.00 a.m.

Cavendish Road in Norwich was a quiet street. Ordinary and suburban. A row of what had once been prosperous Victorian villas, complete with basements, lined one side of the road. They were now mostly divided into flats and bedsits. The other side, slightly later and more modest terraces, occupied for the most part by young couples buying their first home.

The street behind Cavendish Road, Sullivan Avenue, still retained its sense of grandeur. Tree-lined, habited by prosperous family houses, Edwardian semis with sweeping bay windows and cramped but well-paved driveways.

At the end of Cavendish Road itself stood a terraced block of five, divided from the rest by an alleyway. Their small rear yards backed on to the gardens of Sullivan Avenue. This was a neat, red brick row, each with a little forecourt, net curtains at the windows and a couple of steps leading up to the front door.

Theo Howard stood on the steps of the end one of these five, clasping her pink towelling robe tightly closed over her half-dressed body as she bent down to collect the morning's milk. Despite the robe, she looked neat and wide awake. Her thick grey hair was already combed and her make-up carefully applied to make the most of her large blue eyes.

She straightened up and took a moment to survey the street before turning back inside. Watching as the milk float trundled its noisy way around the corner. Waving briefly as her neighbour got into his car and left for work.

A few of the older children were already on their way to school, wandering towards the main road to catch their bus. She watched as the boy went by. His dark hair needed cutting again and his trainers, as usual, bore the traces of last night's football game. Theo almost lifted her hand to wave to him, but resisted at the last moment, knowing there would be no response. He was far too aloof to hope for that. Instead she smiled and, clutching the milk bottle with both hands, ducked back inside and closed the door.

Davy was already engrossed in the morning papers.

'More tea?'

'Thanks.'

A lock of dark hair had fallen forward across his forehead, reminding her of the boy, making Davy look even younger than he was. She flopped down in the chair opposite and reached out for the teapot. Sitting there, his mind absorbed by breakfast and the morning news, Theo could watch him at her leisure.

Admire the dark curls and the smooth, clean-shaven face. The way the muscles of his jaw dimpled and the brows creased as something in the paper caught his eye.

Theo shook her head, laughing inwardly at the butterfly feeling in her stomach that happened every time she looked at him. If only, she thought with a deep and wrenching sadness, these moments could go on for ever.

She gave herself a little shake and looked around for distraction from the melancholy that threatened, glancing instead at the headlines on the morning paper.

'Oh!' she exclaimed. 'Aston Park.'

'What?'

'The headlines on the paper,' she pointed them out. 'Another girl. Whatever is it all coming to?'

He nodded. 'You take care tonight. Get a taxi back from night school if you decide not to drive yourself.'

'Oh, I will, I will. Not that anyone's going to bother with an old thing like me.'

She caught Davy's smile from across the table. 'Fishing, Theo?' he asked. Then put the paper down and drained his tea. Even at fifty-two, they both knew that Theo could still turn heads.

'Got to go,' Davy said. 'Take care today. I mean it.' He came around to her side of the table and kissed her lightly on the cheek, avoiding her lipstick. Then gathered up his coat and briefcase, his mind already on the day ahead.

'What did you do to your face?' Theo asked him. 'You never did get around to telling me.'

'Oh,' he said, touching a finger lightly against his temple. 'Cupboard door at work. Some fool left it open.' She watched him go, finishing her tea, the pleasure brought by Davy's company dissipating as she thought of her own day.

Sighing, Theo got to her feet and took the pots over to the kitchen sink.

'Oh damn,' she said suddenly, looking out of the window to see if Davy's car had already gone. She'd meant to remind him to be home on time. John Tynan had telephoned the evening before and confirmed, after all, that he'd be coming to dinner.

She reached into the pocket of her robe. Inside was a folded piece of paper covered with neatly written words. It began: 'Right now; I do not need to be told truth.'

* * *

The boy with the unruly hair and dirty trainers hesitated at the corner of the road and stared, frowning towards Sullivan Avenue. His frown disappeared as the girl came racing around the corner. She stopped, catching her breath as she got to him and fell into step.

'God, I thought I was going to be late. Trying to get my homework finished. I've been up since six. You done yours?'

Terry shrugged. 'Got the maths done. English doesn't have to be in till tomorrow.' He scuffed his feet. 'I looked for you last night at the recce. Waited till nearly nine.'

'Yeah, I'm sorry,' Sarah told him. 'I did say I didn't think I could get out and my dad was fussing round, looking at my work and stuff. You know how he is.'

'Sure.' He fell silent for a moment, then brightened. 'Still on for Saturday?'

'Course it is. I'm going Christmas shopping with Maddie in the afternoon so I'll be getting changed at her place. We'll go to the party from there.'

'What have you told your parents?'

'That I'm going out with Maddie and the rest of the crowd. I mean it's not really a lie, is it? Most of them will be at the party.'

He shrugged, but said nothing. The bus was coming and they had to run to make it to the stop in time.

* * *

From the window of the flat Judith watched her son walk down the street and pause at the corner of the road.

Terry was old enough to get his own breakfast, but she got up and had coffee with him, needing some kind of kick to get her started on her day. She waited till he'd gone to have her first cigarette. She knew it was stupid, but somehow hated him to see her doing anything that she felt was slightly wrong. He'd had such a rough time, been away from her so long . . .

Sighing, Judith moved away from the window. She made herself a second cup of coffee, took it and her early morning cigarette into the bedroom and turned on the radio. She listened with half an ear to the morning news as she smoked her cigarette and sorted out her clothes for the day. A staff uniform for the local supermarket hung behind the door. Four nights a week, Judith spent three hours stacking shelves. Another five mornings she acted as receptionist for a wood merchant's across town. It was a family business, and the daughter-in-law took over in the afternoon when her kids went to nursery school. Judith was dreading them starting full-time, knowing it would probably mean the end of her job. Piss poor though the pay was, it was something. Family credit topped up a lousy wage and made sure she got help with paying rent on the two-bedroomed flat, so they managed. Just. Though she dreaded every new expense that came along.

She fished a dark skirt out of the wardrobe and went to fetch the iron, pausing by the bedroom door. Unhooking the uniform from the back of the door revealed a cheap, distorted mirror.

'My God, just look at yourself,' Judith muttered, leaning forward to examine the dark shadows beneath her eyes.

8.30 a.m.

Stacey was dressed and ready to leave. She sat beside the hospital bed in a high-backed chair. Her long blonde hair was drawn back from a pale bruised face, and the marks from the attack showed clearly on her throat.

Mike sat down on the bed. 'Hello, Stacey,' he said. 'I'm Detective Inspector Mike Croft. I was here last night.'

She looked at him and managed a weak half-smile. 'I don't really remember,' she said. Then, 'They say I can go soon. I'd like to go home if that's all right?'

He saw her swallow nervously and nodded. 'Of course. I'll keep this short. Is someone going to pick you up?'

'My mum and dad. They'll be here soon. Look, I told everyone everything I could last night, do I have to go through it all again?'

Mike shook his head. 'If you want me to go away and leave you alone, I will,' he said. 'If you want someone with you while you talk, then that's fine too.'

She stared at him for a moment, then took a deep breath and nodded her head. 'I'll be all right,' she told him. 'I'm sorry, it all happened so fast. I never thought I'd fight like that, but I just knew that I was going to die and every time I close my eyes I'm there again, with his hands round my throat and his breath on my face and . . . They gave me something to make me sleep last night and it was worse than if they hadn't. He kept chasing through my dreams, his hands all over me and I couldn't wake up enough to get away.'

'I'm sorry,' Mike said softly.

They both fell silent for a moment, Stacey biting her lip and staring at the floor. A nurse hovered discreetly in the background, folding the sheet corners of another bed and smoothing the covers.

Mike began again. 'Is there anything more you can remember, Stacey? Something really small maybe that came back to you?'

Still staring at the floor, she shook her head. 'No, nothing. I told them all I knew last night.'

Mike decided that he would get no further. He could see her parents walking down the ward, anxious looks creasing their faces.

'You've been given the numbers to call if you need anything or if there's anything you want to add?'

She nodded again. 'You're the one investigating?' she asked. 'It is you?'

'My boss, Superintendent Flint, he's the one in charge,' Mike told her. 'But . . .' he smiled.

'You'll be the one doing the work,' she finished for him, trying to smile properly this time.

Stacey's parents had reached the bed. Mike introduced himself again, but they remembered him from the night before.

'We can take her home now?' Stacey's mother asked. 'She'll be better off there.'

'Of course.' Then a thought struck him. 'Stacey, the man who attacked you. How did he smell? I mean, was he wearing aftershave, anything like that?'

She looked puzzled, frowned, really trying to think.

'No,' she said. 'No, I'm certain of it. He smelt kind of clean, if you know what I'm saying. Not over-scented or anything, just kind of soapy and clean.'

Price had waited for him in the corridor. When Mike got to him he was leaning against the wall, gazing out of the opposite window, a plastic cup of coffee in his hand and an expression of complete boredom on his face. He was trying to ignore the sound of Christmas carols drifting out of the children's ward.

He brightened when he saw Mike. 'She remember anything more, guv?'

Mike shook his head. 'She looks like the others, small and blonde.'

'She's the first one you've met, isn't she?'

'Yes, but I've had a good look at the pictures.'

They left the hospital and walked across to where they had parked the car. 'So, what do we have?'

'Six victims,' Price said. 'Age range fourteen to twenty-two, though the youngest was all made up to go on the pull and could have looked older and the eldest could easily have passed for seventeen. This one had her eighteenth birthday just last month. Make of that what you like.' He frowned. 'We've got an eighteen-month span timewise.'

'As far as we know.'

'As far as we know, and the attacks have been more violent as time's gone on. The fourth and fifth girls could have died.'

'So could this last,' Mike observed.

'True. But it seems to me he only got really vicious when she tried to fight him off. She hurt him, he retaliated.' He paused. 'Look at it the other way, mind, girl number four, Tracy Wilding, she didn't fight. She stayed passive, tried to keep him calm and got her head caved in for her trouble.'

They reached the car. Price slid into the driver's side and started the engine.

'No sign of him using a weapon this time,' Mike observed. The two previous victims had been hit with something hard and blunt-edged.

'Just his hands. No, but it's not the first time we've seen that. Tracy Wilding had choke marks round her neck, if you remember?'

Mike nodded. 'Then we've got two of the victims mentioning some kind of scent or aftershave. This one described him as clean and soapy.' He paused, picturing in his mind the street map pinned to his office wall and the six pins marking the places where the attacks had taken place. 'All open, public places,' he continued. 'Four parks, one common and one multi-storey car park. We know each time the attacker went some distance on foot, but there's nothing to say there wasn't a car parked close by, or that he hopped on a bus.'

'Not after attacking Tracy Wilding and Debbie Hall, he didn't. There'd have been too much blood.'

'OK, so it's likely he used a car. So he's fully mobile.'

He waited thoughtfully before continuing. 'So, what does he do? Cruise around looking for small, blue-eyed blondes or does he pick his victims first and wait for an opportunity?'

'Not very likely, guv. Way I see it, he gets the urge and goes hunting.'

'How many hunts before a strike? And if he doesn't find what he's looking for, what then?'

Price glanced at him. 'You reckon the more violent attacks came after a few failures?'

'I think it's possible, yes. And then, then we have the letters. IF they're genuine.'

'If they are, it could be the one thing we really have going for us. This need to show off, laugh in our faces.'

'He hasn't fallen over his ego so far,' Mike commented.

CHAPTER SEVEN

8.30 a.m.

DCI Charlie Morrow rubbed his hands together. 'Right, boys and girls, and what do we have on our fire this bright morning?'

'We totalled twenty-seven calls following the radio news this morning. Mostly missing persons. Two from drivers on the Devizes road last night, saw someone trying to hitch a lift.'

'Heading which way?'

'Back towards Malmesbury. About three or four miles from Kennet.'

'Description? Or is that too much to hope for?'

Sergeant Cooper shrugged. 'Male,' she said, 'average height, slim build.' She grinned. 'Apparently looked very wet.'

Morrow grunted what might have been a laugh. 'Well, he bloody would be, wouldn't he? What we have to hope is he looked wet enough for someone to take pity on him and pick him up.'

'We've got the same name coming in twice on the missing persons.' DC Stein had spoken this time. Morrow turned to fix the officer with his usual malevolent stare. 'And?'

'Well, sir . . .' The younger man was starting to blush, Morrow noted. 'Well, sir, it seems a bit odd, sir.'

'Well, sir, it seems a bit odd, sir,' Morrow mimicked viciously. 'Well, constable, maybe you'd like to do follow-up on that one.' He turned back to Sergeant Cooper who was eyeing him with open disapproval. 'Any "Mispers" we don't already have on our list, Beth?'

She nodded. 'Twelve, all from outside our area. Five of those known or thought to have been headed in this general direction. Usual mix, couple of New Age sorts travelling together. Teenager who had a holiday down here last year. Ran away from home and her parents are trying every direction. One mental patient, known to be suicidal. That one looks promising actually, sir; same age range, height and blood group as our victim. The fifth is a woman reported missing by her husband. Says she disappeared after a row and he knows she had relatives someplace hereabouts.' She paused. 'But he doesn't know where or what their names are.'

'Well, get on to his local plod station and tell them to go dig up his garden! Next?'

'The other Mispers are the usual "hoped-fors" I'd guess,' Beth Cooper continued unperturbed.

'Hoped-fors?' This from Stein, who was obviously trying hard to stand the Charlie Morrow test.

'Hoped-for result,' Morrow told him abruptly. 'Hell of a lot of folk out there would rather know for certain someone's dead and gone than spend the rest of their lives waiting for them to walk back through the front door.'

'But surely, sir . . .' Stein began and coloured red again.

'But surely, nothing,' Morrow told him. 'Now stop blushing like a frigging virgin and get some checking done. Start with that twice-reported Misper.' He glanced across at Beth Cooper once again. 'I take it she's one we've already got on our list.'

Beth nodded. 'Yeah, name of Marion O'Donnel. Funny thing though, the new report comes from a name we didn't have as a contact before. I checked.'

'Interesting,' Morrow said. 'Well, you'd better go along with Stein. Hold his hand for him while he talks to these newly concerned friends.'

'Sir.'

'Any questions?' He glanced around the room at the dozen or so people he had allocated to him. He looked from the assembled officers to the stack of paperwork on his desk, the lines of enquiry that needed following. Callers that needed talking to, names to be checked and dead ends to be weeded out. Not enough bloody resources, he thought grimly, as bloody usual.

'OK, back at sixteen hundred hours. Bear in mind if you please that the Chief Super's yelling for results and after my backside.' He paused, fixing Stein with his discomforting gaze once more. 'That's supposed to be incentive to succeed, blushing boy, not to let things slide.' There was brief laughter and Stein coloured again. Beth Cooper awarded Morrow a look that would have burned ice before guiding the embarrassed constable towards the door.

It was cruel, Morrow knew, but some people were just made to be wound up.

He watched them go, then crossed to the white board on which was pinned the photographic record of the case so far, staring hard at each of the stark and brutal images.

'Who are you?' Charlie Morrow asked the dead woman. 'And who hated you so much that you had to die that way?'

* * *

Stein looked uncomfortable out of uniform. He was one of those people, Beth found herself thinking, who was happiest when he had an appearance of authority to hide behind.

Their destination was a neat terrace in Devizes itself, not far from the brewery. Beth got out of the car and glanced up at the house. Weak sunlight was trying to battle through thick grey cloud. Light caught the edge of the open transom window in an upstairs room.

'Well, looks as though someone's in,' she said. 'Hopefully, they're up and dressed.'

They were. Moments later she and Stein were introducing themselves to two neat, grey-haired women — 'The Misses Thompson' — who examined their IDs before ushering them both inside.

'So she was a regular visitor?' Beth checked as she took her cup of tea from the low coffee table that occupied most of the centre of the room.

She was conscious that they had been shown, as potentially important visitors, into the front parlour. Tidy with disuse and slightly chill, until the fire had been on for several minutes.

'Regular? Yes, I suppose so, since she moved back this way. We'd always kept in touch, you see. One of my best students. It took a lot of persuasion to get her father to agree to university. I know it seems funny in this day and age, but he was an old-fashioned man and couldn't see the point of girls having that sort of education. Always argued that all they did was get married and have babies whatever you taught them, so why waste time?'

'But he agreed in the end.'

'Oh yes, and he was there — we both were — the day she graduated. Dear Lord, I thought the man would burst, he was that proud.' She shook her head, laughing. 'People can say what they like on a general level, you know, but when it's their own — oh well, that's very different.'

'She was Dolly's final year,' her sister put in. 'Dolly went back, you see, after she'd officially retired. Taught part-time for another seven years.'

Edith, the younger sister, sounded more than a little in awe.

'Oh, do give over, Edie dear,' her sister told her. 'I enjoyed every blessed minute of it. But yes, Marion was one of my last students.'

'Is this her, Miss Thompson?' DC Stein was asking. He'd got up and was examining a graduation picture of a pretty, curly-haired girl dressed in gown and mortarboard.

Dolly Thompson nodded. 'Yes, that's Marion.' She sipped at her tea and then looked hard at the young woman opposite. 'You think it might be her, don't you?'

'Oh, Dolly,' her sister began. She fell silent as Dolly raised a hand to silence her.

'You think it might have been her in that car.'

Beth Cooper set her cup carefully on the edge of the table before replying. 'Why did you call this morning?' she asked. 'Had something happened to make you suspect it might have been Marion in that car?'

The older woman continued to regard her in silence for a moment longer, then she said, 'I suppose you'd call it instinct. Intuition, perhaps. I knew, we both knew. Oh yes we did, Edie,' — this as the sister began to protest — 'that there was something not quite right the last time Marion came. She seemed distracted, anxious, and when she left her bag behind I began to wonder.'

'She left some things behind?'

'People do that all the time,' DC Stein put in.

'Yes, but generally they go back for them, especially when the things are so obviously personal.'

'What was in the bag, Miss Thompson?' Beth asked her.

'Just a few things. Letters, a cardigan, some keys I think and a poem. It was rather pleasing as I remember. Don't worry, dear, you won't have to ask. I'll give you her things before you leave. And her address too and that of her aunt. Her father passed on some two years ago now. Not an old man. It was very sad. But she has an aunt still living, sister of her mother's. And a small flat of her own in Malmesbury, if the landlord hasn't assumed she's done a moonlight and let it again.'

'Miss Thompson,' Aiden Stein was asking, 'why did you take so long before you reported her missing?'

'We didn't, dear, not really. You see, as I was about to tell you, Marion called on us about once a month. Usually the second Thursday, her day off, you see. When she left the bag behind I called her. She'd come and fetch it, she said. But there was nothing that couldn't wait and they had a rush on at work. Oh dear. I forget what it was.'

'Stocktaking or something,' Edie said helpfully.

'Yes, yes, well, whatever. So it wasn't until she didn't arrive on her usual day. And she hadn't called us to change her plans. We kept the day clear for her, you see, so she always called if she couldn't come.'

'Marion was like that,' Edie said. 'Always thoughtful.'

'So we left a message on her machine. In fact we left several messages. And called her aunt as well, but she seemed to think that Marion had gone away for a few days. Something about a new man in her life. When Marion didn't get in touch and she couldn't reach her, she did finally talk to the police. But your people just told her Marion was an adult, there was nothing they could do.'

She hesitated as though uncomfortable about something. It was Edie who said, 'She wasn't that good a judge of men, you see. Always did pick the unreliable ones. Her aunt was worried. We were worried. It was the way she didn't like talking about the man that concerned us.'

Dolly glanced gratefully at her sister. 'It made sense then, her not getting in touch. If she'd got herself involved and was worried we might not altogether approve. If this man wasn't quite right in some way. So . . .' She shook her head sadly. 'So, we did nothing and then I heard the news this morning and I just felt . . . there was no reason, dear, not really. Just an old woman's intuition I suppose.'

'How long since you last saw Marion?' Beth asked gently.

'I looked at the calendar, dear. It was two weeks. Exactly two weeks.'

'And when did you last speak to her, Miss Thompson? You said you called.'

'Yes, yes. It took a few attempts to get her. She didn't always leave her machine switched on and she was often out, so it was the Monday after her last visit. Ten days ago . . .'

'And how did she seem?' DC Stein asked.

'A little strange,' Dolly Thompson said. 'I thought about it a lot. I wondered if she just seemed strange in retrospect. You know, as if I'm adding that to the way she was because that's what I'm expecting her to be. But no. She *was* a little odd. A touch distant and impatient to get off the phone. She said she was expecting a call.'

'Maybe she was. From the new boyfriend perhaps,' Aiden Stein suggested.

'Maybe so. Maybe so.'

Dolly got up and went into the other room, returning with a macramé shoulder-bag lined with a bright blue print.

'This was hers,' she said. 'I glanced through, I was worried there might be something she might need inside. But it's all just as she left it. And you should have this.' She handed them another photograph of Marion O'Donnel. Written on the back were two addresses, her flat and her aunt's house. Along with her date of birth. Beth noted that she was twenty-five.

It was obvious that the interview was at an end. That Dolly Thompson wanted now to be left alone with her sister. Beth took the bag from her and smiled encouragingly at the women. For the first time since their arrival Dolly Thompson looked her age, as though the handing over of the bag had forced the last piece of the puzzle into place. Made it certain that their Marion was dead and gone from their lives for ever.

DC Stein drove and Beth Cooper radioed in to Charlie Morrow. The DCI told her to look in the bag, give him a resume of its contents and then report back to the station.

'It's a bit of an odd collection, guv,' Beth told him. 'A white cardigan, cable knit, a couple of paid utility bills, both for her flat by the looks of it.' She glanced more closely. 'Must have paid them at the post office in Devizes from the look of the date stamp. Then there's a letter.' She slid it carefully from the envelope, touching as little as possible. 'Signed Auntie Nora. That must be the other address we've got. Sounds like she's Marion O'Donnel's only relative.'

'Well, you'd better talk to her next,' Morrow instructed. 'Anything else?'

'Mmm, bunch of three, four, five keys,' she said, leaving them where they lay in the bottom of the bag. 'And another letter. No sorry, guv, it's not a letter, it's that poem Miss Thompson mentioned.'

'A poem. Right. Handwritten?'

'No. Typewriter, or printer. I'd say more likely printer, there's no indentations on the paper and it's pretty thin stuff.'

There was silence over the radio as Charlie Morrow processed the information.

Beth waited.

'Go and talk to the aunt. Show her the stuff, she might have some idea. Maybe her niece wrote poetry. What's it about anyway?' he added impatiently.

'Well, that really is the interesting part,' Beth told him. 'It seems to be about West Kennet and a fire being lit up on the hill.'

CHAPTER EIGHT

9.15 a.m.

They had not printed his letter. The morning paper carried an update on the latest attack, the revelation that the young woman had fought back and might have marked her attacker's face, but there was no mention of his letter.

The woman sitting across the breakfast table poured more tea and pushed the cup in his direction. He murmured thanks and continued to scan through the inside pages.

It wasn't there, no mention anywhere.

Perhaps it had simply been too late for the morning edition; he'd pushed the letter through the door the night before, and it had been late. Too late maybe for it to be printed in the morning.

He reached out and picked up his cup, sipping tea and allowing the loose page of the paper to rest against the teapot.

His face was sore where the girl had clawed at it with her key. Little bitch! There were bound to be stupid jibes from his workmates when they read the paper. Bitch! he thought again. His sudden surge of anger making his hand shake, he splashed his tea on to the blue-checked cloth.

* * *

The morning was chill and damp, the overnight rain soaking the fallen leaves and making the paths greasy underfoot.

Mike and Sergeant Price arrived at Aston Park at nine forty-five, slipping through the cordon, watching the search that had already been underway since first light.

The sergeant in charge crossed over to them.

'Anything?'

'Not a sausage. The rain's washed out any prints. We've got crushed grass and broken branches where the struggle took place but bugger all else.'

Mike nodded, he'd expected nothing more. In this instance the best hope for forensics was the victim herself.

He watched a little longer, the slow, thorough process of finding and bagging fragments of rubbish, examining ground too wet to hold a decent print, then he turned to go.

'The *Chronicle* offices next,' he said. 'See what Tom Andrews is excited about, then we'll go and find out if they've resurrected my car.'

Price rolled his eyes. 'Local garage got Jesus working for them have they, guv?'

* * *

Tom Andrews, senior staff reporter on the *Chronicle,* passed the letter in its plastic bag across to Mike and sat back waiting for the questions to begin.

'When . . . ?'

'It was there this morning, hand-delivered, near as we can guess between eleven last night and three this morning.'

'Oh?'

'Last shift cleared out just after eleven. Sid the security man picked it up and put it on the front desk at about three, so . . .'

'So maybe our man works shifts?'

'Or was coming home from the pub, or out walking the dog.'

Mike nodded and read the letter again. The typeface was clear and uniform. Daisy-wheel maybe but more likely something like a bubble-jet printer. At least, that's what documents had said about the other two. Plain white sheet of typing paper and a cheap manila envelope, easily picked up at any stationer's or post office and a lot of other places besides.

And if it was like the other two there would be no prints — except, presumably, for Sid the security man's. With that in mind he said, 'I take it this Sid of yours has gone off duty?'

Tom Andrews nodded. 'He'd gone and his day relief was on by the time this was passed to me. You want to talk to him?'

'Get him to call in to divisional. Have his prints taken for elimination, that should be it. He can give a brief statement as well, just to keep the record straight as regard to time, but there's not much else.' He paused. 'You've taken a copy of this?'

'It's news, Mike. Look, we held off printing the other two because Flint strung us the line that the case was about to break. Didn't want the investigation jeopardized. So OK, we went along with him even though I knew he was lying through his teeth, but I mean, Mike, you can't expect the editor to hold off for ever. This is news, and there's bugger all else happening with this business yet.'

He regarded Mike thoughtfully. 'You've got an angle on this, I'll play it for all it's worth, but it goes in the next edition whether, which or how.'

'And the other two letters?'

Andrews nodded. 'Along with our reasons for sitting on them this far.' He smiled suddenly, the deep wrinkles creasing around tired grey eyes. 'Anything new come out of this latest attack?'

Mike leaned back in the chair and stretched his long legs. 'Plenty. Too much maybe. It's being weighed and sifted as they say.'

Tom Andrews gave him a shrewd look. 'Something on your mind?' he said encouragingly, then laughed as Mike shook his head.

'You know better than that, Tom.'

'I can always hope. Even DI Croft has his weak moments. If you want me to play an angle on this you'll have to let me know fast. I've got an editorial meeting in fifty minutes.'

Mike got to his feet. 'I'll give you a call.'

Tom Andrews watched him go, his eyes narrowing slightly as the tall man went through the swing doors and strode out into the car park. He had known Mike Croft some two years now, had come to like and respect him in that time, and had learnt to recognize when there was something preying on the man's mind. Something new and something very big.

As Mike got into the car, Price asked, 'He's going to publish?'

Mike nodded, took the plastic-wrapped letter and envelope from his pocket and handed it to the sergeant.

'And he's right,' he said. 'Nothing I can say that's reason enough to stop him.'

'Flint will not be pleased.'

'Superintendent Flint is never pleased. You're right though, but that's the least of our worries.'

Price handed the letter back to him and started the engine. This letter, which like the other two taunted the police for their lack of progress and threatened further incidents, was only a small part of what worried Mike. Tom Andrews had been right. Mike did have much more on his mind. There had been blood on Stacey's keys and on her clothing that had definitely not been her own. Blood was something they hadn't had before, but they'd typed the attacker from serology tests done on semen left at two of the previous crimes. The serology had shown the attacker to be type O.

The blood, of which there was sufficient quantity to leave no doubt, had been type A.

It had been a shock to Mike to realize that he had been dealing with two rapists and not just one. He was not yet ready to let Tom Andrews in on that fact.

* * *

Max Harriman took a slight detour on his way to work. He liked the two till ten shift best of all. It gave him his mornings free and didn't end so late that he was unable to indulge in other activities in the evening.

His detour took him through Aston Park, within a few yards of where the girl had been attacked last night. A police cordon had been thrown up around the area and Max could see the search team still probing the bushes for clues.

Max stood and watched them for a couple of minutes. He wasn't the only one; others paused too, fascinated by this glimpse into another official world. Then he walked on slowly, his gaze drifting from the three men poking around in the bushes to the other two standing a little apart, looking at a map.

Max wondered what they'd found so far. He looked around, making certain that no one could see, then he lifted his hands close to his face, first fingers and thumbs at right angles as though framing an image. Smiling to himself, Max panned his imaginary camera across the scene.

CHAPTER NINE

3 p.m.

Terry sat in the big chair in the corner of Maria's consulting-room. He was restless, moving constantly as though the chair was uncomfortable and he couldn't work out how to sit. His dark hair flopped forward over one eye as he stared down at his feet, turning them this way and that as though examining the laces.

Maria, sitting over by the window, the angle of her chair set obliquely to his, ignored the fidgeting. She had grown used to it; this sense of pent-up energy Terry exuded was symptomatic of a boy impatient to get away in time for football practice and had little to do with any clinical problem he might have.

Personally, she hardly viewed these sessions as therapeutic, or as making the best use of her psychiatric skills. The boy was in no need of medication, little need of deep therapy. Any trained counsellor could do what she was doing with him. He talked freely about his experiences and his feelings, trusting her, now, in a way that was very satisfying. In view of what he had been through, his mental balance was extraordinarily good. So good in fact that Maria was forced to wonder occasionally if she was missing something. If under the very moderate, very ordered facade lurked a clever manipulator. A psychopathic personality conning the expert.

Mostly, she preferred to believe that he was a very ordinary teenage boy, emerging from a bloody awful past with far more determination and courage than could reasonably be expected. She held out great hope for Terry.

He had finally told her about Sarah and about 'some old woman' he had befriended who lived up the road from him.

'Her shopping bag broke,' he told Maria. 'I gave her a hand with her stuff and we kind of got talking.'

He stopped fidgeting for long enough to look up and meet her eyes, a Terry sign that this was important.

'She's all right,' he said. 'Used to be an actress, she's got books and books of cuttings, you know, all her reviews and stuff. We got talking about it. She even played on Broadway once.'

Maria nodded. 'And you've been to her house?' Terry looked uncomfortable. 'Yes, like I told you. She showed me her scrapbooks and stuff.' He fidgeted again but tried to hold Maria's gaze, something she knew he found terribly hard. 'Look, I know I should have told you about her and about Sarah, but I mean, do I have to tell you everything?'

'No, of course not.' She smiled. 'I know, sometimes it's hard to explain, the way a complete stranger can become a friend almost overnight.'

He regarded her suspiciously for a moment, seeing if she was testing him, winding him up.

Then he nodded. 'Yeah, it's kinda hard. But I like her. And there's Sarah too.' He frowned suddenly. 'Do they have to know, I mean about . . . ?'

'That's not for me to say, Terry,' Maria told him. 'But you should have a chat to your social worker about them both, especially Sarah, if things get serious.'

Terry frowned again. 'Nobody "chats" to Mrs Williams,' he said irritably. 'I suppose if I don't say anything, you'll have to tell.'

'No,' Maria shook her head. 'What you tell me is confidential, you know that.'

Terry stared at the floor, his shoulders tense. Maria knew how important these fledgling relationships were to him. Knew he was waiting for her to comfort. To encourage. Instead, she remained silent and waited for him to speak.

'I will,' he said at last. 'I will talk to her, but not yet. It's too soon. I don't want to ruin everything.' He gave her an odd sideways look as though challenging her to go against his wishes. The expression in his eyes caused Maria a moment of real doubt. It was so hard and so very cold.

* * *

7.55 p.m.

Sarah had been doing homework at a friend's house after school. Her mother collected her in the car rather than let her catch the bus home alone with all the worry of the recent attacks.

'I don't mind too much if there's two of you together,' Paula, her mum, had said in familiar refrain, 'but you're not coming home alone.'

Friday night was her mum's aerobics night and Paula collected her on the way to the class. It meant an hour of watching sweaty women in multi-coloured, multi-stretchy sports gear leaping around to the strains of a badly setup tape player, but Sarah had her magazine and figured she could cope.

The aerobics class was held in the gym of Fairfield Community College. They arrived just before eight fifteen, the evening wet and already cold, the car park yellow with the glow of sodium, discolouring the soaking tarmac.

'Oh, look after this, will you?' her mother asked her, dragging the mobile phone and her Visa card out of the glove compartment. 'And don't let me forget, I've got to get some petrol on the way home.'

'OK.' Sarah took the card and posted it absently into the pocket of her jeans. Her mother plucked her sports bag off the back seat, almost spilling her towel and after class clothes on to the floor of the car as she stuffed the mobile phone inside. 'Hurry up now,' she said, shivering in her Lycra with just a sweatshirt pulled down over the top. 'I'm freezing.'

They crossed the car park and pressed the buzzer next to the glass doors, waiting for the light to flash in the gym so someone would come and let them in.

Moments later, a woman in pink Lycra and silver trainers came running down the hallway, pressed the button to release the catch and greeted Paula effusively.

'Are you joining us tonight?' This to Sarah.

'Oh no, our Sarah's not into aerobics,' her mother said. The two women laughed as though at some big joke and Sarah's mother smiled at her, a private smile, as though to apologize that they found it funny. Sarah smiled back, falling behind the two of them, following them to the gym with her magazine rolled tightly in her hand. She glanced at her watch. Ten minutes before the class began and then another hour. She wondered, not for the first time, why perfectly sane women — and, generally, she actually liked her mother — behaved like idiots when they got together.

She seated herself at the end of one of the benches in the gymnasium and settled down with the problem page of her magazine. Half an eye watching as the women took off their sweatshirts and coats, talking noisily, comparing, she thought with more amusement than cruelty, the sag of their respective tits and bums.

'OK,' the instructor called out, clapping her hands then bending to turn on the tape. 'Ready for the warmup. One and two and side and stretch . . . get those knees higher girls . . . Remember, this is the last workout before Christmas.'

Sarah watched with half-attention.

Then the blue light began to flash.

'Reach higher, girls, higher . . . Oh, get that for me will you, love? Probably Debbie, she's always late.'

Sarah glanced across at the flashing light. She shrugged. 'Sure,' she said. She put her magazine aside and went to open the door.

8 p.m.

John Tynan turned into Cavendish Road. He had been looking forward to this evening. Theo was always good company and the young man, David, who had been lodging with her for the past eight months or so had proved to be very pleasant too in his own way.

He had been thinking earlier in the day about just how long he had known Theo. Most of her life, probably. Her older sister, May, had been at school with John's wife and the two had stayed friends all their lives, the two women dying within months of each other as it turned out, and from different versions of the same bloody illness.

May had lived all her life within five miles of where she was born, but Theo had always been a wild one. Wanted to be an actress and going full pelt to achieve her dream. She had run off to London and worked at anything and everything while she auditioned, until she'd finally got her first break with a little rep company that travelled doing one-night stands all over the country.

She'd done well for herself in the end though. In work more than out of it and playing small but useful roles on the television later in her career. Theo had stayed with sister May between engagements and kept in touch with old friends despite being away so much of the time.

It had been a great surprise when she'd come back home to stay. Must have been close on a year before, thought John.

He turned the corner into Cavendish Road to find his way blocked by a police car parked diagonally across the nearside lane and a uniformed officer waving the traffic around the cordon. Blue lights flashed eerily in the darkness pooled between the streetlights.

Theo's house. The cordon was around Theo's house. What the hell?

Anxious, John drove a little way on and parked at the side of the road, then walked back, taking in the two cars with their flashing lights. The constable standing by the slightly open door, the small crowd beginning to gather on the other side of the street and the curious watching discreetly from their curtained windows.

'You can't come in here, sir. I'm sorry, but there's been an incident.'

'But I'm expected,' John said, startled.

'If I could have your name, sir. And, you say you were expected?'

John took control of himself. 'My name is John Tynan, ex-Detective Inspector Tynan. Theo Howard is a friend of mine and I'd like to know what's going on.'

The young officer's expression had changed a little as he took this in. He opened his mouth to speak, but whatever he had in mind was interrupted as the front door was flung open and Davy threw himself out, grabbing at John's arm. His face contorted with emotion as he cried out, 'She's dead, John. Theo's dead!'

Tynan barely had time to react before Davy had been ushered gently but firmly into a waiting police car. He turned back, reaching a hand towards the closed door as though to push it open. It was white, he noted, as though seeing it for the first time. White replacement uPVC, with an ornate brass handle and a little stained-glass panel just above the letter box.

The young constable on duty was speaking to him, John realized, but it was not until the PC reached out and touched John's arm that he really took in what the man was saying.

'Are you all right, sir?'

'Yes, yes, I'm fine.'

'Was she a close friend? If you could just come and sit in the car for a moment . . .'

Another car had pulled up parallel with Theo's house. John saw it out of the corner of his eye and recognized Maria's silver Mazda. Mike was in the passenger seat.

John raced down the steps towards them, talking almost before Mike had a chance to get out of the car.

'Theo. They're telling me Theo's dead.'

'Steady, John, slow it down. What are you doing here anyway?'

'Theo, I told you, I came to see Theo.'

'She was a friend of your wife's,' Maria remembered as she eased herself out of the car. 'I remember you talking about her.' She frowned. 'Wasn't she an actress at one time?'

'Yes, yes. That's her. But they're telling me she's dead. I was supposed to come to dinner tonight. I got here to find the place cordoned.'

He took a deep breath as though realizing how close to hysterical he must sound, holding out a hand as though to fend off their concern. 'I'm all right, Mike. Really I am. It's just a bit of a shock.'

Another car arrived. The police surgeon got out, greeted Mike and nodded to John Tynan. 'Thought you were retired. Can't they keep you away?'

'Look,' Mike said, 'Maria will take you back home and stay with you.' He glanced across at her for agreement. 'Give me your keys, John, and I'll drive your car back later when I wind up here.'

For a moment Tynan's expression hardened as though angry at being dismissed. Then he nodded. 'But I want to know, Mike. I want to know what happened. Theo, she had no family, not since May died, same year as Grace you know. She was a good friend. A good friend.' He allowed Maria to open the passenger door for him and got into the car, the age showing on his pale face as they drove away.

Inside, the house was tidy, no signs of a struggle. Unusually for a terraced house of this kind, there was a small hallway with the staircase going off. A little table, no larger than a plant stand, stood at the bottom of the stairs, supporting a red-shaded lamp.

Three doors led off the hall. One at the end, open to reveal the kitchen. The front room had been turned into a dining-room. Mike was directed into the rear living-room. It was not a large room. French doors led into a neat garden. A three-seater sofa, covered with a cream throw, stood against one wall with stacks of bright cushions propped against the ends. An old chesterfield with a drop-down arm stood at right angles to the first settee. It too was draped with cream, and blue cushions lay beneath the woman's feet.

Her shoes had been removed and placed tidily beside the sofa. Other than that she was fully and smartly dressed in a dark green suit and cream silk blouse.

There was, Mike noted absently, a tiny ladder in the left foot of her tights.

Her head was supported on another blue cushion and her eyes were closed. Theo Howard had grey hair. It was shoulder-length and loose and there was something about the way it had been combed out across the cushion that made Mike look twice. One hand rested across her stomach, the other fell awkwardly towards the floor, but from her position, neatly propped upon the sofa, and the casual arrangement of her limbs, she could almost have been sleeping.

Almost.

The reek of vomit and alcohol filled the tiny room. An empty bottle lay upon the floor and streaks of vomit ran from her nose and the corner of the woman's open mouth, pooling beside her face, staining the blue of the cushion a fetid brown.

'She's holding something, Mike,' the police surgeon commented.

With gloved hands he gently opened the woman's hand. The fingers were still flexible, lightly clenched about the paper. Someone held an evidence bag for him and the surgeon eased the paper into the bag, drawing it flat as he posted it inside.

Mike took the sealed bag, moving away from the body as the surgeon continued with his work. Temperature of the body, temperature of the room, pronouncement of death at twenty thirty-two. Directing the photographer as she moved softly about the scene.

Mike read, his lips moving silently as he took in the words.

'Anything interesting?' the police surgeon asked.

'It's a poem,' Mike told him.

'A poem. Well, that's a new one.'

He packed his equipment away and prepared to leave. 'You can move the body when she's finished the family snapshots,' he said, nodding towards the photographer.

Mike thanked him. He glanced back at the paper in his hand and read again.

'Right now; I do not need to be told truth . . .'

CHAPTER TEN

8.40 p.m.

Charlie Morrow sat in the one and only armchair, trying not to think how long it had been since he last slept, and surveyed the rest of the room. It was a tiny flat. One small living-room, an equally small bedroom. Bathroom with a shower but no bath, crammed into a space that should have been a cupboard. A screened-off area at the end of the living-room that held a Baby Belling two-ring cooker, a sink and half draining-board together with a couple of wall cupboards and a yellow Formica-covered table that must have to double as a work surface.

Marion O'Donnel rented the place part-furnished apparently. The kitchen stuff was owned by the landlord, as was the bed — she'd supplied her own mattress. The two-seater sofa also came with the flat. It had a missing castor and its limp side was supported by folded cardboard torn from a cornflakes packet padded around a strip of wood.

The chair in which Charlie Morrow was seated, the pine desk standing under the window and the nest of square teak-effect tables were hers, it seemed. As were the assorted, cheaply framed posters and the flatpack bookshelves with their burden of paperbacks and magazines. Charlie Morrow had glanced through them earlier. She had eclectic tastes, he thought. A few thrillers, the odd romance. Cheap edition classics shoved, careless of any order, between science fiction novels, travel guides and women's magazines.

On the top shelf were framed photographs. Herself and two old ladies who must be the Misses Thompson. An old photograph of a man and woman, standing awkwardly together, the woman squinting into the sun with a hand raised to shade her eyes.

Another of the same man, older and alone, seated in the armchair that Morrow now occupied.

Others of Marion and younger people. College friends, he assumed. She looked relaxed and happy, laughing into the camera.

Charlie Morrow shook his head and sighed. 'Didn't know what was coming to you, did you, girl?' In his mind there was no doubt but that the dead woman was Marion O'Donnel. They'd contacted her dentist, got the dental records; it was only a matter of time until forensics confirmed what Charlie was certain he already knew.

Marion worked in a bookshop. They had tried to contact her when she hadn't turned up for work, but that was all. She had holiday due to her, had taken two weeks of it and then not come back to work.

'Was that in character?' Charlie Morrow had asked. Her employer had shaken his head. No, she had generally been reliable.

And you didn't think to report her missing? Morrow had questioned. The man had looked awkward. Shrugged vaguely.

'She was an employee, Detective Morrow. I don't think of myself as my brother's keeper; never mind my employees'. She was a nice girl, obliging and friendly with the customers. I'd had no complaints.'

'Until?' Morrow asked.

'Well, she'd . . . it was as if her mind wasn't on the job, suddenly. She came in late, pleaded sick and went early on, oh, a dozen or more occasions in the month before she took her holiday. And she started to forget things. Orders didn't get done and customers were complaining about her behaviour.'

'So you suggested she take some holiday?'

'I thought she might have problems. Need some time to sort them out . . . I don't know. She'd been a first-rate employee before, I didn't want to part with her if there was a chance she could straighten herself out. When she didn't come back, well, I thought . . .'

'That it was easier than having to get rid.' Charlie Morrow nodded, ignoring the man's indignation at his lack of tact.

'Was she close to anyone at work?'

Apparently not. She was friendly enough, but it was a small shop. Just himself, Marion and three part-timers. She had formed no close friendships with any of them.

Morrow took their names and addresses and arranged for interviews. By then it was getting late and he had come here to her flat, just as forensics were finishing up. Morrow looked at the stack of documents lying neatly on the desk.

She had been very ordered, he thought. Everything filed and kept. Bank statements arranged by date. Phone and other utility bills sorted according to type and held together with paperclips.

Personal letters in yet another folder.

There was nothing hidden between the pages of her books. Nothing slipped between the magazines. Her rent had been paid in advance and was up to date, or had been until two weeks before. The landlord, thinking she had been away, had let it slide for a week then dropped her a note through the door and, later, left messages on her answering machine.

'I thought there must be some good reason,' he had told Charlie Morrow. 'Eighteen, nineteen months she'd been with me. Paid her deposit good as gold and never so much as a day late. I decided she must have, maybe, family trouble and couldn't get back. So I said to my wife, I said, we'll take the rent out of her deposit money this month and she can make the deposit up again when she comes back.'

Charlie Morrow nodded and placed his own interpretation of events around the story, guessing it to be essentially the same but with a little of the altruism removed.

The landlord had been more worried about having police cars outside the converted house than he had been about the loss and possible death of one of his tenants.

There was a knock on the door; an officer came in and began to pack the sealed evidence bags into a plastic crate for transport.

Thoughtfully, Charlie Morrow reached out for the evidence bag lying on the table close to him. 'Here, you'll be wanting this too,' he said.

For him, that single sheet of paper was the most significant find of the day. A second poem, this one also untitled. It began: 'Right now; I do not need to be told truth . . .'

Charlie Morrow had been about to leave when DS Cooper and DC Stein arrived.

'Thought we might catch you, guv,' Beth said. 'We've just come from the aunt's place.'

'Anything useful?'

Beth shook her head. 'Not so far. The aunt was the father's sister; after Marion's dad died they didn't see a lot of her. No conflict or anything, just drifted apart.'

'Did the aunt know about the new boyfriend?'

Beth shrugged. 'She knew there was one, but that was about all. Thought his name might be Jack, but no last name and she'd never met him. Said Marion was a bit tight-lipped about this one. She reckoned that was unusual, Marion was generally full of it.'

'And the last time she saw Marion O'Donnel?'

'Was the Friday before Miss Thompson spoke to her on the phone.'

'And in her opinion, was her niece upset about anything?'

'Hard to say,' Beth shrugged. 'Marion stayed for maybe half an hour. Had a cup of tea, talked about work and family and then went on her way.'

'And did she mention the boyfriend then?'

Beth nodded, 'Briefly, only to say that she was still seeing him. The aunt seemed to think he might be a married man. I think, because she was reluctant to talk . . .'

'And she said it wouldn't be the first time. Her last was a married man,' Stein put in.

Morrow nodded. 'That fits in,' he said, 'with what the Misses Thompson told us. That her choice of men left something to be desired.'

CHAPTER ELEVEN

8.40 p.m.

Sorting through the latest submissions to 'readers' wives' was not the most satisfying of deals. These, the static equivalent of mucky home videos — Jake got a fair few of those too, sent through his various agents — were always a mixed bag. Some of them, he thought, should have been wearing a bag. But on the other hand, he'd found some real hot sales that way.

She had been one of them. Vinnie had passed her photo on, he remembered. Vinnie had a good eye. She was a classic blonde, firm curves and that look. A little uncertain, a tiny bit shy, as though she didn't know the full score.

Whatever her boyfriend had been thinking when he took the shots, Jake saw pound signs.

And he'd groomed her, pampered her, dressed — and undressed her — right. Had her photographed by the best in the business. She could have had anything her little heart desired. But it hadn't been enough. She had to stick her pretty nose in where it wasn't wanted. Not satisfied with what she'd got.

For some people, he thought bitterly, nothing was ever enough.

Well, time to see how his latest project was doing. Jake set the photographs aside and went down into the basement.

When Jake first moved into the house the basement had been a damp and dismal place, crammed with the debris of generations of successive owners. He'd cleared it out, run power and heat and water into all three rooms and replastered the walls, hiding the cold stone behind a colour wash of broken white. The basement was virtually soundproof, warm, and each of the three rooms was decorated in its own distinctive style. Jake did a lot of his work from here and he needed comfort and variety, though he doubted the young man lying bound and blindfolded on the narrow bed had any appreciation of the effort he had gone to.

Jake had bound his victim's hands and feet and covered his eyes with thick grey ducting tape, but he had deliberately left the mouth uncovered. There was no need for silence. The man could scream himself hoarse and there'd be no one able to hear. And Jake had learnt the hard way how easy it was for someone to choke on their own vomit if you covered their mouths too tight.

He said nothing as he set the camera on its tripod, turning it towards the young man, checking he had the whole body in frame. The crotch of his jeans, Jake noticed, was wet, the damp patch spreading down one leg and on to the sheets.

'Who's there? For Christ's sake, who's there?' Voice cracked with desperation.

Jake said nothing. Panning down the body, then back to rest upon the face.

'Why don't you say something? I know you're there. For Christ's sake, why don't you say something?'

His voice broke and Jake could hear the young man trying to control the sobs that rose in his throat. His face contorted with fear; his body writhing on the narrow bed as he struggled to turn his head, straining for the slightest sound.

Jake listened to him pleading, the voice thick with tears and the body twisting and convulsing with mental agony and the physical pain of arms tightly pinioned.

And Jake filmed it all, regretting only that he could not see the tears that would have stained the young man's face.

CHAPTER TWELVE

9.05 p.m.

Sergeant Price arrived at Fairfield just after nine. Sergeant Mason, his opposite number in the uniformed section, greeted him at the entrance. 'It's probably a waste of time you being here,' he said, 'but the mother's practically hysterical and two of the previous attacks took place not half a mile away.'

Price nodded. 'And the girl just went to the door and hasn't been seen since?'

'S'right. A blue light flashes in the gym when someone wants to come in. The door's released by this catch here. Gives you five seconds to get out before it closes again.' He shrugged. 'Not that it's much of a problem. The door lock can be blocked with chewing-gum — often is when the kids are in school and half the time in hot weather they prop it open with a litter bin. Unless the alarm's actually armed, and it won't be while the building's in use, there's nothing to tell anyone the door's been left unlatched.'

'Very security-conscious.' Price laughed without humour. 'But tonight it was properly closed?' He glanced up at the security camera above the door. 'Do we have the video tapes yet?'

'Someone from the security company's being sent over. Should be here within the hour. There's that camera there and another two trained on the car park.'

Price looked towards where he pointed. 'Which anyone with half a brain cell could avoid by staying close to the walls.'

Mason nodded. 'Set up to deter car thieves, and petty vandals,' he said. 'I imagine they give a good view of the car park and the first-floor windows but not much else. And this porch affair makes that camera less than useless once you're underneath it.'

Price nodded. 'Well, we'll have to hope we get lucky. You'd better take me to the mother.'

Inside the gymnasium all was quiet. A small knot of women in training gear gathered around a woman sitting on a bench. A WPC, looking strangely out of place in her dark uniform, was taking statements. She saw Price and came over to him. The woman on the bench watched anxiously. Her hands clutched at the sweatshirt draped around her shoulders and her face looked pinched and tired.

'She's certain it's the sex attacker,' the WPC said. 'I keep telling her it's way off his MO, but the idea's got fixed in her head.'

'Any reason, I mean particularly?'

The WPC sighed. 'Because Sarah looks like the rest, sir. Fifteen years old, small and blonde and slightly built and because the mother's scared out of her wits. Wants any answer. Though it beats me, sir, if she's more afraid of her daughter being grabbed by some pervert or of going home to her old man and telling him about it.'

9.30 p.m.

Mike was getting nowhere.

'I know nothing, Inspector Croft,' David Martin was insisting, as he had been since the interview began. 'I came home around 7.30, the door was unlocked. I thought it was strange, but Theo's like that. It's one of those doors that you have to actually remember to lock. It doesn't latch on its own.' He looked at Mike as though for confirmation. 'Sometimes Theo just forgot.'

He paused, studied his hands clasped in front of him on the table. 'I called her name and I went through to the back room. She was just lying there. Just lying there the way . . . I thought she was sleeping. But she'd been sick . . . and then I saw the bottle.'

'And you tell us Theo had had a problem, but that she no longer drank at all.'

'She couldn't!' David Martin's voice rose again. 'I told you, Theo had a problem. A big problem, but she'd been sober more than a year. Completely dry for almost thirteen months.' He broke off and hammered with both fists on the table. 'And then your lot arrived and dragged me here. I should be with Theo, not sitting here with you going over the same bloody ground over and over again. I did nothing! I saw nothing! She was like that when I got there and I don't know what the fuck happened.'

Mike was silent and for a moment there was no sound in the room except for David Martin's laboured breathing. Agitated, David dragged his fingers through his hair and then rubbed both hands across his face, pulling at his skin as though trying to wipe reality away. 'She's really dead?' he asked, his voice cracking. 'Theo. She's really dead?'

'You were close friends?' Mike questioned.

'We were more than friends. Theo and I, we'd been lovers for, well, close to a year. She moved here and I followed on a couple of months later. I had some things to sort out first.'

'Things?'

'A . . . a job, that sort of stuff.' He lifted his gaze to meet Mike's and his voice rose angrily again. 'I had a living to earn. I wasn't going to sponge off her. And don't think I don't know what you're thinking. Younger man. Older woman. Just using her for what he can get.' He fell silent again, twisting his hands, his anger burning itself out once more.

'But no one knew of your relationship,' Mike reminded him. 'Why was that?'

The young man's eyes flashed. 'Because she was afraid. Scared of what everyone would say about us. Everyone like you, thinking the worst. Cheapening what we had.'

'Close friends would have understood,' Mike said quietly, thinking of John Tynan.

'Theo had no close friends. There was only me. The rest. The rest meant nothing to her.'

Mike let it pass. The young man's hands had grown still now and lay flat upon the table. He stared down at them, his gaze intense, but blank.

Mike let the silence sit for a little longer, Then: 'That scratch on the side of your face, Mr Martin. How did you get it?'

CHAPTER THIRTEEN

Saturday, 17 December, 3 a.m.

Although it was now the early hours of the morning, the noise of the argument continued unabated. It had been interrupted, briefly, by Price's arrival, but soon resumed and as he went into the hallway to use his phone he could hear the parents railing at each other even through two closed doors.

The noise became louder momentarily as the WPC who had been left to cope with the grieving parents slipped out after him.

'They been like that all the time?' Price asked her.

She nodded, wearily. 'More or less. I gave up trying to calm it down. I might as well not have been there for all the notice they were taking, so I thought that as long as they weren't actually coming to blows I'd let it burn itself out.'

Price gave her a wry smile. 'Grief takes people in different ways. That's what my old sergeant used to say when I was just a probationer.'

'Right sir; if scoring points off each other counts as grief, well, I'd say they're drowning in the stuff.'

Price grinned at her, his hand resting on the phone. 'Was there something you wanted to tell me or did you just need a breather?'

'Both! But yeah, there is something Mrs Myers told me about ten minutes before you got here. I'd have called it in, but I'd been told you were on your way and she seemed pretty keen on keeping it from her husband.'

'Oh?'

'The kid, seems there might be a chance she's taken it into her head to do a runner. I mean, if this was going on all the time . . .'

'She wouldn't get far, no money.'

'That's just it. She had her mother's Visa card.'

'She had what? She stole it?'

'No. Her mum didn't want the bother of taking her handbag, she'd just got her sports bag, so she asked Sarah to look after it for her. Sarah slipped it in the pocket of her jeans. She had it with her when she left.'

'Fucking hell! Why didn't she mention this hours ago?'

'Says she was too distressed and just forgot.'

'Forgot. All right, all right. I've got to call in about the video tapes. You go back to the battle of the bulge. I'll be there in a couple of minutes and we'll deal with this.'

She rolled her eyes. 'Thanks a lot, sir.'

Price, his hand still resting on the phone, nodded slowly, listening to the continued arguments. Silently, he hoped the kid bankrupted the pair of them.

Price was surprised to be put through to Mike Croft. 'What the hell you doing there, guv? Thought you were off tonight.'

'So did I. Suspicious death. What's your excuse?'

'Misper. Christ almighty, we're never going to get the overtime on this. I've clocked up thirty hours so far this month alone.'

Mike laughed briefly. 'So tell me another one. A Misper, can't the new relief deal with it?'

'Well, it got a bit complicated.'

He explained briefly the details of Sarah Myers' disappearance. 'The mother's convinced it was the sex attacker. It's looking more and more as if the kid simply took off with her mum's credit card.'

'Anything useful on the video tapes?'

'Nah, not a lot. We've reviewed just the half hour either side of her going. It's the usual over-used tape and grainy pictures and it's dark and raining and the sodium lights create one hell of a glare. You know the problems. The girl left with someone, probably male, looks tall, but as Sarah Myers only stood about five two in heels anyone's going to look tall.'

'Probably male?'

'Well, it was wearing trousers, but so was Sarah. No, looked vaguely male but the hood of the coat was pulled well up so it's hard to tell anything more.'

'Anything to suggest she was being coerced?'

Price sighed. 'My instinct says no. But he had hold of her arm and at one point she pulls back, glances towards the door. So . . .'

'Right. Well, I'm just about to wrap up for the night. What's left of it. This one's going to turn out a little difficult, I think.'

'Why's that?'

'The dead woman, she was a friend of John Tynan's and he's going to be pushing for some answers.'

'Ah. Nasty. Is it definitely murder? Anyone in the frame yet?'

'I've got the lodger here making a statement but we don't even know what we're dealing with till I've got the PM report. The look of it is, she got drunk and choked on her own vomit, so . . .'

'Right. Well, I'm going to have to get going. I need to find out if this credit card's been used since the girl disappeared and if she has any relatives in the south of France she might have run off to.'

He signed off. Behind him the noise continued unabated. Price took a deep breath and went back to join the adult Myers.

3.40 a.m.

Maria had dozed off in the chair. She woke to find John bending over her, a mug of hot chocolate in his hand.

'I made us both one,' he said. 'But you ought to go to bed.'

'I'm all right. Sorry, John, I'm supposed to be keeping you company, not falling asleep on you.'

'I don't need a baby-sitter, my dear. I'm quite all right.' He paused, sitting down opposite Maria on the old sofa. 'I just wish he'd call.'

'I know, John. I know.'

Maria leaned back in the chair and sipped her chocolate. It was still too hot to drink properly. Her gaze travelled around the comfortable sitting-room that was so familiar now. The massive, carved wooden cupboard that took over one wall. The sagging, tapestry-covered furniture, chosen by John's wife years before and well past its retirement age and all the random collection of books and pictures and knick-knacks accumulated over long residence. Recently, a new photograph had joined the collection on the bookshelves. Herself and Mike, taken on a day at the seaside in July. She was in a summer dress, the skirt blowing in the usual east coast wind. Mike was in cream trousers and an open-necked shirt, head slightly bent to the side and that lost look he always had when someone took away his jacket and tie.

'He'll call, or be here, before long. I'm sure he will.'

John Tynan nodded, the lines gathering about his eyes as he tried to smile at her. 'It's just so hard, my dear. I want to be out there, doing. Not stuck here like some spare part unable to help, to influence a damn thing.'

3.45 a.m.

Money had been withdrawn from Mrs Myers' Visa account. Discovering that it had not been drawn until one fifteen that morning and that the transaction could have been blocked only added to Phillip Myers' anger.

'And it never occurred to you to mention it? Never thought it might be important, I suppose?' he shouted at his wife.

Why the hell does she put up with him? Price thought. He exchanged a glance with the WPC and said quietly, 'Did Sarah know your PIN number? Kids often see their parents drawing money. Do you think she would have known your number?'

Paula Myers nodded. 'Probably,' she said. 'I mean,' she took a deep breath, 'yes, of course she did. She'd been with me when I drew cash, I'm sure she would have seen.'

'And remembered?'

'My daughter is not a thief, Sergeant,' Phillip Myers said stiffly. 'Someone abducted her from the leisure centre and that same someone must have used the card.'

'You think they forced her to tell them the number?'

It was interesting, Price thought, that Myers found it so much easier to accept that his daughter had been kidnapped and forced to reveal the number of his wife's Visa card than it was to accept that she might have drawn the money herself.

'They wouldn't have had to force it out of her,' Myers said heavily, glaring at his wife.

'Oh, Phillip, please.'

'I'm not sure I understand, Mr Myers.'

Phillip Myers exhaled slowly. 'My wife,' he said heavily, 'as you cannot fail to have noticed, is not the brightest of people. Amongst other annoying little habits, she forgets her PIN numbers. I scratched her number on to the corner of her card so she wouldn't forget it yet again.'

'You did *what*?' Price could hardly believe it.

'And there was no damn need,' Paula Myers was saying. She had been seated at the dining-table, agitated fingers playing with the white lace cloth, but now she rose to her feet, her eyes blazing, more anger powering her slight body than Price had seen her display all night.

'I make one mistake with the card and you treat me like a complete fool. It's something anyone could get wrong, but no. It's just one more proof to you of your goddamned superiority. Well, let me tell you something, Phillip. That wasn't the only mistake I made. The biggest one, the first and most damning one, was marrying you and the second one was letting you have anything to do with raising Sarah. If she's run away it's because of you. Your fault.'

She laid a shaking hand on her narrow chest, breathing hard. 'Not mine. *Yours,* because she hates you just as much as I do and what's more she's bright enough that no one had to teach her how to do it.'

Phillip Myers stared at his wife, momentarily silenced.

Price wanted to applaud; instead, he glanced appraisingly around the dining-room at the expensive and perfectly matched yew-wood suite and the display of fine china on the dresser shelves. Money, he thought. Money and stuff bought for show. Because they went well together not because there would be any pleasure in their use.

Phillip Myers had recovered himself and was about to begin again. Price turned back to him with a question he'd been wanting to ask since he'd first arrived and seen lurid scratches on Myers' temple.

'Where were you on Thursday night, Mr Myers, between about six and nine?'

4.10 a.m.

Mike arrived at Tynan's cottage just after four. The place looked to be in darkness and he breathed a sigh of relief, wanting rest rather than questions he couldn't answer right then. A tiny crack of light at the heavily curtained living-room window made him groan out loud. It had been too much to hope, really, that John and Maria would have gone to sleep, content to wait till morning for the news.

They must have heard the car because the door opened, flooding yellow light on to the step. The rain had stopped and the air smelt fresh and clean as Mike got out of John's car and walked wearily to the open door. He fancied he could almost smell the sea on the freshening wind. It was very cold and he was very tired.

'Not much I can tell you, John,' he said as he stepped into the narrow hallway, ducking his head instinctively under the crooked lintel above the door.

'How did she die?'

'We don't know yet, but it may well have been an accident.' He was aware that he had lowered his voice, dropped into that careful cipher he used for the distressed and the newly bereaved. Aware too, from John's face, that he had recognized the tone and resented it.

He apologized at once. 'I'm sorry, John. It's been a bloody night. Has for all of us.'

He shrugged off his coat and turned to kiss Maria who had emerged sleepily from the living-room. 'Mind if I make some tea? I've had three cups tonight, all of them cold and with that foul stuff in the plastic cartons instead of milk.' John Tynan nodded, going into the kitchen to fill the kettle and setting it on the stove. Maria followed him, perching herself on the table edge, and Mike leaned against the doorframe, watching the gas flame lap around the kettle, willing it to boil quickly.

'You knew she had a drink problem?' he asked John.

'Yes, she told me when I took wine over to dinner. The first time I went to dinner with her. Before David went to live there.'

'Well, it looks as though she could have started over again. There was an empty bottle of scotch on the floor and she'd been sick. Until I get the PM report I can't say for sure, but . . . it happens. She was lying on the sofa as though she'd been taking a nap. If she was too drunk to wake up properly . . .'

John Tynan nodded. 'I see,' he said. 'And David?'

'He's made a statement. Until we know the time and cause of death there's nothing more to be done.'

The screech of the kettle's whistle tore into the quiet of the kitchen. John lifted it from the stove and switched off the gas. He turned away from them as he poured water into the large brown pot, stretched the absurd woollen cosy over the top and shook it gently as though that might speed up the process. Mike could see that for all his calm his hands were shaking and his lips were bloodless.

'She was one of the last, you see,' John said with quiet resignation. 'Mine was not a job that made for socializing. Well, you know all about that. Grace kept in touch with people but when she died, well, I wasn't much good at it. Theo was one of the last of our mutual friends. People we'd both grown up with. It's a shock. She was so much . . . alive.'

He took a deep breath and straightened up, began arranging cups on the tray and sugar and milk. His hands shook a little and he was showing his age far more than usual.

'And what about David,' he asked. 'Where has he gone now? Presumably not back to the house?'

'No, we've got a cordon round the house until cause of death's certain. As I understand it he's gone to a hotel for the night. There's another thing, though. Our people arrived practically on his heels. Suspected break-in at the same address. Neighbours'd seen a teenage boy running away, climbing over that back wall and into the garden of the house behind.'

'Any connection with Theo's death?' Maria asked.

Mike shook his head. 'There's no evidence of a break-in. No disturbance that we could see. Of course, we can't be certain there was nothing missing.'

'You'll have David to check later on.'

Mike nodded, flexing his shoulders in an effort to clear some of the exhaustion from his body. He was very tired, but his mind was jumping and he knew he would be unlikely to sleep.

'Did you know they were lovers, John?'

'What, Theo and David?' He paused, poured the tea with a much steadier hand. 'I didn't know. Not for certain, but I did wonder. And if that's true, then I'm glad. I know that David made her very happy and if they were more than friends, well, all I can say is good for them.'

CHAPTER FOURTEEN

7.30 a.m.

Jake held the cup to the young man's lips and told him to drink. His victim was whimpering now, pleading hysterically to be released, so frantic that he could hardly swallow. He choked on the water as Jake tipped the cup too fast, coughing and spluttering with the liquid pouring back out of his mouth and through his nose. Jake moved aside to protect his clothes, frowning slightly.

'Now, drink,' he repeated, tipping the cup again. The blond man managed to swallow this time, gulping convulsively. 'Don't want you dying on me quite yet,' Jake told him. 'Not quite yet.'

He moved out of camera shot, setting the cup down. The man was still blindfolded, but for the sake of the film, Jake had covered his own face. He wore a black ski mask and combat gear. A knife in his belt and an AK47 replica propped against the wall. This one would probably end up as just one brief sequence in the finished film, but Jake liked to participate from time to time, bit parts that extended his enjoyment of the make-believe. There was enough genuine footage around, available dirt cheap if you knew where to find it, for him not to be too worried about providing major scenes and he often doubted that his buyers would know the difference anyway.

He returned to the bed and checked the bindings around the wrists and ankles. The tips of the fingers were cold and slightly blue, but not enough to cause immediate concern, and the ankles were puffy either side of the bindings. He took the knife from the sheath at his belt and laid it coldly against the blond man's throat.

'Can you feel this?' he asked.

No reply.

Jake pressed the point harder, just drawing blood. 'I said, can you feel this?'

'Yes, yes, I can feel it. I don't want to die. I just don't want to die . . .'

9.15 a.m.

The bell rang as he pushed the door of the small artist's supply shop and the girl looked up from the counter.

'Oh, hello, Mr Phillips, not your usual day, is it? I'll tell Freda you're here.'

Jake Bowen smiled at her. 'No, I don't usually make calls at the weekend, but I was passing and it's going to be a couple of weeks before I'm this way again.'

The girl nodded and went into the back of the shop to tell the owner that John Phillips had arrived. Jake put his briefcase down on the counter and began to sort out the supply catalogues Freda Hurst had requested. She was hoping to expand, was in the process of buying the shop next door and planned to add photographic and darkroom equipment to her stock. John Phillips, her usual rep, was all in favour.

Freda came through from the back of the shop, her face wreathed in smiles.

'Thanks for calling in,' she said. 'I hope it's not put you out?'

'Not at all, glad to help.' He placed the catalogues on the counter. 'Just give me a ring if you need advice.'

'OK, will do.' She was holding a newspaper in her hand and waved it at him. 'Dreadful business,' she said, pointing to the front page and the updated report of the attack in Aston Park.

Jake nodded sympathetically. 'It won't be long before they get him though, he's getting too cocky for himself if you ask me.'

Jake had seen the report earlier and he meant what he said. Back in his car he glanced at his own copy of the paper. So the prat was sending letters to the police now, was he? Jake shook his head. Amateur, he thought.

10.30 a.m.

Max Harriman had Saturday off. He lay in bed late, propped against the pillows, smoking a cigarette. He was as individual in this as he was in all things; cigarettes were an indulgence he allowed only before he took his morning shower. Max might like to smoke, but the stale smell of it on hair and clothes was something he found intolerable.

On the wall opposite the bed were pinned a series of images. They were nothing if not eclectic. There was a centrefold, the staple marks carefully smoothed away so as not to spoil the look of the woman's skin. Her name, according to the title at the top, was Marianne — though Max knew different . . .

Next to that was a picture cut from a full-page advert in a magazine. The blonde woman with the perfect smile and the blood-red lips gazing out at him. And positioned above them both, pictures taken with a motor wind of a teenage girl. Her blonde hair flying loose as she ran.

There were others too, of places Max had lived and people he had known. Obsessions he'd once had that had played themselves out on a much bigger screen than a mere still camera could embrace. An historic catalogue of Max Harriman's life and work.

The other one had taken those pictures for him, the ones of the young girl he'd liked so much and been torn away from before his time. Jake was good like that, he never said a word, just provided the images for Max's fantasies. Gave him the title and then watched him run with the story. Time to time, he'd even used the raw material Max could provide. Max was proud of that.

Max drew deeply on the cigarette. It was his third that morning, chain-smoked. He would allow himself one more. Then shower and dress and begin his day properly.

He was proud of his sense of discipline. It was important to be ordered, in most things at least; Jake had taught him that.

But even Jake broke loose sometimes from his strictly self-imposed rules. The first two girls here in Norwich, for instance, they had been his. The fourth one too, but the others had belonged to Max.

A tribute to the master one might say.

Max smiled, shook his last cigarette from the package and lit it from the butt of the last.

CHAPTER FIFTEEN

11 a.m.

Mike had been so certain that Theo's death was a tragic accident that he had not even called in to chase up the post-mortem.

He was well aware that, regardless of what TV dramas liked to portray, anything short of a dead cert killing had to wait in line with the other routine body count: the cot deaths, the sudden heart attacks, the collapses and the suicides and the unidentified. Theo's death would be lodged somewhere on this list and wait until someone could get around to dealing with it.

It was with deep surprise, therefore, that he took the call, standing in John's hallway in the middle of what he'd hoped would be a peaceful morning.

'I put her on the list for my students to take a look at,' the pathologist was saying. 'I like to give them a little variety and this was a good one. I'd got a couple of them doing preliminary exams and when they told me what they'd found I was certain they must be mistaken.'

'I thought you'd decided it was probably asphyxia?' Mike questioned, acutely aware of John's hovering presence in the background.

'That's right, but this is slightly off kilter. There's evidence of minute conjunctival haemorrhage. I've brought her to the top of my list, Mike, but from the early indicators, your lady was smothered.'

'The haemorrhage you found, it's not consistent with asphyxia caused by vomiting?'

'If there's vomit in the lungs then, yes, it's possible. Drowning on your own puke when you're blind drunk isn't that uncommon, as you well know, but it doesn't normally lead to the kind of pressure needed to rupture blood vessels in the eyes. It's more consistent with what we'd expect to find in strangulation or, as I think we've got here, smothering.'

Mike listened a while longer, thinking of the way Theo's body had been positioned. The bottle on the floor and the scattered cushions . . . Blood alcohol had been found at 275mg per 100ml of blood. Enough to cause unconsciousness, Mike thought. Theo was very, very drunk. Killing her would have been easy.

He put the phone down and turned to face John. He didn't need to say a word.

'She was murdered, wasn't she?'

'We can't be certain yet.'

'You'll be bringing David in for questioning again?'

'When we get confirmation, yes.'

John nodded slowly. 'And the boy seen running away?'

'We've no news yet. I don't know, John, he could be completely unconnected.'

John Tynan took a deep breath and shook his head. 'I know you have a job to do but go easy on David.'

'I'll treat him the way I'd treat anyone else.'

'I know, I know. But I can't believe he's involved in this. I believe he loved her.'

Mike nodded. 'The number of killings committed by strangers is pretty small, John. You're as much aware of that as I am. You didn't even know the pair of them were lovers until I told you. We still don't know that's true. Who can tell what their relationship was really like?'

'I saw them together. I knew Theo well.'

'But not David Martin. About him you know next to nothing. A few meetings when he showed you what he wanted you to see.'

'I'm not a fool!'

'No, no, you're not. But you are a friend.' He paused. 'Theo's dead, John. We don't know for certain that we're looking at murder, but if we are, I'm going to find out who and why, and there's no more that I can say.'

11.10 a.m.

Maria was catching up with the morning news when Mike came in to say he'd have to go. He explained quickly about the phone call.

'How's John taking it?'

'How do you think?'

Maria smiled. 'You're going to watch the PM?'

'Yes, I was wondering . . .'

Maria took the car keys out of her bag and handed them to him. 'We're going to book a day off, Mr Detective Inspector Croft, and we are going to take that junk heap of an estate car and see who's stupid enough to give you a trade in on it.'

She turned the local paper towards him. 'Have you seen this? Oh, and there's a piece on Theo's death on page two.'

Mike took the paper from her. 'Yes,' he said. I've already read it.' He skimmed the front page again. Tom Andrews had played it very fair, he thought, though Superintendent Flint hadn't seen it that way. Mike had spoken to him on the phone earlier while Maria had still been catching up on sleep. 'Flint was not amused,' he said. 'Thinks all journalists should be operating under a D notice or kept to reporting on village fetes.' He read out loud from the sections of the letters Tom Andrews had published.

There will be others.
The police will never find me.
I can run rings around them.
I don't even have to try.

'Your man believes in short sharp sentences,' Maria commented.

'Hmm, and that's not all, he lays them out like poetry, you know, double-spaced, each sentence on a new line . . .' Mike frowned, reminding himself of what Tom Andrews hadn't yet been told. As he now knew there were two attackers, which one was responsible for the sending of the letters, and why? The thought came fleetingly that the author of the letters might be deliberately taunting the other man. Hoping to goad him into further action. He turned back to Maria, bending to kiss her goodbye, enjoying the way she smelt, fresh from the bath. Marry me, he thought, but he didn't say it. Instead, he asked, 'And what does this say to your keen psychiatrist's brain then, Dr Lucas?'

'Well,' she said, taking back the paper, 'I should say, Inspector Croft, that what you have here is a bit of a nutter.'

2 p.m.

Charlie Morrow had long ago given up worrying about paid overtime, or weekends. The truth was, he didn't have a great deal else to fill his time. He had no family — a brief and broken marriage without children. Few friends outside the workplace — and there were those who would argue he had fewer in it. So, to find him working overtime on a Saturday was not so unusual.

Rain lashed at his office windows. December rain falling from a heavy sky. The office lights were on in an effort to offset the grey, but, somehow the yellow cast only made the room, with its threadbare green carpet and stained white walls, an even gloomier place.

Charlie Morrow sighed and put down the address book he had been studying. He'd worked his way through, so far, from A to E — including D for dentist — phoning through the list. Giving out a standard spiel. Introducing himself and his business and explaining who he was trying to trace. So far, the Thompson sisters were the last people who claimed contact with Marion O'Donnel. Idly, Charlie Morrow played with the scenario that the sisters might have done away with the young woman themselves. He could just picture the headlines:

'Thompson Twins in Inferno Murder', see himself arresting two twittering, grey-haired old ladies for a brutal killing.

Then he stopped laughing and got up, stretching. He was hungry and humour didn't work on an empty stomach.

He eased himself back into his jacket. It seemed to be going the way of all others and getting too small again. And, he thought, glaring out of the window, it was still bloody raining. Maybe that was the problem with his jacket, too often wet, it was obviously shrinking.

He packed the evidence bags away into his drawer and locked it. Dragged his green, waxed cotton raincoat off the hook and put it on, another button coming off between his fingers as he tried to fasten it.

Swearing to himself, Charlie Morrow dumped the button in his pocket along with the other junk, and went out to brave the rain.

6 p.m.

Outside, it was still raining. Charlie Morrow had reached T in Marion's address book. One thing he had learnt about Marion: she had an odd way of ordering her phone numbers. They weren't listed in any form or order that Charlie Morrow could figure out.

OK, he could understand D for dentist instead of the man's name, and GP for doctor was reasonable, but more often than not people seemed to be listed under their first name instead of their last, or according to some other reference he could only guess at.

He looked up the first entry under T and dialled the code and then the number. The phone was picked up on the third ring.

'Good evening,' he said. 'I wonder if you can help me. My name is Charles Morrow and I'm a detective inspector with the Devizes police. That's Devizes in Wiltshire,' he added, realizing that he had no idea which part of the country he was calling. 'I'm trying to contact someone I believe may be at this number. Someone called Theo Howard.'

7.30 p.m.

By the time Mike arrived back at John Tynan's house he was very tired. The post-mortem on Theo's body had brought surprises and now, Mike realized, they were dealing with a whole new ball game. Driving through the twisting country roads back to the cottage, his mind played with the facts.

Fact number one, Theo Howard had been murdered. Fragments of blue fibre had been found in her mouth and nose and even the upper part of her lungs. The fibres matched the blue cushions on the sofa. The one on the floor next to the empty bottle had been stained with vomit.

Someone had killed Theo Howard by pressing the blue cushion over her nose and mouth and holding it there. Mike could imagine the final struggle for breath. Drawing only the soft, airless fabric into her nose and mouth.

Would she have known what was happening to her? Mike hoped not. The amount of alcohol she had consumed would have made it very easy for the killer.

Easy for Theo too, he hoped.

Fact number two had taken everyone by surprise. It seemed that, murdered or not, Theo could have expected little more time on this earth. She had a massive and malignant tumour behind the posterior lobe of her liver. Her body was riddled with secondary infection. Theo had been dying.

He had returned to her house looking for medication. There had been none.

He had chosen not to bring David Martin in for questioning that night. The evidence against him was, at best, circumstantial and, besides, Mike felt that if he didn't get some rest soon he'd be sleeping on his feet.

Even more strange, perhaps, was the reaction of Theo's doctor. He'd been informed of her death, of course, but when Mike called him he professed ignorance of Theo's condition. So concerned was he that his memory might be failing him that he had checked through Theo's record.

'No,' he said. 'I'm glad to say dementia isn't setting in. Theodora Howard has seen me only three times in the past year. Once for a sprained ankle. Once for a throat infection, oh, and the third time I told her that she had a rather virulent influenza virus. That one was a call out. She'd been up all night with sickness and a high temperature and someone had got worried. I've a note here that I was called out by her lodger. Would that make sense?'

But surely, Mike had asked, she must have been in pain. She must have been diagnosed. She must have known.

The doctor had just shaken his head. 'I've not seen Miss Howard in the last six months,' he said. 'If she knew, if she was receiving medication, well, it wasn't from me.'

Mike had spoken to John Tynan a couple of hours before, filling him in on the bare facts, aware that waiting for news was putting a great strain on the older man. He was glad that Maria was there.

Fact number three, Theo must have started drinking from the moment she had walked through the door. A neighbour had seen her come home at about five o'clock. She had parked her car easily enough in the small space left in front of the house, so it seemed a fair bet that she was still sober. Davy claimed to have found the body at about twenty to eight. The boy had been seen running away about thirty minutes before. All in all, Theo must have died some time between five and, say, seven thirty.

The pathologist's estimate based on body temperature couldn't put it much more accurately than that, the best guess being about seven o'clock. And that made sense. She'd need time to have drunk so much.

Arriving at John's house he cut the car engine, sitting back in his seat for a few moments to gather his thoughts before going inside. Maria was right, he thought. He would have to change his old car. He'd just been putting it off for far too long. Driving hers was a sheer delight and one less thing to worry about. Twice now, his had died on him. Once at a set of traffic lights when he'd already been late for a meeting and once in the middle of nowhere. He'd had to get it towed to a garage.

He got out of the car, aware that the front door was open and John was waving to him.

'Phone call for you,' John shouted.

'Oh God, what now?'

He hurried into the hall, pausing to kiss Maria on the cheek as he passed her by.

'Croft.' He listened in silence, then thanked the speaker and put the receiver down.

'Well?' Maria asked him.

'That was Price. There's been an odd development in the Theo Howard case.'

'One you haven't told us yet?' John said gruffly. 'I thought we'd had enough surprises for one night.'

'So did I. Price has just got off the phone with a Detective Inspector Charles Morrow. Based at Devizes in Wiltshire.'

'Wiltshire, what's that got to do with Theo?'

'That's just it, we don't know. But it seems he's been heading up a murder enquiry. The body's only just been identified and Morrow was going through the woman's effects. Theo Howard's telephone number was among them.'

9 p.m.

It had taken a lot of ringing around and more than a few threats, but Phil Myers had finally got the location of the party his daughter was supposed to be going to.

Paula Myers was outraged. 'She told me she was going to the pictures and staying over at her friend's afterwards.' She looked at her husband, anxiety replacing anger. 'You don't seriously think she'll turn up there, do you?'

'I don't know. But her friends must be able to tell me something.' He paused, then got up and resumed his earlier pacing around the room like a trapped animal. 'I can't believe she'd go off like this. Just go. I mean, if she had problems I could understand it, but . . . why couldn't she just talk to us?'

Paula's eyes focused on him and she shook her head. 'When was the last time either of us could talk to you without getting our heads bitten off?' she said. 'You've built a wall so high round yourself we can't even see you these days, never mind try to talk.'

She could see him bristling with anger, ready to resume the fight that had raged off and on all night and most of the day. Paula didn't think she could take any more of it. Instead, she shook her head, lifting tired hands to rub her face as though scrubbing it clean.

'No, no. It wasn't just you. Neither of us really asked her anything, did we? It was always "How was school, Sarah? Do you have any homework, Sarah? Do you really think you can make up good enough grades at that ordinary school, Sarah?" My God, I'd listen to us sometimes and *I'd* want to switch off too. No wonder she didn't talk to us.'

'We weren't that bad!' He crossed to the table and sat down opposite. For a moment she thought that he would reach across and take her hand, but he didn't.

He said, 'We care about her, that's all. Is that so wrong?'

'No, of course not, but — I don't know, maybe we were so busy trying to get it right we forgot why we were doing it?'

He got up and went through to the hall. She could hear him, visualize him taking his coat from the hook and looking in the hall mirror to straighten his tie. Then she heard the front door slam.

CHAPTER SIXTEEN

9.10 p.m.

The Parishes had gone away for the weekend leaving their two teenage sons behind. The oldest was nineteen and the youngest in the same year as his Sarah. Phillip Myers had worked this out from the assorted bits and pieces of information he had gleaned from Sarah's friends.

The Parishes' house was a nineteen-thirties bay-fronted semi at the end of a quiet cul-de-sac. He had not been able to find out the number. The kids he'd talked to knew where it was, but not unimportant details like addresses. He had hoped there would be evidence of a party going on, remembering, with a guilty start, the parties of his late teenage years. The complaints of neighbours. The desperate efforts to clean up before parents got back. The housewarming when he'd moved into his first bedsit flat and, long before independence, that one, humiliating time when the police had been called to a friend's place because of the noise and someone hadn't been smart enough to flush their stash down the toilet in time. He still remembered the horror of having to explain to his folks why he hadn't been home all night.

'But I was older,' he told himself. 'I was a student then.'

And yes, he had been, all of two years Sarah's senior. Somehow, in the drive over to the Parishes' house, that two years had ceased to be such a great divide. Now all he wanted was to get his daughter back.

The cul-de-sac was so quiet he thought he had to be mistaken, or that his informants had deliberately misled him. He drove slowly to the end of the road. Two houses stood together. No car in the drive of one, and lights on in the front room and the front bedroom. The other house appeared to be in darkness.

He got out of the car and looked around. The cul-de-sac was empty. The rain had ceased to fall and now the wind was rising, blowing the clouds across the moon. Lights glowed behind closed curtains, television pictures flickered across uncurtained glass. Phillip began to walk towards the semi at the end. Dimly through the thickly curtained bay window of the house, he could hear music.

His footsteps were loud on the gravel of the drive. Phillip stood for a moment in front of the wooden door. What if she wasn't here? Was it really likely that she would be?

He raised his fist and began to hammer on the door.

Phillip Myers had lost his temper. Lost it in a big way and even by the time Price arrived had not yet fully recovered it.

Phillip had not bothered with introductions. As soon as the door opened, he had pushed his way into the house, marched into the front room from which the music was escaping and turned off the CD player.

The silence was absolute within seconds. Then broken as the protests began.

'Oh come on, man, we weren't making that much noise.'

'I'm here to find my daughter,' Phillip announced loudly. 'Some of you, one of you has got to know where she is and you're going to tell me. You're going to tell me now.'

Graham, the eldest Parish son, stepped forward, still sober enough to put two and two together and not wanting anything to spoil his show. He tried to be placatory.

'You must be Sarah's dad. Look, I'm sorry, mate, but she's not here.'

Phillip turned on his heel and walked from the room, calling Sarah's name.

'Look, we told you, she ain't here.'

'Sarah!'

Phillip pushed into the kitchen, opening doors, shouting loudly as he did so.

'Sarah. I know you're here, Sarah!'

He stormed up the stairs, shoving anyone aside who got in his way.

'She isn't here! Look, mate, if you don't get out of here, I'm going to call the police.'

Graham raced up the stairs after him. He grabbed Phillip's arm as he reached the top of the stairs preparing to search the bedrooms, the bathroom, even the attic if there was a chance Sarah might be hiding there.

As Graham reached out and touched Phillip's sleeve the man turned on him, jerking his arm aside, hitting out reflexively with his other fist. He missed the young man by a mile, but his fist made contact with the landing window. Glass shattered, breaking the silence outside.

Thrown aside by Phillip's sudden movement, Graham lost balance. Arms flailing, he toppled backwards down the stairs.

A girl began to scream. People were dashing in all directions. Some to help Graham, some scattering away from Phillip Myers and others leaping forward to try to restrain him. Amidst the chaos, someone had the presence of mind to call the police.

Price was not amused. He had been about to go home when he was told Phillip Myers had been arrested.

He was even less amused now, an hour and a half later having seen Myers' hand patched up by the duty surgeon and spent a further forty minutes with him in the interview room getting his version of what was going on.

'Look, Mr Myers,' he said at last. 'We're all sympathetic. We all know what you must be going through, but if you had information you should have passed it on. Then we could have checked out this party, made sure your daughter wasn't there without all this unpleasantness.'

Phillip Myers looked at him, a cold anger in his eyes. 'I want to find my daughter, Sergeant. I want her back home safe and, frankly, I don't give a damn who I upset or how much "unpleasantness" I cause doing it. And as to calling you lot in, one thing I have learnt, Sergeant Price, is just how bloody little use that would be.'

He stood up and began to move towards the door. 'I'm leaving now. I've got more important things to do.' Price got to his feet also, the officer sitting near the door moving to block Myers' exit.

'Sit down, Mr Myers. I said, *sit down.*' Reluctantly, his gaze drifting from one to the other of the two men, Myers sat.

'Now listen to me. You were brought here on an assault charge. If you keep pushing we'll add breach of the peace to that and you'll be spending the night in the cells, and with the crowd we've got in here tonight, you'll be spending it up to your armpits in piss and puke. I have had about two hours' sleep in the last two days and, frankly, the sympathy angle is wearing just a little thin. As it happens, Graham Parish hasn't said yet that he wants to press charges. He's being understanding, which, in his position, is a darn sight more than I would be. You want to think yourself lucky that Mr Parish bounced or you'd find yourself up in court on Monday morning with a count of GBH on your record.'

He paused to draw breath, and, seeing that Myers was about to start again, held up a hand to silence him.

'That's enough. Now get off home. If we or Graham Parish, or his parents for that matter, decide to press charges then we know where to find you, don't we?' Phillip stood up and walked stiffly towards the door. 'My car?' he said.

'Is where you left it. I suggest you take a cab.'

Price sat for several minutes after Myers left. He was thinking deeply. Myers had never really explained the scratch marks on his face and he had shown tonight that he was capable of violence.

He shook his head. It was hardly the same. A flailing attack against a young man who'd got him riled was hardly the same as deliberate sexual assaults on girls as young as his own daughter.

Price gave that some more thought. Sexual violence? Was that why Sarah had run away . . . ? It was worth following up. At this point in time, anything seemed worth following up.

11.30 p.m.

The woman had dark hair and deep blue eyes. He'd been with her before, many times, and always there had been a pleasing simplicity to their lovemaking.

She had a good body, strong and supple and infinitely satisfying. Her mouth and hands soft and warm, and what she might be lacking in skill she made up for in familiarity and a willingness to please.

'Will you be gone again when I wake up?' Her voice sleepy and content.

'I don't know. Perhaps I'll stay.'

She smiled then and stretched luxuriously, turning on her side before going to sleep.

There had been only two women in his life who had ever behaved that way, been so relaxed and fearless in his presence. So unconcerned and unworried about appearance. And the other was dead now.

He swung his legs over the side of the bed and switched on the television set. The hotel had satellite and he flicked aimlessly through the channels. He kept the sound turned down, the woman's soft breathing the only noise in the room.

He found himself listening closely to the sound. Hearing her every breath, in and out, slower and deeper, deeper. He found himself breathing in time with her, matching her rhythm, his own breath slow and deep, a sleeping, dying breath.

What if it stopped, what if he slowed his own breathing, caught her rhythm, made it his own and then made it stop?

It never ceased to fascinate, this fine line between what was living and what was not.

This woman lived; the other one did not. There had been that final moment when the breath was no longer breath and the something that set her apart from death was gone for ever.

He sat for a minute longer, watching the woman sleep, waiting for the moment when he might decide if she should live or she should die.

Then he sighed, gave up the game and began to dress. He took his cheque book from the inside pocket of his coat and wrote a cheque, leaving it on the dressing-table weighted down by the glass ashtray.

He left so silently the woman would not wake.

Walking swiftly down the hall.

Remembering to breathe.

CHAPTER SEVENTEEN

11.40 p.m.

Jake had returned home and gone straight down to the basement. He could hear the man crying as he went through the second room. He'd been struggling to free himself and had fallen off the bed. He had stayed where he fell, lying at an awkward angle with his face pressed against the bare floor.

Jake had not had time to change for the benefit of the camera this time. He was dressed casually in jeans and open-necked white shirt. But he took time to don the ski mask before dragging his victim by pinioned arms and dumping him back on to the bed. The man screamed in agony as he hauled already cramped and swollen limbs back against the joints.

'Where did you think you could get to?' Jake asked him gently. 'No one leaves here walking, you know, my friend. No one.'

'Please. Let me go. I don't know who you are. I haven't even seen your face. I wouldn't tell anyone. Not a soul. I swear it, on my mother's life, I swear it. I haven't even seen your face . . .'

For a moment Jake paused, bending over him, smiling behind the mask. Then slowly, and with infinite care, he pulled the tape from the man's eyes. They struggled open, lashes fighting the adhesive left from the tape and the sudden blinding brightness. Jake stepped back out of shot and removed his mask.

CHAPTER EIGHTEEN

Sunday, 18 December, 9 a.m.

Mike put the phone down and returned to the breakfast table. 'That was Price,' he said. 'Checking in before he leaves for Devizes. He's dropping in on the Myers on the way out. It seems they called demanding to see him. He's going straight from there.'

'Anything new?' John enquired.

'Beyond the fact that David Martin appears to have done a moonlight, no.'

'David? What do you mean?'

'I mean he's left the hotel. He left a cheque in his room for payment of the bill and phoned them this morning to say he'd checked out. They called us. Apparently, he slipped out through the back way at some point last night.' He paused. 'It doesn't look good, John.'

Tynan sighed. 'Stupid fool,' he said. 'No, you're right. It's hardly a good way to proclaim his innocence. But I still find it hard to believe he could have harmed Theo. It just doesn't feel right.'

'What's this, cop instinct?' Maria asked. She smiled. 'I know, John. Maybe he'll come to his senses and turn himself in.'

The morning papers crashed through the letter box. Mike was closest to the door and went to get them. He scanned the front page as he walked back into the kitchen. Two stories competed for front-page space: an update on the sex attacker following the printing of the letters and the report on Sarah's disappearance from the leisure centre. The report kept to the broad lines of the release put out by the police press office. It was accompanied by photographs of the missing girl and an appeal by Mrs Myers for her daughter to come home. 'There's nothing we can't sort out,' the woman said. 'Nothing that can't be put right.'

There was, Mike noted, no mention of the girl having her mother's Visa card.

He dropped the paper on to the kitchen table and continued with his breakfast.

9.30 a.m.

The path to the Myers' house was original to the building. Black, white and red tiles laid out in an ornate geometric design. It was also well worn and, in the pouring rain, treacherously slippery as Sergeant Price ran towards the front door.

Paula Myers opened it as he reached the step. Price stood in the hall, wiping his feet energetically on the doormat.

'She has a boyfriend,' Paula Myers announced, with as much horror, Price thought, as if she'd just found her daughter mainlining drugs.

'Well,' Price countered, 'she's of the age when girls often do.'

'She has no time for boyfriends.' Phillip Myers emerged from the dining-room. 'Sarah's studies are what's important right now. I want her to get somewhere in life, not—'

'Quite, sir.' Price cut him off mid-flow. 'Look,' he said, more than a little annoyed. 'You got me out here on what you said was an urgent call. Made it sound as though you'd had contact with Sarah at the very least. You can sort out your differences with your daughter later. What's more important is does the boyfriend know where Sarah is?'

Myers stared, then shook his head and sank down into one of the high-backed chairs that stood either side of the dining-room door. He looked tired and suddenly quite grey. It was, Price thought, the first real emotion he had yet seen Myers display.

'Have you spoken to the boyfriend, Mr Myers, Mrs Myers?'

'No. No, that's just it,' Paula Myers told him. 'We found out from one of her friends, Maddie. She didn't want to tell, but I suppose she was more worried about Sarah than about what we might think.' She glanced meaningfully at her husband, who looked away, angrily. 'She gave us his name, Terry. Terry Ryan. He lives on Cavendish Road, right around the corner. But we don't know where . . .'

Her face crumpled suddenly and she began to cry, very softly as though embarrassed. 'We were going to knock on doors. Ask if anyone knew him.' She looked up at Price as though waiting for him to sort it. He reached out and patted her awkwardly on the shoulder.

'It's all right,' he said. 'We'll find him and I'll call you the moment we have any news.'

She nodded bleakly, seemed to be waiting for him to leave before she completely broke down. Her husband sat still, gazing at the floor.

'I'll call you, straight away,' Price reiterated, then tugged the front door open and stepped out into the rain.

It hadn't taken long to trace Terrence James Ryan. A call back to divisional to get them to check the voters' register and he had the address of Judith Ryan, Flat 2, on the top floor of a converted house at the end of Cavendish Road.

Price drove around the corner from Sullivan Avenue. The cordon was still up around the Howard home, but there was no one on the door. Retreated inside, no doubt, out of the foul weather. It was wrong, he thought, what they said about lightning not striking in the same place; the Howard house practically backed on to the Myers' garden.

The address he wanted was at the other end of Cavendish Road. A tall, imposing house, similar in design to the Myers', but this had a neglected, run-down look to it. Paint peeling from the front door and rust from the iron railing that blocked off the basement flat, staining the pavement.

There were five names, written in faded ink behind a perspex panel. No doorbell and no security. The door opened easily by an external handle, stairs straight ahead of him. Two doors leading off the hall, one to his left and one at the end of the hall. Both had Yale locks and doorbells.

Letters from the previous morning post lay unsorted on a narrow table. Price leafed through them. Mainly bills and circulars; nothing for Judith Ryan or her son.

Price glanced back at the front door. Not exactly the most security-conscious of places he'd ever been in.

The stairs were thinly carpeted and the polish on the wooden banister had more to do with the rub of hands than regular cleaning. There was grey-blue paint over faded wallpaper on the dusty walls.

Judith Ryan's flat was on the second floor with a small rug spelling 'Welcome' set outside. Price knocked and rang the bell, holding it down for the count of five before letting go. The door was opened as he took his finger away and a red-haired woman who looked too young to have a teenage son stared out at him. Her eyes were red too, Price noticed, and she looked as though she'd had little sleep.

Price had his identification in his hand. 'Police,' he said. 'I'm . . .'

'It's Terry, isn't it? You've found him. What's happened? Please, he is all right?'

Price was taken aback for an instant, then he caught on. 'Terry's missing?' he said.

Judith looked blank. 'I thought that must be why you'd come?' she said. 'I mean, you see, it's not like him.' She took a deep breath. 'Terry didn't come home on Friday night.'

9.30 a.m.

Max Harriman was reading the morning paper. Looking at the image of Sarah Myers on the front page it crossed his mind that this might be one of Jake's; she certainly had the blonde looks and slightly innocent air that Jake was specializing in at the moment, like a younger version of what Marion had become.

Max frowned slightly at the memory. Marion had not been good for Jake. Max had known, from the moment Jake had become so excited about those pictures Vincenza had sent him, that Marion would not be good for him.

It was true, Marion had inspired some of Jake's most beautiful work, some of his most original stuff, especially in the final scenes — Max couldn't wait to see that final film — but she had involved Jake much too closely, made him think of her as something more than just another star. It had become personal and that was always a mistake.

Max sighed and shook his head. In one thing, one perception, he was well ahead of Jake. Max had learnt long ago that their type, people like himself and Jake, they weren't made for the settled life with the one-to-one commitments that went with it. It didn't do to get involved like that, it took away so much of your objectivity.

To be a great artist, Jake had once said, you have to be both passionate and detached about your creativity. It had been a great phrase, Max thought. The local press had thought so too. And it should have been good — it had taken Jake all day to think of it and not exactly been the easiest of speeches to slip into the conversation.

Max put his paper down and riffled through the stack of cuttings books stacked on the floor. He knew just where to find the piece he wanted, flipping open the page to show a picture of two teenage boys grinning out at the photographer and the single paragraph beside it describing the award that they had won.

The headline spoke of 'Budding Film-makers' winning a top award and went on to tell how Jake Bowen and Nick Jarvis had won second place in a national competition for young film-makers — documentary section — for a film made about a local factory strike.

Nicholas Jarvis. It was a very long time since anyone had called him that.

He looked closely at the two boys. Excited smiles, lousy haircuts, standing on the steps of the terraced house belonging to Jake's parents.

They had been fifteen years old. The camera borrowed by their English teacher from a local community group. The teacher had fussed and nagged the whole time they were making their film, Max remembered. Always getting in the way.

Max smiled. Life had seemed so full of possibilities even then.

9.40 a.m.

Mike was still at John Tynan's when Stacey rang the police station. The memory had come to her in a dream, and for a little while after waking she had lain still and thought about it. Trying to fit the dream memory into what she knew to be real.

Painfully, she re-ran the entire thing, from her storming away from Richard to the moment he had found her and driven her attacker away.

The tightness in her chest, the panic that this evoked was almost more than she could bear, but she knew that what she thought she remembered could be crucial. She had to go through it, sort it out.

Finally, she sat up in bed and pushed the covers aside. The telephone was downstairs in the living-room. Stacey pulled on her dressing-gown and made her way down, repeating the words in her head as though they might escape her again.

This was no dream. Stacey was certain of that now. The words had come hard on the heels of a dream, but they had come into her mind in that time between sleep and waking and now she had prodded the memory, felt the pain of it, she knew that it was real.

Her mother called to her from the kitchen as she went by. Walked silently past her father as he came into the hall. Made her way straight to the telephone and dialled the number on the card that she had been given.

She was startled to find that Mike wasn't there.

'Oh!' Stacey said. 'Well, look, can you get a message to him, get him to phone me? It is important, yes. Tell him it's Stacey. Stacey Holmes. And that I've remembered something.'

CHAPTER NINETEEN

10 a.m.

'Do you mind if I smoke?'

Price shrugged. 'It's your house.'

'I know, but some people don't like it. Terry doesn't, I tend not to when he's here.'

Price smiled. 'Difficult things, teenagers,' he said. 'Think they can tell you everything.'

'Do you have children?'

Price shook his head. 'No, not me, never found anyone daft enough to have them with me.'

There was silence for a moment or two, then Price said, 'You reported him missing Friday night? You got a visit, I presume?'

'Yeah, a young constable. A quarter past one, it was.' She smiled. 'He looked a bit lost himself; funny, you know what they say about policemen getting younger . . .'

She trailed off, looking away from him and taking a cigarette from the pack. Her hands trembled a little as she lit the match. She was, Price thought, holding herself together very well now that he was here, but the pale face and red-rimmed eyes told a different story.

'I thought you'd come to tell me something,' she said. 'I thought . . .'

'No, like I said, I didn't even know your son had gone missing. Uniform deals with most of the Mispers, the older ones anyway.'

'Mispers?'

'Missing persons. Sorry. You see, when they get to Terry's age and there's nothing suspicious, well, the thing is, most of them go off in a strop and turn up again the next day. Starving hungry and ready for another round of parent-baiting.'

He watched her closely, not certain he was taking the right road with her, but she smiled slightly. 'Yeah, I suppose you're right,' she said. 'I mean, Terry's not a baby, but he is my son and he's never done anything like this before, you see. And it wasn't like we'd argued or anything. I saw him go off to school on Friday morning and he was fine. He was just fine.' The tears were back, threatening to overflow as she blinked rapidly.

'This girl, the one that's missing too. Sarah. It wasn't uniform that dealt with her?' She looked up sharply at him, the unspoken accusation clear. Was this girl more important than her son?

'Yes, it was. As I told you, she went to let someone into her mother's aerobics class and never came back. There was a worry at the time that she might be another victim . . .'

'Of this sex attacker?'

'Yes. You see I've been involved in working on that one. She fitted the profile, fifteen years old, small and blonde.'

'But Terry doesn't even know this girl,' Judith argued. The protest faded as soon as it was made and she sighed, 'He never mentioned her.' She shook her head.

Suddenly she sounded angry, frustrated. Price probed carefully, sensing that there was something more than just a son careless of what he told his mother.

'Did he talk much about his friends?'

'Of course he did!'

Obviously he'd touched a raw nerve. She recovered herself immediately, consciously. 'No, not really. I mean, we haven't lived here all that long, five, six months or so. And it's not, well, not the sort of place you bring friends back to . . .'

'I think it's very nice.' Price looked around at the poorly furnished flat. 'You've done a lot to make it homely,' he said gently and found that he really meant it. There wasn't much in the flat that hadn't come from a second-hand shop or cheap discount store, but the walls had been colour-washed and rag-rolled and finished with a pretty border. There were books and magazines and flowers in a cheap glass vase. An effort to make the place like home. But he could see she might feel sensitive, and if she had known about Sarah, known about the way she lived . . . The Myers house might be only round the corner but it could just as well have been a world away. It could have been a reason for Terry not to mention her, if he knew how his mother felt.

'And he never mentioned Sarah?' Price asked her again.

'No, I told you. He never did.' She hesitated, then said, 'You see, Terry and I, I guess we were getting to know each other again. I'd got divorced, you see, and Terry didn't live with me for quite a while.'

Price waited. There was more, but he clearly wasn't going to get it now. He got up ready to go. Terry had no local family, she had said. No family at all, in fact. Except his grandparents, her parents, and they'd just moved abroad. No friends he might have gone to, nowhere to go.

Judith had seemed awkward and uncomfortable then. It was as though she had suddenly realized how little she knew about her son and she was shaken by the knowledge.

She'd get back to him, Price thought, when she'd had another chance to think it through.

'I'll call you as soon as I know anything,' he said, as he had done with the Myers a short time before.

'The hall phone doesn't always work,' she said, 'and I don't have one. Not here.'

‘Ah, right. I see.’ That explained why Mr Myers hadn’t been able to trace Judith himself. He’d make bets that Myers would have made a beeline for the phone book the moment he had Terry’s name.

He took a plain white card from his pocket and scribbled his name and number on it. As an afterthought he added DI Mike Croft’s as well. ‘He’s my boss,’ he said. ‘Give me a call if Terry gets in touch.’

She took the card and nodded, tears beginning again as he took his leave.

Price walked back down the four flights of stairs and let himself out of the front door. There was something very wrong with this whole scenario, he thought. He just wished that he could work out what.

* * *

Stacey’s message was phoned through to Mike at John Tynan’s cottage.

‘She didn’t say what she had remembered?’ he reiterated.

‘No, sir, insisted on talking to you. Shame to spoil your day off though. We could send a uniform round.’

‘No, no, I’ll go to see her. You said there was something about the missing girl?’

‘Yes. A bus driver called it in. He’d just picked up his morning paper and recognized the girl. He’s sure he dropped her off at Hoton about ten o’clock last night.’

‘At Hoton? He’s certain?’

‘Seems so.’

‘No more news on David Martin, I suppose?’

There was not. Mike hung up thoughtfully.

‘Hoton?’ Maria asked him.

‘Our runaway. A bus driver thinks he remembers dropping her off there about ten o’clock last night.’ He glanced at his watch. ‘I have to go, I’m afraid, see this girl, Stacey.’

'Right. Look, I'll head back to Oaklands, I'll give you a call later.'

* * *

Stacey told him about her dream that was not a dream. She went through it calmly and in careful detail. She might, Mike thought, have been describing a shopping trip or her holiday plans, until you looked at the way her hands were shaking.

'And you're sure that's what he said?'

'Quite sure, Inspector Croft.' She took a deep breath and said the words again. 'He said, "I know you want it, Marion. I know you do. I know you do." '

Her words were flat, deliberately devoid of all feeling or tone.

'And the name was Marion. Not Mary or Marie or anything similar? You're absolutely certain about that?'

Stacey nodded. 'It's not a common name,' she said. 'I mean I know two Maries and even a Mary, though she's older than me. But Marion. I don't think I've ever even met a Marion. So I know I've got it right.'

Mike thanked her and got up to go.

'Do you think it will help you?' Stacey asked him.

He nodded. 'Yes, I really think it might. As you say, Marion isn't that common a name. It could be very significant. And I want you to know, I think you're handling this brilliantly.'

She half-smiled at him. 'I don't feel brilliant,' she said. 'Only I keep telling myself, he didn't really hurt me and I wasn't raped. Not like those other girls. I keep telling myself that.'

Mike left her, his mind a turmoil of possibilities.

No, Marion was not a particularly common name. Unusual enough to be distinctive. And he could not help but make the connection. Marion had been the name of the woman whose death Price was now following up, and Marion O'Donnel had Theo Howard's number in her book.

* * *

2 p.m.

John Tynan was astonished to find David Martin on his doorstep.

'You've got to let me in, John. I have to talk to someone.'

'How about talking to the police?' John questioned. 'They're looking for you.'

Davy shook his head. 'I know, at least, I guessed they must be.'

John Tynan looked thoughtfully at the young man standing on his doorstep. He was unshaven and rumpled; his clothes looked as though he'd slept in them. Very different from the smartly dressed figure John had usually seen at Theo's.

'You'd better come inside,' he said. 'But I'm warning you, David, when you've talked to me, I'm taking you into Norwich. You've got to turn yourself in.'

'You going to make me?'

For a moment, John thought he was going to hit out at him. Then he shook his head. 'No, you're right. I've got to go back and I know that. But I've spent all night going through this. I needed time. And I need to talk to someone first.' He gave John a look of such desperation that the older man was moved, despite his instinct towards caution.

Tynan said, 'See it from their point of view. From mine. Theo is found dead, murdered in her own home. You disappear, no word of explanation, you just skip out through the back way like some common thief. And you ask us not to think badly of you? For all I know, you might well have killed Theo. For all the police know, you probably did.' He shook his head. 'You've got half an hour; Davy. Long enough to have a cup of tea and give me your version of events before

I drive you to the station. Talk to me and let me take you in and I'll do everything I can for you. But you run out again and there'll be no one believes you're not implicated. You must see that.'

David nodded. 'Yes, I do. I do. Thank you, you won't regret it. I promise you that.'

CHAPTER TWENTY

3 p.m.

It had been a long drive and the light was already fading when Price arrived. Morrow suggested they go straight out and view the crime scene while there was still daylight left to see. Dental records had provided the final confirmation that the body was that of Marion O'Donnel.

Morrow drove. An experience Price vowed he was never going to repeat, tearing along the curving down-land road as though it was a slalom course grafted on to a race track.

He pulled the car into a farm gate close to a small cottage and pointed.

'Up there, that's where we found her. The gate was opened. Somebody had cut through the chain.'

'They came prepared then,' Price commented as he climbed out of the car, trying not to notice that his legs were shaking from all the compensatory braking he'd been doing.

Charlie Morrow nodded. 'Oh yes,' he said, 'I think they came prepared.'

The place where the car had burned was the widest point of the track, before it narrowed into a single file walkway between the fields. It was unremarkable, just a barren area of rutted mud and grass and a rough oblong of charred earth showing where the car had stood.

Morrow had talked almost non-stop during their drive, bringing Price up to speed on his conversation with Mike. He had, Price discovered, a disconcerting way of turning to look at his passenger while he talked rather than concentrating on the road. Price was certain he'd made most of the curves on a mixture of memory and instinct. It certainly hadn't been by sight.

He flipped through the photographs of the crime scene that Morrow had provided for him, trying to match the pictures to the reality. The photographs showed what must have been a wet, foul-tempered night; they revealed little of the surrounding landscape.

'What's that over there?' he asked, his attention attracted by a large conical hump that rose out of the flat earth on the opposite side of the road.

'Silbury Hill,' Morrow told him. 'I'll take you up there later; when you've more chance of getting a view. It's fenced off now, problems of erosion, but we still get the odd tourist braving the barbed wire, looking for crop circles or something equally psychic I suppose.'

'You're not into that sort of thing, then?' Price grinned wryly.

Charlie Morrow grunted. 'Not so's you'd notice,' he said. He gestured towards the rise behind them. 'Want to go and take a look?'

He set off up the path without waiting for a reply.

Price followed.

It seemed an oddly appropriate place to contemplate a murder; Price thought. The mist was coming down, much as it must have done the evening that the woman died, and it would soon be dark. The dampness seeped through his clothes and into his bones, but he hardly noticed it. Despite himself, he was captivated.

Morrow had led him into the tomb itself. West Kennet Long Barrow. Thousands of years old, and Price could feel the weight of every one of them pressing down on him through what looked like precariously balanced rock.

Someone had lit candles inside the tomb. He commented on them.

'People come here all the time,' Morrow told him. 'Religious feelings they're supposed to have for it or something.'

He sounded dismissive, but there was something in his voice that made Price look at him suspiciously. It was at least an edge of affection; it might even have been a touch of awe.

It was in the tomb and the flickering candlelight that Morrow, with an unexpected sense of the dramatic, gave Price the two sheets of folded paper.

One was the poem Price already knew, a copy of the one found in Theo Howard's hand.

'It was in the dead woman's flat,' Morrow told him. 'Is it the same?'

Price nodded slowly. 'The other one was found in her bag. It seems to be about this place.'

He unfolded the paper and began to read.

I spent the night beneath the stones, he said,
But didn't sleep,
Their whisperings kept my thoughts alive,
And held my mind from dreams.
I spent the night beneath the stones, he said
And watched the beacon lit upon the dead man's hill.
And when the night had fallen full,
I spent the night beneath the stones, he said
I spent the night beneath the stones, he said,
But did not sleep.
Your voice within the beacon kept my thoughts alive.
And held my mind from dreams.

At the bottom of the sheet were written the words, 'With love, David.'

CHAPTER TWENTY-ONE

5 p.m.

Harriman was preparing his evening meal. He took chicken breast from the styrofoam package with an old fork he kept specifically for meat and placed it on a grill lined with foil. Potatoes were already baking in the tiny oven; he had to turn the flame up high to get the skins to crisp the way he liked. He had already prepared the salad, slicing everything neatly and arranging carefully on his plate.

Max liked to cook. He knew his workmates had found it a little odd when he'd admitted to this in an unguarded moment, but the fact was, it gave him great satisfaction that he knew exactly what went into his body.

His mother had always cooked, drumming into him from an early age how important it was to treat your body right, and Max had taken her advice to heart. He kept himself fit with regular exercise, his body well fed and his mind active, and he was meticulous about the details.

Max crossed to the sink and washed his hands once again. The third time during his ritual of food preparation.

Then he examined his hands and nails with the greatest care.

Max did a manual job operating a lathe, and the hands of his fellow workers were calloused and stained in a way that Max could not allow. He wore gloves at work and kept his hands very clean at other times. In addition, twice daily he massaged them with a cream used, so the advertising said, by Icelandic fishermen to combat the effects of cold.

It had earned him some odd comments the first few weeks at this job, but he did his work well enough to silence the criticism and the 'he's a bloody poof' jokes had faded when they had spotted the pictures taped to the inside of his locker.

It was, Max thought, the sort of thing that Jake would do to throw others off the track. The women he attacked would remember his hands as being soft and smooth — if they remembered anything at all — not rough and hard like the skilled manual worker that he was.

He went back to the sink and scrubbed at his nails once again, shaking his head. There were still marks. Stains around the nails and on his knuckles, but it would have to do.

He thought of Jake. Jake had never laughed at his neatness or his meticulous habits. Jake had been the only one Max's mother had ever really liked, but then, Jake always knew the right thing to say.

Staring at the table with its blue-checked cloth, carefully set and clean enough for his mother to be proud of, Max remembered how it had been when Jake had come to call for him.

'Your house, it always looks so nice,' Jake would say, and Max's mother would award him one of her small, tight smiles and let Max go out without another word.

Max's face grew dark as another image imprinted across the first. His mother dead on the kitchen floor, her small, tight smile replaced by a bloody grin that split across her cheeks from ear to ear.

5 p.m.

Judith had walked for a long time before finally getting up enough courage to go to the Myers' house. Their number was in the phone book and had taken only moments to find. The house was only a ten-minute walk from her flat, but it had been close on an hour before Judith had finally been able to bring herself to go to the door.

Paula Myers replied quickly to her ring, her pale face anxious and the faint hopefulness in her eyes fading as she saw the stranger on her doorstep. She had been expecting news. Judith didn't look like news.

'Yes,' she said. 'Can I help you?'

Judith swallowed nervously. 'I'm sorry,' she said. 'Sorry to bother you. It's just that I thought maybe we should talk; if we put our heads together, we may get some idea.' She broke off, aware of how jumbled her words must sound and of the woman's cold stare.

She began again. 'I'm . . . I'm Judith Ryan,' she explained. 'Terry's mother. I just wondered, have you heard anything?'

For a moment Judith thought Paula Myers was going to fly at her; the look of rage and pain that crossed her face was so strong and so obvious. Then it faded. The two women gazed at one another with red-rimmed eyes. 'I think you'd better come in,' Paula said.

'It's a lovely house,' Judith said. She was seated at the kitchen table cradling a mug of very hot coffee between her hands.

'Thank you. You live on Cavendish Road . . . it's a nice road, Cavendish.'

Judith half-smiled. 'We live at the other end, in one of those tall three-storey places. It's flats now. Terry and I, we have the top floor.' She sipped her coffee. 'It's all right really, and it's our own place. That's what matters.'

Paula didn't really know what to say to this woman now she was inside the house. They had spent the last ten minutes like this. Dodging around the questions each one wanted to ask. Trying not to step on feelings that were so bruised already one more hurt would make little difference.

'I didn't know about Terry,' she said.

'No, neither did I. I mean about Sarah. He never told me.' Judith hesitated. 'I thought we'd got a good relationship,' she said. 'Thought he told me things. But he never mentioned Sarah. He didn't mention many of his friends really, but I never noticed somehow. Not till now.' She smiled wryly, trying not to feel too uncomfortable with the admission.

Paula smiled back. 'Nice to know we're not the only ones facing that conclusion,' she said. 'God, but I feel so helpless just sitting here. Maybe Phil was right, at least he did something.'

'Did something?'

'Yes, well, it turns out they were going to a party yesterday. Both of them.'

'Terry as well? He didn't say a thing. Well, he talked about going out . . .'

'Oh, don't fret. Sarah spun a yarn about staying at a friend's. Seemed to think we'd disapprove if she'd told the truth.'

'Would you?'

'No! Of course not. Sarah's . . . Probably. I mean yes. I suppose we would if I'd thought she planned to be out all night. Anyway, Phil found out where this party was supposed to be. His going round there didn't do much at the time, but this morning one of the girls phoned us. Said, did we know about Terry?'

She paused. 'The parents are away, where this party was, so you can just imagine.' She smiled bitterly. 'I mean that's just it, isn't it? You can just imagine, more to the point you can remember.'

Judith thought back to her rather strict upbringing. Actually parties at sixteen without adults present were not something in her experience, but there had been other things that probably more than made up for that.

'But I mean, we could have compromised. Picked her up at midnight or something. I don't know. And it doesn't explain why they ran away.' She looked awkwardly at Judith. 'I'm sorry to ask this, but was Terry in some kind of trouble or worried about something? I mean, I know how that must sound . . .'

Judith was shaking her head. 'No. I'm certain not. He was happy here. Settled well in school. It had been a fresh start for us.' She sighed deeply. 'I don't know why he would go off like that.' She looked hopefully at Paula. 'Sarah, she had no problems, I mean . . .'

Paula shook her head. 'I don't know. She was doing well at school, seemed to have plenty of friends. The usual worries, I suppose, but nothing . . . She didn't get on with her father.' The words came out almost unbidden and immediately she felt she had uttered a betrayal. 'I mean, a lot of teenagers have problems with their parents, there was nothing. I didn't mean . . . Oh God, I'm making this sound much worse than it is. He's gone out tonight,' she added irrelevantly. 'These days he's always going out.'

She looked up suddenly as though a thought had struck her. 'Terry's father. He wouldn't have gone to his father? No, I suppose you already thought of that.'

Judith sat quite still, the coffee cup still clasped tightly between her hands. 'Oh no,' she said, keeping her voice as steady as she was able. 'We're divorced, you see. I mean, obviously you realized that. Terry's father walked out of our lives when Terry was just six years old. Terry wouldn't even think of going to him.'

5.30 p.m.

The search warrant had been applied for as soon as David Martin had debunked. It had been granted in a special session and served mid-afternoon. Mike's beeper went when he was halfway back to Tynan's place. He pulled over on to the grass verge and called in, then turned his car around and headed back to Norwich.

The search was well under way by the time he got there. White-clad figures, their hands covered in surgical gloves, moving from room to room giving the impression that they really knew what they were looking for.

'The lady was an actress then,' someone commented. Mike took the proffered book of clippings and reviews. There were, he saw, glancing across at the shelves, about a dozen such books.

A shout from upstairs distracted him. He went up to the second bedroom. David's room, he thought, seeing the men's clothes lying on the bed and the shaving gear on the shelf. He thought about Davy's assertion that they had been lovers, wondering how much this room had seen.

The magazines were nothing unusual, soft-porn top-shelf editions, and Mike was ready to dismiss them, but one edition was being thrust into his hands, open at the centrefold. It had been marked by a bulky envelope slipped between the pages.

'Bit of a looker, guv! Marianne,' he commented, looking at the name that headed the page.

Mike opened the envelope and tipped the contents carefully on to the bed. About a dozen photographs fell out. Polaroids of the woman in the centrefold. The poses were amateur and the photography of questionable ability, but there was no doubt but that it was the 'Marianne' of the centrefold. Blonde hair, blue eyes, her body more graceful than voluptuous. She gazed out at the photographer, her expression slightly uncertain. A quality of innocence, despite the lewdness of some of the poses, that was highly charged. Genuinely seductive, Mike caught himself thinking.

He shoved the thought to the back of his mind and took a pen from his jacket pocket. Used it to flip the photos over. With the third, he struck lucky. There was a date, some eighteen months previous, and a name.

'Marion,' Mike said softly.

CHAPTER TWENTY-TWO

6 p.m.

Price and Morrow had retreated to the Red Lion in Avebury. It was still early enough for the dining-room to be relatively empty and they found a table at the back of the room where they could talk about the case in privacy.

'Nice this,' Price commented, looking around the comfortably furnished dining-room with its heavy beams and warm lighting. The food was good too, he thought, realizing just how hungry he was and how long the day had been.

Outside, although it was only six o'clock, the night was closing in, fended off slightly in the pub yard by the only street-light in the entire village.

Morrow was eating with great enthusiasm and didn't seem to want to be interrupted. Price got on with his own meal in equal silence. He was beginning to like Morrow. The man was blunt to the point of rudeness, drove like a maniac and seemed terminally prone to bossiness. But he had an energy and drive that Price guessed he was going to enjoy, and a commitment to the job that matched Price's own.

Morrow's large hand reached into his pocket, withdrew a small carton of single cream, opened it and dumped it in his coffee. He'd pocketed about a dozen of these little cartons when they'd been ordering their meal, and about the same amount of sugar, brown and white in little packets.

Price waited for the sugar to emerge from the big man's pocket. He was disappointed. Morrow drank it without.

'Tell me something,' he said. 'All that stuff you half-inched. You a klepto or what?'

Morrow slurped his coffee noisily. 'Probably,' he said. 'But I'm getting help.'

'Oh?'

Morrow nodded solemnly. 'I'm training my sergeant,' he said. 'So far she's only got the hang of sugar. Women have stupid pockets, have you noticed that? No room for anything but a lipstick and a pack of tissues. I mean, what the hell use is that?'

Price shook his head. 'Yeah, but they have handbags,' he pointed out.

'Not our Beth. Doesn't believe in them.'

He wolfed a few more mouthfuls of steak pie, sucking up more coffee without first swallowing the mouthful of food.

Price shuddered inwardly and looked away, half-nauseated, half-amused.

Morrow swallowed again, then said, 'She died of smoke inhalation but there was enough of a cocktail of drugs and drink in her system that I doubt she knew much about it.' He paused, prodded at his pie once more. 'Bloody hope she didn't know anyway. Hell of a mess.'

'There was enough soft tissue left for the tox results and blood typing then?' Price enquired.

Morrow nodded. 'Practically pickled, she was, probably had been for days, the surgeon reckons. All body tissues saturated.'

'Well,' Price observed, 'she sure as hell didn't drive there.'

Morrow guffawed, at least that's what Price thought it was. 'The car she was found in was stolen two or three days before her death. The owner was away so there were no reports, but witness statements have given us a rough fix. It was a BMW 3 series before they killed it,' he said with feeling. 'Quality. Whether that says anything or not I couldn't tell you.'

He paused, chewed thoughtfully for a moment or two, then said almost wistfully, 'Amazing things women's bodies. I mean, if she'd been a man we'd have known a whole lot less about her.' He looked deliberately at Price, leaning forward slightly, and said, 'Did you know that the womb is often the last thing to be destroyed? Symbolic that, don't you think?'

Price laughed, he couldn't help himself, then he sobered. 'The question is,' he said, 'who killed her and what the hell does she have to do with Theo Howard?'

6 p.m.

Davy had given John no trouble. He had driven him back to divisional HQ at Norwich and delivered him quietly to the front desk. The custody officer had taken over from there.

John, waiting for Mike to finish Davy's interview, had made a statement telling how Davy had arrived on his doorstep. Then he'd drunk several cups of tea with the desk sergeant in the tiny, untidy room behind the front office.

'You miss the job?' the desk sergeant asked him. He knew John, had been around long enough to remember him as a serving officer.

Tynan nodded. 'Old habits and all that, but I fill my time one way or another.' He smiled. 'It's hard though, wanting to get stuck in and being kept on the sidelines like some damned civilian.'

'You knew the dead woman.'

'Theo, yes, my wife and I grew up with her, well, her older sister really.' He paused, settled himself more comfortably in his chair. He had no real right to be here, aware he was trading on his past reputation and on Mike's friendship. But what the hell, it was a quiet Sunday evening and the opportunity to talk shop with old colleagues didn't come up all that often.'

'So,' he said, 'anything new on this other business . . . ?'

* * *

Mike sat down at the table and started the tape, going through the usual formalities. Time of interview and those present. 'Mr Martin has not requested the services of a lawyer,' he said, 'but understands that he may do so at any time and that the interview will then terminate until such time as one can be made available.'

He looked across at David Martin. 'You have been made aware of your rights, Mr Martin?' Mike asked quietly.

'Yes, yes, thank you, yes.'

'And you understand the information that you have been given?'

'Yes, I understand,' Davy said. 'I understand it all.'

Mike tipped the envelope from the evidence bag and emptied the photographs on to the table top.

'Do you recognize these, Mr Martin? For the record, Mr Martin is being shown photographs found in his room at Miss Howard's house. They will be listed as exhibit B1.'

Davy looked at the pictures and swallowed hard. 'Yes, I recognize them,' he said. 'I took them.'

'And the woman in the picture,' Mike asked. 'Who is she?'

'A girlfriend. She was a girlfriend. Ex-girlfriend now of course.' He laughed nervously.

'Why "of course", Mr Martin?'

David Martin looked surprised. 'Well, because of Theo, of course. I never looked at another woman after Theo.'

'And your relationship with Theo Howard, for the record?' Mike asked him, slightly shifting tack.

'We, we were . . . I loved her.'

'You were lovers, Mr Martin, is that what you are telling me?'

'You know it is.'

'And this other woman, this former girlfriend.' Mike changed direction once again. 'Can you tell me her name?'

David was looking puzzled now. 'I don't see . . .' he began.

'Just answer the question, please.'

'But it's not relevant. Look, I told you, I never looked at another woman after Theo. These pictures, she asked me to take them. She meant nothing to me after Theo.'

'She must have meant something for you to have kept the photographs,' Mike said. 'Her name please, Mr Martin.'

For a moment David Martin stared at him, then he said, 'It's Marion. Marion O'Donnel. I knew her for a little while when I was living in London. She asked me to take them for her. Some magazine she wanted to get into. I don't know. She did some modelling or something for them afterwards.'

Mike took the second evidence bag from his folder and laid the magazine on the table. 'This magazine?'

Again Davy swallowed hard and nodded that it was.

'For the record,' Mike intoned, 'Mr Martin is nodding.'

'What does this have to do with Theo?' Davy was asking. 'I came here because of Theo, not because of some other woman.'

There was a knock on the interview room door, a whispered consultation between someone outside and the PC sitting in on the interview. Mike was called out. He returned moments later with a second envelope and added its contents to those already on the table.

'Did you also take these, Mr Martin?'

David stared in silence at the images strewn across the table. Pictures of Theo in various stages of undress. She had taken care of herself and her body was still well-shaped and firm. She laughed playfully into the camera as though it was all some huge joke. These pictures were not pornographic, merely intimate, and Mike felt suddenly too much like a voyeur.

'You took these also, Mr Martin?'

'Yes, I took them. Theo asked me to.'

There was a catch in the younger man's voice. Tears caught in the back of his throat. Mike pushed forward.

'And now Theo's dead,' he said softly. 'Dead, Just like Marion O'Donnel. Strange coincidence, don't you think, Mr Martin?'

CHAPTER TWENTY-THREE

8 p.m.

Max turned the pages slowly. The books were like old friends to him now. His closest confidants.

He rarely saw Jake, to speak to anyway, though he followed his career closely through the newspaper reports and the work that Jake put out. Jake always made sure Max Harriman had his copy of a new work. Jake always knew where Max could be found no matter how many times he moved.

Max could not say the same. It was years since he had known exactly where Jake made his home. He had a flat in London; Max had borrowed it a time or two, he had a key. Marion had used it too when she worked there, and, Max knew, others went in and out, using the place as a letter drop and collection point. But that was not where Jake lived. As far as Max knew, it was not even a place where Jake spent the night.

He missed Jake, missed the closeness of their early years when he and Jake and the rest had been the best of friends. He often thought about them, the kids he'd gone to school with. Had them in his cuttings books too, when they'd done anything worth recording.

One was inside. Armed robbery, three counts. Others had gone their own, more respectable way. He had the notices of marriages and births and even deaths of half a dozen others he and Jake had known. But it was only Jake that had made it to the big time. Jake who'd seen the greater picture, known that nothing really mattered so long as you were following your own particular star.

He turned the pages, pausing at one particular entry. Jake's first really successful film. It was the story of a police raid on a sex shop and the seizure of some special stock that Jake had provided for them.

It had been tame beside the stuff he was producing now, Max thought, but he still had his copy, he hung on to it knowing it would be worth an absolute packet some day.

* * *

Jake stared out into the garden through his conservatory window. He had a night sight in his hand and had spread food on to the lawn hoping they would come back. The badgers had made his garden a regular stopping-off point and Jake had come to like watching them. They were a family group, both parents and three little cubs. He liked to watch them as they came snuffling through the long grass near the hedge and nosing around at the scraps he put down for them. They argued over the food like nursery school kids at a Christmas party.

Jake liked the creatures far more than he liked the average human.

He scowled suddenly, remembering Marion, how close she could get to them before they ran away.

It soothed him a little, remembering that, though his pride still hurt at just how much he had misjudged her. But he knew he must let the anger go now. If things as wild and fey as the badgers could be taken in by that stupid, nosy cow, then it was not so bad that Jake could make that same mistake too.

It would be the last time, though, Jake made that promise to himself. The very last.

8.30 p.m.

Sitting in the Myers' house had brought back so many memories for Judith. It was, in many ways, so like the house her grandparents had owned. Tall and imposing, in truth a little in need of modernization and repair, but a place Judith had loved.

She remembered the big kitchen, the two halves of it, divided for the preparation of milk and meat. The long wooden table. The family gathered, generations of it, at Sabbath, at festivals.

Judith's father had married outside his faith and Judith had been their only child. It had been hard on her grandparents, she knew, but they had accepted it. Her parents had divorced when she was three and Judith spent holidays with her father. Mostly with her grandparents.

With her mother, she lived one life. At her grandparents' house she lived another, one steeped in ritual and tradition. In music and stories. Sometimes, she thought, the stories had seemed far more real than the everyday world of school and her mother's home. She had loved the stories, told in her grandfather's sonorous voice. Elaborate tales to be narrated slowly, savoured like a fine wine.

Judith winced at the analogy. The strongest thing she allowed herself these days was coffee and it would stay that way. For Terry's sake.

She remembered that day clearly, so clearly. That final Pesach she had spent with them. Terry had been five years old, the youngest child present. Her grandfather the patriarch, in his dark suit, sitting at the head of the table. Judith herself heavily pregnant with her second child and deeply, deeply unhappy with the way her world was turning.

Terry, the youngest child, a little shy because it was the first time he had played the role, going to her grandfather and asking the question. Asking why they were celebrating with the bitter herbs and the salt and the Passover Lamb. His great-grandfather sitting him on his knee and telling the story of the flight from Egypt and the days his people had spent in the wilderness before they came finally to the promised land.

'Were you there?' Terry had asked him, his eyes round and innocent.

'No, I'm not quite that old, my boy.'

And then the final words, the pledge to celebrate the festival next year in Jerusalem. Next year. And Judith could remember her feelings of utter and complete despair. Remember also how much she had craved a drink, the partial oblivion that alcohol would provide.

Next year in Jerusalem. She'd heard that every bloody year since she could remember and that next year had never, ever come. Not for her grandparents, not for her father not for her.

Her grandfather had told her once that Jerusalem represented a dream. The image of fulfilment and the precious treasure of the soul.

She could remember his face when he had said those words. The conviction in his eyes.

'You'll find your Jerusalem,' he'd told her. 'You will see.'

But Judith knew that, search as she might, she never would, unless she glimpsed it briefly in the bottom of a glass.

She remembered how she had excused herself then. Got awkwardly to her feet with the weight of the second child wanting to drag her down. Had hurried from the room and sneaked into the kitchen. A half-empty bottle of whisky lay hidden at the bottom of her bag. She took a teacup from the cabinet and poured herself a large measure, drinking it down almost without tasting.

Then another.

Judith could taste it now, sitting in her tiny kitchen, hugging a cup of cooling coffee between her hands. Disgusted with the memory of herself, craving oblivion in spite of her disgust. Looking out of the window at the pouring rain, she thought of her son. Of what had happened with Terry.

8.30 p.m.

Davy lay on his back on the bench in the police cell and thought of Theo.

He had touched her when he'd found her dead. He'd told no one that. Touched her face, her hair, the curve of her breast and hip, imagining the flesh beneath.

He had felt no disgust at her death, at the smell of sick and alcohol, only a strange sense of detachment that this woman, lying so still on the couch, was the same woman that had shared his bed. Finally, Davy had taken a comb from his pocket and combed out Theo's hair, arranging it across the pillow. He had still been holding the comb in his hand when the banging on the front door had broken the spell. Then the police had been there and life had become so much more complicated.

He fell asleep and dreamed of Theo. Theo lying beside him, her body still warm and the grey hair tangled about her face. She reached out, wrapping him in her arms, drawing him close, her body curving against his. And he, responding so strongly to her touch that even in his sleep he felt himself grow hard. Wanted her. Breathing in time to her rhythm, breathing her breath as if they were a single being.

Then Theo dissolving, becoming another woman with fairer hair and lips stained so red they seemed to drip with blood. The woman pressing her mouth against his, sucking the air from him as he wrapped her tight, pinning her to the ground.

He felt her body writhing beneath his own. The arousal and the fear blending into a single emotion as he held the woman hard enough to cause her pain, pulling away from her kisses that were not kisses and threatened to suck the breath from his lungs.

In his sleep, Davy cried out, struggling to control her. He'd never felt so much strength in anyone, man or woman, as he felt now. She had one hand free and he fought to catch her wrist again, throwing his whole weight down on top of her.

With a cry of pain, Davy woke, just as the woman's red tipped hands flashed out to rake across his face.

11.15 p.m.

It had taken only an hour or two to find her, but then he knew the places to look now. Had watched her enter the pub with her friends, followed them inside, sat drinking only feet away from them all evening without them paying any notice. The pub crowded enough for a lone drinker not to draw too much attention, and anyway, he'd gone through the pretence of waiting. Looking at his watch, showing reluctance when someone wanted to use the chair next to his. He'd been too clever to be noticed, he was sure of it.

He had left just before the group had broken up, the first couple going off just about the time he did, turning towards the main road, too preoccupied to pay him any mind.

He'd made certain that the girl had been alone. No boyfriend, one of four in the group who'd obviously been singles.

Then he'd waited, parked in a side street with a view of the main door. She could have left the other way, of course. And if she had, slipping out of the side door, then that would have been it. But he was certain she would not.

His waiting time paid off. She came out of the main door with two other friends. He waited some more, breathing shallow with anticipation as they stood a minute or two and talked on the pub step. Then the couple turned one way and the girl the other.

Yes! Yes!

He followed slowly, waiting until she had walked almost out of sight before starting the car. Would she go left towards the bus station or turn right down the side road towards the park?

Right towards the park.

Right towards the park.

He drew the car into a side street and got out quickly. His feet in their soft-soled shoes made little noise on the pavement. He followed, keeping the same distance behind her all the way until she reached the spot he wanted, where the road swung left and there was a small patch of derelict ground.

Then he ran, grabbing her from behind and using his momentum to take her down.

This one wasn't like the last. She didn't fight. Just lay there, stunned, her mouth opened in a silent scream, her breath stinking of alcohol and cigarettes.

The smell nauseated him so he hit her anyway, striking again and again at the side of her head until it lolled back at an awkward angle, blood staining the lips an even deeper red.

CHAPTER TWENTY-FOUR

Monday, 19 December, 3 a.m.

Terry woke up cold and stiff, realizing that the fire had burned itself out.

He swore under his breath and eased his arm from around Sarah's shoulders, feeling the familiar pins and needles sensation in his fingers. He'd been in one position far too long.

Sarah opened her eyes with a start. 'What's going on? Oh, it's freezing.'

'The fire's gone out.'

He tried to get it started again while Sarah scraped around for more kindling and fuel.

'What time will it get light?' she asked him.

'I don't know. It's getting light when I get up usually, so I suppose about seven.'

'Right.' She fell silent, hugging herself against the cold and staring into the fire as though willing it to burn. She didn't need to voice what they both were thinking. That was hours away, and it looked as though it was still going to be raining. Then, even when they got to Oaklands, there was no guarantee that the woman Terry wanted to see would be there. She hadn't been there yesterday morning and they hadn't dared to go back again twice in one day. Would she be back today? Sarah didn't feel she could spend much longer cooped up in this freezing cold semi-derelict house. She was hungry and tired and fed up with being damp and cold.

With an effort, she tried to put her doubts aside.

'My gran had a real fire,' she said. 'In her old house, before she moved to the bungalow. We used to make toast on it sometimes, in the winter.'

'Wish we had some bread, we could give it a try. I'm starved.'

'Yeah.'

'There's that little village not far up the road. The shops'll be open soon.'

Sarah sighed heavily. It all seemed so unreal; home seemed so far away.

'We've got to call home,' she said. 'They'll be worried sick.'

'I know.'

They fell silent again, guilt creeping in and preventing words. Then Sarah asked him, 'Why did you run away? I mean really.'

He didn't look as though he was ready to answer. She pushed harder.

'Look, Terry, I've stuck by you all through this, I'm not going to run out on you now.' She paused, listening to the rain outside, waiting. 'I think I deserve to know, don't you?'

Terry shook his head. 'You wouldn't understand,' he said.

'Try me! God's sake, Terry, I think you owe me that much.' She paused, reached out and took his hand. 'Please.'

He looked sideways at her, then moved closer, sitting side by side, staring into the fire as he began. He really liked Sarah, a lot. Wanted her to be his proper girlfriend, and he knew he could only do that if he was honest with her.

But still, it was so hard. The habit of silence so ingrained that it was near impossible to break. Doctor Lucas had been easy to talk to. She'd made it clear from the start that she was used to hearing stuff, all kinds of stuff that might shock other people. And she had never shown anything either in her face or in the tone of her voice that had made him feel that she was judging him, hating him the way he knew so many people would.

He took a deep breath. 'I had a baby brother,' he said. 'He died when he was only two weeks old.'

He pulled away from her, turned so that he could see the expression on her face. 'They said I killed him, Sarah.'

CHAPTER TWENTY-FIVE

7.45 a.m.

Price woke up in a strange bed, his usual early morning confusion mitigated by the untuneful shouts coming from the bathroom next door.

For a moment Price thought that Morrow was in pain, then he realized that he was singing in the shower. Splashing energetically and bellowing something unidentifiable at the top of his voice.

Price groaned, dragged himself out of bed, pulled his dressing-gown on and went in search of a cup of coffee. The clock said a quarter to eight but it felt like only five minutes since he had dragged some sheets on to Charlie Morrow's spare bed and just managed to collapse into it before falling asleep.

He found the kitchen on the second try. The first door had revealed a through lounge with a dining-table at one end and a three-seater sofa with matching chair at the other. There wasn't a great deal in between and what there was seemed veiled in a layer of long undisturbed dust. There was one clean area in the room, which told him a lot more about Charlie Morrow. The alcove next to the fireplace and opposite the solitary armchair was occupied by some remarkable looking hi-fi, stacked on several levels of custom-built racking. And it was clean, spotlessly clean.

Price found the kitchen at the next try and was relieved that, if not up to the pristine standards of the hi-fi, it was at least less dirt-ridden than the rest of the living-room. There were cups in the drainer and a kettle on the side with a tea caddy and a large blue jar marked 'Coffee.' The morning, thought Price, was looking up.

Somehow, he wasn't surprised to find the sugar bowl crammed with little packs of sugar, or the fridge piled up with tiny cartons of half cream and UHT milk.

Curious, he opened a cupboard door. Plastic packs of ketchup and mayonnaise, tartare sauce and French mustard showered down on him.

'Shit!' Price muttered, picking stuff up and pushing it safely back behind the cupboard door just as the man himself walked in.

'Find everything?' Morrow said, grinning broadly.

'Is there anything you don't pinch?' Price asked him irritably.

Morrow's smile broadened. 'Believe me, Sergeant, my criminal tendencies are very specialized. Sleep well?'

'Not bad.'

'Right, how about breakfast?'

Price eyed him cautiously. 'You mean you actually have *food* in this kitchen?'

Morrow looked offended. 'Don't be silly,' he said. 'We'll head over to Mickey's place. What I've got in store for you this morning, Sergeant, you'll need a good breakfast inside you.'

Price took his coffee and went off to get dressed. He wasn't quite sure he wanted to know what Charlie Morrow had planned.

7.45 a.m.

Max was watching the video again. The one he'd first seen all those months ago.

'Marianne', as she was billed simply in the credits, had been the most beautiful thing he'd laid eyes on. That thick golden hair and pale skin and the way she'd reddened her mouth so much her lips seemed coated with fresh blood.

She was dressed in black. A tight gown that clung to every curve. The two men with her, undressing her, seemed to peel the dress from her body as though she was shedding a second skin. He watched as she lifted her arms above her head, turning towards the camera, rejoicing in the way the camera adored her body.

He imagined he held the camera in his hands now, reviewing every frame as though through an imaginary lens. Panning shots, close-ups, focusing on his favourite poses as Marion moved across the room, the two men with her caressing her body, stroking down the length of it, guiding her towards the king-sized bed.

Then, abruptly, he switched off the video. He was growing bored with these pictures of Marion, tired of the same old image.

He picked up the remote and flicked through the channels, trying to find some local news. Would they have found the body yet? Not likely, he supposed, that would be to expect efficiency from the police and he'd seen no evidence of that so far.

He switched back to the video, letting the film run while he showered and dressed. He liked this, playing after-dark film like this in broad daylight, even if he did still have his curtains closed. Enjoyed the secrecy of it. That feeling that he could go where others would not go. Do what others dare not do. Think about his next move in his game even while he went about the day-today, the ordinary. The mundane.

7.50 a.m.

Mike had spent the night at Maria's. He was woken by the insistent ringing of the telephone; the collator back at divisional HQ was phoning to tell him that yet another force had called in about the sex attacker and possible links.

Mike listened. 'Manchester area, about five years ago. They're faxing the stuff down to us.'

'Right,' Mike said. Then after a pause he voiced what had been on his mind for some time now. 'Why hasn't this been cross-referenced before?'

'We did make a start after the third attack,' he was told, 'but Superintendent Flint was convinced this was a localized event. Didn't want to start a panic. Anyway, this new stuff's five years old. You know how it is, takes a lot to jog memories when you've already got a backed-up case load. If a perp goes quiet for a while we all breathe a sigh of relief and don't ask too many whys. It's only when stuff gets national coverage like this that the little grey cells start nagging. Looks as though our man has history anyway.'

Mike thanked him and was about to ring off when a thought struck him. It was pure impulse, but he said, 'Pull anything we've got on Phillip Myers, will you, Bill. It's probably nothing, but his alibi for the last attack was what you might call flimsy. He claims he was just driving around after another row with the wife. He says that she was the one who scratched his face as well. But you never know. And run a previous address check on both him and David Martin going back the last five years. Get someone to track down their work records too, see if either had a job that let them be where we need them to be at the relevant time.'

'OK. Will do. Anything else?'

Mike asked briefly about David Martin and was told that he was on the roster for the duty solicitor to see him first thing. Mike had left him in the cells to think things over for the night, but knew that he either had to charge him with something definite soon or let him go. Frankly, he didn't think he had a hope in hell of getting anything to stick as far as Theo's death was concerned. The timing was all wrong. David Martin had been at work until a half-hour before discovering Theo's body, and it would have taken close on that time to get home even at the tail end of the rush-hour.

So unless he had slipped away from work, committed the crime and then gone back and finished his afternoon, Mike had to admit that he was off the hook.

He'd held him overnight, questioned him until late, then left the statement-taking to the night shift. His alibis for the nights the women had been attacked had been shaky, but, Mike had to admit, if he'd been asked to account for his actions on five separate occasions over a twelve-month period he'd have needed help piecing it together.

David Martin had been willing to have a blood sample taken and that could be compared to what they already had. And they could run a match on the DNA, though that would take time. It could be said that his willingness to give blood was a point in David Martin's favour, but he wouldn't be the first criminal to think himself too clever for the police no matter how much help he gave them. In the meantime, all Mike could do was accept that Martin would be released that morning and have him watched.

If Flint would assign him the manpower.

If David Martin didn't skip out on them before that could be arranged.

Irritated, he shook his head, wondering if he was barking up the wrong tree anyway.

'Penny for them,' Maria said.

'Not worth that much.' The phone was by the bed and she was still stretched out beside him. For a moment he was tempted to say sod the day and stay with her. Forget the problems and the responsibilities for a little while. Then he sighed, swung his legs out of bed.

'Got to go.'

'You're headed for London?'

'That's right. Magazine publishers. I'm having a last word with David Martin first, in case he's thought of anything else, then to the publishers. See if they featured Marion O'Donnel in anything else. And, for that matter, if David Martin sold them anything else.'

'He says not, presumably?'

Mike nodded. 'According to him, he took the pictures, kept some she didn't want as souvenirs and off she went. He claims that was more than a year ago, before he even knew Theo Howard.'

'Do you believe him?' Maria asked.

Mike hesitated for a moment, then nodded. 'As a matter of fact I do,' he said. 'I also believe, for what it's worth, that he loved Theo. And I'm being forced to the conclusion that he probably didn't kill her.'

* * *

'You've got something for me?' Mike said as he arrived at the police station.

The collator nodded. 'It's about our other runaway and his mother. The Ryans,' he said. 'Took a bit of rooting, I'm afraid, but this is what I've come up with.' He handed the printouts to Mike, who leant comfortably against the wall and began to read.

'As you'll see, Mrs Ryan was arrested almost three years back for being drunk in charge. In fact she's only just got her licence back. She had a drink problem but she'd been on the wagon for a good eighteen months, only fell off again when she was refused custody of her son, Terry. He'd been living with his grandparents, been in care before that, going back to when he was six years old.'

Glancing through the printout, Mike could visualize the circuitous route his colleague must have taken to put all this together. Communication between different departments was not what you might call good at the best of times.

'The grandparents didn't oppose their daughter's claim on her son but the courts did, the first time she applied, anyway. It must have been one hell of a disappointment. She was absolutely soused when they picked her up. Amazing she was still conscious, never mind able to get the key in the ignition and the car started.'

'What about the father?' Mike scanned but found no trace of him. 'She said he'd left them when Terry was about six . . . What's this?'

'I thought you'd be impressed. The inquest ruled an open verdict on the child's death. There was just the possibility that the padding round the cot wasn't tied properly and simply fell down, but there were doubts. I've included the summary. You want the court records it'll have to be tomorrow morning.'

Mike nodded. 'There was talk that Terry did it,' he said.

The collator shrugged. 'The kid was six. Just six, it was his birthday. And if the mother was drunk then, who the hell knows what went on? Still, makes you think, don't it?'

Mike nodded. 'Thanks. And let me know if you find out anything about Myers,' he said.

He closed the file. The teenager seen running away from the murder scene. Was that Terry?

9 a.m.

Mike arrived at Judith's flat just as the rain had begun to fall again. He parked the car and ran inside, closing the door on the downpour. Judith was in. She came to the flat door with a half-anxious, half-expectant look on her pale face. Mike introduced himself.

'Oh,' she said. 'You're that other one's boss. Does this mean you've heard from Terry?'

'No, I'm sorry. May I come in?'

She stood aside, directing him through into the living-room with a gesture of her hand.

'Please sit down. Can I make you any coffee? Tea?' Mike shook his head. 'Terry hasn't called?'

'No . . .' The question hung in the air. 'Have Sarah's parents . . . ?'

'She called them, yes, I heard just before I came over. She didn't say much, apparently, just that she was sorry and that she had something important to do. They think it was something to do with Terry.'

'With Terry? What could Terry possibly have to do?'

'A bus driver thinks he saw Sarah, and that Terry was with her,' Mike said. 'Saturday night about ten o'clock. He's sure he dropped them off just outside Hoton. Can you think of any reason he might be going there?'

Judith shook her head. 'Hoton?' she said. 'I'm not even certain where that is.' She hesitated. 'Isn't Oaklands out that way?'

'Oaklands?' Mike questioned.

Judith nodded slowly. 'Terry's had a few problems. He goes out there to see a counsellor. A woman called Dr Lucas.' She hesitated, then went on. 'He's a good boy,' she said. 'I don't know why they think he needs to see her. He's fine, no problems now. Just gets on with his life.'

She met his eyes deliberately, her expression implying that she thought that Mike should let him do the same. Mike's brain was working overtime. Terry went out to see Maria?

'Would you like to talk about it, Mrs Ryan? If I understood why Terry needed therapy, I might have more idea of why he ran away.'

Judith shook her head. 'It's nothing to do with him running away,' she said. 'Nothing at all.'

'If Terry had problems . . .' Mike began again, but Judith was on her feet now, clearly ready for him to go.

'Look,' she said. 'He did have some problems, but we've sorted them out and he's just fine now. Ask that psychiatrist woman, she'll tell you just the same. Terry deserves to be left alone. Allowed to get on with his life and not be hassled by every official Tom, Dick or Harry who has nothing better to do. Now. You've told me all there is to tell me and I'd rather you went.'

Mike rose to go. 'If that's the way you want it, Mrs Ryan,' he said, surprised at the anger he seemed to have provoked. 'We've only Terry's interests at heart though. All of us.'

Judith said nothing, she had turned away from him, blanked him out as though he was no longer there.

'I'll let you know if I hear anything,' Mike said quietly and left.

9.15 a.m.

Maria had just reached her office when Mike got through to her on his mobile and told her what Judith Ryan had said.

'Actually,' he said, 'she told me that Terry was fine, didn't need the likes of you and me nosing around and practically threw me out on my ear.'

'Wise woman. Bloody policemen.'

Mike could hear the smile in her voice as she said it, imagine the dark eyes laughing. He sighed.

'Have you spoken with Judith Ryan? I assume you have.'

'Once. At Terry's initial assessment. Terry's not one of my usuals, you know.'

'Really.' Mike thought of the mix of schizophrenics and bipolar depressives that made up the bulk of Maria's case load. Oaklands had three in-patient wards and a small secure unit. But these were separate from the old building in which Maria lived and which housed offices and out-patient clinics as well as flats for the on-site staff and rooms for those on call.

Maria rarely dealt with juveniles.

'So, how did you come by Terry?'

'He's just turned sixteen; in legal terms he's not yet an adult, but in terms of funding he's come to the end of the line as a juvenile. It took a bit of fiddling, but his social worker, Mina Williams, she was convinced Terry would benefit from further intervention. The kid had just come to live with his mother, and the pair of them were doing their best to come to terms with all the changes. To abandon him, take away all support systems now seemed, well, stupid.'

'But I thought you said all funding had dried up.'

Again, he could hear the smile in her voice. 'I had a free hour or so. Enough private patients in between the national health ones to pay for the car, so . . .'

'So Terry's a charity case?'

'The Americans would call it Pro Bono. I think that sounds so much nicer.'

‘I see.’ He laughed. ‘But I suppose the confidentiality clause still stands whether you’re getting paid or not.’

‘Got it in one. Look, talk to his social worker, she’ll be able to point you in the right direction at least.’

Mike had to leave it at that. Clearly, he wasn’t going to get any cooperation from Judith and Maria couldn’t help him. Mike had met Mina Williams on several occasions. She’d been present in loco parentis when he’d been interviewing juveniles. He liked her, but she was a tough lady, client’s rights coming first in her book. What was she going to tell him that Maria would not? Until an hour or so ago he’d assumed he was just dealing with a sixteen-year-old Misper. Now he thought of the boy seen running away from Theo’s house and he was not so sure.

* * *

Judith stood beside the window, looking down at Mike Croft’s car and willing him to drive away. The big old estate car seemed to dominate the street, to mark her house out for special attention, and she wished fervently that he would go.

She had played it all wrong. Lost it at the very moment when she should have been cool and calm, or even just upset by Terry’s going. He could have accepted that, she thought. Understood it.

But she was so sick of all the prying and the fussing. Even now, when everything was going so well and she had begun to feel that she and Terry finally had the chance to lead a normal life, everything was going against them.

‘Oh, Terry,’ Judith whispered, suddenly angry with her son for jeopardizing it all. ‘What the hell did you have to run off for?’

CHAPTER TWENTY-SIX

9.15 a.m.

They had talked through the night. It had been hard, at first, seeing the shock on Sarah's face, so hard that he'd wanted to run out into the storm and get far away from her. Then the shock had faded.

'I don't believe it,' she had said. 'I don't believe they could think that about you. And besides,' she'd added as though this made it impossible, 'you were just a little kid.'

'I don't remember much,' Terry said miserably. 'If I did it, I don't remember doing it. I know I was jealous of Nathan, but I mean, lots of kids are jealous, aren't they?' He didn't look at Sarah, but felt her nod, he willed himself to carry on. 'I remember I'd gone into Nathan's room and I shouldn't have been there. They'd given him my baby toys. Said I was too grown up for them and that I should give them to him. I didn't want to. I cried. I remember that. It was my birthday. I was six and they'd given me all this new stuff to make up for taking my baby things away. They'd had a birthday party, all the family, that sort of thing. Then, when everyone had gone away Mum and Dad had started arguing about something. They were always fighting. I sat on the stairs for a long time listening to them. Then I went into Nathan's room.'

He clammed up again. Sarah hunted around for something that would keep the conversation going, wanting him to open up to hen

'What were you looking for,' she said, 'in Nathan's room, I mean?'

Terry hesitated. 'You'll laugh,' he said.

'No I won't.'

He glanced sideways at her, then dug a hand into his pocket, pushing through a hole he'd made in the lining. 'It was this.'

Sarah took the proffered object with something close to reverence. 'It's a mouse,' she said, then laughed. 'Where's its other ear?'

Terry shrugged. 'Lost it a long time ago,' he said. 'I don't know how come they let me keep it really. I guess in the panic no one noticed.' He hesitated, embarrassed. Sarah could see the back of his neck and his cheeks begin to redden. He said, 'When I was really little, I didn't want teddy bears or any of the usual stuff but Mouse always slept under my pillow. When they made me give it to Nathan, well I guess it must have really pissed me off.'

He fell silent then, drawing into himself as the memory played itself out. His parents' angry voices coming up the stairs and his father slamming the bedroom door. He'd hidden behind the big cupboard in Nathan's room, afraid of his mother. She had come unsteadily into the room, leaning heavily against the bedroom door, pushing herself off from the doorframe as she lurched towards the baby's cot. She'd been drinking again. Even at six years old, Terry had understood that.

Terry had pressed himself closer to the wall, peering around the corner, watching.

Nathan's cot had also been his once. It was a white, drop-sided affair trimmed with white drapes and lace-edged bumper cushions all around the sides. From his place behind the cupboard, he lost sight of his mother behind the drapes as she bent towards the cot. Then she began to scream. A piercing, tremulous sound that had Terry cowering in the corner and his father dashing from the bedroom and bursting through the door.

Nathan was dead, one of the bumper cushions from around the cot pressed across his face.

'I was six,' Terry told her. 'It had been my birthday. But it does happen, you know.' His voice rose with a nervous edge to it. 'I mean, don't you ever listen to the news? Being a kid doesn't mean you can't kill someone. Nathan's dead, Sarah. And so's Theo.'

CHAPTER TWENTY-SEVEN

9.15 a.m.

Tom Andrews had received another letter and this one worried him far more than the last. Like the others it had been hand-delivered. It was printed on cheap paper and had been addressed to him directly. That last was no real surprise, Tom's by-line appeared on a weekly column and regularly on articles and reports. He was well known locally. It was the content of this last letter that troubled him so deeply.

He picked up the telephone and called Divisional. Inspector Croft was not there, he was told. On impulse, he called Maria, who was getting ready for her first patient. Mike wasn't there, she said. Off to London.

Tom knew better than to ask why; it was a concession to him that she told him that much.

He tried to reach Price, then remembered that Price too had gone elsewhere, and there seemed little point attempting to reach Mike on his mobile. He could hardly turn around and come right back just because Tom Andrews would rather deal with him.

Reluctantly, Andrews called divisional HQ again and asked to be put through to Superintendent Flint.

He was brief and to the point. 'I've received another letter' he said. 'He claims he's killed someone. Name of Marion.'

* * *

Davy breathed deep. It was raining, but the air was cold and clean, and after a night cooped up listening to the town drunks the sound of rain and traffic was the most welcome sound in the world.

Theo's house would still be cordoned off. He had the few things with him he had collected for the night he had spent in the hotel, and his bank and Visa cards.

The duty solicitor had seen him signed out then gone on to his next case. He'd been ushered out like a guest who'd overstayed his welcome and insulted his hosts.

Davy began to walk, not knowing where to go or how to get there, his mind dwelling on the facts that seemed most important to him.

Marion was dead. Theo was dead. Two women he'd been involved with, murdered within only a few days of one another.

God, if he'd been the police, he'd have been suspicious of him, Davy thought bitterly.

He quickened his pace, turning up the collar of his coat against the rain and moving with a sudden determination.

Twice in the past year he had seen Marion. Something he'd failed to tell the police and really didn't feel he wanted to tell them now. Reason told him that his disinformation would count against him should he ever be found out, but right now Davy really didn't care.

The first time he'd seen Marion had been brief. He'd called into the bookshop where she was working, just to say hello. The second time, she had called him, had insisted they meet at Avebury, well away from anyone that might see them.

They'd walked among the stones. It had been raining and the ground was soft beneath their feet and slippery with fallen leaves. Marion's mood had seemed to match the weather, dull and miserable, but she had failed to tell him what the problem was. Seemed to regret her impulse to call him and, when he really pressed, told him it was only man trouble.

At the time he'd accepted that. It was easy to accept Marion having trouble with the men in her life. Now, he wondered. Realized he was probably withholding material evidence or whatever they called it.

He should go back really. Sort it out.

Davy hesitated for a moment but couldn't face returning to the police station and the hours of questioning that would follow. Not yet.

They had had coffee, he remembered, in the barn cafe, and when he had paid the poem he had composed for Theo had fallen out of his wallet. Marion had picked it up, that poem that he had written especially for Theo, and she had smiled properly for the first time.

'You wrote poetry for me once,' she had said. 'That one about the fire on Kennet Hill. You know, I really liked that.' He had only realized much later that she had not given Theo's poem back.

Theo and Marion, such different women. They had known about each other. Davy was open that way, not liking secrets. The two women had even spoken once when Marion had called him about something.

Different women, but he linked them. He had known them both and, surely, he must somehow have drawn the thread closed between them.

There was only one link he could think of. The photographs. The magazine.

He glanced around before crossing the road, wondering if he was being tailed. Then decided it didn't matter if he was. They had nothing they could charge him with and there was no way they could keep him confined. Running across the busy road, Davy hopped on to a bus, the first that came along, looking back over his shoulder as it pulled away.

9.30 a.m.

The weather seemed to have broken at last. Grey skies had lightened and there was even a suggestion of sunlight about the day. Price was not destined to see much of it.

'Arrived late last night,' Morrow said over breakfast, producing a series of faxes from his pockets. 'Thought it best you got a bit of sleep before immersing yourself in muck for the day.'

Price took the papers from him and laid them on a spare bit of table.

Mickey's Cafe was Morrow's regular watering-hole. It fell somewhere between an old-fashioned transport cafe and a continental bar. Formica-topped tables that could have survived the fifties and old cigarette ads framed on the walls, together with a selection of film posters and painted art deco mirrors.

'This is the Howard woman,' Price commented, surprised at the poses and Theo's state of undress.

'And that's Marion O'Donnel,' Morrow confirmed. 'Interesting, don't you think?' He waved a greasy knife in Price's general direction. 'Starred in her own feature, by the look of things. July's special. So I've arranged for a root around in our "lost and found", see if the young lady was more than a one-hit wonder.'

'Marianne,' Price commented, reading the curvy lettering at the head of the page. 'You think she was a pro, then?'

Morrow took a large swallow of his tea. 'Who can say? Your boss is paying a visit to the publishers, but I thought we'd see what we've already got in stock. I've cleared it with Vice.'

Price folded the faxes and handed them back to Morrow. 'So you and I are going to spend the day looking at mucky books?'

'And the odd video.' Morrow grinned. 'Anyway, it won't be just the two of us. I've got a couple of assistants lined up.'

Morrow settled down to finishing his breakfast. Two little helpers, he thought happily. Beth Cooper was a trooper, she'd not turn a hair at anything she saw, but he was looking forward to seeing just how red Stein could get during the course of the day.

* * *

Beth Cooper did a lot to improve Price's day. He put her in her middle twenties. Five five, somewhere about a hundred and twenty pounds and none of them wasted. Blonde curls, cut a bit too short for his liking — but then, she hadn't asked his opinion. Blue-grey eyes.

The young man who crept in with her was another matter. He was still a probationer, Morrow told Price. Seconded from uniform because Morrow needed bodies. 'He's all they could spare me,' Morrow had complained.

He sidled into the room, sandy-haired and pale-faced, looking far too uncertain even for a probationer, Price thought. But he remembered his own time as a police rookie far too well to pass judgement, yet. And the thought of a probationary year under a Charlie Morrow was enough to make anyone a little green about the gills.

It was funny, Price thought, after the first ten minutes of flicking through skin mags, just how boring it got, how unsexy. The women in the pictures ceased to be women, just images to compare with the pictures he had of Theo and Marion. He'd thought it unlikely that Theo would be featured in any of them. After all, she might be in good shape, but she wasn't exactly a spring chicken. He'd mentioned the thought to Morrow.

'You ever work Vice?' Morrow had asked him.

'Only briefly and it was drugs rather than porn.'

'Right. Well, I have, sonny boy, and I'll tell you for nothing. I've seen skin flicks and magazines featuring anything with a body from six months to Methuselah.'

Price tried hard to concentrate, realizing that images were just skipping by. From across the room he heard Beth Cooper laugh. Now if he was looking at her . . .

He put the thought aside. Jesus Christ, and he didn't think these things affected him . . . He shifted uncomfortably in his seat, trying not to think of Beth Cooper and convinced of Morrow's piercing gaze upon him.

'I see brush salesmen are still in vogue,' Beth commented. 'God, Charlie, you should take a read of some of this stuff.'

Price found himself skimming through the pages of text. Sure, he'd read these things when he was younger. Not quite behind the bike sheds, but the equivalent. He was surprised to see how little they had changed.

He'd had a friend at college who had supplemented his grant writing this stuff. He'd fallen lucky and placed quite a bit with one magazine or another. Price vividly recalled one of the rejections he had got too: 'Sorry, but we're steering clear of the pseudo-lesbian stuff this month.'

It had paid better anyway than working in the student bar.

Sighing, he realized that the last few pages had just passed him by. Either woman could have been there, everything exposed, and he would not have seen them.

He went back for a second look.

'See something you like?' Charlie Morrow bellowed at him. Price's thoughts drifted to Beth Cooper sitting across the room. 'Oh yes, guv, plenty,' he said.

* * *

The collator could not get hold of Mike. He knew that Mike generally dumped his mobile, switched off, in the glove compartment when he was driving and it was no use trying to get him that way. He paged him anyway and then went straight to Flint with the information.

Phillip Myers had a record. An old one, for sure, but still a record.

Flint read it through. 'Two counts of possession,' he said, 'and one count of indecency.' Satisfaction was written large on Flint's face.

'Bring him in,' he said.

CHAPTER TWENTY-EIGHT

12.20 p.m.

Terry and Sarah had finally fallen asleep and it had been late morning before they woke up. The rain had eased to a light drizzle, but the skies were still leaden and threatened more. At first they had tried to keep off the roads and walk parallel to them across the fields, but with the weight of mud dragging on their feet this had proved too much. And hedges crossing the path made the trek impossible.

There was little traffic. They decided they would risk walking on the road and hope that no one took an interest.

Sarah had taken hold of Terry's hand as they left the house, surprising him. Most of the night had been spent talking and, despite the rain, Terry felt more hopeful than he could remember in a long, long time. Up until now, the only people that knew his story had been his grandparents and his mother and the various social workers and other professionals that had seemed to dog their lives.

The village Terry had spoken of was just ahead of them. 'Look,' he said, 'it might be better if we don't both go inside the shop just in case the police have put out a report or something. You wait round the corner. There's a bus shelter, I think, and I'll go inside.'

Reluctantly, Sarah agreed, delving in her pocket for some of the damp money she had obtained with her mother's card. 'I think you watch too many spy films,' she said. 'They won't be interested in looking for us. Too many crimes to solve.'

'Please, Sarah,' he said.

She bit her lip. 'OK, I'll wait round the corner, but don't you think of running out on me or anything.'

'Don't be stupid.'

He left her at the bus-stop and crossed the road, disappearing inside the shop. Anxiously, Sarah watched.

He took so long that Sarah was beginning to think he really had run into trouble. Then he came out, carrier bag in hand. He walked slowly, with exaggerated casualness, until he reached the bend, then he ran.

'Come on,' he hissed at her. 'We're in the papers, both of us.'

1.45 p.m.

The main gate at Oaklands stood open and they walked through unchallenged.

'I thought there'd be security,' Sarah commented.

'Not on this part. The hospital bit, where the inpatients are, that's across the other side and I think it's got its own gate.'

They walked on up the drive, Sarah looking around with interest. 'A lake,' she said, pointing.

'Yeah, there's acres of parkland and woods and stuff, even deer. Can you imagine owning a place like this?'

Sarah grinned at him. 'Fancy cutting the grass?'

Terry was straining to see up ahead, then, suddenly, he was smiling. 'She's here,' he told Sarah. 'I can see her car.'

'Well, come on then!' Grabbing Terry's hand, Sarah began to run.

* * *

'It's all right, Pete, I know them,' Maria said.

The caretaker looked unsure, but nodded. 'OK, if you're sure.'

Terry looked gratefully at the tall black figure standing at the top of the long oak staircase. Beside him, Sarah drew a quick startled breath. However she had pictured Dr Maria Lucas, it was not as someone who could have made it as a supermodel.

She clasped Terry's hand more tightly and walked up the stairs. Maria smiled, then opened the door to her flat and ushered them inside.

'Coats off,' she said. 'You look soaked through. Get yourselves in front of the fire and I'll make some coffee, or would you like tea or chocolate?'

'Er, anything, anything would be just great,' Terry was saying.

'And Sarah?'

Sarah nodded. 'Oh, sorry. Chocolate please.'

'How do you know Sarah's name?' Terry asked suddenly.

Maria shook her head. 'You don't want publicity then remember to put a little X in the box.' She picked up a copy of the *Chronicle* and tossed it over to him. 'Now, get warm and read about yourselves.'

She went through to the kitchen and they could hear the kettle being filled and the rattle of pots. Terry seemed to have frozen to the spot, staring at the newspaper, the real shock sinking in for the first time.

Sarah took it from him and pulled him over to the fire. 'God's sake, Terry, what's the matter with you? You think people don't read the papers or something? You saw it back in that village. You knew what it said.'

He looked really scared, she thought. She was just relieved that they had made it here. But neither of them, Sarah realized, had given much thought to what they should do afterwards, or even what Maria Lucas would say to them.

She sank down on the small sofa beside Terry, laying her head against his shoulder. At first he sat stiffly, then he unbent a little and put his arm around her.

Maria came back into the room and sat down opposite them. 'The kettle will soon boil,' she said. 'Then we can talk and you can tell me what you came all this way for.'

She raised an elegant eyebrow in Terry's direction but the boy said nothing. Instead, he sat staring at the carpet as though its pattern fascinated him.

'Terry!' Sarah nudged him, then when it was clear she'd get no answer, she turned to Maria. 'Terry said you could help him.'

She nudged him again, uncertain of how much to say, then, hesitantly, 'It's about that woman, the one that died, you see. Terry thinks they're going to blame him for it.'

She stopped there, not knowing what else to say without at least Terry's tacit approval.

Maria nodded slowly, careful not to let anything of what she was thinking show on her face. So that was why he had run. He knew Theo Howard. Of course, the 'old woman' he had helped with her shopping, and Theo was an actress. Stupid not to have connected them before. And with what Terry had been accused of in the past . . . She remembered the teenager Mike said had been reported running away. 'I thought you'd come here, Terry. I rather hoped you would,' she said quietly.

'Oh?' Sarah questioned.

'You were seen,' Maria told them. 'Getting off a bus at Hoton late Saturday night. Hoton isn't far away. I thought you might be coming here.'

The boy looked up, briefly meeting Maria's eyes.

'Don't know why I did,' he said. 'Nothing you can do.'

'Are you sure of that?'

'Terry!' Sarah said again, nudging him harder this time. 'You've got to tell her.'

Maria smiled at the girl then got up and went back through to the kitchen. 'I'll get those drinks,' she said. As she disappeared through the kitchen door she could hear Sarah haranguing her friend. Telling him he'd have to talk. She closed the door quietly, hoping that Sarah would have got through to him before she went back in. It would make things so much simpler if she did. She set about preparing the drinks, arranging biscuits on a plate. Trying to give Sarah time to work on Terry.

There was a telephone in the kitchen and for a moment she thought of calling Mike, at least to tell him that the kids were safe. She was reaching for the phone when a sudden shout from the other room turned her around and had her heading for the door.

'You've got to talk to her,' Sarah had been saying. 'You can't just sit there, Terry. You just can't.'

'How did she know about the bus?' he said.

'I don't know. Maybe it was in the paper.'

'It wasn't. I looked.'

Terry raised his head, staring into her face. She had never seen such desperation or such fear.

'Terry. . .' Sarah laid a hand on his arm.

He jumped to his feet. 'I shouldn't have got you into this. I'm sorry. What if I did do those things? If I did it to Nathan then maybe . . . What if I did it, Sarah?'

Sarah stared at him. Of course you didn't do it, she wanted to tell him. Of course you couldn't do anything like that, but the words just wouldn't come out. They seemed frozen somewhere in her throat and she couldn't get them to budge.

Just when had he started thinking like this? Had this horrific self-doubt been playing on his mind all the time that they had been together?

Suddenly, Sarah was afraid, his doubt transmitting itself to her. The fear must have shown itself on her face because Terry moved then, looking around him urgently for an escape. His gaze fell on Maria's car keys lying on the table near the door. He'd grabbed them even before Sarah realized what he was doing and was heading for the stairs. Then Sarah was on her feet as well and chasing after him, screaming out his name.

Her screams brought Maria running.

By the time Maria reached the top of the stairs Sarah was standing by the big front door. As she ran down the stairs, she heard a car engine surge into life, revving far too fast, then a sudden screech of tyres spinning on loose gravel.

She reached the door in time to see her Mazda fishtailing wildly as Terry, not understanding power steering, swung the wheel sideways. He tried to pull it back on line again, and veered far too much the other way.

'Terry!' Maria's shout joined Sarah's screaming. 'Oh shit!'

'I tried to stop him. I tried.' Sarah was grabbing at her arm. Maria hardly heard her. She was running down the long drive after the speeding car, Sarah close upon her heels.

He'll never make that bend. Oh God, he'll never make that bend . . .

The drive swept a graceful left and then back right in another sweeping curve. Terry still didn't have the hang of the steering. She could hear from the change in engine note that he must somehow have managed to shift to second gear. 'He's not going to make the bend.'

She almost covered her eyes, but couldn't tear her gaze away as the car, in a shower of mud and gravel, veered wildly out of control and left the road heading towards the lake.

For an instant Maria stopped dead, horrified by what she saw.

'Terry!' Sarah cried again. 'Terry!'

Just for an instant, the Mazda seemed to stop dead, poised with its wheels free of the ground, a creature of the air. Then it plunged forward and dived nose-first into the lake.

CHAPTER TWENTY-NINE

1.45 p.m.

Max Harriman was on his way to work and thinking about what Jake would be doing next.

Trying to second guess Jake Bowen was a full-time occupation and Max was pretty good at it, though he had to admit that Jake gave him a little help. Small hints here and there in the details of his attacks or the content of his films. Details that emerged from a shared past and that Max was certain few others would be able to see. Like the vicious red he drew upon his women's lips and that vampire image Jake had used now in three of his best films, mouths filled with blood sharing kisses deep enough to touch the soul.

Max smiled to himself as he remembered looking on his mother's face and that blood-red smile. Of bending over her face, his lips touching . . .

Max pulled the thoughts away. The truth was he felt restless now that he had killed the woman, eager to find another image, another story to play out.

It was lucky that Jake had come up with the last one. The Marion story had been one of the best that Max had ever told himself. Now it was time to move on, to start looking again.

* * *

Jake was driving along the Devizes road. He was dressed in his working clothes, his jacket hanging from the loop near the back window, briefcase on the passenger seat, the very image of a perfect sales rep.

He had two more calls to make today, then he could head for home.

His road took him between the ridge of Kennet Long Barrow and the conical rise of Silbury Hill. He glanced sideways as he passed, seeing the bright orange tape of the police cordon flapping in the breeze and the dark oblong of the grass where the car had burned. It had been at the back of his mind to use the location from the moment he'd seen that poem Marion's old boyfriend had written her. It had, Jake thought, worked out well in the end.

Now Jake passed Kennet by without a second glance. He had enjoyed his time with Marion, the brief interval they had been lovers, but he had always known it couldn't last. Jake's was not a lifestyle that could easily be shared.

He shrugged lightly, his mind already turning to his next delivery. Pity she hadn't been able to keep her nose out from where it had no right to be. The day he'd found her in the second editing suite he had set up at Vinnie's place had been the day he realized their time was over. Nothing was wasted though; those final days he'd kept her in the basement had given him some useful footage and it had been good to be able to add another fire sequence to his repertoire.

Jake had been raised to let nothing go to waste.

* * *

Terry thought he was going to die. Then he stopped thinking, had no time for thought, as the car tore itself from his already minimal control and headed towards the lake.

He heard himself screaming, lifting his arms instinctively to protect his head. Then the stunning blow as the car hit water that felt like iron and he was thrown forward against the restraint of the seatbelt.

Winded, Terry lowered his arm and looked around in panic, blessing the ingrained habit that had made him fasten his belt. The front of the car had hit the water first and was sinking fast. In the darkness, Terry couldn't tell how far.

How deep was the water? How the hell was he going to get out?

The car had landed at a slight angle, sinking obliquely, pitching the driver's side most deeply into the water . . . He dare not open the door. He tried the window, feeling along the door panel for the handle, then realized that Maria's car had electric windows. Frantically he tried to find the button, but when his fingers touched it, pressed it hard, nothing happened.

The water, he thought. It must have short-circuited. Nothing was working. He'd never get out. He had to get into the back. Try and climb out through the back somehow.

He began to wriggle around, easing himself past the steering-wheel and into the space between the seats, grazing his leg against the gear-lever, jamming for a moment between the gear-shift and the handbrake, panicking as his clothes caught on them. He thought he'd never get himself free.

Then, he heard the hammering on top of the car.

* * *

Mike took the opportunity to try to reach Maria, hoping she had heard from Terry. He stood for a long time, listening to the phone ringing, the sound hollow in the empty flat.

He rang John Tynan and asked him to keep trying Maria, to see if there was any news of Terry.

'I was planning on going out there anyway. Maria promised me a drink after work,' John told him. 'We've got your mobile and pager numbers. I'll get back to you, soon as I can.'

* * *

'Terry? Can you hear me, Terry? Keep away from the window. Keep down.'

Her face pressed as close to the window as she could get, Maria could just make out the dark shadow of Terry's body inside the car. He seemed to be wedged between the seats. For an awful moment she wondered if he was even still conscious. Or if he had been badly injured in the crash. She tried again. 'Terry. Keep your head down and your face covered, I'm going to break the glass.'

She thought she saw him move, couldn't afford the time to be sure. Standing up to her waist in freezing water, her feet sinking into deep, foul-smelling mud and with the car sinking further at every moment, Maria knew she didn't have time for much finesse.

Were rear windows laminated, like front windscreens? She didn't know. She couldn't risk trying and then failing. The car was sinking far too fast. Hoping that Terry would have the sense to cover his face, she moved around to the side and slammed the rock she was holding with all her weight behind it into the glass.

It took three attempts before it broke. The water restricted her movements and the mud sucked at her feet, throwing her off balance, but finally she made it through. Shouting at Terry, trying to find out if he was all right, even as she used the stone to break the sharpest edges from around the window frame. The force of her blows against the glass was making the car shift, sinking even faster into the mud and slime. Finally, she was satisfied that she could get him out. She reached a hand inside. 'Terry, come on, Terry. Let me help you out.'

Almost reluctantly he unwedged himself from between the seats. His face was white. She grabbed his sweater; tugging him forward, making him turn his body so he would fit more easily through the gap she'd made. He reached forwards, trying to help himself now.

'That's it,' she encouraged. 'Keep going. That's it.' Terry pushed against the seats with his feet. His hands reaching out, trying to get some purchase on the outside of the car. Maria pulled on any part of him she could get her hands around. Tugging at his shoulders, his sweatshirt, the belt of his jeans, until eventually he fell forward, splashing into the water on top of her, dragging them both down.

Maria struggled to stand upright, pulling the boy with her. He seemed stunned, unable to co-ordinate, and she found herself having to support him as they waded to the bank.

Sarah was there, shouting encouragement and reaching out to help them on to shore. They fell in a muddy, shivering heap, gasping for breath.

'Are you all right?' Maria demanded. Then: 'God almighty boy, no one would have blamed me if I'd let you drown! Now, come on, on your feet before we all freeze to death out here.'

By the time John Tynan arrived about half an hour later, they were back inside Oaklands. Sarah was taking her turn in the shower. Terry was wrapped in an old dressing-gown that Mike had left at Maria's place. There were cuts from the flying glass on his face and arms, but he'd been lucky; wedged between the seats, he'd been protected from the worst of it. Maria herself, muddy clothes dumped on the bathroom floor and a towelling robe wrapped around her, was trying to clear up some of the mess.

'Oh, John. Just the most welcome person. Please, make some tea or something, will you, and make sure he stays put.'

John looked at Terry, then at Maria, taking in the muddy feet emerging from beneath the towelling robe and the mess of filthy, stinking clothes she was holding in her hands.

He decided that this was not the time for questions.

From the bathroom, Sarah emerged, wrapped in Maria's dressing-gown, towelling her hair.

'Better?' Maria asked her.

The girl nodded. 'Good. You'll find the hairdryer on the shelf in the bedroom. The one next to the door. This is John Tynan, he's going to make some tea. And I'm going to get clean.'

She marched off, her pent-up anger charging the atmosphere until it almost hummed.

John surveyed them both thoughtfully. 'Terry and Sarah,' he said. 'It might be worth knowing that I've never seen her that annoyed. Just what did you two do?'

'We, Terry . . . Her car,' Sarah began. 'It's in the lake.'

John took a deep breath and exhaled slowly.

'Tea, I think,' he said. 'Strong tea.'

* * *

Mike had done his time as a probationer in King's Cross, his beat taking in the station, the seedy little hotels and the back-street strip clubs. It was a long time, though, since he'd had to drive in London, and he had forgotten just how much he hated it.

He'd managed to squeeze into a parking space, partly blocking an alleyway, beside the building that housed Primart Publications Ltd. The December day, grey and miserable, cast grimy shadows over the city street.

Mike went inside. Primart was on the second floor. He was well off his home ground here and had, as a matter of courtesy, informed his local opposite number . . . that he'd be coming. They'd filled him in on Primart's background.

Primart Publications produced books and magazines, sex aids, videos. The usual stuff, all legal and above board. Squeaky clean, was the way it had been described to Mike, and very profitable.

They used girls from a series of agencies. Drew up official contracts with each one they used and actually went to the trouble to insist on proof of age.

'They are totally professional,' Mike's informant had told him. 'For that matter most of the bigger skin publications are. Can't afford to be otherwise. The editor was busted ten years ago for printing pictures of a fifteen-year-old girl. I saw the pictures and you'd have sworn she was five years older. They cleaned up their act after that and their processing of models. Only deal through agencies now.' It was useful to know. If Primart was concerned with its reputation it would be more likely to cooperate.

Mike had taken the stairs. He found himself facing a pair of glass doors leading to a surprisingly plush lobby, with an elderly, blue-rinsed receptionist seated behind a solid wood desk. The lobby was decorated with potted palms and comfortable armchairs. Mike did a doubletake. It looked more like the entrance to a small hotel than to a company specializing in soft porn. He found himself checking the logo on the glass doors — and his own preconceptions — before crossing to the woman at the desk and asking if the editor might be available.

He laid his identification in front of her. She took her time, putting on her glasses and reading carefully before returning it to him.

'You're a long way from home, Inspector Croft,' she said cheerfully. 'If you'd like to take a seat, I'll see if he's free. May I tell him what it's about?'

Mike reached into his overcoat pocket and produced the magazine, withdrew it from the evidence bag and laid it open at the centrefold.

'This woman,' he said. 'I need to know if she did other work for you beside this.'

'May I?' Mike nodded and she flicked back to the front, checking the date. 'Miss July this year,' she said. 'Well, it will all be on file. All our young ladies are registered, you know.'

Mike nodded. 'I'm sure.'

'She's not in any trouble, I hope?'

'If you could just tell him I'm here . . .'

'Yes, of course.' She spoke into the intercom, telling the listener that a police officer needed to speak with him. Moments later, he was being directed through to the inner office.

Darren Prestwick had been editor of the three magazines put out by Primart Publications for the previous five years. He had learnt early on that image was everything. He was a businessman and wore a business suit and an air of competence and authority that he felt went well with the job.

He listened to what Mike had to say without comment, then got up and crossed to a second desk housing a computer.

'We keep everything on a data base,' he said. 'Cross-referenced under real name and any they might have appeared under in our magazines. All of our girls come to us through an outside agent, and this one, if I'm not much mistaken, came in through Mr Vincenza.'

'Vincenza? Vinnie Vincenza, used to have a basement office, back of Holland Park?'

Darren Prestwick smiled. 'He still does,' he said. 'And a second model agency in Bristol, though he no longer runs the main business end himself. He has managers to do that.'

'Things must be looking up for him,' Mike commented.

Prestwick was manipulating the data base. 'Ah, here we are. Yes, I was right. Vincent Vincenza, came in through his London office apparently. If you give me a moment I'll print out for you. It looks as though she just did the one edition. Our monthly feature.' He frowned. 'We had her booked for a shoot last week too, but she didn't show.' He swung his chair around and gave Mike an interrogative look. 'Is there some kind of trouble, Inspector Croft? Because if there is, I'd like to know. We want our girls to have a clean background. Insist on it.'

'Did you meet Marion O'Donnel personally?' Mike asked.

'No, generally I don't. Their agents deal with ours and they do the shoot, usually in our studio out at Victoria Dock.

We've got a converted warehouse down there. I approve and select the finished shots.' He paused. 'I'd like to know what your interest is, Inspector Croft.'

Mike frowned, took the magazine back and replaced it in his pocket. 'There's a good reason Marion O'Donnel didn't turn up for that second shoot,' he said. 'By that time she was dead.'

2.15 p.m.

'That was your governor,' Morrow announced as Price returned from lunch. 'He's been to see the publisher. Seems Marion O'Donnel did only the one shoot for them. Didn't live long enough to pose for any more.'

'Any mention of David Martin?'

'No. The original shots were sent in by one Vincent Vincenza. Alias Mr Brian Hammond. Offices in London, Bristol and maybe bloody Rome as well for all I know. Your boss is planning on paying him a call this afternoon.'

'What's he driving?' Price asked automatically, thinking about Mike's wreck of a car and wondering if it would make the distance. 'No, never mind.'

Morrow gave him a puzzled look. 'He says he knows Vincenza from when he worked the King's Cross beat. He was small time then but things have been looking up for Vinnie this last year or so, bought a place out Malmesbury way. Lives there with one of his ex-models.'

'So,' Price asked, 'what's Vincenza been up to that pays so well since then?'

'That's what your boss wants to find out.'

Price glanced at the magazines stacked on his desk. 'Not much point in going through the rest of these then,' he commented.

'Not for the moment, no. Croft checked on Theo Howard, but they denied all knowledge, so, for the moment, we've drawn a blank. This afternoon though, I've got something else lined up. Took me a while to get it set up and it might not even be relevant.' He paused, frowning. 'There's just been something puzzling me ever since I saw the crime scene, the way it was laid out. Reminded me of something Vice brought in a month or two ago.'

* * *

Mike reported in, bringing Flint up to speed on his investigations.

'I think you're wasting your time looking for a link,' Flint told him. 'Martin knew the girl, just happened to give her his number. What could be more natural than that?'

'Probably nothing,' Mike agreed. 'But there's still two suspicious deaths. We have to look at all angles.'

'And one of them not even on our patch. Seems to me you're wasting resources, Croft. Anyway, we've finally got a breakthrough on our rapist.'

'Oh?'

'That's right. That file you wanted pulled on Phillip Myers? Well it panned out. He's got previous.'

'Myers has? What?'

'Conviction for indecency and a couple for possession. Agreed it's a long time ago. His student days . . .'

'And nothing since? And what exactly was the charge?'

He listened as Flint filled him in. 'It hardly adds up, sir,' he protested. 'A student prank and now a series of very violent attacks with nothing in between . . .'

'We don't know that. Myers isn't stupid. Anyway, like you said yourself, we have to check it out.'

He paused — Mike could hear voices in the background — then Flint spoke again, his voice grave. 'There's been a development. A woman's body's just been found on wasteland close to Aston Park.'

'Same MO?'

'Looks like it. I've got to go. Look, check in later with anything you turn up your end. There's something else, too. David Martin's done a bunk,' he paused. 'It was a risk we took in letting him go, but you said yourself you couldn't pin anything on him.'

'I thought you'd put a tail on him.'

'For God's sake, Mike! We don't have the manpower, you know that. Look, if we need him we'll find him and bring him in. Meantime, we've other fish to fry.'

CHAPTER THIRTY-ONE

3.15 p.m.

Mike called the office again on his mobile and asked to be put through to the collator.

'Anything come through from either of the other areas?'

'I take it you've heard about Phillip Myers? Flint's been like a bloody dog with two tails since I gave him that one.'

Mike laughed humourlessly. 'I'll just bet he was. Even if Myers is our man, it still leaves another bastard on the loose, or is he planning on Myers being blood type O as well as A?'

'God knows. He'd probably give it a go. Anyway, this might interest you more. We've got two possibles so far. Neither is a perfect fit, but not bad for a beginning. One's a feller called Osbourn. Served three years of a five-year stretch for serious sexual assault. Released three years ago, faded into the woodwork since then. Originally from Manchester. He's no good for our first two victims, but those two could well be down to our other unknown. He's the right blood group for the last four and Marion O'Donnel too. We don't know about the dead woman until the path reports come in.'

'Sounds promising,' Mike said. 'And the other one?'

'The other one was sent through from Bristol. A more interesting proposition. Three charges of serious sexual assault and a series of public order offences. Seems he became obsessed by some young girl. Fits the description of our attack victims, blonde hair, blue eyes, small. She was still at school at the time, used to follow her there. Follow her home, sit outside her house until all hours. He never touched her, just made a nuisance of himself; when they finally got the evidence to pull him in on the assault charges, he disappeared. The thing was, guv, all the girls he attacked fit the same broad description. We're running it through PNC and Voters, see if he's turned up here under his own name or any of his known aliases.'

'You've informed Flint?'

'Told him we're tracking, not a lot else to tell him yet unless our man surfaces here.'

It was a long shot, Mike knew, but it sounded more likely than Phillip Myers.

'The other thing, Mike, the kids have turned up. We had a call from Oaklands. Uniform's on its way out there now.'

4 p.m.

The project Morrow had in mind was a series of videos. Morrow, Price, Beth Cooper, Stein and an officer from the vice squad crowded into the tiny projection room.

'Where the hell did you get these?' Price thought he had seen everything, but the films he had witnessed in the last hour had been beyond belief.

Stein had looked sick. He gripped the arms of his chair tightly. 'Are these snuff movies, sir?'

For once, Morrow hadn't tried to put him down.

'In a way, I suppose they are,' he said. 'The thing is, we know that these are real.'

He turned to Price, answering his question. 'We've had four of them turn up over the last year, year and a half. We checked with other forces; similar numbers have turned up all over the country, some duplicated, and still others what look like salesman's samples. Made up of clips of other films, complete with titles and order numbers.' He shrugged. 'These things go in fashions and the open market follows the black market pretty damn closely. You remember a while back, the fuss that was made about the executions video? Well, we think that's pretty much what we have here, but with, shall we say, overtones that the straight version didn't have.'

Price felt sick. He glanced across at Beth Cooper. Her gaze was fixed carefully upon the screen and her features smoothed clear of all emotion. Tension showing in the fixed gaze and the way she held her pen, hard enough almost to break.

He switched back to watch the film. In the last two hours he had seen beheadings and amputations. Strangulation. A man dying in breathless agony, his lungs full of mustard gas, three-quarters of a century ago. Another; present-day in a small white room, an execution, Price guessed in some nameless American jail, the camera panning across the room to show the witnesses behind the plate-glass window.

Another scene, a kneeling man, the camera closing in on his face as realization dawned that the man dressed in combat gear and ski mask, with the gun in his hand, was for real. That he was going to die, here and now and without the hope of reprieve or mercy. A moment later and the man was dead. Brains and bone blasted across the lens as the camera came in close for the final shot. And intercut with it all, dancing shadow figures superimposed across the screen, the couples and singles and groups involved in sexual acts as varied and as starkly brutal as the many ways of dying Price had seen.

'It's this last scene I want you to look at.' Morrow's voice was oddly serious for him.

The final piece, a car, stationary upon a grassy hill, the camera panning across the scene then zooming in to show the courting couple in the back seat. Price felt every muscle tighten in anticipation and from across the room he heard Beth Cooper gasp. He wanted to look away, not to see it, but he found himself involved in the incident. Wrapped up in the plot in a way that both attracted and appalled. He couldn't look away even as he saw the flames begin to lick beneath the car. The flames begin to rise higher as the camera drew back far enough to show the entire scene. The couple in the car on the hill, the stillness of the summer's day.

'Why don't they move? Why don't they get out? Don't they know what's happening to them?' Stein's voice drawn thin with anguish. 'Why don't they get out?'

It seemed to last for ever, but Price knew that was just illusion. Less than half a minute had passed from gathering their first impression of the scene to the moment when the car exploded into flame. 'It was rigged,' he whispered. 'It was bloody rigged!'

He looked at Morrow who was nodding slowly. He'd seen this before but the shock of it never left him and it showed now on his face.

Vaguely, Price was aware of Stein pushing himself from his chair and running from the room. Price's gaze was fixed upon the television screen as through the smoke he glimpsed the bodies burning up inside.

CHAPTER THIRTY-TWO

4 p.m.

Jake was editing his new film, the first section of the plotline already put together by actors, of a young man being kidnapped. In the film, he was hitching along a lonely road. It was night-time, but there was enough light to catch the blond of his hair. He was quite tall, slender, dressed in the ubiquitous blue jeans and a dark top.

A car pulled up just ahead of him and he began to run towards it, then, when he reached the car and bent to look inside, it became clear that something was not quite right. The young man began to back away, then to turn and try to run, but already two people had emerged from the car and grabbed him. Pinning his arms behind his back they bundled him inside.

Jake re-ran the sequence, checking to see that there were no clear shots of the blond one's face. He'd use the same actor later for the final sequences, and for the major sequences up to the middle of the film; the face of the man he had down in the basement would be either covered or filmed obliquely. It would be easy enough to substitute the head shots later.

The initial sequence, Jake decided, would do. It didn't have the stark tension he would have liked, the real fear factor, but then even the best actors couldn't substitute for the real thing, the genuine terror of someone who's trapped with no way out and a growing fear that they are going to die.

Jake skimmed through to the later sequences, classic S & M skin shots, unremarkable but sound enough. The young man from the kidnap scene was doing what he was good at now. Jake flicked back through the script and the rough storyboard that he had put together to organize his shots. According to the brief he'd been given, the young man abducted in the early scenes, after a period of torture and humiliation, would not just cooperate with his captor's sexual desires — but would actively participate. It was, Jake thought, unimaginative and a little old-fashioned these days. A new take on the rape victim that was really gasping for it, hardly artistically demanding or particularly stimulating. But it would sell, and who was Jake to argue with the demands of economics?

He had begun to cut what were for Jake the interesting scenes. Those with Blondie in the basement. Jake didn't know the guy's name, he wasn't interested, though he was mildly surprised that the man hadn't volunteered it. Most people these days saw enough TV drama and police reconstructions to know that you should try to make direct contact with your captor's psyche. Make yourself real for them. A person, not just a piece of meat, though such distinction would have been wasted on Jake.

He ran the sequence he'd been working on, something he'd shot that morning. It would need tightening up, but he figured he had enough footage not to have to do another take.

He had the sound turned down; soundtracks would be dubbed on afterwards by someone who was better at the words than he was. Jake was purely an image man. He made a note that Blondie's voice would need to be dubbed too. In some ways he was a bit of a disappointment. Not enough reaction. Jake needed him to plead and scream a whole lot more.

4.15 p.m.

Flint was still trying to get to grips with Myers. The man seemed to have worked himself into a loop and nothing Flint could do would break him out of it.

'I have done nothing,' Myers said in answer to almost every question.

'How did you get those scratches, Mr Myers?'

'I have done nothing, Superintendent Flint.'

'Where were you last Thursday evening, Mr Myers? From about six o'clock. Were you home? We could bring your wife in perhaps. Ask her.'

'I have done nothing wrong, Superintendent Flint.'

'And these other occasions? You're a businessman, an engineering consultant, isn't it? You must keep records, an ordered man like yourself. Where were you on March the twenty-fifth of this year? On April the nineteenth? On July the seventeenth?'

'I have done nothing wrong, Superintendent Flint. Nothing at all.'

'That's not what your record shows. And these young women, Mr Myers.' He laid a series of photographs on the interview room desk. 'These badly beaten, frightened young women. Recognize any of them, do you? Or did they all look different before you tried to bash their brains out through their ears?'

Flint paused. Myers continued to regard him steadily. He was furious, Flint knew, but keeping himself well under control now.

'I have done nothing wrong,' he said again.

And so it went on. It was only when Flint told him that they were going to search his house that Myers showed any emotion.

'You have a right to be there, of course,' he said. Phillip Myers' eyes flickered with resentment, but he answered calmly. 'I have done nothing wrong.'

4.15 p.m.

The two uniformed officers listened to Terry's version of events. Maria was sitting close by, quietly encouraging. 'I went into the room,' Terry said, 'and she was just lying there. I thought she might be asleep at first; coming in through the door I could see her feet propped up on a cushion on the end of the sofa. But then I could smell it.' He hesitated for a moment, looking up at Maria as though needing encouragement.

She nodded. 'Go on, you're doing fine.'

The boy continued, his voice low and artificially steady, sitting on Maria's couch with Sarah beside him, clasping his hand tightly. Maria and John facing him. She had dimmed the lights. Only a single table lamp, casting more shadow than illumination across the scene, like some Italian chiaroscuro painting, all depth and light with little in between.

'I could smell the booze,' Terry said, 'and the sick.' His lips twisted in a look of disgust. 'I knew she'd had a problem; we'd talked about it.' He looked up quickly at Maria as though again needing approval. 'Because of my mum, you know. I couldn't get her to talk to me. She said I wouldn't understand, but Theo never ever said that. She treated me . . . like I was important to her, you know. Like an equal.'

He hesitated, and they all waited. At last Maria said, 'The last time we spoke, you mentioned Theo and I had the impression this was a new friendship. It wasn't though, was it?'

Terry shook his head. 'Months ago,' he said. 'In the summer. I . . . I liked her, Dr Lucas. I really liked her. I didn't want anything to spoil it. And it's always been the same, every time I made a friend, somebody would interfere. Try and break it up.' He licked his lips nervously, fidgeted with

Sarah's hand. 'I even told her about me, about my mum, about Nathan. I thought she'd hate me, but she didn't. I knew my mum would go up the wall if she found out, either about Theo or Sarah. She would have hated it; she always got so scared when I made friends in case they found out. But Theo listened the way you do, but she didn't judge me.'

'I've never judged you, Terry,' Maria said steadily. 'You know that.'

'Yeah. But you're paid not to. Theo just didn't.'

Maria nodded slowly, not bothering to correct him.

Terry had no idea that her involvement with him was voluntary; she'd always figured it would just add to the burden of guilt the boy already carried.

She said, 'So what did you do, Terry? What happened then?'

'I went in. I thought, if she'd been drinking then it would have to be something really bad to make her start again, so I thought . . . she'd been to see the doctor. I thought it must be bad news. I'd promised to come round before David got home and see how she'd got on.'

'The doctor?'

'Yeah, some specialist in London, not her own doctor. She'd been to him when she lived there. When she was still an actress.'

Maria exchanged a glance with John. Even David had claimed not to know of Theo's illness. Had she confided in Terry?

'This doctor, Terry, did Theo tell you his name, or what she was seeing him about?'

He shrugged. 'Abbot or something. I don't know really. She usually just called him the specialist. She said she had pain, here.' He touched his stomach. 'I thought she just meant an ulcer or something. My grandad had an ulcer. But she said it was more than that. She said she'd brought it on herself with the drinking and stuff. I told her that was stupid.'

He fell silent then, staring at the simulated flames on Maria's gas fire. She found herself wishing, not for the first time, that the fire was real. That would have been more comforting, somehow.

'What did you do, Terry, when you found her? What did you see?'

The boy shuddered as though suddenly cold. Sarah moved closer to him and gripped his hand tighter. 'Tell them, Terry,' she said gently. 'Tell it like you told me.'

He nodded. 'It was like the other time,' he said.

John glanced at Maria, his look questioning. Other time?

'When Nathan . . . when Nathan died. The pillow was over her face. I was so scared.' He was almost whispering now, his gaze fixed and staring. It had been like reliving a nightmare. He had reached out, he told them, not daring to get too close, afraid of seeing Theo's face, blue-lipped like the baby's had been. He had reached out with fingertips, grasped the corner of the pillow and tugged it aside. Theo had been lying there, her eyes half open and her mouth gaping, and he had known, without going any closer, that she was dead.

'Then I ran away,' he said simply. 'If they'd found me there no one would believe I hadn't hurt her. Just like they didn't believe me about the baby. About Nathan.'

He raised his head, looked desperately at Maria. 'I'm sure I didn't do anything, Dr Lucas. But I'm scared. Sometimes people do things and then they don't remember, do they? One therapist I had, she said people shut things out they don't want to think about. She went over and over, trying to get me to say I'd shut it out. Killing Nathan. She kept telling me it would be all right. That all I had to do was say I was jealous of my baby brother and that I killed him. Then they could help me. She kept on at me and on at me and so did my mum and everyone else that in the end I didn't even know what I really remembered any more and what I thought I did. So what if they were right? What if they were and I don't remember? I need locking up if they were, don't I? Don't I?'

There was silence. John, new to this, not knowing how to respond; the possibility that for the first time he had a proper suspect for his friend's murder hadn't escaped him.

He forced himself not to react. To reserve judgement until he had some more of the facts.

Maria paused, then, professional tone carefully in place, she began quietly. 'I don't know what happened, Terry . . .'

But Sarah, who had been silent through all of this, seized on something he had said.

'You saw the baby's face. You said you saw the baby's face.'

They all stared at her. Sarah reddened but carried on. 'That means you must have moved the pillow, but you told me, when the baby was found, it had the bumper pad over its face.'

Terry stared at her, his eyes horrified as though in that simple deduction she had just confirmed his guilt.

'So I killed him,' he whispered. 'I must have done.' He tried to get to his feet, to pull his hand away from hers, but she was yelling at him that she wasn't saying that.

'No, she isn't,' Maria said, realizing where Sarah was leading him. 'She means you saw the baby's face after he was dead. That maybe Nathan was dead even before you went into his room. That maybe you saw him, like you saw Theo and knew you had to move the bumper pad from his face. Even quite small children know about smothering. Maybe you moved it then. Saw him, dropped it back when you heard your mother coming.'

Terry was staring at her, his face a conflict of emotions. 'I don't know,' he whispered. 'I just don't know. Maybe it was like that and maybe it was just an accident, but what if I did kill Nathan? What if I saw his face because I'd lifted the cushion up just to make sure that he was dead?'

CHAPTER THIRTY-THREE

4.30 p.m.

Vinnie Vincenza, alias Brian Hammond, had made a big thing of remembering Mike.

'Things have been looking up for both of us since you went away,' he said. 'I don't think you'd even made it to sergeant then.'

'Just,' Mike informed him. 'I'd just received promotion. A lot of water's passed under since then, Vinnie. I hear business is good. You have a place out of town these days.'

Vinnie laughed. 'Just like the old days,' he said. 'Always up with the gossip. Yeah, I've got a little place out Malmesbury way, though the truth is I only make it down for the weekends.' He grinned. 'This is still where the action is.'

Mike took the pictures of Marion from his pocket and laid them with the magazine on the table.

'I'm told she's one of yours, Vinnie.'

Vinnie picked up the polaroids and flicked through them with an air of professional interest. 'She was,' he said. 'Not any more though; this is a tough business we're in. You've gotta be professional.'

'And Marion wasn't?'

Vinnie shrugged expansively. 'Didn't turn up for a shoot. You're letting a lot of people down if a girl fails to show, doesn't do a whole lot for a man's reputation, so I crossed her off my list.'

'Did she give any explanation?'

Vinnie's eyes flickered sideways for the merest instant, then met Mike's again. 'Never a word,' he said. 'I left her messages, told her to give me a call, but nothing. That's the way it goes sometimes.'

He shrugged again, more reflectively this time. 'It was a pity. She had just what it takes to make it. Right to the top.'

Mike let the unconscious use of past tense go. Vinnie wasn't going anywhere at the moment and he didn't want to scare him off. He had no doubt that Vinnie either knew Marion was dead or suspected it.

'Did she do work for anyone else?'

'A little glamour work, that sort of thing. But she had a regular job and wasn't into selling herself cheap.' He wrinkled his nose. 'Choosy, you know. What she's been doing since she left me, I've no idea . . .'

Mike nodded and got up to leave. There was a lead here, he could feel it, but push too hard now and he might lose what edge he had. Better to use the local force, they'd have the background info.

Vincenza was seeing him to the door. 'You haven't told me what this is all about?'

'No, I haven't, have I?'

'Aw, come on, Mike . . . OK, OK, always the tight one, weren't you? Well, if you happen to run across my girl, tell her the door's always open.'

'I thought you didn't give people a second chance.'

'You know Vinnie. Always a soft touch.'

Mike left him, walking purposefully back towards his car parked two streets away. He paused once out of sight and back-tracked carefully, waiting ten minutes in the shadows of an alleyway behind a small hotel. Vinnie didn't show. Any longer and he would attract far too much attention.

Reluctantly, Mike made his way back to his car and the long drive home.

Maria called him just after he'd left Vinnie's and told him about Dr Abbot.

'I've already looked him up in the register,' she said.

'OK, give me the address and I'll fit him in before I come back.'

5.30 p.m.

Price and Morrow had returned to the place where Marion O'Donnel had died. Their mood was sober; Morrow had driven and had only terrified Price once.

They had left the car parked near Silbury Hill and climbed through the wire, Morrow puffing with exertion by the time they reached the top.

It was already winter dark but by the time they had reached the summit, Price's eyes had adjusted to moon and starlight. Around them lay fields, brown with winter earth, flecked with the white of the chalky landscape.

'They used to play cricket up here at one time,' Morrow commented.

'God help anyone that hit a six.'

Price walked to the edge of the flat-topped hill, looking across towards the village of Avebury.

'What about Vincenza?' he said.

'No evidence he's anything more than a two-bit creep. And, according to what he told your boss, he sold the pictures on elsewhere.'

'But the magazine thinks they came direct from him.'

'Maybe he sold them twice, or rather, sold Marion. Whoever hired her would do their own pictures, I presume. Or video,' he added, thinking of the stuff they'd seen that afternoon.

Price looked away. 'Yeah, could be she was into more than the odd centrefold.'

He turned back to Charlie Morrow, who seemed to be staring at something moving in the grass.

'Do we believe Vincenza?'

Morrow shrugged. 'Best we can hope for is apply for a warrant to search his place at Malmesbury and both offices. Could take a bit of time unless we get something more definite. It's going to involve three separate forces and God alone knows how many sub-divisions.'

Whatever it was that had attracted Morrow must have moved. Morrow edged towards it.

'What have you spotted?'

'Rabbit,' Morrow told him.

'Can't we just buy dinner at the Lion?' Price asked plaintively.

Morrow laughed briefly and inched towards the little animal. 'Lot of them still have myxie round here. Pitiful it is.'

'Myxie?'

'Myxomatosis. Used it to control the population.'

'Sure, but I thought that was years ago.' He watched, fascinated as the big man inched towards the rabbit.

He'd picked up a large stone in his right hand. The animal didn't move.

'You going to kill it?' He could see the animal clearly now. Milky eyes, unable to stand and with patches of fur hanging from its body. 'Christ,' he said.

Morrow brought the stone down squarely on the creature's head, then got back to his feet again and wiped his fingers on a bunch of serviettes he'd filched from Mickey's place that morning.

Price looked away.

They didn't speak again until they had reached the car, then, to break the silence, Price said, 'Beth Cooper. Attached, is she?'

Morrow gave him a predatory grin.

6.45 p.m.

Theo Howard's London doctor had his surgery in a quiet square in St John's Wood, amazingly quiet after the bustle of King's Cross. Mike could hear the birds sing.

'Yes, I saw Theo last week,' Dr Abbot told him. 'I'd been seeing her for years, usually minor complaints, a little depression from time to time. I gave her a medical once a year, that sort of thing, but until this, Theo had rarely ever been ill.'

'You knew what was wrong with her? You made the diagnosis?'

'I suspected what was wrong with her. Theo . . . Theo drank perhaps rather more than she should have done over the years. It became very serious at one time, but she was a tough lady. She worked her way through it. When she came to me I thought at first it was liver damage purely alcohol-induced. I sent her for tests. She had a tumour on the posterior lobe. It was operable but we suspected there were secondaries.' He frowned. 'You see, she put off coming to me until the pain began to get very bad. It wasn't that she was afraid of the pain, or even of dying. But she didn't want to die. She told me that she had met someone. Someone very special. I believe that for the first time in her life, Theo Howard had fallen in love.'

The two men were silent for a moment, then Mike said, 'We found no medication in her house. I would have thought . . .'

'I gave her pain-killers, this time. She's refused them every time before and you know, Inspector pain is a funny thing. Some people have a high threshold. I think Theo must have been one of them, but it would not have lasted for much longer. The disease was spreading and there was nothing any of us could do. If you found no medication, well, I don't know.'

As Mike was leaving the doctor said, 'There's another thing. It might be unimportant but . . . Theo said she wanted to leave something for Davy to remember her by. Pictures, I think she said. She didn't want him to think of her as she was going to be in the end. She wanted to leave him something special. I thought she meant one of these makeover portraits at first. You know, there are studios that specialize in those things. She thought that was really funny, I remember. She seemed very excited about the whole thing. Like a child. Said she had something far more special in mind.'

10.00 p.m.

Flint had news when Mike got back to Norwich. The first check on Voters had drawn a blank, then Bristol had sent through a list of other aliases their suspect had used.

'They were used in different offences,' the collator explained. 'He was done for kiting, passing forged cheques, about seven years ago. Bristol dug around for the names he used then and guess what?'

'You've got a match on Voters.'

'Might not be connected, of course. Max Harriman might be just that. But he fits the general time frame, came here two months before the first attack occurred and is A blood group.'

'We're bringing him in,' Flint confirmed.

The call came a few minutes later. No Harriman, but the landlady lived on the premises and had let them in.

'He's our man, guv,' the officer's voice broke up a little. 'The walls are plastered with stuff. There's pictures of Marion O'Donnel and another woman and also some young kid. And books of press clippings. Looks like the man's into souvenirs.'

'Then we wait for him to come back,' Flint said.

'No need, guv, we've got his workplace. The landlady insisted on a reference for him before she took him on. He's working shifts, finishes at ten.'

Flint looked across at Mike. 'Croft,' he said. 'You want to do the honours?'

CHAPTER THIRTY-FOUR

10 p.m.

Less than a street away from one another, it felt as though Terry and Sarah were at opposite ends of the earth. Terry, seated at the kitchen table, stared morosely out of the window, trying at least to look as if he was concentrating on his essay.

For the last two hours he had tried to work. His mother had been so busy pretending that this was just another normal day, that Terry felt compelled to do the same. She had been dusting and polishing and bleaching the already spotless flat, filling the air with the stink of cleaning fluids and the atmosphere of angry busyness until Terry felt he could take no more.

His mind was full of questions that he couldn't ask her. Worries that he couldn't voice. He tried hard to write something sensible, but the essay he was writing seemed so far from any of the problems racing through his mind that he couldn't concentrate.

What if they decided it was him? What if they sent him away, to prison, to a young offenders' centre? To some secure psychiatric unit, locked up with the loonies.

He wasn't mad, he wasn't. He wasn't guilty either; he was sure of that . . . wasn't he?

Over and over again Terry ran through the twin events in his mind as if the two were linked, superimposed one against the other. A mess of images and impressions that merged and flowed and interrupted one another until he could no longer separate them out. Theo's face, Nathan's face. The fear he felt when he heard his mother coming.

Angrily, he tried to drag his thoughts back to Lenny's problems in *Of Mice and Men.* His hand wrote about the prejudice that Lenny suffered, the bright hot sunlight and the dim-lit barn and the woman taunting him, pushing him too far. In his mind, Lenny and he became one. The misunderstood. The odd one. Lenny, killing. Terry, killing. Lenny not understanding. Terry not knowing. His mind worrying at the problem like a puppy with a rag. His hand writing ordered words.

And outside, it was raining.

When Judith came into the kitchen he could bear it no longer.

'Did I do it?' he asked her, desperate for absolution. 'Did I kill Nathan?'

* * *

Sarah watched the rain lashing against her bedroom window. From this angle, she could see the back of Theo's house and, if she stretched on tiptoe, the rooftops of the taller houses at the end of the street where Terry lived.

She wished desperately that she could talk to him but knew her parents wouldn't hear of it. They had been by turns sympathetic and furious, still not understanding why she had gone off with 'that boy.'

They were madder than hell with her because she wouldn't tell them what Terry was running from. They knew it had something to do with Theo's death and Sarah knew that her own mother and Terry's had talked, but she was certain they knew nothing about Nathan.

Sarah could just imagine the scenes that would be played if ever they found out.

Finally, she had been sent to her room and her mother had made a show of fastening the window locks in Sarah's room and taking away the key.

Sarah stared out through the wet glass, wishing, even, that she was back at school. Wondering when the blasted rain was ever going to stop.

10.35 p.m.

Jenkins' was an engineering company. Mike took three uniformed officers as back-up and went in quietly, but even so, the presence of one plain-clothes and three uniformed officers was not something to be easily hidden.

Other officers had been assigned to the three exits from the building.

'He's a lathe operator,' the night supervisor told them. 'Look, what the hell's going on here?'

'If you'll just point him out to us, sir,' Mike said quietly. Now they'd found their man they didn't want to lose him. He didn't feel it was the time for explanations.

'I'll take you through,' the supervisor said.

Quite what alerted him, Mike was never afterwards quite sure. Events seemed to fall in upon one another in quick succession. One moment Mike was aware only of the noise of the machine shop, of having to shout over it to make himself heard as the supervisor pointed to the man in yellow ear-defenders working at the lathe down at the far end.

Then the man turned and saw them and he was running.

He had a head start, the full length of the engineering shop. Mike began to run, shouting to the officers who followed him to split up, try to head the man off. He didn't know if they had heard, but saw them move, hoped that someone would be in time. Trying to second-guess the route his suspect would be taking.

Beside him, the supervisor was gesturing. 'The fire escape. There's a fire escape that way.'

Had they anyone waiting there? Mike tried to visualize the layout of the building but was uncertain where the men outside would have taken up position.

He couldn't leave it to chance, he had to get to the suspect before he made it to the door.

Around him was the roar of machinery, the sound of people shouting. Faces, gestures. Awareness that his leg, badly broken a few months before, was really not up to this. Then he saw the man ahead reaching for the fire escape door. Bursting through. The sudden rush of night air as the outside wind, damp with rain, surged in. Then Mike was through. Shouting ahead, hoping to make enough noise to alert whoever might be waiting below. One hand on the rail, one clutching his radio. Trying to predict where the fire escape might come down.

There was a sudden shout. The suspect dropped suddenly as though the ground had fallen out from beneath him. Mike looked down. The escape ended a good six feet from the ground.

'Damn!' He could see the man running down the back alley towards the main road. He expected to see officers come down the other way towards him, but at that moment there was no one. 'Where the hell is everyone? Suspect has reached the alleyway, repeat, reached the alleyway. Headed in the direction of Alden Street. Repeat Alden.'

Behind him one of the other officers crowded close and for a second Mike considered moving aside, letting him go ahead, but there was little room for manoeuvre. Mike swung himself out into empty air and dropped ungracefully into the alleyway. He could feel his leg protesting at the strain. Stumbled, then ran on, limping badly.

'You all right, sir?' The uniformed officer had landed beside him.

'Yes. Just get after the bastard.'

Then it was all over. At the end of the alleyway, Mike could see three officers, the suspect on the floor.

He steadied himself against the rough brick wall, then limped towards them, his leg and hip screaming every step of the way.

11 40 p.m.

Phillip Myers collected his things from the custody sergeant and walked out of the building without a word. He felt in his pockets. He had his front door key, a handkerchief, a little change. For the first time in years, he didn't even have enough to hire a cab.

He shivered. He didn't have his coat either.

There was a call box on the corner of the road and Myers crossed over to it, oblivious of the traffic. He had enough change to call his wife.

'They've let me go. No charges,' he told her. 'Do you think, I mean, could you and Sarah come and fetch me home?'

11.40 p.m.

Mike had settled down to what was going to be a long night. A half-hour into the interview and Max Harriman was already causing problems. He wanted to confess to everything, he said. But wouldn't even let them know his real name.

'Names are unimportant, don't you think? They tell you nothing about the man. It's actions that are really important, not just names.'

Mike sighed. 'All right,' he said. 'For the moment, Harriman will do. Now, Mr Harriman, you were telling me about the woman that you met last night.'

* * *

An hour later they took a break in the interview. Flint was convinced that they could pin the whole series of attacks on their suspect, he seemed so willing to talk, to boast about what he had done. 'Forensics won't stand up to that, sir,' Mike reminded him. 'We know the first two attacks were carried out by someone with O group blood.'

Flint paced the room irritably. 'I know, I know,' he said. 'But God knows it's tempting. Anyway.' He brightened a little. 'We've cleared five of the eight girls — the path report on the latest victim just came in — and getting this one might well scare our other perp off our patch.'

'So he can become someone else's problem,' Mike said wryly.

'Oh, get real, Mike. You know his type as well as I do. He was someone else's problem before he was ours, and will carry on being someone's problem until either he gets caught or gets too old to get it up. People like him — for that matter scum like him in there — they don't stop, they just go on and on until something puts a stop to them or they get too old for the chase.'

Mike fell silent. Then: 'What about Myers?' he said.

'What about him?' Flint shrugged. 'Dammit, Mike, if he wants to complain we'll feed it through the usual channels. It was a legitimate suspicion you had.'

'I had.'

Flint nodded. 'All right, *we* had. And I'm behind you on it all the way.'

20 December, 12.45 a.m.

Jake had been making a delivery when he saw her and for a moment thought she looked like Marion. But no, at second glance, the similarity was superficial. Marion had a different way of moving, an indefinable quality that this girl didn't have.

He turned his back on her and locked the garage door.

This would be the last drop tonight. He rarely made deliveries himself these days but from time to time liked to check on security, in this case a strong-box hidden beneath the garage floor. They never knew when a delivery would be made. He demanded payment in advance, delivered the goods within ten days, but no set day and no set time. And no more than three issues to a set. He didn't believe in leaving merchandise in bulk, too much loss if someone got careless and the stuff was seized, and the price this stuff went for, he didn't have to deal in bulk.

He thought about Marion again as he got into his car. She could have been quite something if she hadn't got too stupid and threatened to give the game away. Talking of stupid, he had only himself to blame. First woman in a long time he'd allowed to get that close and it could have been an expensive mistake.

He wondered vaguely if Vinnie had any more like her on his list. The new editions would come out in a few weeks' time. Marion at her best, and no one would ask too many questions about where the pictures came from.

And later on, there would always be the new video.

Switching on his radio, he heard the first news of the other one's arrest. It was vague; talk of a police raid on an engineering firm and a suspect being interviewed about last night's murder and the previous attacks.

He was not surprised. Max was getting careless, always trying to impress. Jake had a feeling the man would try to cop for all the previous assaults, even Jake's score. He was that sort, liked to play the numbers game when, they both knew, Jake out-classed and out-scored him every time.

Jake turned the radio up, started the engine and drove away.

2.15 a.m.

The police photographer had finished at Harriman's flat and the cuttings books and pinned up clippings removed and brought to the police station.

Mike was told as soon as they came in. He took them to the interview room and laid the cuttings books out on the table in front of Harriman. There were eight in all, the last not yet complete.

Max looked at them but made no attempt to touch the books wrapped inside evidence bags.

'Are they yours, Mr Harriman?'

Max looked across at him and smiled. He had, Mike thought, a truly appealing, ingenuous smile that creased the corners of his eyes and lit his entire face. It was a strange thing to think about a possible murderer.

'I collected them,' Max told him. 'For posterity.'

'Posterity?'

Max nodded. 'You see, Inspector Croft, we've been making history here, and now,' that smile again, 'now you're a part of it too.'

Mike ignored the boast. 'These young women, Mr Harriman. You were telling me about the attacks on these young women.'

Harriman nodded.

'We know you're not responsible for them all,' Mike went on. 'No, no we *know* you're not.' This as Max began to protest. 'There were two separate blood types you see. O and A. Yours is A, and, much as my boss would love to see this whole thing cleared up in one go, we know that someone else attacked two of those girls. You can't take credit for them all, Mr Harriman.'

Max Harriman smiled and he shrugged his shoulders as though conceding the point. 'I had a good teacher Inspector Croft,' he said. 'He set a fine example for me to follow.'

Mike let the implication sink in. 'You know the other man?' he said.

Harriman merely smiled.

2.15 a.m.

After leaving the police station, Davy had ridden the bus to its terminus before he'd even thought of what he had to do next.

Finally, he had walked back to Theo's house, but the police seal was still across the door, a reminder that they still did not know who had taken his Theo's life.

There was, he thought, nothing left for him here, but he had no idea of where to go or what to do.

Finally, he had taken a taxi to John Tynan's cottage and retrieved his car. Tynan wasn't there — Davy was relieved about that. John would have been full of more questions that Davy didn't know the answers to. Then he had begun to drive.

Close to dawn and he sat on the stones at the mouth of West Kennet Barrow. Uncertain what had brought him here, but glad that he had come.

Inside, someone had lit candles and their faint glow lit the barrow forecourt. It was beginning to rain once more, a slow, steady drizzle that would soak him to the skin.

Davy knew that he should move and go back to his car, but the rain continued to fall and Davy sat, his hair dripping water down on to his face. Davy no longer knew what was rain and what was tears.

11.50 a.m.

Terry had not gone to school on Tuesday. Late morning, he took a break from work. He watched as his mother buttered bread for sandwiches and made tea. She had barely spoken to him all day and when she had it had been with that false brightness that Terry hated. That 'Let's just forget everything and get on with life' brightness that had nothing to do with the way either of them was feeling.

'Can I go to the funeral?' Terry asked. The question had come out of the blue, taking even himself by surprise. He had been thinking about it off and on all morning. Theo's funeral. He knew that he wanted to go.

His mother ignored the question. 'Do you want pickle with this?' she asked him. 'Or mayonnaise?'

'I asked you something,' Terry said. 'I want to go, Mum. I want to go to Theo's funeral.'

The knife stopped moving. His mother halted what she was doing, her hands limp on the kitchen counter.

'Do you honestly think anyone will want you there?' she said, her voice hoarse with emotion. 'She'll have family, friends. What makes you think they'll even want you there?'

Terry stared at her, hurt and angry. 'I was her friend, Mum.'

His mother turned on him. She slammed the knife down on the counter and whirled around to face him, the tension and strain of the weekend suddenly breaking over her.

'Your friend,' she hissed, 'that woman was your friend, was she? You think she'd have been your friend if she'd known about you? Known what they said about you. Known all the gossip we've been trying to protect you from. Me and your grandad and everyone?' She stopped suddenly, wringing her hands in desperation. 'You can't have friends like that, Terry, love. People like that who might talk and not understand you. I wanted you to understand that for yourself, not have to do everything for you. You have to grow up, Terry, realize that however much you try, however much either of us try, it can't be normal and easy and all the things I know you want. Life's not like that, Terry. It never was.'

Terry stared at her. 'You knew about Theo?' he said. 'Mum, did you know about Theo?'

'Of course I knew. Not because you told me either. Always creeping around the way you do, keeping things from me, but I knew about her and about that girl.'

'You followed me?' Terry was incredulous. He thought he had been so careful.

'I was going to tell her,' Judith said, her voice falling almost to a whisper. 'Tell her to keep away from you. I didn't want you hurt if ever she should find out.'

Terry shook his head. 'Theo did know,' he said. 'I told her. I told her about the night Nathan died and about how everybody thought I might have done it and how you started drinking and all the things you never wanted to talk to me about. I told Theo, Mum, because I knew she'd listen to me and help me sort out what I really felt and what I thought and what I couldn't understand. And she did. She didn't hate me and she didn't think I was some kind of creep. And you know what she said? She said she didn't believe I could have done it. She said that accidents happen and that maybe the padding just wasn't tied up right. And something else. She said I was still the person she had known before I told her and it wasn't her way to hate someone just for being honest about what had happened to them. That made me feel good. Better than all the secrets and all the . . . everything.'

He'd run out of words, he could see his mother's face, cold and white with anger. 'After all I've tried to do for you,' she said. 'All I've tried to protect you from.' She walked unsteadily to the table, pulled out a chair and sat down.

'I love you, Terry,' she said softly. 'You know that, don't you? I really love you, kid.'

'Oh Jesus, yes I know you do.' He went over and stood beside her, pulling her close to him, holding her tightly as though he was the adult and she was the child.

CHAPTER THIRTY-FIVE

Tuesday, 20 December, 10 p.m.

Terry crept downstairs to the hallway. It was almost ten at night, but he couldn't think of what else to do. His mother had been so odd, talking little that afternoon and evening and when she had spoken it had seemed like nonsense.

At last, she had seemed to make up her mind about something and had told him to call Maria Lucas.

'But it's so late,' Terry had objected. But she had insisted.

Maria listened to what he had to say. 'All right,' she said finally, reacting more to the distress in his voice than to his confused words. 'I'll be there in about an hour. You just hold on till then.'

John had spent the evening with her and planned to stay over, as he'd drunk a little too much wine. She'd put him up in one of the rooms they kept for the overnight staff.

She padded along the hallway and tapped lightly on the door, then went in.

'John,' she said. 'I've just had a call from Terry, he seems pretty upset, something about his mum. I need you to go with me.'

11.15 p.m.

'I only went to talk to her,' Judith said softly. 'I knew about you and that woman. I'd seen you talking to her. Believe me, Terry, all I wanted to do was talk to her. Tell her she wasn't wanted. That we didn't need her kind. I went into the house. I'd tried knocking on the door but there was no reply, but I knew she was in there. When I'd come home I'd seen her go inside. So I tried the door.'

She paused, looking up at Terry, fixing him with an intense gaze. 'I went into the room and I saw her lying there. Blind drunk and I thought, this is the woman who my son looks up to. The woman he'd rather spend time with than me. This disgusting drunk, lying there in her own stink.'

Terry stared at his mother. 'You killed her?' he whispered. 'You killed Theo?'

Judith nodded slowly. 'It didn't take much, really, it was so easy. I couldn't stand to think of her with you.'

'And Nathan?' Terry whispered.

Judith looked away.

'So what happens now?' Terry asked as his mother was led away. He looked exhausted, Maria thought. Utterly spent.

'For tonight,' John said, 'I can offer you a place to stay. Tomorrow, we can talk it through, decide what's best.'

Terry nodded. All he really wanted to do now was sleep. His head just couldn't get around it all.

'Do you think she did that too?' he whispered softly. 'Do you think she killed Nathan?'

Maria clasped his hand gently. 'I don't know, Terry,' she said, meeting John's eyes. 'I just don't know.'

Midnight

Harriman was getting bored. He had wanted to take Mike through his cuttings books, and for a while Mike had listened carefully to all he had to say. It had become clear, though, that it was not what this stupid policeman wanted right then. He had failed to see the significance of it all.

'Vinnie Vincenza,' Mike repeated patiently. 'You were telling me about Vincenza.'

Max sighed, turning his gaze to the ceiling. 'Vincenza sells pictures,' he said. 'He's a little man, with little ideas, and will never be any more than that.'

'This woman.' Mike turned the centrefold picture of Marianne back to face Max and laid the polaroids that Davy had taken beside it. 'This woman,' he repeated. 'Vinnie Vincenza sold her pictures to this filmmaker. This Jake Bowen you told me about?'

Jake's name caught Max's attention once again and he smiled sweetly at Mike.

'Jake is not a little man,' he said. 'Not like Vincenza. Jake is a maestro.' He reached out again for one of the cuttings books. 'It started with one little film, all those years ago. We were children then, you know, just children, but the vision was there . . .'

* * *

Jake was editing film, making the cuts to the closing sequences.

Marion's last film was ready for distribution now and he was pleased with it. He'd included something very special in the final run. Those last seconds of film, showing the car well ablaze, Jake had taken with a long lens. He had let his eye rest on the flames, the black smoke billowing through the open window and into the damp air, and then that final moment he had hardly dared to hope would come about when for an instant the smoke had cleared and Jake had seen her face.

Jake sat back and reviewed the end of the kidnap film. He'd finished with Blondie in the cellar, disposed of him earlier with a single shot at point-blank range. Jake had let the blond one watch the preparations. Covering the floor and walls with plastic sheet to make the cleaning up easier. Jake had taken time to explain it to him. How it would be in the end, and had finally got the screams of fear that had eluded him so far.

In the final analysis it had turned out well.

Jake's mind turned briefly from the job in hand to wonder what Max was telling the police.

CHAPTER THIRTY-SIX

Wednesday, 21 December, 8.30 a.m.

They had little sleep that night. Terry had collapsed straight away, but had been awake and restless again an hour later and the adults had fared no better. By the time Mike arrived along with the morning post, they were sitting at the breakfast table feeling very sorry for themselves and Maria knew she had a busy day ahead of her.

'My mum,' Terry began. 'She all right?'

Mike nodded slowly. 'Your mum was taken to the hospital last night, Terry. We got the doctor in to see her and they decided she'd be better off there.'

'Which one?' Terry asked him. He swallowed hard. 'I mean, can I see her?'

'I'll find out what I can this morning. I promise you.'

Terry nodded and fell silent, stirring his tea. Mike began to speak again, wondering what to say to the boy, but Maria shook her head and he left well alone.

'What's in the post?' she said.

John was reading something, his face drawn and pale.

'John?'

'It's from Theo, my dear. Written on the day she died.' He picked up the padded envelope and glanced at the postmark. 'Though the package wasn't posted until Friday.' He reached inside the envelope. Inside was a video. John laid it on the table.

'It's for David,' he said. 'A final gift. She says she made this film over thirty years ago when she was just starting out and needed money. She says she wants me to keep it, give it to Davy when . . .' He paused, then read on:

'But I've never regretted it, John. The girl I starred with went on to take far bigger roles than I did. You might recognize the face. In those days, we all seemed to do at least one blue film. It paid the rent and I've never felt ashamed or that I needed to apologize.

'When I knew that I didn't have long left, I felt so dreadful, John. Not because death frightens me. It never has. Life has always been the hard bit. But there was Davy and I loved him so much, you know. I always intended to finish things myself, before the pain got too bad. I didn't want Davy suffering. I wanted him to know me, to remember me, not as I knew I would be in the last days and weeks, but when I was young and vibrant and just starting out.

'There was a young woman Davy used to know. She'd called a few times and, well, you know how it is, we'd got talking. She told me about a friend of Davy's who could help me and so I called his friend, Mr Vincenza.'

'His friend,' John laughed harshly.

'And he helped me to make this happen and he had the film transferred on to video for me.'

'And this is it,' John said, fingering the video as though he had a precious relic lying on the table.

* * *

Jake woke early, feeling relaxed and content with the world. He had some holiday due to him from his regular job and felt that now would be a good time to take it. Escape from the winter and get some sun. He made a mental note to book the time off later that day.

He'd disposed of Blondie's body. Jake had been undecided as to what to do with him, but finally decided to take him back where he'd found him. Leave him in the alleyway at the side of the nightclub. Occasionally, but only occasionally, the love of risk got the better of him.

11 a.m.

Morrow led the way, Stein and Price in tow, following the instructions given on Vincenza's tape.

The search warrant had been issued early. The Vincenza house was impressive. Mock Tudor, complete with swimming-pool and billiard-room. Officers combed the house and grounds but Morrow was going straight for the jugular.

The store room backed on to the billiard-room. A second safe had been sunk into the floor beneath false boards.

Vincenza had the combination but claimed he had no knowledge of what had been left inside. He never looked, he said. His fear of the filmmaker he called Bowen was tangible even through the medium of tape.

Morrow knelt and lifted the boards, took the paper from his pocket and began to turn the dial.

The doorway was narrow. Price leaned against the frame, watching. Stein waited just outside.

'Right, this is it, boys,' Morrow said. He sat back on his heels, his heavy body sagging. Then reached down and pulled the door.

A sheet of flame shot through the narrow room and caught Morrow with full force. Threw Price off his feet and backward into the billiard-room. He heard his own voice, screaming, then shouting Charlie Morrow's name.

Pulling himself to his feet, he struggled forward. The drapes had caught and cardboard boxes piled against the wall. In the centre of the room something still living writhed and fought in agony. Price could hardly breathe. Fire in his lungs, they burned so much. He tried to throw himself towards the thing that burned to pull it free before the fire caught even fiercer hold, but his body didn't want to move and everything seemed to be so slow.

Somehow, he grabbed Charlie Morrow's arm, screaming as the fire bit naked hands. Beside him, Stein had hold of him the other side and they dragged the big man from the room. Then Price fell to the floor, retching, hardly able to breathe, dimly aware that there were others now, helping him outside.

It was rigged, the voice whispered in his head. It was bloody rigged.

* * *

At a Travel Inn on the M25 Mr John Phillips checked in for the night. The news was full of it. The arrest of the Norwich rapist. The big copper who'd been blown up in the raid on Vincenza's house, they didn't know if he would live or die, it said.

Jake Bowen smiled. Pity he wasn't there, he thought. It would have made fantastic film.

PART TWO

1999

18 June, 1999

They had been forced to leave the car parked at the head of the lane and carry their equipment along the narrow track.

From the top of the hill they got a view across the valley for the first time, the high hedges either side of the road having blocked any sight of the landscape as they had driven up. It was a beautiful but claustrophobic place.

Liz pointed across to the opposite rise. 'That's the farm where we asked directions. See, it's marked on the map and this' — she nodded towards the house at the side of the lane — 'must be the Jacksons' place.'

Macey nodded, swinging the camera bag across his shoulder. 'Through there,' he said, pointing to a narrow opening between the trees.

Neither spoke as they pushed their way along what was little more than a rabbit track through a tangle of trees and across a plank bridge over a tiny stream. They reached the second stile, beyond which was Forestry Commission land. Here, they both paused. Liz exchanged a glance with Macey, not needing to say a word. The tip-off had come in a couple of hours before. If this was for real then, they had a very good idea of who had brought them to this place and suddenly, being here, just the two of them, didn't seem too bright.

'Maybe we should have waited for the police,' Liz suggested tentatively.

Macey shook his head. 'And have them get here to find it's all a wind-up?'

Liz gave him a shrewd look. Macey didn't believe the hoax theory any more than she did. He just wanted to be there first, before the arrival of the local police pushed them back behind the usual barriers. Macey had followed every angle of the story as it had been reported in the nationals and now this had happened on his home ground. If it was for real, it could be his break into the big time.

Macey made the first move, handing his equipment to Liz while he eased himself over the stile, then helping her across. Behind them, the mixed woodland they had left was alive with the noise and rustling of wildlife. Here, in this dimly lit conifer plantation, there was an uncanny stillness.

'I don't like this place,' Liz whispered, expecting one of Macey's usual acerbic rejoinders. But for once the big man was silent.

They looked around. Behind them, the hill continued to rise, densely planted and very dark. The path itself was wider than it had been but dropped off to the right, falling down the hill into a steep gully.

Below, in the gully, there was only a chaos of fallen trees and deeply channelled earth eroded by last winter's rains. Liz looked again at the sketch map. This was definitely the place.

She and Macey began to scramble down. It took all their attention just to keep their footing and protect their camera equipment from being slammed against the rough ground and exposed roots. They did not see it until the trees thinned and the scene was suddenly there, exposed in all its terrible beauty.

The body lay, naked, on a rough bed of fallen branches and fresh flowers. All around, on every low branch, every niche that could be used, stood tiny candles, their white stems gleaming in the flickering light.

CHAPTER ONE

Mike Croft turned away from the crime scene and walked along the head of the gully towards the second stile. Beyond that, the path broadened out, allowing an avenue of sunlight to break through between the tall trees. He climbed over the stile, relieved to get out of the darkness and into the warmth of the early summer's day. The sudden heat on his back was enough to persuade him out of his jacket.

He held a large-scale OS map in his hand and referred to it now. Further along, the path apparently turned into a gated road leading back towards Honiton.

Which way had Jake Bowen come in? Mike wondered. The narrow road and rabbit path that Macey and Liz Corran had taken or this other road? And had the woman been alive when he brought her here?

Mike leaned heavily against the fence post next to the stile, facing into the sun. This last six months, he felt, he'd done nothing but live and breathe Jake Bowen, especially since he'd been seconded to the operation eight weeks ago, along with practically anyone who'd ever had dealings with the killer. Mike had found himself dragged over half the country, chasing one short-lived lead after another, finally fetching up here — the middle of nowhere and a long way from home.

'Penny for them?'

Mike turned with a slight smile. 'Not worth it, sir. I was trying to work out the last time I had a weekend off.'

Chief Superintendent Mark Peterson returned the smile. 'Probably about the same time I did,' he said. 'And it's not likely to be this weekend either.'

'No, I suppose not. I'd arranged for Maria to come down.'

'Ah. I'll tell our man to improve his timing.' He paused for a moment. 'Look, Mike, get your lady to come anyway. Unless something breaks fast, you'll be able to wangle a couple of hours free.'

'Thanks. I'll do that.'

Peterson leaned against the fence and gazed out, eyes squinting, into the sunny space between the trees.

'I've got someone walking in from the other end, looking for tyre tracks, anything out of the ordinary.'

'Doubt they'll find anything. Last two weeks have been too damned dry. I asked one of the locals,' Mike added by way of explanation.

'You been down there yet?' Peterson gestured towards the gully.

'Briefly. I came back up top, let the photographer and SOCO do their bit. There's enough bodies down there as it is.'

Peterson laughed gruffly at the unintended humour. 'We'd better get back and join them,' he said, 'they've just warned me the surgeon's on his way.'

A sound overhead made both men look up sharply. A squirrel, its tail flying out behind it, leapt between trees. Peterson laughed again. There was relief in the sound of it. 'You know, Mike. I'm not a man given to all that much imagination, but if, when we find this bugger, he's got hooves and a forked tip to his tail, I'm not going to be surprised.'

A shout from behind them in the gully told them that the police surgeon had arrived. Mike eased himself over the stile and they made their way back along the path. Peterson's comment had come as no surprise; everyone was as jumpy as hell. He glanced sideways. The man's rather round face, reddened by too much sun, had gained lines these last weeks. Peterson was a robust man, taller than Mike's six two and heavier, but the strain of the Bowen hunt was beginning to tell on him and recently he seemed to have shrunk in on himself.

Some fifteen years older than Mike, Peterson was a career copper who'd made it up through the ranks. His present title, Chief Super; was being phased out in one of the 'reforms' sweeping through the service and men like Peterson, who seemed to belong to another time, were finding it hard to make their way in the new order. Promoted sideways to head up 'Operation Final Frame' — Mike wondered who made these names up — this was likely to be the last thing Peterson would see through before he retired.

DI Mike Croft had grown to like and respect the man a great deal and knew it was an opinion largely shared by the rest of the team. Under other circumstances, Mike would have enjoyed working with this large, bluff man with the overgrown moustache. Under these circumstances, Mike wished himself anywhere but here.

It was not an easy scramble down into the gully. Tree roots reaching from the dry ground and hard, rutted furrows cut by the last heavy rains then dried by the summer heat threatened to undermine every step. The scene, when they reached bottom, was pretty much as Macey and Liz had viewed it. It looked, thought Mike, like a scene from a low-budget horror flick, but this was real. The woman's long hair was carefully combed out across the bed of flowers on which she lay, her hands folded prayerfully between her breasts, and a long, thin line of blood had flowed from the artery in her throat down across the flowers. White roses stained a rusty brown.

'Bled her like a bloody pig,' Peterson said.

CHAPTER TWO

'Death confirmed at four thirty-five p.m., Friday 18 June. And before you ask, a quick estimate just from body temperature, ambient conditions and all that rot, I'd say she's been dead maybe four, five hours.'

'That would make time of death around midday.'

'No, that would make my rough estimate around midday. When was the body found?'

'Two fifteen, two twenty or thereabouts. The call came in at two thirty-seven. Mobile phones don't do so well around here. The pair who found her had to go back to the farm on the main road and call in on a land line.'

Peterson frowned. 'They claim to have received their tip-off at around one this afternoon. The call was made from a telephone box in Honiton.'

Mike had been looking more closely at the trail of blood. 'I'd have expected more spattering. More spread. The blood's run in just this one stream.'

The police surgeon looked impressed. 'I was coming to that. You're quite right, arterial blood usually spurts in all directions. Maybe our man was intent on not getting his clothes dirty. Maybe to keep to our timescale, he couldn't allow himself time to change.'

'So she was already dead when he brought her here?' Peterson asked.

'No, I didn't say that. What it probably means is that he reduced the pressure sufficiently for it not to spurt. My guess, and it's only a guess as yet, is he wanted the effect without getting himself covered.' He paused, his mouth curved with distaste. 'To put it bluntly, he drew off sufficient to lower the pressure before he even got her here. Then he arranged things neatly and finished the job.'

Mike felt sick. Murder he had dealt with many times, but Jake Bowen had the knack of going well beyond previous experience.

'Well, then, we've answered one question,' Peterson said harshly. 'Poor kid certainly didn't walk here.'

He turned away and Mike followed him back up onto the path.

'The Jacksons are letting us have use of their barn as an incident room. Just as well! We'd never get a mobile up those narrow lanes and I'm pulling in all the extra bodies they'll let me have, posting a twenty-four-hour, two-man patrol to keep the trophy hunters at bay.' Mike nodded. 'I don't envy the night shift,' he commented. 'This hole's bleak enough in daylight.'

'What daylight?' Peterson gestured. 'It's all just bloody dead. Downright weird if you ask me.' He paused again as though not sure how to say what he had in mind. 'Do you believe in spirit of place, Mike? You know, you'll go somewhere and it'll feel wrong.' He went on without waiting for an answer. 'This place. I mean, it's like it's been waiting here, all this time, just for something like this to happen.'

He laughed, trying to dispel the notion.

'I've known places like that,' Mike said quietly. 'There was one I came across when I first worked in East Anglia. A place called The Greenway. It was only a pathway, with these damned great hedges either side of it, but there was always this feeling about it. Something that said we didn't belong there.'

Peterson smiled. 'It's getting to all of us, isn't it? We know so much about this man and yet the more we know, the further away he seems to get. Damn it, Mike, we even know the bugger's name. No wonder the bloody press are making us a laughing stock. Four deaths and he's pre-warned us about each one. And we're no bloody closer.'

Mike nodded in silent sympathy. It had all been said and he had nothing to add, but Peterson wasn't finished.

'It's the sort of thing you'd expect to see in some American slasher movie. You know, some place where crossing the county line actually means something, and with so much bloody space the states are like separate countries. But I mean, look at this. A goddamned wood in the middle of Dorset and we're chasing this psycho who even has the cheek to send us photo locations before he commits the crime.'

He reached into his pocket, withdrew copies of three photographs and held them out in front of Mike, who didn't bother to look.

'It could have been anywhere,' Mike said quietly. 'A few fallen trees and a bit of a bush. Nothing to set it aside from a thousand other places across the country, not until you see the real thing.'

Peterson shook his head and continued to regard the pictures, comparing them to the actual scene. Then he shoved them back in his pocket. 'I know. You're right,' he said. 'Hindsight's a wonderful thing, but you think our bosses are going to look at it that way? Or the media? Or Joe Public? Damn it, Mike. One man and he's got most of the population locking themselves in after the *Six o'clock News* every night.'

He sighed, rubbed tired eyes with the heels of his hands, then straightened himself up. 'Get yourself back to Dorchester, find out how the interviews with our friends from the press are going. I'll see things are finished up here.'

Mike nodded. 'One thing's for certain,' he said wryly. 'Mr Ed Macey finally got his exclusive.'

CHAPTER THREE

The murder in the woods near Honiton, just above the Jacksons' farm at Colwell Barton, had made the national evening news. At that point, no connection had been made between this and the three others attributed to Bowen, but, as had become typical, Jake Bowen himself had drawn public attention to his latest escapade.

The pictures of Liz and Macey standing in the woods surrounded by half-burnt candles appeared in two of the morning editions of the tabloids.

Liz found Macey staring at the front pages scattered over the top of his desk.

'You've seen them then?'

'What do you think?' He looked up at her, then pushed an office chair in her direction. 'Sit down before you fall down. Christ, you look bad!'

'Thanks a bunch. I didn't sleep, OK? You got a cigarette?'

'Thought you'd given up.'

He pushed the packet towards her. Liz was new to this game, a mere trainee. He wondered, looking at her pale face and red eyes, if she'd be changing her mind on a career in journalism. Most kids at her stage of the game were writing Local Notes on the village fete, not encountering dead bodies in remote woodland. Her hands trembled as she sparked up and she drew a deep, unsteady breath before managing a weak smile.

'I'll be OK,' she said.

'Sure you will. Sure you will. We've been summoned to another chat with Detective Inspector Michael Croft later this morning. Dumb shit probably wants to accuse me of taking these.' He gestured angrily at the tabloid pictures. 'God, Liz, but I wish I bloody had. I truly do.'

'You don't mean that.'

'Don't I? All my working life I've waited for something like this. It falls in my lap and I can't take advantage. There's no justice. No bloody justice at all.' Liz said nothing; she was learning to take little notice of Macey's bluster. Instead, she pulled the pictures towards her, trying to be calm.

'He'd have to think you were some kind of cool shit to have taken these,' she said. 'Stood there with a dead body, set the camera on a timer and posed with that real shocked look on your fat face.'

She broke down then, covering her face with her cigarette-free hand and sobbing bitterly, still deep in shock.

'He was there, Macey. There in the woods watching us all the time. We could be dead by now, don't you understand that? You're going on about missing the chance of a lifetime and we could be fucking dead.'

Macey reached out and put what he hoped was a comforting hand on Liz's shoulder. She was right; he just didn't want to tell himself that. The two pictures that had been spread right across the front pages of the morning news showed the clearing in the gully shadowed by trees and slightly unfocused, as though to preserve some sense of decency. But clear enough and in the foreground, the shock and disbelief on their faces so plainly written, stood Liz and Macey.

June 19

The morning news was full of it. Maria Lucas had watched it on the television: the pictures of the latest Bowen outrage and the predictable responses from anyone and everyone who could wangle a little airtime.

Library pictures showed Chief Superintendent Peterson speaking at an earlier press call and Mike Croft, almost out of shot, looking as though he'd slept in his suit and had not shaved for at least a week.

It was, Maria mused, about the only time she got to see him these days. Brief glimpses caught as he sought to avoid the press photographers or the TV cameras. She knew from the odd times they had managed to talk that the strain of conducting this investigation so much in the public eye was becoming unbearable.

The phone rang. She picked it up on the second ring. 'Oh, good morning, John. Yes, I saw him. I guess this puts paid to our plans this weekend.'

She could hear John Tynan's smile. 'That's the penalty for being involved with a policeman, my dear. Seriously though, it's a nasty business.'

Maria sighed. 'Isn't it always? I was going to give you a call later anyway, see if you were free tonight.'

'Yes, I think so. What did you have in mind?'

'Essie,' Maria told him. 'Jo's still in the hospital, likely to stay there until this baby's born, and, as you know, Essie's still at my momma's place. I thought I'd give everyone a break and take her to see the latest Disney or something.'

'And you're not keen on facing it alone? No, certainly I'll come. I'd love to. Essie's a pleasure, though are you sure Disney isn't a bit tame for her? I thought space aliens with big guns were more up her street.'

Maria laughed. 'Probably, but as she's only five I think we might have problems getting her in. Anyway, I'll find out the times and give you a ring around lunchtime. That's if I get a lunchtime.'

'Heavy workload?'

'You wouldn't believe it. Prozac must be the in fix this season.' She glanced at the clock. 'OK, got to go, John. Catch you later.'

She rang off and began to get her notes in order. Maybe, she thought, if Mike was going to be tied up all weekend, she should offer to have Essie. Maria's sister, Jo, was expecting her second child and, with high blood pressure and oedema, was having something of a rough time. It would be a load off everyone's mind if Auntie Maria stepped into the breach.

* * *

Mike and Peterson watched the officers file out after the morning briefing. The barn which had been commandeered as their incident room was hardly ideal. No animals, but the place was still half-filled with hay bales and feed sacks piled against one wall. The flagstone floor struck cold even on the summer morning and Mike was glad that at least this was not happening in the middle of winter.

There was electricity in the barn, or rather there were two overhead lights. A generator was promised for later that morning to power essential equipment, and it had not yet been decided if this should be set up as a long-term incident room or just a temporary feature. That would depend on what was found at the crime scene, what witnesses came forward and on Jake Bowen's next move.

Two cats lounged in the patch of sunlight that poured through the open door. Eight thirty, but the last of the mist had evaporated and the day was already hot. The bright sunlight threw the rest of the barn into deep shadow and Mike turned the pin-board he was setting up towards the light to give himself a clearer view. He was pinning up pictures of the scene in the woods and of Jake Bowen's previous known victims. There were others, still unproven, filling a stack of files and untold disk space back at Honiton and elsewhere, but, Mike figured, to display that would take more than a pin-board and be a task too depressing to even attempt.

Peterson pulled out a chair, reversed it and sat down. He'd let Mike handle the morning briefing and assign the search teams and two local mobile units to carry out the door-to-door inquiries. Neighbours were well scattered, a few along the single track road, more placed well back along rutted lanes or accessible only on foot.

It was a task complicated by the number of visitors. The farm across the valley and a couple of others further along the road had been given over to the tourist trade.

Folk just there on holiday and intent on relaxing and enjoying themselves probably wouldn't notice the unusual if it got up and hit them in the face. Many would be in residence only at the ends of the day, not be around to see murders committed at noon. Add to this, as they'd found out the night before, that there were at least four well-established footpaths into the woods, with as many offshoots from each one. When Jake Bowen had chosen what looked like a public time and a public place, he'd certainly known exactly what he was about.

Peterson looked across to where Mike was pinning the photographs.

'Four murder victims,' he said, 'in five months.'

'That we know of.'

'Don't make life complicated, Mike. OK, four that we can prove. And not a bloody thing to connect them.'

'We can add the Norwich rapes,' Mike persisted, carefully aligning one of the photographs with the edge of the board. 'Three of them anyway, and the woman at Kennet in Wiltshire, Marion O'Donnel, all late last year. Whatever else he might be, our man's no slouch.'

Peterson got up, came across to where Mike was standing and began to sort through the notes and pictures lying on the table. It had been Mike Croft's involvement with a spate of violent attacks on women on his home patch of Norwich that had first brought him into contact with Jake Bowen. That had been at the tail end of the previous year. Peterson himself had become involved in early February of this, when a young woman had been found brutally murdered in a Bristol park. With the turning of the year, Jake Bowen had moved west.

'You spoke to the two reporters last night,' Peterson said. 'First impressions?'

Mike thought about it. Ed Macey and Liz Corran's statements had been analysed at the morning's briefing. Peterson was after a personal response.

'The caller asked for Macey,' he commented. 'That's typical Bowen behaviour, pick on someone specific, someone local, someone who's likely to want to get involved.'

'Wouldn't that go for any reporter?'

'Maybe, but Macey's been working on provincials all his life.' Mike shrugged. 'Some people would like it that way, but I think not Edward Macey. He talked last night about looking for a break into the big time before it was too late.' He paused, pinned up an enlargement of the wound in the victim's throat. 'The young woman, Liz Corran, I think we can see her presence as incidental to Bowen's plans. I'm sure he wanted Macey as a witness and went to great lengths to get him there.'

'Which, betting on Bowen following his previous pattern, means he might well make contact again.'

'He might,' Mike agreed. 'The officers who interviewed Macey's associates say he's apparently in the habit of mouthing off in his local when he's had a few. Goes on about how he could have been working on one of the nationals if he'd had the right breaks or the right connections.'

'And that's just the thing Jake Bowen would be on the lookout for.' Peterson nodded. 'And asking round here if there'd been any strangers in the local pubs would get us laughed out of court. We're in the middle of the bloody tourist season.'

'Not quite.' Mike smiled wryly and went to fill the kettle from the tap on the wall. They hadn't asked, but had assumed that this was drinking water. At any rate, it tasted all right in tea. 'The real tourist season begins when the schools finish. That's the third week in July around here, so it's worth asking. We'll get a list of conflicting information a mile long, especially as Macey's "local" could be any one of three or four pubs, but I've got a couple of officers on to it.'

Peterson nodded. 'Have you spoken to Maria yet?'

'No. She was out when I called last night. I'll have another go mid-afternoon. She generally grabs ten minutes or so then.'

Peterson shook his head. 'I think my wife's forgotten who I am,' he said. Then, 'So what do we have? A woman caller. Asks for Ed Macey and gives him a map reference and a time and tells him that there'll be something useful waiting for him.'

'Yes. She sounded drunk, Macey said, and wouldn't answer any of his questions.'

Peterson took a copy of Macey's statement from the table, glancing through it. 'He mentions that she kept giggling and breaking off to confirm with another person that she'd got it right.' He dropped the statement back on the table. 'I mean, anyone else would have reckoned it to be a wind-up and put the phone down.'

'But not Macey. He *wanted* this to be real. The caller only had to mention Jake Bowen's name and he'd be there, on the line with the worm in his mouth.'

'I agree.' Peterson frowned. 'We know how thorough our man is. It's obvious he's talked to Macey or at the very least observed him.'

Mike shrugged. 'Macey is not what you'd call a quiet man,' he commented. 'My guess is, with a few pints inside him, you could sit way across the saloon bar and still not need to read lips to know what was on his mind.'

'So that leaves the woman. The call came in at one p.m. and we're assuming our victim had probably been dead for around an hour by then.' He paused and reached across to see to the kettle, which had just come up to the boil. 'So we have to ask ourselves, does Bowen have a friend or relative living in the area? Someone to make the call for him. Did he meet some woman in the pub and get her drunk, tell her it was some kind of a prank?' He dunked tea-bags in the mugs and then handed one to Mike. 'I don't like what you're thinking.'

Mike took the mug. 'Neither do I,' he said, 'but we both know Bowen's record. He's too thorough, too organized, to use someone he just picked up in a pub, unless he was very certain they'd not talk about it. A friend? Relative? Maybe. My bet is, though, whoever made that call is going to be Bowen's next kill.'

CHAPTER FOUR

Mike drove out to Dorchester to speak with Liz and Macey. He found Macey sitting in a side office behind a desk piled high with newspaper clippings and handwritten notes.

'All the stuff I have so far on Jake Bowen,' Macey told him. 'I've even got you in amongst that lot somewhere.'

'Oh?' Mike queried.

'Your work on the Norwich rapist,' Macey told him. 'Or should that be in the plural?'

Mike poked a cautious finger at the stacks of paper perched precariously on the edge of the desk. 'You've done your homework,' he commented.

'Some good it's been. I'm there, literally in the picture, and some bastard on the nationals gets all the credit for it. Didn't even have to do the work for it either.'

Mike found a free chair and sat down. 'You'll have them beating a path to your door and you know it. First impressions. The inside story from the man who saw it all.'

Macey snorted. 'Yeah, maybe.' He was reluctant to confirm what Mike had said, but he was feeling a whole lot better than he had done earlier in the day. Already the phones had been buzzing; big names wanting to get on the inside track. He looked sharply at Mike.

'So, what's your line this morning? Have you come here to make sure I don't talk or to accuse me of taking those flaming pictures?'

Mike smiled. 'You watch too many bad films, Macey. No, I'm here because we think you may have had contact with the killer at some time, maybe in the last week or ten days.'

'Contact? With the killer?' Macey's face turned purple and then pale. 'Now look here, Detective Inspector Croft, if you're accusing—'

'No one's accusing, so cut the outraged voice-of-the-people act.' Mike paused and rubbed a hand across tired eyes. He couldn't remember the last time he'd been anything but tired. 'Look, you might have talked to him in passing. Talked in front of him. Complained too loudly about not getting a piece of the action. Anything, as simple as that. Jake Bowen's got a peculiar sense of humour, that much we do know, and all it might take for him to involve you in his game could be the odd word in the wrong place at the wrong time.'

Macey's mind was working overtime. Random thoughts that had plagued him through a sleepless night now started falling into place.

'He asked for me by name,' Macey said. 'It could have been anyone, but he asked specifically for me.' Mike sat forward suddenly.

'Now wait a minute. It was a woman who made that call.'

Macey shook himself. 'Sure,' he said. 'But it was a man who spoke to reception. It was only a woman on the line when it was put through to me.'

'A man,' Mike said heavily, 'and you didn't see fit to mention this in your statement?'

'I didn't know, not until this morning, when I started to ask around. Talk to the girl yourself. You'd better hurry, though. Once she starts putting two and two together and realizes she was chatting to a murderer, she'll be off like a flash. You mark my words.'

Mike wondered if Macey always talked in clichés. 'I'll be talking to her,' he said heavily, 'just as soon as I've done with you, Mr Macey. The fact that he didn't speak to you himself, that could be significant.'

'You mean I might have known the voice? Yes, I'd considered that. Look, I'll give it some thought.'

'You'll give it more than some,' Mike told him. 'I want to know. Anyone strange or anyone in one or other of your local watering holes who might have shown an unusual interest in you or what you have to say?'

'Aw, come on, Inspector. I work for a bloody newspaper. Look, knowing that — and, believe me, most of them do where I choose to drink — well, most people it takes in one of two ways. Either they shut up tight when I'm around or they won't bloody give over. It's all, "Oh, I've got a good story for you, mate," ' Macey mimicked. 'Or, "There's something going on at such and such a place you ought to be looking at." Then when they find out I'm a bloody photographer they all want cheap rates on their kiddie portraits. It's like being a frigging doctor — no such thing as off-duty. There's always someone got something suppurating they want you to take a look at.' He pushed back his chair and got up, pacing the little space there was left in the room.

'I mean, what does this fellah look like?' He waved an impatient hand towards his stacks of paper. 'A good half-dozen descriptions you've got there and not one of them the same. He's got blond hair. He's got dyed black hair. He's clean-shaven when he hasn't got a beard or an occasional moustache. He's got blue eyes that might be brown and a Geordie accent according to some vicar in Berkshire who might be talking about the Lord God himself for all the reliability of it. You've got some forensic shrink that profiles him as a lorry-driving loner and a wannabe Doris Stokes spiritualist medium that claims she's in contact with him on a higher plane. Fuck it, Inspector. You know the man's name. You think he might be from up north because you've got a couple of Jake Bowens up there you haven't been able to track through the voters' register and that's about it. Oh, I'm sorry, you know he kills people and likes to make artistic films about it. He probably even takes a starring role. And you can take a guess that he's going about his business under an assumed name.'

Mike opened his mouth to speak, his own anger and frustration beginning to break through, but Macey hadn't finished.

'I talk to a lot of people, Inspector Croft. You do in my game and a lot of people ask me a lot of daft questions about what I do.' He sat down again and reached across for a stack of papers. 'I'll tell you something for nothing. This guy's not going to hang around waiting for you to get a fix on him. He's mobile and he's smart and, you mark my words, he's done what he set out to do. He's long gone.'

Mike shook his head slowly. 'I think you're wrong,' he said. 'I've seen the way Jake Bowen works and he's not finished yet. Those pictures, they were just the beginning. He caught you on film. Just one frozen moment, but that won't be enough for Jake Bowen. He likes his pictures live and moving or spectacularly dead. I'll make a bet with you, Macey, he's already got an archive on you that would make what you've got on him look like a kids' dictionary put beside the *Encyclopaedia Britannica.* You might hope he's left, but Jake Bowen makes feature-length editions and so far all you've contributed are a few stills.'

* * *

Mike had a swift word with both Liz and the receptionist who had taken the call, but his patience was short and he did not want to push it further. He normally saw himself as calm and controlled — *too* controlled, Maria was always telling him — but Macey had reached under his skin and he had reacted.

Liz had little to add to her previous statement. She was clearly still shaken and was chain-smoking cigarettes in a non-smoking office as though to make up for the weeks when she'd been trying to give them up.

'I'm OK, though,' she told him. 'Damned if this thing is going to get to me.'

The receptionist had nothing useful to tell. 'An ordinary voice,' she said. Not a local accent, but not one that she could place either.

Mike made a note to get an officer sent out to take a formal statement but held out little hope that it would get them anywhere. Ordinary voice. That was just the trouble with everything they knew about Jake Bowen. Much of it was so damned ordinary.

It was mid-afternoon before Mike managed to talk to Maria and suggest that she come down to see him that weekend.

'Oh, Lord, I'm sorry, Mike. I thought with all this business going on you'd be tied up and I've volunteered to have Essie.'

'Oh.' He knew it was inadequate, but it was all that he could manage. He tried again. 'There's no one else? I take it Jo's still in hospital?'

'I'm afraid so. Look, I'll ring Momma, see if I can come down on Sunday at least. Or,' she said tentatively, 'I could bring her with me?'

Mike hesitated. He was loath to bring a child to where Jake Bowen might be, even though he knew that was probably stupid, as Bowen could be just about anywhere. Rather hesitantly he explained this to Maria, half expecting her to laugh at him.

'I see what you're saying, Mike. OK. Look, I've not said for certain I'd be able to have Essie at the weekend. I'll try and sort something out and make it up to everyone another way. I'll drive down Friday night if you can book me in somewhere. It's going to be late, but at least we'll have the weekend together.'

'It's a long drive, love, and I can't promise I'll be there all the time.'

'I'll be fine. Anyway, I'm missing you.' She laughed suddenly. 'Maybe I should bring John with me. Kind of family reunion.'

'Don't even think of it. Much as I'd love to spend some time with him, I need time alone with you more. I'll ring you tonight.'

He listened as she put the phone down before switching the mobile off and starting back towards Honiton, thinking about Maria. Having her say she missed him was precious. He'd known her almost two years now and found it impossible to imagine life without her, though it still amazed him that someone as beautiful could choose to be in love with him.

Mike carried her picture in his wallet. He had always thought that a rather sentimental thing to do, but now he found it comforting to be able to open it and see her smiling at him, head slightly to one side. Her smile raised dimples in the richness of perfect black skin and her dark eyes sparkled with mischief. She wore her hair close-cropped. Before Maria, Mike had always preferred hair to be long. But that was then. Now he viewed everything about her as perfect.

It would be good to see her at the weekend, even if only for the briefest of times.

Though the strain still showed itself around his eyes, Mike was actually smiling as he drove down into Honiton.

* * *

When Liz went to find him, Macey was still poring over his Jake Bowen archive. He'd spent the hours since Mike had left on the phone, returning calls, chatting to editors whose names he'd previously only read at the head of their columns. Macey was one of an increasingly rare breed. He might work for the *Dorchester Herald* as a photographer but he'd done his time as a journalist and that made him a one-man band, ready and eager to produce the goods for whoever wanted to pay.

He'd agreed to a couple of interviews, but what he really wanted was the by-line and finally he'd forced tentative agreements from a couple of tabloid editors. Find a new angle and we'll publish. Macey's rational side told him that such verbal contracts weren't worth the proverbial paper they were written on, but he didn't care. This was going to be it and it was Mike Croft who had given him the germ of an idea. The angle. If Jake Bowen hadn't finished yet with Macey, well maybe he could use it to his advantage. A genuine inside story with Macey as the leading man.

And the *Herald* wanted their share of the glory too. The editor was determined that Macey should not sell them short and, going back over his notes, he thought he had just the thing to satisfy.

'Charlie Morrow,' he announced as Liz came through the door.

'Charlie who?'

'Morrow. He put two and two together about Jake being the killer movie-maker he was after. Specialist stuff. Very select audience. Used the one-shot casting principle.'

'The what? Macey, what the hell are you on about?'

'His actors. You get to feature in a Jake Bowen special, it's likely to be your one and only chance of stardom. You burn bright, but by God you have a short career.'

'You're talking about the snuff movies this guy is supposed to have made?'

'No supposed about it, Liz. They're real enough and they're still out there, getting more valuable by the frigging day. This guy, Morrow. He was a DCI from what I remember. Led a raid on one of Bowen's studios and got himself blown up for his trouble.'

'And?' Liz queried.

'You and I are going to talk to him. See how he's getting along.' He grinned at her. 'Editor says we need a good story for the local rag, something the big boys haven't covered, and my feeling is that Charlie Morrow could be it.'

Liz frowned. 'If it's such a good story, how come no one else has touched it?'

'Because up until about a month ago he was still in hospital, specialist bums unit, and they weren't about to let hordes of journos clutter up their waiting room. Anyway, after all the initial fuss was over and he failed to die from his injuries, the story kind of faded out.'

'And you think you can revive it?'

'Sure I can. Few phone calls — well, actually every bloody nursing home in Wiltshire or near enough — and I've found him.'

'And they told you he was there, just like that?'

'Well, no, not just like that. I called and asked to speak to him. Number five and I struck lucky. They put the call through to his room.'

'And he talked to you?' Liz was caught between outrage and astonishment.

'Well . . .'

'He told you where to go. Words that start with F and end with off by any chance?'

Macey laughed. 'That was his first reaction, but I talked him round. Told him who I was, mentioned Jake Bowen's name.'

'God, Macey, I'd think that was the last thing he'd want to hear.'

'Ah.' Macey tapped gently on the side of his several-times-broken nose. 'That's where you're wrong. Ex-DCI Charlie Morrow is very interested in Jakey boy's latest escapade.'

'Jakey boy! Christ, you make me sick sometimes.' She shook her head. 'I still can't believe he's agreed to see you.' She looked more shrewdly at Macey. 'He hasn't agreed, though, has he? *Has he?* This is all just so much pie.'

Macey pushed himself to his feet with an air of injured importance. 'Not yet, my girl, but he will. You just mark my words.'

CHAPTER FIVE

June 20

Friday morning was as hot as ever, even at eight o'clock, when Mike set out from Honiton. He was lodging in a cramped room above a pub. The accommodation was basic but adequate, and Mike was quite content with it. All in all, it was probably more comfortable than his flat in Norwich, a one-bedroomed affair he had rented half furnished and to which he had added very little in the two years he had been there.

He was on his way to see Max Harriman. Mike reprised what he knew about the man. Harriman had been a close friend of Jake when the two of them were growing up and he'd maintained contact with him in a distant way ever since. He had regarded Jake as something of a hero, mimicking his actions, though he lacked Jake's innate caution and sense of purpose. He had finally been arrested when his imitation of Jake had gone too far. He had raped and then killed in December of the previous year.

Harriman was still on remand awaiting final psychiatric assessment before going to trial, the wheels of the judiciary moving as slowly as ever. He was presently being held in a secure psychiatric unit and Mike had been seeing him several times a month since then, sometimes at Harriman's instigation and sometimes his own.

Harriman should have been their key to Jake. It was because of him that they knew Jake's real name and anything about his background, but, Mike reflected as he drove out on this latest visit, that still didn't amount to a great deal. Harriman had played them like an expert over these last months and many times Mike had felt like threatening to withdraw his visits, which seemed to lead to nothing but frustration and only fed Harriman's sense of self-importance. His superiors, though, had said he must carry on. Mike had been the arresting officer and, for whatever reason, Harriman had chosen him to be the one he'd talk to. From time to time he'd let slip some little detail; some fragmentary clue to the way Jake thought or the way he might behave. It was enough to make them consider cultivation of Max Harriman worthwhile.

Beside Mike on the passenger seat lay a large folder. Inside were copies of the cuttings books Max had kept over the years, with material from local papers, from the nationals, even from the occasional glossy magazine. Max must have spent a fortune on his news collection. Not all of the articles concerned Jake and Max; it was an eclectic mix. Max had taken care to record noteworthy incidents in the lives of anyone he had once known and grown up with: the weddings of one-time friends; births of their children if they appeared in the paper; even the small achievements of those children, such as the time one had won first prize in a dance competition or another been a May Queen's attendant at the local fete.

Everyone mentioned in Max's books had been traced, interviewed, tagged and quietly turned inside-out, on the off-chance Jake Bowen might still be known to them.

Macey had been wrong in what he'd said the day before. They knew a great deal about Jake Bowen: the young man growing up in what had been a pit village just outside York;

the young man who had shown such promise at school — when he could be bothered to attend. They knew about the teacher Ian Wright who'd borrowed the super eight cine camera on Max and Jake's behalf and helped them make a film that had won a prize in a national competition, and, unknowingly, set Jake on a career that would make him the most hunted and probably the most feared man in Britain.

Jake Bowen had been just fifteen years old then and his picture, with Max, in the local paper was the last image they could be certain they had of him.

They knew that Jacob Alastair Bowen had been born on 9 November 1959 to Millie and Alastair Bowen. He was an only child, though Millie had suffered two miscarriages in previous years. Jake Bowen had grown up in the next street to Max Harriman. There were rows and rows of terraced, back-to-back houses with quiet roads between where the kids had played. The Bowens had a proper bathroom added to their home in 1964 and a downstairs extension at the back. The Harrimans had beaten them to it by a year and been the first in their street to have a pink suite.

Harriman's reminiscences had been full of details like this.

Jake had gone to the local school, built originally as a Victorian Board School a few streets away. It still had the words carved above the doors denoting separate entrances for girls and boys. Mike had visited the school about a month before and it was still a Victorian Board School, for all that the staff had dressed it up inside, making the place more bright and cheerful than its founders could ever have intended. The holes in the tarmac of the school yard, Mike thought, were probably the same ones that Jake Bowen had fallen over, splashed in when it rained and played marbles in all those years before.

It was ordinary, recognizable. Mike himself had grown up in similar surroundings, geographically about a hundred miles south but in look and spirit very little different.

Police officers had converged on the little community over the past months, ostensibly mapping Max Harriman's career, but really more intent on tracking Jake. Mike knew that it would be only a matter of time before Max's connections with Jake Bowen came out, then the few details the police knew, but the press and public did not, would be splashed across every front page in the country. He could just visualize the headlines, the glaring spotlight trained on this small community when it finally became known that not one murderer but two had emerged from its quiet streets.

It was a two-hour drive to the prison even using the motorway and another half-hour dealing with the bureaucracy of the visit. Mike sat behind the wooden table in the bare room where it and two chairs were the only furnishings and laid out the cassette recorder he used during these interviews and the photocopied cuttings books.

The copies had been spiral-bound for ease of handling. Max Harriman's original books had been sugarpaper scrapbooks, of the sort that could be bought in any stationer's or post office. Stapled together and bound in stiff card. Harriman had made them more robust by covering the outside in sticky-back plastic.

The originals had been stashed away as evidence, but Max had been given a copy of each one in the hope that it would prompt him to make further disclosures. In practice Max spent more time bemoaning the loss of his originals than he did adding to their information. He would complain from the moment Mike came through the door, as he did today.

'You haven't brought my books. I told you, I wanted my books.'

'Good morning to you, Max. Sit down.'

Harriman sat down and shoved Mike's spiral-bound books away from him as though he found them distasteful.

'I told you, I don't say anything until I've got my books.'

'They're evidence, Max. You know that.'

'You've got copies. Use those as evidence.'

Mike didn't bother to reply this time. Instead he opened one of the books at a page he had previously marked and turned it so that Max could see.

'Last time I came to see you, we talked about Jake's parents.'

'No, Inspector, *you* talked about Jake's parents, I just listened. I told you, I can't do it without my books.'

'What happened to them, Max? Where did Jake's parents go to? We've got this one picture and nothing after that.' He leaned forward to see better and read the caption. ' "New lay preacher, Mr Alastair Bowen, at St Bartolph's Parish Church."' He looked expectantly at Max, who said nothing.

'It's an odd thing for you to have saved, Max. A little clipping from a church magazine. Especially as neither you nor Jake could have been more than seven when it happened.'

Max glanced at him, then at the picture. 'It isn't mine,' he said.

'It was in your book.' Mike frowned. 'It's a funny thing, though, it was in one of the later books if I remember.' He flipped the cover over to check. 'Yes, I thought so. You must have added it later and not had room in the original book, so you put it in here. Five years ago, Max. What happened five years ago that you suddenly acquired this?'

'It isn't mine. I told you.'

'Then whose is it, Max? Are you suggesting that I made it up? Stuck it in a book and copied it just to fool you?'

Harriman gave Mike an almost pitying look. This was a routine they had repeated many times. Max sometimes even refused to acknowledge that the copies of the cuttings books bore any resemblance to the originals or had anything to do with him.

'If it were in my book I could tell you about it,' Max told him. 'That thing, it isn't mine.'

Mike shook his head thoughtfully. 'I can't let you have the originals, Max, you know that.'

'Why not? You've got copies. Lots of copies.'

'So you agree this is a copy of your book? If it's a copy and you recognize that it's a copy, why can't you tell me about this clipping?'

Max sighed and leaned back in his chair; gazing up at the ceiling. Mike had learned over the course of many such sessions that the best thing he could do now was carry on, continue to talk, allow his conjectures to become wilder and wilder until Max was finally provoked enough to contradict him.

He pressed on. 'So what happened, Max? We know that the Bowens moved to York when Jake was twenty-one and that Jake went with them. We know that Jake was working in a printer's, that he was a plate maker. Very good, from what I'm told. We've traced them on the voters' register until 1982, when Jake would have been twenty-three, and then they drop out of sight. Now why was that?'

He sat forward, turning the book towards him. 'Where did the Bowens go to?' He let the silence sit for a little, then, as though thinking out loud, he said, 'It's strange, though. Alastair Bowen was a keen churchgoer all his life. Avid, you might say. Sang in the choir as a boy, joined an evangelical chapel as a young man and was a lay preacher at St Bartolph's right up until a month before they moved to York.'

'So?'

It was the first positive response of the morning, so Mike treated it with care. 'Well, doesn't it strike you as a little odd? I mean, we've absolutely no record even of church attendance in York. And I know, because I've talked to the minister who had the living at the time, that Alastair left the church quite suddenly. From being a mainstay of church activities to nothing, literally overnight, doesn't that strike you as strange, Max? Even a *little* strange?'

Max Harriman was sitting very still, his focus having switched from the ceiling to the wall behind Mike.

'And there's another thing. The minister from St Bartolph's said it was as though Alastair Bowen was afraid of something. Ashamed and afraid. That suddenly he wouldn't even speak to anyone from the church. Wouldn't let them into his house or take their calls when they phoned. Odd behaviour, don't you think? And I have to ask myself, Max, what was he afraid of? If the minister was right and he was ashamed of something, what do you suppose that could have been?'

Max blinked rapidly, as though awakening to Mike's presence again. 'He was a stupid man,' he said. 'Never understood.'

'Understood? Understood what?'

'Why —' Max laughed and looked at Mike disbelievingly — 'Jake, of course. What Jake did, what he was, was beyond anything their small minds could understand.'

'Jake was special, then?' Mike pressed on, keeping his voice level and noncommittal, though he sensed they might be on the verge of something important.

'You know Jake was special. He always was, always will be to those of us who understand. Who have the vision to see beyond the act and look to the purpose.'

'And what purpose would that be?'

Max smiled at him, two bright spots of colour burning in an otherwise pale face, and his hands moved excitedly as though turning invisible pages to search for the right entry in the book.

'What happened to Jake's parents, Max?' Mike asked, hardly daring to raise his voice above the softest whisper. 'And Jake, where did Jake go to? Where did he go to next?'

Max's hands stopped moving abruptly, as though he had suddenly realized that the pages he was turning were unreal. What he was searching for wasn't there. 'I can't tell you without my books,' he said. Then he got to his feet, pushing the chair back so that it scraped loudly across the floor. 'I want to go now. I have nothing more to say. I want to go.'

It would be useless to press him further. Max could sit in stubborn silence for hours at a time once he'd set his mind against speaking. Mike watched the guard escort Max away and sat quietly, trying to assimilate what had and had not been said. He had come here today quite convinced that Jake Bowen had murdered his parents and had hoped to get some kind of confirmation from Max. Now, unaccountably, he was not so sure. What he had said to Max about having spoken to the old incumbent of St Bartolph's Church was a lie. The old minister had been dead and gone at least a dozen years.

It had been guesswork on Mike's part, built on the slight evidence that Alastair Bowen had resigned from his position as lay preacher, but it looked as though he'd hit a target not so far from the truth.

Mike flipped open one of the other books. If the clippings held any clues, then Jake was already at least involved in the sex industry by then. Max's clippings recorded raids, in 1983, on two sex shops in the Bradford area, and another one, curiously, in Cardiff, where a quantity of magazines had been seized.

The evidence had long since been used to prosecute and would then have been destroyed, but from police records most were S&M mags of a particularly violent type. The report also stated that the pictures were very graphic, extremely realistic in their evocation of torture and of pain, and were taken by an obvious professional. It seemed that Jake Bowen knew his business even then.

Mike gathered his paperwork together and removed the tape from the machine. He glanced up as one of the guards who had escorted Max back to his cell came in.

'I hoped I'd catch you,' he said. 'Harriman got very excited when we were taking him back, wanted me to come and tell you something.'

'What was it?'

'Well, it's a bit odd really. He said to tell you that Jake sent him the picture five years ago and that you were right, he didn't have room for it in his proper book. Then he said I'd also got to tell you that his mother was a whore and the day she died was the only time he ever saw her smile.'

* * *

Mike got back into the car and turned on the radio. Peterson had held yet another press conference earlier that morning and details were given in brief on the lunchtime news, which Mike caught the tail-end of. Peterson was saying that he recognized the need for media exposure, that he realized public feelings were running high, and once again he appealed for help. Mike winced, knowing how Peterson really felt about all the media involvement, how much of a struggle it had been to keep anything under wraps.

Mike flicked the radio off and dialled the incident room number on his mobile phone. 'I'm on my way back,' he said when Peterson came on the line. 'I just heard you on the radio.'

Peterson snorted. 'Total farce,' he said. 'But you have to make the right noises. Anyway, we've got a development. I'm not going to say much over the air, but we know who she is. And she's been missing close on twelve weeks.'

'How?'

'Got lucky with a missing person's report. We're trying to locate kin. I'll fill you in when you get back. But the big question is, where the hell's she been all this time?'

CHAPTER SIX

21 June

Mike had arrived in Lyme Regis at ten o'clock on the Saturday morning to find that Maria had already left for the beach. Their hopes of a romantic weekend had been dashed the night before. Her mother had called her literally as she had been about to leave with the news that Jo had gone into labour. She had to go to her, as Jo's husband, a sales rep, had been notified but would not be able to make it home for hours. Please could Maria help out?

She had called Mike immediately but had been unable to reach him. Undecided, the best she could manage was to leave a message telling him that she would be coming down but bringing Essie.

'They left about an hour ago,' the woman at the boarding house told him. 'The little girl was so keen to get to the beach.'

Maria had left instructions as to where they were likely to be and Mike went to see if he could find them.

He wasn't dressed for the beach but for the interview with the bereaved relatives he knew he would be meeting at some point that day. The girl in the woods had been called

Julia. Julia Norman. Her parents, after weeks of anxiety, had finally been persuaded to spend a few days away with friends somewhere in the Midlands and it had taken time to track them down.

Julia had been a fine arts student. She had walked away from her course and the house she shared with four others without so much as a goodbye, taking only some clothes and the box containing most of her art equipment. That had been almost twelve weeks before and was the last anyone saw of her.

Anyone except Jake Bowen.

Mike loosened his tie and slung his jacket over his shoulder. He felt conspicuously overdressed among the shorts and T-shirts of the holidaymakers. He walked down the steep hill from the boarding house and cut through a shaded alleyway towards the beach. Maria had said they would be on the short stretch of sand close to the breakwater, looking out towards the Cobb. He strolled along the seafront, enjoying the bright sunlight and the blueness of the water, looking ahead and scanning the crowd for them.

It was Essie who saw him first. He heard her shouting his name.

'Uncle Mike, Uncle Mike! We're over here, Uncle Mike!'

Mike grinned and waved at the small figure in the red swimsuit. Her braided hair decorated with blue and yellow beads swung about her face as she leapt up and down trying to attract his attention. Water, sparkling like diamonds, splashed all around.

Mike strode across the stretch of sandy beach, picking his way between the sandcastles and sunbathers. Essie ran to him, arms outstretched. He hoisted her up, almost losing his jacket in the process, and her wet arms and plump sandy legs locked around his body.

'I love you, Uncle Mike.'

Mike cuddled the child close, inhaling the warm sunshine scent of her skin. It was a long time since his son Stevie had been this age and he had held him like this.

'I love you too, sweetheart,' he told her, looking over her head at Maria, who was walking up the beach towards him. She looked spectacular, he thought. Blue denim cut-offs and a white shirt open at the neck and tied below her breasts.

'Hi. I'd forgotten what you looked like.' Smiling, she kissed him, then looked with mild disapproval at his suit and tie. 'You're not dressed for making sandcastles, Uncle Mike.'

'I know, but I'm sure I'll manage.' He set Essie down and watched as she scampered back into the sea, aware of the damp patches on his shirt from wet, sandy limbs.

'You're likely to be called in?'

'They've identified the murdered girl. We finally managed to contact her parents late last night and they're expected back in Exeter this morning. Peterson's going to give me a call when they've made the formal identification. I'm really sorry love, but I don't know how long I'm going to be.'

Maria slipped an arm through his and kissed him again. 'I knew it would probably be like that,' she said. 'Don't worry, we'll be just fine. Exeter, you say. She was a local girl then?'

Mike nodded. 'Born and brought up in Exeter. Studied at art college there, even lived in a shared house not two miles from her parents' home. Quiet and rather shy, according to her teachers. Then suddenly she breaks the pattern and takes off without a word.'

'Maybe no one knew her as well as they thought?'

'Maybe.' Mike sighed. He was dreading meeting the parents. 'Anyway,' he went on, 'I've got a while with you, and I can't tell you how good it is to see you.'

* * *

Mike had a little over an hour with Maria and Essie before the inevitable call came through. As brief a time as it was, it helped get his mind back into gear and his life back into perspective. As he allowed himself to relax and play with Essie and chat with Maria, he realized just how much tension had built up over the previous weeks and how heavily Jake Bowen weighed upon his mind.

Peterson's call, when it came, was brief and to the point. The parents had identified Julia and were insisting on seeing where the body had been found. Mike was to meet them at the crime scene with Peterson.

Mike frowned as he slipped the mobile phone into his pocket and told Maria he had to go.

'Is that unusual?' she asked. 'For people to want to see the place?'

'It happens, though usually later rather than immediately, but you can never tell what a bereaved family are going to do.'

He hugged Essie goodbye, getting wet again. He slipped his jacket on over the sand stains on his shirt and kissed Maria, promising he'd see them later; then walked back to find his car.

What had possessed a girl like Julia Norman to disappear as suddenly as she had and make no attempt to contact anyone? Or had she been unable to do so?

Twelve weeks of captivity was an awesome thing to contemplate. Mike wondered just how soon into that time she had known that she was going to die.

Mike was first to arrive back at the incident room in Colwell Barton. He spent the waiting time taking down the pin-board covered with the pictures of the dead girl and hiding it behind the hay bales in the corner, then tidying any other evidence out of sight. He heard the car pull up on the gravel outside only a few minutes later.

The Normans were middle-aged, a little older than Mike would have anticipated. He stood stiffly, shoulders squared as though to attention, his gaze deliberately concentrated on whoever might be speaking, while Mrs Norman could hardly bear to meet anyone's eyes.

Peterson made the introductions.

'I really am terribly sorry,' Mike found himself saying, hating himself for the meaninglessness of such platitudes but at a loss as to what else he might do.

Mr Norman nodded briefly and his wife murmured something that might have been thanks.

'You'll want to be getting on with this,' Peterson said brusquely. He'd spent time with them already and realized that sympathy at this stage was more than either of them could take. 'Mike, if you'd maybe lead the way. The going's a bit rough, I'm afraid,' he added, glancing down at Mrs Norman's summer sandals.

'If we could just go.'

Peterson glanced across at Mr Norman. 'Of course,' he said. 'Mike, would you . . .'

Mike led them along the narrow rabbit path and across the stile into the first patch of oak wood before they reached the Forestry Commission land. It was hot and still, silent but for the song of birds and their footsteps, half muffled by the grass. Peterson followed directly behind Mike after the first stile, leaving Mr Norman to help his wife. Her skirt and heeled sandals made it awkward for her to climb and Peterson had no wish to make her feel uncomfortable by having him watch her struggle.

Mike paused as they reached the second stile. 'It's just through here,' he said quietly. 'Are you certain you want to do this, Mr Norman? Mrs Norman?'

It was Julia's mother who answered, with surprising firmness. 'I need to see it,' she said. 'I won't believe it till I've seen the place.'

Reluctantly Mike led them on.

The gully was steep even for those in flat shoes but Mrs Norman would allow no one other than her husband to help. She laddered her tights and scratched her legs on the exposed tree roots, but she made it down.

The place where Julia's body had lain was still cordoned off, the yellow plastic of the tape seeming to glow in the semi-dark. Mrs Norman stood as close to the cordon as she could and stared at the rough altar of branches and now wilted flowers on which her daughter had died. Her gaze took in the dozens of tiny candles, burned down to mere stumps, that decorated the branches of the trees and travelled upwards to the dark canopy of leaves blocking the sunlight overhead. Then she let out a little cry before covering her mouth tightly with both hands.

'Are you all right, Mrs Norman?'

She nodded, hands still tight over her mouth as though she wanted to be sick. Her husband circled his arms around her and pulled her close.

'It's the same place, isn't it?' She pulled away enough so that she could look up into his face.

He nodded. 'Yes, I think it is.'

'The same place?' Peterson was questioning. 'Same place as what? You've seen this before, Mr Norman?'

'It's in a painting,' he said slowly, his voice thick with tears. 'At Christmas, Julia gave us a painting. One of hers. It was beautifully done, but it was not like her usual work.'

'A painting of this place?'

'Yes. This place. We knew it would be, that's why we had to come. We knew when you told us where she died. The flowers and the candles and all the things you told us, we had to come and be sure.'

'This painting,' Mike asked, 'it was more than just a landscape?'

'Oh, yes,' the father said softly. 'It was more than just a landscape. There was a woman lying on a bed of flowers. Lilies and white roses all painted so clearly you could tell what every one was meant to be. All stained with blood.'

CHAPTER SEVEN

22 June

Sunday morning brought a surprise in the shape of a phone call from Charlie Morrow. He and Mike had spoken during the earlier investigation and Mike had visited him several times while he had been in hospital receiving treatment for the severe burns he had suffered. He'd had a call from a couple of reporters, he told Mike. They'd done a good job of tracking him down and wanted to do a feature article on him.

'My first reaction was to say no, but I've been thinking about it and it might do some good. You've not exactly been getting sympathetic coverage.'

Mike laughed. 'No, it's been more like, why don't those useless coppers get off their backsides and get their collective fingers out. Seriously, though, do you feel up to joining the media circus?'

'I feel well enough to be bored out of my brain and very left out,' Charlie told him. 'I've been lying on my bloody back in hospital for months. No television in case it upsets me and no one willing to tell me a damned thing. I learned more interrogating Macey on the phone for ten minutes than I've pieced together in the past six months. Seriously, Mike, it's been the most frustrating time of my life.'

Mike sympathized and promised that he'd try to get to see him. He still wasn't used to the slight slur in Charlie Morrow's voice when he spoke. The burns to the right side of his face had tightened the skin and scarred his upper lip badly enough to have necessitated grafts.

'I've had a lot of time doing nothing but think and there has to be something I can help on.'

'If I could offer you anything, Charlie, then you know I would. Lord knows we need the extra brain-power, but while you're officially on the sick . . .'

There was silence for a moment at the other end of the line. The truth was that it would be a long time, if at all, before Charlie Morrow returned to full duty. 'Charlie, I'm sorry. I really am.'

'Yes, I know. I know. But it rankles, Mike. I figure I owe that bastard one.'

* * *

Mike returned to Lyme to spend some time with Maria. They walked at Essie's pace along the shoreline out towards the headland jutting like a rocky finger into the sea. It was rough going over stones and heavy boulders, especially as Essie insisted on taking the hardest way across and shouting for Uncle Mike to look at every fossil that she found embedded in the rocks. Finally, they paused at a spot where the boulders gave way to flat rock, covered with weeds and broken by shallow pools full of shrimp and tiny fish. Essie was delighted, dipping her hands into the warm water, trying to catch the darting fish or sorting among the pebbles for the fossils that Mike had shown her how to identify.

The adults took the time to talk — a conversation interrupted every few minutes by another of Essie's finds, but still much more than they had enjoyed for many weeks.

Jo had given birth to a baby boy the night before and Maria looked forward to seeing the new addition to their family.

'You ever thought about having children?' Mike asked, surprised that he had never asked before.

Maria laughed. 'Are you proposing something?'

'Maybe. I don't really know. Sometimes I think, yes, I want to settle down again. Have kids before it's too late and I get too cynical or just too old.'

'Poor heading-for-middle-age man that you are.'

'Exactly that,' he said with a grin. 'Other times I think of Stevie, of how it felt when I lost him, and I know that I'm afraid of it happening again. Of having something as precious as a child and losing it.'

Maria reached for his hand and squeezed it tightly. She was about to speak when Mike stood up abruptly, turning to face the cliff and shading his eyes against the sun.

'What is it?'

'I thought I saw something. A flash of light, like something reflecting off a lens.'

Maria shrugged. 'Probably twitchers. There must be a ton of bird life up on the cliff.'

'I suppose you're right,' Mike said, but he continued to scan the clifftop, looking for the source of that elusive flash of light.

Maria touched his cheek, turning his face towards her. 'You're really spooked by all this, aren't you?'

'Anyone would be.'

'Of course they would, but, Mike, you've got to let up a bit or I'm going to be seeing you professionally.'

Mike tried hard to make light of it. 'I didn't think the rules allowed that,' he said.

Maria half-smiled in return, but her eyes were worried. 'I'll have to bend the rules, then,' she said.

CHAPTER EIGHT

23 June

At the briefing in Honiton on the Monday morning Peterson unveiled the painting Julia Norman had given to her parents. He set it on a table leaning against the wall.

It was stunningly beautiful, Mike thought. A large canvas, some three feet tall by two across, the towering pine trees almost black against a glimpse of pale sky, with broken shafts of sunlight filtering through the branches, bleaching the colour from the ground.

The woman seemed to be at one with the scene. There was nothing anomalous about the figure lying prone upon a bed of flowers. The entire painting had a magical quality that allowed anything to happen within its frame.

Mike bent to look more closely at the figure. It was undoubtedly a self-portrait, with Julia's auburn hair and pale skin, her full lips curving in a slight smile. She looked as though she could have been dreaming.

Peterson had pictures of the crime scene, blown up to the same size and pinned to the wall beside the painting. He'd had them taken from as close to the same angle as he could get and it was obviously the same place, down to the details of the fallen trees and the light filtering onto the forest floor.

He turned towards those assembled.

'Your thoughts, please,' he said.

'She must have been there.'

'Maybe, or she could have painted from photographs.'

'So, did she take the pictures or did Jake Bowen?'

'It was a gift to her parents, sir?'

Peterson nodded.

'Well, it seems a bit of an odd thing to give your mum and dad. A nude self-portrait, I mean.'

'They thought it strange,' Peterson acknowledged. 'They said it was not like her usual stuff.'

'Have you seen any of her other work?' someone asked.

Peterson nodded. 'A couple of pictures they had at home. Most of it's still at the college and back at the house she shared. I'm having Mike collect it later this morning, but from what I've seen a lot of her work was semi-abstract stuff she was doing for her degree project. This is definitely not typical.'

'So why did she paint it?'

Mike took a few steps back, standing so that he could see both the painting and the photos of the crime scene from the same angle.

'It's summertime,' he said.

Peterson looked blank for a moment and then realized what Mike had said.

'And I'd say early summer,' he added. 'The greenness of it and just the general look. She either painted it last summer, in which case they'd probably have seen it at home — a canvas this size is not exactly an easy thing to hide — or she did it after she moved out in the autumn from pictures or sketches made earlier.'

'Her parents have no recollection of her coming here,' Peterson said thoughtfully. 'But, as you say, if she took the pictures herself or made working sketches, she must have come to the site well before her course began in October. She was only in her first year at the college. I've had a list made up of friends and associates, Mike, I'll leave you to go through it with the parents and identify those who are pre-college, so we can do a follow-up. Conningsby and Pierce, when the rest of her artwork gets here, see if she sketched this place or anything like it.'

'And we should look out for portraits,' Mike added. He indicated the painting. 'She obviously had some skill in that direction.'

'You think she might have drawn Bowen?'

Mike shrugged. 'We should be so lucky. It's possible. Anything's possible.'

'What if Bowen took the pictures? If she did the painting from those?'

'She could have got her reference material from anywhere,' someone else put in.

'But if Bowen did provide it, then it points to him coming here a full year ago. Maybe he took a holiday?'

'So, check all the local holiday properties for June and July.'

There was a general groan from those assembled.

'I know, I know. There must be tens of properties and hundreds of visitors, plus all the B&Bs and camp sites. Look, break it down. Start with those closest. Christ, I don't need to tell you how to do your jobs.'

He broke off as the phone rang. Mike picked it up.

'The front desk have got your wife on the line,' he said.

* * *

Peterson's usual beat was Bristol. He lived at Somerton with his wife, his two daughters having left home, one for university, the other married with three young children of her own. Jenny, the eldest, was there with her children when he and Mike arrived at his home an hour later and his wife met them at the door.

'Jenny's terribly upset,' his wife told him. 'I know I should have called the locals, but well, when you see the pictures, you'll know. It's got to be something to do with what you're working on.'

Peterson's daughter and three grandchildren were waiting in the kitchen. Only the oldest child, who was seven, seemed to have any comprehension of what was going on. She stood beside her mother's chair, clinging to her arm, while the other two played with Lego on the floor, arguing between themselves.

'Oh, Dad!' Jenny got to her feet and almost collapsed into her father's arms. 'I've been trying to get hold of Roger but he's out on site somewhere and his mobile's not switched on.'

'Did you tell them what was wrong? At Roger's work, I mean?'

She shook her head. 'No. Just that there was something urgent. He'll probably think one of the kids is ill, but I've left word that I'll be here. I'm not going back home, Dad, I'm not.'

Peterson held her tightly and then led her through to the living room, while his wife took charge of the children. Mike followed.

'Sit down, Jen,' Peterson said.

She did as she was told. 'They're in there,' she said, pointing to a plastic freezer bag sitting on the table. 'I opened the envelope, obviously, and I looked inside, but as soon as I realized what it was I tried not to handle it too much. I just shoved everything in the bag and drove over here.' She smiled weakly. 'The way I was driving it's a wonder I didn't get arrested.'

'Never a policeman around when there should be.' Peterson returned the smile, then reached for the plastic bag and carefully emptied the contents onto the coffee table.

'These came with the normal post this morning?'

Jenny nodded. 'This, a postcard from a friend on holiday and the phone bill.'

With the eraser end of a pencil, Peterson moved the six pictures around, spreading them out on the table. Three of the images seemed innocent enough: the children playing in the garden at their home, one on the swing, the others on the climbing frame; a bright summer afternoon, blue-skied and filled with sunshine. But the everyday images had been scanned into a computer and subtly changed so that at first it was not clear that there was anything wrong. You had to look closely to see the ligature around the neck of the youngest; the empty, bloody sockets of the oldest's eyes; the missing hand . . .

Peterson stood up abruptly and crossed the room, standing by the window and staring unseeing at the world outside. Jenny got up and joined him, clinging to his arm as her own child had done earlier to hers and hiding her face against his chest.

Quietly, Mike took plastic gloves and an envelope from the pocket of his jacket and gathered the pictures together, opening the envelope and hiding them inside.

* * *

Macey had been a little surprised when Charlie Morrow had agreed to see him, despite his assurances to Liz that he'd be unable to resist.

Charlie had kept him guessing until late on the Sunday night, then called to say he could fit him in on the Monday morning.

'Fit him in.' Macey had laughed at that. As if the man had anything better to do.

Macey had some trouble offloading his scheduled work, but he managed it and arrived at the nursing home, Liz in tow, just after eleven.

Charlie was waiting for them in the lounge, positioned so that he could watch them arrive through the half-open door. He watched Macey's reaction as the nurse pointed the way through and the journalist caught sight of him, the livid scars puckering the right side of his face and the pressure bandages on his hands and upper body just visible beneath his shirt.

He gave Macey eight out of ten for control, the way he put aside his shock and strode forward, businesslike and brisk, with his hand extended. The girl following behind was less able to hide her reaction, but Charlie didn't object to the frank way she looked at him. Anyway, she had pretty eyes and a body that invited equal notice, so he considered it a reasonable trade.

Macey sat down opposite Charlie and glanced around. 'Posh place,' he said. 'Private, is it?'

Morrow laughed. 'My wife took out health insurance years ago. We've been divorced for more than a decade so that'll tell you how long. The payments went out direct debit and somehow I never got around to cancelling. I thought it was time they gave me something back.'

'Not public money, then? Police charity fund or something?'

'No, so feel free to splash it across the headlines. Hero cop goes private.'

Macey made a show of writing it down, then grinned at Liz. 'Grab that table and bring it over here,' he said to her. 'That's unless you'd like to go somewhere else, Charlie?'

'No one's going to bother us,' Charlie assured him. 'I'm an acerbic bugger and they leave me alone. Now, what have you got for me?'

It had been a condition of Macey's visit that he bring Charlie up to date on the Bowen case and Liz had spent a good two hours with the photocopier, making a record of Macey's archive. She'd piled it into a black pilot's case, which she now proceeded to empty onto the coffee table. Charlie eased forward in his chair; eyes gleaming with anticipation.

'Your copies of everything I have,' Macey told him. 'Enjoy. Now, do you mind if I tape this, or should we make Liz do her bit with the shorthand?'

* * *

The incident with Peterson's family had disturbed Mike deeply. He left them comforting each other and discussing the safest course of action while he tried to get through to Maria on his mobile phone. She was with a patient, he was told, and couldn't be disturbed. He thought about insisting, but it seemed a little pointless. What could he tell her beyond the fact that she should take extra care?

And that she should check on Essie.

He had Maria's mother's number somewhere, he remembered, but it was back at his office and, anyway, the same thing applied. What could he tell them? In the end he called John Tynan and filled him in briefly on what had happened, reluctant to say too much over the air.

'I'll keep trying Maria,' John promised. 'In fact, I'll go over there. She's off duty today at four or thereabouts.'

Mike thanked him. 'I'm probably just being paranoid,' he said.

'No, you're just being human,' John told him. 'And it's human to worry about those we love.'

* * *

'They wouldn't let me see anything or tell me anything in the hospital,' Charlie was complaining. 'I understand why, but it didn't make it any easier. Wouldn't even let me watch the bloody news. Afraid it might upset me. *Upset me!* I'm still a bloody copper, aren't I? He didn't stop my mind working even if he did have a go at blowing my bloody face off.'

Macey grinned at him, sensing a kindred spirit. 'Charlie, my friend,' he said, 'we have to work together.'

Charlie snorted. 'Me? Work with a flaming journalist? Lowest of the frigging low?' Then he smiled, half his mouth pulled crooked by the scars. 'What do you have in mind?'

By the time Macey and Liz left, Macey had promised to provide Charlie with computer equipment and a modem. He had his own phone line in his room — 'one of the perks of going private, though they'll probably crib about the phone bill' — so there would be no problem setting up the Internet access that Charlie would need.

Charlie Morrow might not be able to get out there looking for Jake Bowen on the streets, but Macey had given him another option. Macey had been scanning the news groups on the Net, looking for mention of Bowen and his exploits. There was plenty out there. The police already had people trawling the Internet, but Charlie felt he had a slight edge, something that might lead Bowen to make contact. He'd let Macey write his report, take photographs, give vent to much of Charlie's resentment and pain, and both Charlie and Macey would have put money on Jake Bowen reading every word and responding. Anything, they felt at this stage, would be worth a try. It would give Charlie an in on the action and Macey would write the exclusive. Setting up an email address could be done quickly and it would give Jake Bowen yet another point of contact. Charlie hoped against hope that he would strike lucky and Jake Bowen would take the bait.

'Can you manage a keyboard?' Liz asked anxiously, looking at Charlie's hands.

'Don't worry, love,' he told her, his eyes alive with excitement now he was taking part. 'I'll manage, and I can still point and click a flaming mouse.'

* * *

It had taken Mike a couple of hours to get to Exeter, dropping off the photographs on the way and collecting a WPC to take with him to the Normans.

Julia's parents lived in a quiet suburban road of 1930s houses: twinned, bay-fronted semis with neat gardens. Already an hour late for his original appointment, he had called them on the way to apologize. But as he had become lost in the tangle of side-streets that bore no resemblance to the A-Z, that time had almost doubled.

Frank Norman met him at the door but paid little attention to his apology.

'We'd nowhere else to go, Inspector' he said quietly. 'I'll show you her room.'

No one spoke as the grey-haired man led them up the stairs and along the short landing. Julia's room was at the back of the house, overlooking the garden. He opened the door and then turned back along the corridor.

'If you've anything to ask, we'll be downstairs,' he said. He didn't even glance into his daughter's room.

Mike and the WPC, Annie Poyser, stood just inside the door and looked around. He had intended for her to speak with the Normans while he checked Julia's room, but that no longer seemed appropriate. Frank Norman was intent on calling the shots.

'It's pretty,' Annie commented. 'My mum and dad have a place like this but I was always stuck in the box room and you couldn't swing a cat.'

Mike smiled at her. 'The advantages of being an only child.'

'Tidier than my place too, but I don't suppose she was here that much.'

'They said weekends, sometimes. And Sunday lunch, apparently. They didn't like her missing that.'

Annie laughed. 'Sunday lunch with a hangover,' she said. 'O joy.' She frowned, moving across to the window and glancing out over the lawned garden. A child's swing still took pride of place down at the far end. 'Didn't like her growing up,' she commented. 'And the room, too, it's kind of childish, all pink and white like this.'

Mike looked around with a fresh eye. Annie was right. The decor of the room, with its cake-icing colours and frilled flowery curtains, was almost babyish. It was unsophisticated and shamelessly pretty, only the blue of the bedcover jarring oddly with the rest of the scheme.

'There's nothing personal here,' he commented. 'I mean, even if she only stayed over at the weekends, you'd have expected, I don't know, pictures, ornaments . . . something.'

Annie was opening the dressing-table drawers. A few items of underwear, a comb and a lipstick in one. Nothing in the other. The small chest of drawers was similarly empty, just two T-shirts, a hairbrush, a few cosmetics. The built-in wardrobe still had its hangers and a winter coat. There was an overnight bag on the floor.

Mike picked it up, set it on the bed and began to sort through the pockets. Annie was taking the lining papers from the drawers, turning the drawers themselves upside down in case something had been taped to the underside, running a hand around the empty spaces left in the dressing table.

Mike gave up on the bag. 'Anything?'

'Fraid not, sir.'

They checked the back of the dressing table and the mirrors, lifted the furniture to look beneath and stripped the covers from the bed and the mattress from the frame.

'Not even the fluff monster,' Annie commented. 'I mean, it's as if the whole place's been thoroughly cleaned. There's not a speck of dust even.'

Mike looked at her and realized that she was right. He led the way back down the stairs. The Normans were in the kitchen, sitting motionless on either side of the table, looking like awkward strangers in what had once been their home.

'Did you find anything, Inspector?' Frank Norman asked.

'That isn't likely, is it, Mr Norman?'

Frank looked across at his wife and reached for her hand. 'I'm sorry,' he said. 'I should have said something. I should have stopped her, but I was only gone a little while, just to the corner shop to get some milk and she'd . . .'

Tears filled his eyes and he pointed out towards the garden. 'Near the swing,' he said. 'There's a steel basket there I use for burning garden stuff.'

Mike gestured for Annie to go and look, then he drew another chair close to the table. 'Why did you burn her things, Mrs Norman? What was it?'

'She even took the bedclothes off the bed,' Frank told him. 'Burned the lot. It was the pictures. Julia like some cheap . . .' He shook his head. 'Not our Julie,' he whispered. 'Not our girl. Then, well, I knew you wanted to see her room. I knew you'd be coming and I thought—' he looked at Mike. 'I thought, it's not my Julie they're after. If I made it look like it was supposed to, odd bits she might have left behind, then you wouldn't pry. There's enough been done to her already, Inspector, we just wanted the rest left alone now.'

'It's still destruction of evidence, Mr Norman. It was still something that might have helped us find your daughter's killer.' He broke off. Anger was pointless now.

He walked down the garden to where Annie was sifting through the ashes, trying not to add to the ruin that had already taken place. It was starting to rain, fat droplets of water splashing onto the back of Mike's neck.

'Photos mostly,' Annie told him, 'but there's quite a bit not burned right through.' She glanced up at the darkening clouds. 'We ought to get this covered up, sir. A rainstorm'll just about finish what's left.'

'There are bags in the boot of the car,' Mike said. He waited in the now heavy rain for Annie to come running back and help him pile the remains of Mrs Norman's bonfire into the black bags, their gloved hands soon slippery with wet soot and their clothes covered with ash, but even in their haste Mike could glimpse the images that had given Julia's mother so much pain.

* * *

Essie's grandmother May Richards, went to collect her from school. It was a small building, red-brick, slate-roofed, built in the 1920s. Mobile classrooms had been added as the population had grown and these stood to one side of the main building near the Abbot Street gate. Essie's class was in one of them and May could see Essie through the window as she passed by, busy painting at an easel, daubing bright colours onto a large sheet of paper with the frowning concentration of a true artist.

May laughed and risked a wave, but Essie didn't see. She then crossed the playground to the other gate at the Long Street end. The school had outgrown its original capacity and home time was always chaos. To minimize the problem, the smaller children came out of the Long Street gate, where the road was quieter and there was more space for those with pushchairs and smaller siblings to stand.

May was well known. She'd lived all her life in the area, gone to this school and often came with her daughter Jo to collect Essie. She stood chatting with the waiting parents, glancing across the playground now and then, waiting for her grandchild to appear.

Essie was never among the first out. She was a popular child and always slow at getting her coat on and her shoes fastened, because she was too busy playing, so it was only when the crowds of children had thinned and May had already seen several of Essie's friends go by that she began to worry.

Concerned that if she left the gate, Essie might miss her, she hung on, staring intently at each child that passed, asking ones she knew if they had seen Essie, until finally the playground emptied and May hurried across to the mobile.

The teacher looked up in surprise as May burst through the door, 'Mrs Richards? Is something wrong?'

They searched everywhere — the toilets, the grounds, the main school. Staff went out into the street to call after the late leavers straggling their way home.

Then they called the police. There was no doubt of it: Essie had gone.

* * *

A message had been left on Mike's voice-mail about an hour before. Mike had been with the Normans, talking about another missing child, and his messages had been ignored.

This one said, 'She's a pretty little thing, Mike. Very photogenic, don't you think?'

CHAPTER NINE

It was late evening by the time Mike reached Norwich and drove straight to May Richards's house.

He had managed to speak to Maria about an hour after Essie had first disappeared. At that point no one at the Norwich end knew about Jake's message and the hope was still that she might just have wandered away. As out of character as that was, it was the most comforting thought, though from the outset Maria had insisted she tell the investigating officers about Mike and the possible involvement of Jake Bowen. The anxiety and fear were palpable as Mike spoke to the young officer at the front door.

Maria heard his voice and came through into the hall.

'I don't think you should be here,' she said. 'Wait for me at John's and I'll talk to you later.'

'I've driven here to be with you,' he objected.

'And I have to be with my family, Mike, and I'm afraid you're not someone they want to see right now.'

'They blame me,' Mike said flatly.

'I'm sorry. It's not your fault.' But he could hear the doubt in her voice. 'Look, I blame myself. If I hadn't brought Essie with me at the weekend, she might still be here.'

'You think Jake Bowen doesn't know about you? About your family? Do you think it would have made any difference? Maria, he's got the inside track on everyone who's come even close to him.'

'Then no one's safe, anywhere,' Maria said.

She then turned away from him and went back down the hall, leaving him utterly bereft.

'She's just really upset, sir,' the officer by the door said to him, trying to offer comfort. 'Her sister, the little girl's mum, she's discharged herself from hospital. She just can't stop crying.'

Mike nodded and slipped quietly out through the front door. He'd expected blame. Anticipated the raw anger that the situation was bound to generate, but had never thought he would be excluded like this. It was worse than anything he had prepared himself for.

Getting into his car, he thought of Stevie, his son; of the drunk driver who'd taken his child from him and never even stopped to help. It was something he could not recover from and he knew that a little part of him had died along with his son.

But this. For someone to deliberately take a child, to deprive the parents and to let them suffer, not knowing if their baby was already dead or still alive and frightened or in pain.

He thought of Julia Norman and his hands shook as he turned the key in the ignition, barely able to cope any more with the thoughts running through his head.

Mike phoned Peterson from John Tynan's. His daughter and grandchildren had left, he said, gone north to stay with relatives. He wasn't certain it would help, but that was the best they could do. 'I've been promised police protection for them, but it's hard to know what to do for the best. Any news your end?'

'Nothing. There's nothing yet. I feel like I'm in limbo here. I can't get involved in the investigation and I can't help Essie's family. They don't want me around.'

'Then come back here, where you can at least be some use. I'm sorry, Mike, but even if you applied for compassionate leave I'd have to veto it. I can't spare you.'

Mike sighed, guiltily relieved to have had the decision of what to do next taken out of his hands.

'Essie's just a child,' he said. 'She's five years old.'

'And we've no record of Bowen ever attacking children. We have to hope this is just some kind of stunt to get our attention.'

'What about the photographs your daughter received?'

'Photo images, expertly tampered with. Damn it, Mike, we even know what software he probably used. It doesn't mean . . .'

'But the threat is there. Inherent.'

'Yes,' Peterson allowed, the threat was there. 'But for Christ's sake, Mike, if we let ourselves think along those lines . . . We've got to function. If I thought that little girl . . . If I thought about my grandchildren . . .' He broke off.

Mike could think of nothing more to say. Gently, silently, he put the receiver down.

CHAPTER TEN

24 June

It was early on Tuesday morning when Mike called Maria and told her that he would be going back to Honiton.

'If you want me to stay, then I'll stay,' he told her. 'If you want me to, then I will.'

'Go back, Mike. There's nothing you can do here and it's important you keep working on this. It's the best thing you can do for Essie.'

Mike's heart sank. Even though she was right and he remembered Peterson's words of the night before, he had still hoped that she would want him with her.

'There's no more news?' he asked.

'Nothing. That's what's so hard to take. We're just waiting. The doctor's given Jo a sedative and she's sleeping a lot, then she wakes up feeling guilty about going to sleep. And Momma and I, we can't do anything. It's so hard, Mike, we sit around doing nothing and feeling like death, but if one of us puts the TV on or tries to read, we feel as though we're being frivolous or thoughtless, when what we should be doing is giving 100 per cent of our thoughts to Essie and

Jo. I thought I'd cope better than this. I spend my entire life teaching other people to cope.'

'But this time it's you and yours,' Mike put in gently. 'It's not the same.' He paused, then asked, 'Can I at least see you before I go?'

She hesitated for a moment, then said reluctantly, 'I can't leave just now and you can't come here. It would be more than Jo could bear. You must realize that.'

Mike arrived back at the incident room in Honiton after a long, hot drive. He drove badly, far too fast on narrow, winding roads, the miles passing with little conscious thought or recognition on his part.

He reached Honiton mid-afternoon, tired and angry. His shirt was sticking to his back and he was suddenly aware that it had been at least two days since he had last shaved.

Peterson wanted to see him, he was told, as soon as he came in. Mike found him in one of the interview rooms, sitting at the table with a man Mike did not recognize. They were leafing through the copies of Harriman's cuttings books, the stranger poring over them intently while Peterson sat back in his chair as though to distance himself from the other man. He had an air about him of scarcely concealed anger and looked up sharply as Mike entered the room.

'Mike. Good. I want to introduce you to someone.' The other man stood up and turned towards Mike, his hand already extended. As he made the introductions, Peterson's anger began to bubble over; giving a harsh edge to his words.

'This,' he said, 'is Mr Alastair Bowen. Father to the famous Jake. Perhaps you'd like to explain to Inspector Croft just why it took you so long to come forward, Mr Bowen.'

Alastair Bowen's expression was one of total calm. 'As I told you, Mr Peterson,' he said, 'it was because of my wife. My wife, you see, was dying. I had to stay with her and I could not bear that she should know about Jake. Not after all he'd put her through before.' He sighed. 'But she's dead now, after two long years of suffering, God rest her soul, and I can speak. Tell you about my son.'

'We're glad to hear that, Mr Bowen,' Peterson said, 'as, I'm sure, will be the parents and families of those your son has killed these last months, while you were waiting for the right moment.'

Alastair Bowen continued to regard Peterson with the same calm gaze, his grey eyes gentle and unmoved by the outburst.

'I don't expect you to understand,' he said, 'and I have no intention of making excuses that no one wants to hear. But I am here now, Superintendent, and that, believe me, is all that really counts.'

CHAPTER ELEVEN

Mike flicked through the photographs in the folder and laid one down in front of Alastair Bowen. It was five o'clock and the late afternoon sun streaming in through the window mocked the grossness of the images.

'Marion O'Donnel,' he said.

Obediently Alastair regarded the image of the pretty blonde woman set before him.

'And this is how she ended up, Mr Bowen.' He covered the picture with another showing a burnt-out car and the remains of a body curled grotesquely in the driver's seat.

'She was one of his so-called models, I suppose.'

'She was,' Mike told him.

Alastair shrugged.

'You're suggesting she deserved to die like this, Mr Bowen?'

'You lie down with wolves, Inspector.'

Mike let it pass, but his dislike of Alastair Bowen was growing by the second. Two hours they had spent so far, bringing Alastair up to date on Jake's crimes, trying to draw from the man some kind of response, some kind of explanation for what his son was doing. They were looking for a clue that might help them to predict his next move.

'This one's from February.' Peterson laid the photograph of another young woman down on the table. She too was blonde, her long hair wrapped tightly around her throat, hiding the bruises left by her killer's hands. 'We don't even know her name,' he said. 'But somewhere she has family, friends who want to know what happened to her.'

'You believe that?' Alastair questioned. 'In their place I'd prefer to keep my illusions, not be faced with the life she must have led.'

'Whatever life she led, Mr Bowen, she was still a young woman who had the right to live it.'

'I didn't kill her, Superintendent Peterson,' Alastair retorted impassively. 'I don't need your accusations.'

'This next is Simon Caldwell,' Mike went on. 'He was twenty-eight years old. An actor.'

'Is that what you call it? Acting?'

'An actor, Mr Bowen. Jake killed him by forcing a tube down into his stomach and feeding him neat bleach. It's a horrific way to die, Alastair.'

'My wife died of cancer, Inspector. That is a horrific way to die. Death is rarely either clean or peaceful.'

'This is hardly the same as death caused by illness, Mr Bowen.'

'And you expect me to have more sympathy with this actor than with the sick who die of disease not of their making? He chose the way he lived.'

'He didn't choose the way he died.'

'How many of us do? How many of us could?' Mike gave up and pushed the photograph aside. Caldwell's professional name had been a little more anatomically biased. He'd been starring in porn flicks the past five years, making a steady living out of his knack for staying hard as long as the producer wanted. Caldwell had kept his reputation right up until the time he died, and the ligature tied around his penis made certain that he stayed that way.

'Matthew Thompson,' Mike went on impassively, laying the next image on the table. 'Not one of Jake's actors, as far as we know. He was a businessman, owned a chain of retail outlets.'

Alastair Bowen glanced at the picture. 'I remember the news item,' he said. 'The man died in his bath, I believe.'

Mike nodded. 'He'd been tied up. Tied up with a wire noose round his neck. The end had been fastened to the drain hole and the hole blocked with car body-filler. Jake must have been in his flat for quite some time to set this one up. The man had been drugged, presumably while Jake stripped him and positioned him in the bath. Then he'd turned on the taps and left them running. We know Jake watched him die because we have the film.' It was not something Mike would forget in any hurry. 'He watched him die and he filmed every moment, Alastair.' The man struggling to get free before the water drowned him or the ligature tightened around his neck and he choked to death.

Mike thought of Essie, then tried not to think of Essie. He turned angrily on Alastair Bowen.

'There's no pattern to what he does. His victims are all different. Male, female, all ages, no real consistent MO. And we need to get him, Alastair, before he kills again. Before he kills . . . that child.' Mike found he choked on Essie's name.

'And you expect me to explain it to you? You expect me to explain my son?'

'Any light you should shed. We need anything you can give us,' Peterson told him.

Alastair Bowen made no response. He stared at the pictures on the table but seemed not to see them.

'Jake sees himself as an artist,' he said at last. 'He'd do whatever was needed to get an effect. It was always that way.' He looked up at Mike. 'He's also a businessman, Inspector Croft. Surely you lot have worked that out by now? Jake works to commission, he always did. Someone wants a particular script filming and is willing to pay top price for it, Jake will do it any way they want. Life doesn't matter to him. People's lives, their hopes, it's all script to Jake. All part of the storyline.'

'You know this for certain?'

Alastair Bowen pushed himself away from the table, irritated and clearly bored. 'A child could work it out, Inspector Croft. You've detailed Jake's career, you've seen the films. Jake enjoys what he does, but he also makes a killing from it, if you'll excuse the pun, and you can bet your sweet life that he's been doing it for a hell of a lot longer than you credit him with.'

* * *

There had been the problem of finding somewhere for Alastair Bowen to stay, but finally they had settled him at Lyme in the boarding house that Maria had stayed in with Essie. There was a room available only for the next two nights, but there was talk anyway of moving Alastair to a safe house as soon as they went public with him. It seemed logical to assume that Jake would not appreciate his father giving evidence against him.

Mike then made his way slowly back towards the Dorchester road.

It was almost ten p.m. and the sky already darkening over a calm sea. Bats cruised in front of him as he travelled the back roads heading towards the dual carriageway. There was little other traffic and nothing in the blue-grey of the twilight to distract him. Mike was very tired. His thoughts began to wander. Twice he caught himself nodding with sleep, jerking his attention back only just in time as he veered across the road.

He tried to drag his thoughts to the case. Thinking about the fragmentary photographs that they had found at the Normans' house. He doubted they would help further the investigation. All they had done so far was cause more pain to the parents. The few items she had left at the house she shared when she went away had added little to their knowledge. There had been sketches, notebooks for her college projects. No portraits and nothing relating to Jake, not even the odd initialled heart scribbled in the margins. Jake must have been one big secret in Julia Norman's life.

'She was seeing someone,' one of the girls she had lived with had said. 'We knew that, and we thought it must be someone older. But, I mean, Julia went out with a lot of boys, none of them got serious.'

The impression was that Julia had been sowing a few wild oats, breaking free of her parents' rather staid and solid background. When he had put this to her flatmates, one of the girls had laughed. 'Oh, God. Yeah, I guess that's what Julia thought she was doing, but I mean, really, if she had more than a couple of drinks she'd see it as living on the edge.' She'd hesitated, close to tears. 'She was sweet, you know. Innocent.'

The fork for the main road came up out of nowhere and took Mike by surprise. He swerved onto it, blessing the fact that the road was deserted at this time of night. Driving between the trees, it was darker and his mind began to wander yet again. From the corner of his eye he caught movement between the trees like someone running, leaping from the shadow of one tree to the next. He wound the window down and put the radio on, finding some local station playing loud rock music, then flicked the lights to full beam to drive the shadow-men away. For a minute or two it seemed to work, but then he nodded again, his eyes began to close and even the music faded, the names and faces of the dead filling his mind as he drifted into sleep. Julia, Marion O'Donnel, Caldwell, Matthew Thompson. Essie . . . No, his mind rebelled against that one. No, not Essie!

It was the jolt of the front wheel hitting the verge that woke him and the sudden jerk of the seatbelt cutting across his chest. For one God-awful moment Mike thought . . .

Wearily, he stumbled from the car and stood in the road waiting for his breath to slow down and his heart to stop pounding. The car was poised with one wheel above the ditch and the first of the trees only inches away.

CHAPTER TWELVE

25 June

True to his word Macey had taken the computer equipment to Charlie Morrow. He'd arrived early and the morning news was on in Charlie's room. The two men watched in silence as the hastily arranged press conference was aired and pictures of five-year-old Essie filled the screen.

'There has been no word from the kidnapper and, so far, no clue as to why this child was taken. Essie's grandmother and aunt made the following appeal to the kidnapper . . .'

Macey and Charlie continued to watch, listening as the two women made tearful appeals that the child be given back, that she not be hurt, that she be left somewhere for the police to find. They had heard it all before. Neither spoke until the news moved on.

'Poor little bugger,' Macey said softly. 'Not much hope there, I don't suppose.' He frowned. 'But I've seen that woman before. The aunt, I mean, I just can't quite place her.'

‘She’s Mike Croft’s girlfriend,’ Charlie told him, his voice harsh with shock.

‘Then Jake must have taken the child,’ Macey said.

* * *

Mike had watched the appeal on the early news. Afterwards, he had tried again to call Maria, only to find that she had left to go to Oaklands and collect some things. He guessed she also needed time away from the overwhelming tension of it all. He tried Oaklands, where Maria lived and worked, to find that he’d just missed her. Her mobile was switched off, which meant she was probably in her car, and he was forced to give up.

He called her mother’s house again and left a message with the officer on duty, asking him to get her to phone.

‘She tried earlier,’ he was told, ‘but you were in a meeting and she couldn’t reach you.’

Mike smiled faintly. At least she’d tried. ‘Tell her to use my mobile number. And to keep trying. I’ll leave the damned thing switched on.’

He rang off, deeply frustrated. This seemed to be the pattern of their relationship just now, missing one another . . .

* * *

It had taken a long time to persuade Alastair Bowen that he should go public, but he had finally agreed and much of Mike’s day had been taken up with the arrangements.

‘People will hate me,’ Alastair had said. ‘They will hate me for what I am. They will blame me for Jake.’

‘They’ll hate you more if you don’t,’ Peterson told him bluntly. ‘Alastair, you’re the best hope we’ve got, the first real advantage we’ve had on Jake. You appearing on the television may be just what we need to flush him out.’

Finally, he had given in and after that everything had moved with speed. The *Ten o’clock News* saw Alastair Bowen on national television, patched in from BBC Bristol and simultaneously broadcast as a newsflash on all channels. Alastair Bowen pleading with his son to put an end to the killing and the pain.

'I'm asking you to come forward, Jake. There's been enough death and enough cruelty. You need help, Jake, as much as anyone else, you need help and I promise I'll be there for you, whatever you might have done.'

He hesitated, clearly uncertain of how to carry on. 'Your mother's dead. She died five days ago from cancer and I buried her back home at St Bartolph's. I know she missed you . . . son . . . we both did, and thought about you . . . always. It's time to come home.'

Watching from the sidelines, Mike could see the falsity of Alastair Bowen's pleas.

He despises him, he thought. Loathes and fears Jake even more than we do. It was a revelation, a small one, but, Mike felt, deeply significant. He set himself the task of finding out why and when Alastair had first conceived this passionate loathing of his son.

* * *

Jake Bowen had not expected ever to see his father alive and his appearance on the late news caught him by surprise.

Sitting on the large blue sofa in front of the television, Jake leaned forward to get a closer look at the parent he had left behind so many years before.

He swivelled round to regard the small figure lying propped on pillows at the other end of the settee.

'Don't you think he's getting old?' Jake asked the child.

Essie, arms limply at her sides and eyes gazing listlessly into space, never said a word.

CHAPTER THIRTEEN

26 June

Early on the Wednesday morning Mike took Alastair Bowen to see Max Harriman.

Alastair was confident. 'He'll speak to me,' he assured Mike, with that same implacable calm he had displayed when Mike had first been introduced. 'Max loved Jake, doted on him. I'm a link back to their shared past, you see. Max will speak with me.'

Mike was not so sure. Harriman had a mind of his own where cooperation was concerned.

Alastair seemed less blasé about the news reports that had followed his appearance on the television the night before. Every national led with some version of the story, the headlines varying from the lurid 'Father of a Monster' to the insipid 'News Appeal Brings Fresh Hope.' All asked why Alastair Bowen had taken so long to come forward. All seemed certain that he must long ago have known what path his son had taken.

Mike asked him about it as they drove along the M5, keeping just above the speed limit in the centre lane.

'I knew he was involved with filth,' Alastair told him. 'That he made films that decent people would never want to see.'

'Was that what made you break with him?' Mike asked. 'We know he lived with you into his early twenties then you and your wife and Jake seem to drop out of sight. What happened then, Mr Bowen?'

Alastair took time before he answered. His reply, when it came, was obtuse. 'Jake was evil. From the moment he was born, the boy was evil. I told his mother, but she wouldn't have it. No, she was a good woman and could see good in everyone, even Jake. But it was there, that devil's look, right from the moment he was born and I first looked into his eyes.'

Mike glanced sideways at him, the hairs rising at the back of his neck, despite the absurdity of Alastair Bowen's words.

'I don't believe that any child is born evil,' he replied. 'Children are a blank page, it's what the world does to them that makes them good or bad.'

'A *tabula rasa,'* Alastair intoned. He laughed. 'Inspector Croft, I would have thought you'd seen enough of the world to know the lie of that. Sometimes evil is born, made incarnate, and there is nothing you can do to that child, neither kindness nor beating, that can make it not so.'

Mike shifted uncomfortably in his seat. 'And what did Jake have most of, Mr Bowen? Kindness or beating?'

Again the laughter devoid of humour. 'Oh, no, Inspector, you can't lay that at my door. No one can say that Jake was made the way he is by anything I did to him. Jake had what was needed, one way or another, in about equal measure. His mother was too soft with him. Women are. I had to balance that. But he respected me for it even though I knew there would be no saving him. I had to try, you see, for his mother's sake. What woman would want to live with the fact that she'd given birth to evil?'

Mike glanced at the dashboard clock and saw that there would be at least another hour before they reached Max Harriman. He wondered how much more of Bowen's ranting he could take, but there was so much he needed to know. He tried another tack.

'Max's mother. She brought him up alone, I understand?'

He felt rather than saw Alastair Bowen nod. 'The father was killed in a mining accident just before the boy was born. It put her into labour early and they weren't sure she or the boy would have the will to live.'

He fell silent.

Mike persisted. 'Mrs Harriman was killed about the time that you and Jake left the area?'

'That is true.'

'And Max was accused, taken in for questioning.'

'And then released without charge.'

'Did Jake kill Mrs Harriman?' Mike asked.

Alastair was silent, so silent and so still that Mike thought he might even have fallen asleep. He glanced sideways at him once more. The man sat with his hands clasped neatly in his lap and an empty expression on his face, gazing out through the windscreen at the road ahead.

'Mr Bowen?' Mike prompted. 'Do you think Jake killed her?'

Alastair shifted slightly in his seat, but took his time making a reply. 'I never saw that woman smile,' he said.

* * *

Macey paid another visit to Charlie Morrow, this time bringing him a pile of disks; stuff he'd pulled down from the Net.

'Mostly news groups and chat rooms,' he said. 'We know Jake Bowen puts stuff out over the Internet. If he's online then he must have a provider and most providers monitor anyone making an abnormal number of hits to kinky sites.'

'Most, but not all,' Charlie corrected him, 'and there are ways around it. Depends on the route you take through the system. Anyone as smart as Jake Bowen will have thought of that. So, for that matter; will my untoasted colleagues.'

'Right,' Macey said. He'd still not grown used to the way Charlie made fun of his injuries. 'Look, he went on, I've been trying something a bit different. As you know, there are chat rooms and discussion groups on just about anything. I've picked up over a dozen without even trying hard, all specializing in kinky porn, and they've all got something to say about Jake Bowen.'

'With or without prompting?' Charlie asked.

'Bit of both. My whole point is, you can sit on the side, monitor a few. Folk out there still have the illusion that they can say just about anything online, like they forget it's a public place. See what you can stir up.'

He delved into his briefcase and pulled out a computer magazine with a CD still attached to the front.

'*America Online*,' he said triumphantly. 'One month's free connection, complete with helpline. All you've got to do is pay for the calls. Here, keep the mag. Present from me to you.'

Charlie gave him that crooked half-smile that looked more like anger. 'You're all heart, Macey,' he said.

* * *

Max Harriman was not pleased. He had recognized Alastair Bowen almost immediately, despite the years, and his reaction thereafter had ranged from the sulky to the outraged.

'Why bring *him* here?' he wanted to know. 'He doesn't know a thing about Jake. He abandoned him years ago. Some father he was.'

'He's told me more about Jake than you have,' Mike lied. 'Maybe you'd like to set the record straight, Max. Maybe I should tell you what Alastair here's been saying and you can put us right?'

Max sank into an angry silence and refused to be drawn. Mike stood up.

'Well, if you won't talk to me then I think I'll go now. After all, it doesn't look as if we'll be needing you so much now, does it?'

Max was on his feet and yelling loud enough to bring the guards. 'He knows nothing!' he shouted. 'I'm the one that Jake came to. I'm the one that studied him, that followed after him — that understands him. They never did. Never. You need *me,* Inspector Mike Croft, and don't you forget it.'

Mike wondered briefly whether to push his advantage or to let Max simmer. The ringing of his mobile decided for him and he allowed the guards to take an irate Max and escort him back to his cell.

The call was from Peterson, who'd heard from Julia Norman's parents. A video film of her had arrived in the morning post.

The journey back with Alastair Bowen was a very quiet one, both men busy with their own thoughts. It was only when Mike dropped him at the safe house they had put him into after the TV broadcast that Alastair referred to their earlier talk.

'I always thought he'd done it,' he said. 'Killed Emily Harriman. Jake was always round there and the woman liked him.' He paused. 'Women did like him,' he said, 'all women.'

'Why did you suspect him?'

The man hesitated. 'Because of the blood,' he said. 'Jake came home with blood on his hands and the cuffs of his sleeves. The papers said she'd had her throat cut and everyone knows that would send blood everywhere, so I thought I must have been mistaken.'

'And his jacket?' Mike asked. 'Was he wearing a jacket? Mrs Harriman was attacked from behind, her throat cut, and then she was dropped to the floor, her assailant still behind her. Yes, there would have been a lot of blood, but not necessarily all over Jake. Mostly his hands, his cuffs, the sleeves of his jacket.'

'He said he lost his jacket,' Alastair Bowen remarked, staring out of the car window as if absorbed by the scene.

'And you said nothing?' Mike asked him.

'And I said nothing,' Alastair Bowen agreed.

* * *

Peterson was waiting for him in the barn-cum-incident room at Colwell Barton.

'Have fun with Max and Alastair?' he asked.

'Oh, yes, great company. Two of a kind.'

'Maybe they should form a double act when Max gets out. But seriously, did you learn anything?'

'Beyond Alastair Bowen being a religious nut?' He sat down heavily, watching as Peterson set the video player. 'Yes, I learned that Max is jealous and that gives us leverage. And that Jake probably started his career early.'

'With Mrs Harriman, as we thought?'

Mike nodded thoughtfully, but there was clearly something else on his mind.

'I don't like what you're thinking, Mike.'

He smiled at the familiar phraseology. 'It's the way Alastair talked about it. He said that Jake came home with his hands and cuffs covered with blood and his jacket missing. I mean, agreed Jake lived only a couple of streets away from the Harrimans and agreed it was late and dark and probably there was no one to see him on the way home, but why not take time to wash his hands? He must have known it was possible his parents were at home. It was as if he wanted his father to see. A challenge, if you like.'

'If that's so, and I think you may be on to something, why lose the jacket?'

Mike shrugged. 'I don't know,' he said. 'Why do any of the things Jake does? It's as if he was constantly trying to keep everyone off balance even then.'

'It could be you're looking too deep,' Peterson suggested. 'Maybe he just panicked and ran, threw the jacket away and didn't realize how much blood there was until he got home.'

'Maybe. But no, I don't think so. The jacket was never found and the area was searched thoroughly. And you've got to remember, this isn't an affluent area. People might have a work jacket, an everyday one and one for Sundays if they were lucky. I remember my dad had the same Sunday clothes for years.'

Peterson laughed. 'Sounds like me,' he said. 'But I hear what you're saying. Clothes weren't just thrown away and the locals would recognize something that was. It would have led them straight to Jake.'

He sat down beside Mike, playing with the video remote.

'You think he killed before that,' Peterson said thoughtfully, 'and that his father knew about it. That leaving the blood on his hands for his father to see was like saying, "Look at me, there's nothing you can do", something like that?'

Mike nodded. 'Yes. And I think it's important we find out who and when. It might give us the opening we're looking for.'

'It might, and it might just waste a lot more time. Oh, I think you're right, Mike, but we've got enough on our plates dealing with the current Jake Bowen, never mind raking through his distant past.'

He set the video to play.

* * *

Jake Bowen still had to work, no matter what else he was involved in. His filmmaking and other activities he saw as a profitable sideline — very profitable and invested wisely. Jake had learned early, though, that you should always have a good cover story, that people quickly become suspicious of someone with no regular lifestyle or habits or obvious source of income, and Jake had always had a 'proper job' and made certain that, superficially at any rate, he lived within his means.

Jake was content to wait. He was saving hard for his retirement, and planned on making it a long and easy one.

His proper job just now was as a sales rep for an artists' supply house. He enjoyed it. It involved meeting people and selling, two things Jake was very good at. And it gave him opportunity for a little talent-spotting on the side.

Jake knew his stuff. He was way ahead of the game with the latest colours, always knowing which pigment or primer or paper would give the best results; always helpful and willing to go that extra mile to get a satisfied customer. And he was knowledgeable enough to suggest alternatives for hard-to-get supplies or willing to push his buyers into obtaining things for him.

As Mike and Peterson were viewing the video of Julia Norman, Jake was leaving the Fine Arts Department at Exeter University. The young woman who'd been tutor to Julia Norman waved to him from her window as he left, the new samples and colour charts he'd just brought in piled on her desk.

Such a very nice man, she thought idly, turning the ring on her engagement finger and wondering if he was single.

CHAPTER FOURTEEN

There was something like forty-five minutes of film, much of it gently erotic and strangely compelling. The first ten minutes or so were images that could have been on anyone's home movie.

They were shot on a near-deserted beach: a windy day and Julia, her long hair flying loose as she ran towards the camera. She wore jeans and a shapeless blue sweater, the wind strong enough to mould it to her body as she performed, pretending she didn't want to be filmed, but dancing barefoot on the sands, teasing the filmmaker.

Much of their shouted dialogue was lost, whipped away on the strong wind, but Julia chatted to Jake, laughed with him, completely at ease and, Mike thought as he looked into her eyes, clearly in love with him.

They couldn't hear the joke that Julia told, but they heard Jake laugh, the microphone built into the camera easily picking up the sound. Mike was shocked at the naturalness of it, the ease and happiness he heard, as though Jake had not a care in the world, and no plans for anything but enjoyment with this girl.

Other scenes followed, some in which Julia participated with full knowledge, some in which she was clearly unaware that she was being filmed. It was as though Jake wanted to catch her every unconscious movement, her naturalness when she thought herself unobserved. Julia in the park, throwing bread to the ducks. Julia sitting on the steps outside her shared house, chatting to one of her room-mates. Julia brushing her hair and putting on lipstick. Julia painting the canvas she had given her parents that last Christmas.

Peterson paused the film at that point and tried to take it through frame by frame, cursing the scanning lines that ran across the image and his inability to hold the picture steady on the cheap VCR they'd brought with them to the barn. It was good enough, though, to see the photographs and sketches taped to the edge of the painting and pinned on the wall behind: pictures of Julia herself, lying naked on a bed.

As the camera angle pulled back and more of the room came into view, it was clear that this was a studio of some kind: the white walls; the large skylight, angled to give maximum illumination to the room but shaded with muslin against the glare; a glimpse of pictures covering the other wall and a room beyond, dark but for the red glow of a safe-light that had been left on.

'Jake's studio?' Mike questioned.

'It's not the university, and it's certainly not her house or the parents' place.'

'It's worth getting it enhanced,' Mike commented, 'and maybe showing to Max. It's possible he could have been there.'

Peterson nodded but didn't look hopeful. 'He's playing with us again,' he said. 'Showing us so much and none of it's going to be of any use. You just know it.'

'He'll get careless. He has to.'

'I'll be sure and tell him that when we meet.'

Peterson pressed play once more and let the film run. It had changed in character. The same studio, but with Julia dressed only in a green silk robe, standing self-consciously facing Jake. This time they could hear his voice too as he coaxed her into taking off her robe and posing for him: a pleasant, educated voice with the slight twang of a residual accent that Mike could not quite place.

'Come on, Julie darling, I've seen it all before. There's nothing to be shy about.'

'I know, but it's the camera.' She giggled nervously. 'I mean, you might show the film to someone.'

'Why would I do that, darling? Personal consumption this is for. All those long dark nights when you're not around.'

She giggled again. 'And what nights are those?' she asked him. 'I'm here all the time just lately.'

She began to unfasten the belt, biting her lip and looking sideways at him, deliberately provocative as she slid the robe from her shoulders and let it fall to the floor.

'Beautiful,' he said. 'Now move for me, darling, pose a bit, think of it like a life class with a bit of movement.'

She laughed again, posing awkwardly, trying too hard to look sexy and confident, then gradually, as they watched, beginning to relax and play Jake's game.

Her movements became more fluid, more provocative, her eyes on Jake as she touched herself, stroking her own breasts, cupping them in her hands as though presenting them to those watching; her hands moving down onto her belly, and then to the tops of her legs and between her thighs.

Mike swallowed hard, wanting to look away but compelled to go on watching. He felt Peterson shifting uncomfortably in his seat and then get up and cross the room to fill the kettle.

Mike sat still, wishing he'd thought of that first, as Julia Norman played out her role on the screen, totally self-absorbed.

'She's the same age as my youngest,' Peterson commented, his voice gruff with pain and embarrassment.

Mike found himself hoping that Julia's parents had switched off before the tape came to an end.

CHAPTER FIFTEEN

27 June

Against his usual habits, Jake called in sick on the Thursday morning. Alastair's appearance on the television the night before brought a new twist to the game and he had unfinished business to attend to.

The news that his mother had died so recently had surprised him. He had assumed that she had passed away long ago, or at any rate he had given little thought to her still living.

That morning, Jake had spared his mother an hour of his time, the first he had given her in years.

As the clock in the kitchen ticked away, Jake moved his thoughts to his mother's dying. He wondered what exactly had been wrong with her, how long it had taken her to die and if there had been much pain. He made a mental note that he should ask Alastair when they met.

As the clock began to chime the hour Jake sat very still, waiting for the last of the sounds to fade, then he got up from his seat at the kitchen table, ready to carry on with his day, his thoughts of his mother already as dead and gone as the woman herself.

His father, though, was very much on Jake's mind.

Jake walked out of the kitchen and through the garden. It had rained briefly and the grass was damp, the air still early-morning fresh before the heat of the day. He walked barefoot from the house, relishing the coldness of the rain-soaked grass, filling his lungs with the sharp air. He had searched long and hard to find this little house with its disproportionately large cellar and its view of the ocean. It had been in a terrible state, cheap enough to buy for cash, and he'd spent time and money restoring and rebuilding, doing the work himself at the weekends. He'd converted the attic into a studio and darkroom, having to resort to contractors only to install the three large, north-facing skylight windows that flooded the room with daylight.

At the end of his garden was a rose-hedge and a wooden gate that gave access to the clifftop. The cliff path had once run along here, but coastal erosion had made it dangerous and the path had been diverted for a few hundred yards back onto the narrow road that ran in front of Jake's house and then on through the village. The house, the garden, the location, they all suited Jake: remote enough for privacy, but not so remote that people would be unduly curious. In the village they knew him well, or thought they did: Mr Phillips, the sales rep, not there much because of his job but a really pleasant sort. Always ready to take part in parish events, but a bit quiet like. Not married — they'd heard he was widowed and had never really got over it . . . Gossip always ready to fill a vacuum.

Jake stood on the clifftop looking down onto the ocean as it crashed and raged angrily against the rocks. Even at the height of summer the waves were never still. An undercurrent sent the water churning and writhing against the cliff, no matter how calm the water might be further out or how beautiful the day. It was that which had drawn Jake Bowen here, that above all other things, the sound and sight of the restless water grinding away at the land that supported his garden and his house. The slow relentless pounding that had already claimed the old cliff path would one day swallow all that he now owned.

Jake sat down, oblivious to the cold dampness of the grass, and gazed far out to sea.

* * *

Alastair had woken early, his dream still fresh in his mind. He lay in bed, thinking about it, remembering the events that had triggered the image.

He had been walking with his son along the cliff path between Whitby and Robin Hood's Bay. It was a place he had often taken Jake, always being a great one for long, strenuous walks. This time he had something important on his mind.

'I know what you've done,' Alastair Bowen had told his son. 'I know you killed her, Jake.'

Jake made no comment. His father waited, expecting some response, but received none.

'What I don't understand, Jake, what I need to know, is why. Why kill the woman? What had she done to you?'

Jake shrugged. 'Nothing to me,' he said.

'Then why?' Alastair stood still and looked at his son, as though hoping to read something in his face. He shook his head 'You were always evil,' he said. 'That's the only explanation for it. You'll come to a bad end, Jake.'

Jake shrugged again, unconcerned by his father's words. He'd been hearing all his life that he was born the devil's child.

'You think I'm so evil, why don't you turn me in?' he asked.

'You're still my son.'

'Really? I thought my dad had horns and a forked tail, to hear you talk. Nah, you're afraid of what the vicar would say. The pillar of the community with a murderer for a son. You wouldn't like that, would you, daddy dear.'

Alastair's hands clenched spasmodically at his sides. 'It would destroy your mother if she knew,' he said.

'To say nothing of your reputation.'

Jake smiled brightly at his father, his unconcern so blatant. Then, whistling to himself, he walked ahead of Alastair, along the narrow path, head high, daring his father to act.

Jake Bowen was then just fifteen years old.

* * *

Thursday had been a quiet and frustrating day. Mike had spent most of it with the collators, assessing results of the door-to-door inquiries. The mammoth effort had begun to verify the identities of everyone who'd stayed in the holiday cottages the year before. So far, nothing of significance had emerged.

There had been the odd sighting of what might have been Jake and Julia, but could just as easily have been a courting couple heading towards the woods. Then there were a few holidaymakers who were proving difficult to trace — people moved house, Mike reminded himself. The sheer volume of information generated when twenty-odd officers went knocking on a lot of doors was staggering. And all of this had to be fitted in with the normal run-of-the-mill summer problems of tourists and petty crime and stolen cars and domestic trouble that went on regardless of the murder inquiry.

Mike glanced up as a police constable came in and spoke his name. The young man looked excited, obviously pleased with himself, and had a worried-looking woman in tow. He ushered her into the room and found her a chair. She sat down automatically. Mike was on the verge of asking what was wrong with using an interview room, but the officer was already talking. 'This lady, sir, she's the one who made the call to Mr Macey.'

'You're certain?'

'Of course, sir. She'll tell you all about it.'

Mike looked sceptically at the woman. She was in her early twenties, he guessed, with dark hair cut short in a very structured style and blue eyes.

'Would you like a cup of tea?' he asked.

'Oh, yes. Yes, I would.' She looked around uncomfortably. 'I've never been in a police station before.' Mike smiled and gestured to the PC to get the tea, noting with amusement the reluctance with which the young officer stopped hovering and did as he was told. Then he pulled his chair out from behind the desk and moved round to sit on the same side as the young woman, blocking her view of the office activity.

'I'm Inspector Mike Croft,' he said. 'I'm going to have to ask you to make a formal statement in a minute, but for now if you'd like to just tell me about the phone call, Miss . . . ?'

'Watson. Liv — that's short for Olivia — Watson.' Her voice was a little slurred, as though she had started drinking early. She grinned suddenly, nervously. 'Aren't I supposed to ask for a lawyer or something?'

Mike smiled back. 'Not unless I arrest you.'

'You think you might?'

'No. No, I don't think so.' Mike leaned back in his chair, aware that he was being flirted with and a little flattered. 'You wanted to tell me about the phone call Miss Watson.'

'Call me Liv.' She grinned at him again, wrinkling her nose. She had freckles, he noticed, spreading across onto her cheeks.

'Liv,' he said obediently. 'The call?'

She sighed elaborately. 'To Mr Ed Macey, at the paper in Dorchester. There was this man, you see. We'd all been talking to him a few nights before.'

'We?'

'Me and some friends. We'd had a few to drink and this guy, he was chatting to us at the bar. Oh, thanks,' she said, as the PC brought the tea, setting it carefully on the table and then hovering in the background once again.

'Go on,' Mike said.

'Well, Linda, that's one of my friends, she'd got into a row with her boyfriend and gone storming off outside.'

'This was the day you made the phone call?'

'No. No, I told you, this was, I don't know, about three nights before. Linda will remember. She had a row with her boyfriend, like I said, so she's bound to remember when it was, you see?'

Mike nodded patiently, wishing he'd handed her straight on to someone else.

'And this man talked to you?'

'Yeah, he was friendly, you know. Not too flirty but nice. Good-looking too. You'll want a description?'

'You can give it to this officer here, when you make your statement.'

'Oh.' For a moment she sounded disappointed. 'OK, then.' She brightened, switching her attention to the younger man.

'You were telling me about the phone call.'

'Yeah, but you see he'd been there that night.'

'When Linda and her boyfriend had the row?'

'Yeah, and he stopped Linda from storming out, said it wasn't safe and she should at least let him call a taxi for her.'

'And did he?' Mike asked.

'No, Linda's boyfriend got jealous then, said if anyone was going to call a taxi it should be him, and it looked as though it was going to get really nasty. Like I told, you, we'd all had a lot to drink.' She smiled up at the young PC. 'Then we saw him again that lunchtime. He'd spent ages smoothing things over with Linda and her fellah, so we got talking.'

'It didn't turn nasty then?'

'Oh, no, he was a real fast talker. We all ended up having a drink together.' She frowned. 'I can't remember when he left, but I think it was close to chucking-out time. Anyway, this lunchtime, we were all having a drink. We're all on holiday, you see, so it doesn't matter. I mean, we don't drink at lunchtime when we're at work.' She paused, waiting.

'I'm sure you don't.'

'And we were all saying how good he'd been the other night, helping Linda get back with her boyfriend and smoothing over the row, and he said, if we were so grateful, would I help him play a joke on a friend. It was a surprise or something. So I said yeah, why not?'

'And he dialled the paper and you took over after he got past the switchboard?'

She nodded. 'I was supposed to make the call, but —' she giggled — 'I'd had a bit to drink and I couldn't keep the number in my head.'

'You managed to remember the message.'

'Oh, that. He'd written it down, but I kept having to ask him if I'd got it right.'

Mike nodded thoughtfully. 'And you've not seen him since?'

'No, but he said he was on holiday down here, visiting friends or something, so I supposed he'd gone home.' She frowned suddenly. 'Nobody's told me what this is all about,' she said. 'Just that they were looking for someone who might have made a call for someone else to Mr Macey. It was the name I remembered. Mr Ed Macey, who writes for the paper.'

She stared hard at Mike. 'It's about that murder, isn't it? Something to do with the murder.'

'Drink your tea,' Mike told her, 'and then if you could go with this young man here and make a formal statement. You've been very helpful, Liv.'

'It *is* to do with the murder,' she shouted. 'I knew it. I just knew it. I told Linda, this is all about that dead girl.' She stood up suddenly, nervous excitement aided by lunchtime alcohol, looking around as though the murderer might be hiding in the room. 'I want police protection,' she demanded. 'I'm not going to wait until he decides to come back. I want police protection.'

Mike sighed, he'd been surprised she'd not made the connection before, but he'd figured that the alcohol might have softened her perceptions. He reminded himself that when he'd first heard about the woman making the phone call, he'd speculated about her safety. Would she have been Jake Bowen's next victim.

Now, hearing the circumstances, he was inclined to think not, but could well understand why the young woman would be frightened.

'We'll arrange for someone to give you a lift home,' he told her, 'and give you some general advice. Or maybe you'd like to stay with a friend for a few days? But really, Miss Watson, I don't think you have anything to worry about.'

She was still protesting as she was led away to make her statement, the PC giving Mike a look that spoke volumes about his opinion of Mike's protective instincts.

Mike shrugged. The young man was still a probationer and had a lot to learn. He was amused to hear him promise the girl that he'd personally arrange for an eye to be kept on her. In fact, he'd attend to it himself.

Mike smiled. Well, the girl *was* pretty.

Interesting, though, the way Jake had made two very public appearances like that. How carefully had he planned that side of it? Had he worried in case Macey taped his calls? If so, that didn't explain his voice on the video tape of Julia Norman. It would be interesting, too, to see what Jake had chosen to look like this time.

* * *

Jo had awoken screaming, her sedative-induced sleep producing nightmares in which Essie called for her, shouting and pleading for help. Her screams woke the entire household and started the new baby crying.

Maria glanced at the clock on Jo's bedside table. It was one thirty, they had been asleep maybe less than an hour.

Jo's mother and husband were there to comfort her and Maria was surplus to requirements. She picked up the crying baby and cuddled him close, carrying him downstairs and away from all the noise. He was unlikely to settle again until he'd been fed, she decided. Jo left bottles made up in the fridge that just needed warming. She could see to that.

Maria let the baby moan in his cradle chair while she filled the kettle and got the bottle from the fridge. Rocked him gently, chatting to him while the kettle boiled, then stood the bottle in a jug of boiling water to warm through and boiled the kettle again for tea.

From upstairs she could hear Jo, still crying for her lost child, this new one forgotten in her grief. Jo had barely been able to bring herself to hold her little boy in the days since Essie had gone. She had seen every gesture of affection towards her son as a betrayal of her love for Essie. Maria had taken over, glad of something that she could do without seeming in her turn to be forgetting about the missing child.

Maria checked the bottle and then picked up the baby, carrying him around the kitchen as he fed hungrily. She glanced out through the half-open kitchen curtain. The police car was still parked at the front of the house, two figures inside dimly silhouetted. They had offered to take Jo and her family to a safe house or to stay with friends. Somewhere private, when media interest threatened to take over and journalists seemed ready to camp outside their door.

Jo had refused, terrified that the kidnapper might phone and she would not be there to take the call. No one could persuade her otherwise, so they had simply closed the curtains and existed since the Monday night in a twilight world. It had been a relief when, after a couple of days of inaction, the press and television had retreated to camp out in the bar of a local hotel.

The curtains, though, had still remained closed as if the family already mourned.

The baby had fallen asleep in her arms. She put him back in his cradle chair and covered him with a blanket. Poor little thing, she thought, he didn't even have a name yet and no one had gotten around to registering his birth. She must ask Jo if she should do it in the morning, trying to remember if it had to be a parent who did it. She was vaguely surprised that she didn't know.

Maria poured the tea and took a tray upstairs. Jo's husband thanked her. The two women still wept softly, sitting on the bed, May's arms around Jo.

Then Maria retreated once more to the kitchen. She had felt such guilt at having taken Essie with her to see Mike, though common sense told her that, as Essie had been abducted from so close to her own home, Jake Bowen would have traced the child no matter what. Jo blamed her, though, and while she could understand her sister feeling that way, it hurt terribly.

She fished the mobile phone out of her bag and hesitated for a moment before dialling Mike's number. It was after two in the morning and there was no reason he should have his mobile switched on, never mind be pleased at being disturbed, but she needed to talk to him, to hear a friendly voice. He answered on the third ring, sleepy and surprised.

'Sorry I woke you,' she said, instinctively keeping her voice low, even though it was unlikely anyone would hear her from upstairs.

'I'm not,' he said. 'I went to sleep thinking about you. You must have heard me.'

She laughed. 'Maybe I did. How are you?'

'Frustrated.'

She laughed again, then covered her mouth with her hand, in case Jo might hear. It seemed so long since anyone had made her laugh, it was a relief to know that she still could.

'Any news?' Mike asked her.

'Nothing. God, Mike, it's the not knowing that's so hard. Why doesn't he get in touch?'

'I don't know,' he told her. 'If any of us understood Jake Bowen, we might be a lot further on towards bringing him in.'

'What about your famous psychologists?'

'Can't agree between themselves. Oh, I don't mean to insult them, love, but this time they seem as foxed as any of us.'

'And the father, is he any use?'

'Not a lot so far; but I'm hoping.' He paused. 'Look, we're both on mobiles, I'm not keen on saying too much.'

'I'm sorry, I should have thought.'

She didn't speak for a little while.

Mike said, 'Are you still there?'

'Yes. Yes, of course I am. I'm sorry. My head's so full of all this, it's hard to talk about anything else.'

'I know. It must be. Look, give me a time tomorrow, use a call box if you have to, and I'll ring back.'

Two o'clock, she told him, and then the renewed crying of the baby ending her time of peace.

* * *

Jake too had woken from a troubled sleep, but there was nothing unusual in that. He had never been one who needed his eight hours a night; he'd been an insomniac all his life, even as a child getting up at all hours and prowling around the house, enjoying his solitary ownership of it while his parents slept.

He went to look at Essie. She was sleeping but restless and he lifted her, supporting her shoulders as he gave her a drink. She looked up at him with drugged eyes that betrayed no comprehension of who he was or what was happening to her. She had wet herself, too deeply sedated to have bladder control.

Jake brought fresh towels and lay the child on them, taking the soiled ones and putting them into the washing machine. He brought soap and water and washed the small body, drying her carefully. Then he fetched his camera and shot another few minutes of film. The child was so small, he thought, and had such a fragile hold on life. He came close enough to watch her breathing, the rise and fall of the tiny ribcage. He imagined her heart beating, slightly faster each time she breathed in, slightly slower on the out-breath, a pendulum that swung a little too far one way, unable to find a balanced centre.

He sat back on his heels, watching her with naked eyes, the camera put aside, and remembered being five years old and the feel of his fathers hand tight around his wrists: one large hand to hold onto both of his. He remembered the sound of his father's belt being pulled from its loops, the sussussing sound as he tugged it free, and later that day, Jake recalled, he had watched from the window of his room as his father went out into the shadowed yard at the back of their house. There was a raised bed at one end of the concrete surfaced yard that Jake's mother had made with bricks and earth and planted with roses. Jake watched as Alastair dug a deep hole beside a yellow rose and planted what remained of the dead cat inside.

Jake could still taste the salty tang of blood in his mouth.

CHAPTER SIXTEEN

28 June

Jake had three national papers delivered daily and was gratified to see that he figured in all of them. Macey's interview with Charlie Morrow, due out that day, had been sold on to a news agency and picked up by two out of the three dailies that Jake read. The two tabloids led with the story and with pictures of Charlie Morrow, his face turned so that the scarring showed to best effect. The broadsheet had the story as a front-page feature, but what it led with, and what on closer inspection the tabloids had caught onto, was what Jake had really been waiting for. Someone had made the Jake-Essie connection. In less than five days and without the little clue he'd left them.

Jake was impressed.

A closer reading told him that it was Macey himself who had identified Essie as the niece of Dr Maria Lucas, the woman Mike Croft had been dating for the past two years. Their pictures appeared on page three of both of the tabloids, one featuring them next to its daily nude. Jake couldn't help comparing the two women, dwelling on what Maria Lucas might look like displayed on page three. What would DI Croft think to that?

If he could find the right head shot, Jake thought, from those he had taken that weekend at Lyme, then it would be no trouble to arrange it. He had enough black female nudes in his reference collection to make it easy, and all the right software.

Daydreaming about selling a remodelled Maria Lucas to the *Sun*, he set about getting his breakfast. He had already fed Essie some milk and changed the towels again. He still had not decided what to do with her. He'd taken some still shots of her that morning, not particularly provocative but good enough to fetch a reasonable price, especially as the morning news meant he'd have no trouble establishing provenance.

Jake poured his morning tea and stood looking out of the window at the promise of a bright new day. The sky was a polished blue and the sun already glared off the glimpse of sea on the horizon.

What really gave Jake the best buzz was to think of all the effort that was being put into catching him, when every day he was out and about, available, dealing with the public: asking policemen for directions; chatting to people in the street, interacting with them, touching them, liking them and being liked in return. He even formed brief relationships with some of them, relationships of the sweetest and most loving kind. And none of them ever suspected a thing — until it was too late.

He thought of Julia, poor repressed little Julia, so flattered by all his attention and concern. Mummy and Daddy not really understanding the artistic temperament and, to be fair, Julia not wanting them to let go too fast.

She'd been shy, found working in the shared studio at the university so very hard, and when Jake had offered her a place to paint she had jumped at it.

'Don't say anything though,' he'd warned her, as their relationship swiftly became more and more intense. 'I'm supposed to agree not to get involved with the students. My company goes overboard on corporate image and if they found I was sleeping with one of my customers' young ladies that might be the end of my job.'

Jake had never been certain whether she believed him completely, but she liked the idea of a secret lover — so romantic — especially one who took her away for expensive weekends and provided a place to work and materials that she could never afford on a student loan.

He'd let her have Christmas with her family, deliver her painting, and enjoyed imagining their confusion and concern when they studied the subject matter. He knew they were far too polite and well bred to say anything to Julia.

She'd spent Easter with them too. He'd brought her back to the house after the Easter break and told her there was something he wanted to show her in the basement. She had never left it again until the day she died, though he'd let her have her books and drawing things.

Poor Julia, she'd had a lot of talent.

Jake turned back to the table and flicked the paper over to the front page, staring hard at the images of Charlie Morrow.

Jake approved of talent and knew that he had plenty. He took scissors from the kitchen drawer and clipped the pictures of Charlie from the paper, then took them up to his studio and pinned them to the wall, wondering as he did so just how far the burns were likely to extend.

'A real Jake Bowen original,' he said.

* * *

Peterson stormed into the incident room at Honiton and threw the stack of morning papers onto Mike's desk.

Mike moved them off the report he had been reading. 'I've already seen them,' he said.

Peterson sat down. 'Our superiors are not happy,' he said.

'Perhaps if they're so superior they could have told us how to avoid it,' Mike said. 'Someone was bound to make the connection some time and, frankly, I don't see it's done us any good sitting on it. We're still no nearer finding the child.'

Peterson gave him a suspicious look. 'Mike, if I thought you or Maria had anything to do with leaking this, you'd be off this case quicker than I could say Jack Crap.'

'If I'd known that, I'd have leaked it sooner,' Mike said wryly. 'Oh, come off it, we may as well bow to the inevitable. I told Ed Macey nothing. He must have made his own connections.'

'Sometimes, Mike, I wonder about your attitude.'

'Sometimes, so do I.'

Peterson didn't reply to this but stood up again. 'I've got to go,' he said. 'Trouble at home.'

'Oh.'

'My daughter's place. It was broken into. She's been away since those damned pictures arrived so no one's quite sure when.'

'Wasn't the place alarmed?' Mike asked.

'They're out in the middle of nowhere. People don't even lock their bloody doors.' He sighed. 'Yes, it was alarmed. She was upset, thinks she forgot to set it on Monday when they went to get their things. I said I'd go and see what was missing then get back to her. She doesn't want to go herself. She's terrified about going home, Mike. Scared out of her wits.'

Mike nodded. 'I can understand that.'

'Meantime,' Peterson said, 'you'd better go and see our friend Macey. Oh, and we're going ahead with the *Crimewatch* thing. The voice enhancement from that video tape should be ready by then. Maybe the bastard overstepped himself this time.'

'I hope so,' Mike said quietly.

After Peterson had left, Mike went back to what he had been doing, trying to get clear in his mind the various strands of the Bowen inquiry. So many people tied up all over the country by one man. So much information and so little of it that connected or made any obvious sense.

He'd been looking again at the descriptions of Jake that had surfaced. Liv Watson and her friends had him as a man with sandy-coloured hair and pale blue eyes. Freckled skin, they said, and about six feet tall.

The man seen leaving Caldwell's house at the time he must have died was dark, with a beard, and Max Harriman swore that Jake had wavy brown hair and grey-green eyes. He gave Jake's height as being a shade under six feet. That, at least, was vaguely consistent.

There were other sightings, all of them variable, some of them recorded by police artists or computer-generated images, even old-fashioned photofit. There was little match barring Jake's height and his weight — well built and definitely not fat, not even around the middle, as Liv had commented in her statement.

Alastair had confirmed that his son had grey-green eyes and light brown hair, but contacts can be worn and hair coloured, and wigs and false beards no longer had to look as if they'd fallen out of Christmas crackers.

Mike looked at the dozen random images set out on the desk and tried to fit together some kind of composite — the essential Jake that remained even behind the masks he wore.

He picked up the final image as Alastair Bowen came through the door. The picture of Jake at fifteen had been scanned into a computer and aged to give a simulation of how he might be now: Jake at nearly forty derived from Jake as a teenage boy. Mike wondered just how accurate this was ever going to be.

He pushed the images across to Alastair, who regarded them solemnly. Alastair's own features and those of his wife, taken from a photograph of them both close to Jake's present age, had been added to the mix and the artist and programmer who had worked upon it professed to be very pleased with the result.

'You think he looks like this?' Alastair mused.

'I don't think anything any more. I've discovered it's a waste of time.'

Alastair glanced up at him and laughed shortly, then looked back at the picture. 'Handsome,' he said. 'Not flashy, but a good-looking man.'

Mike nodded. 'That comes over in all the descriptions,' he said. 'And he looks younger than thirty-nine. No one placed him older than mid-thirties, most ten years younger than we know he is.'

It was a sharply featured profile. Slightly prominent nose, high cheekbones and a squarish jaw with a small cleft in the chin. The eyes were large and widely set, with heavy but well-shaped brows. Looking at Alastair, Mike could see a definite resemblance. Alastair was a man in his late sixties and the face had become slack with age and two years of worry about his wife, but it was still a challenging face, the eyes intelligent and alert.

Alastair pulled another picture towards him, the one of Jake at fifteen years old. Clutching the super eight camera, the teacher who had helped him with his filmmaking standing behind him and Max Harriman at his side, grinning at the camera.

'This teacher Mr Wright,' Mike said. 'How close was Jake to him?'

Alastair thought before replying. 'Jake used him the same as he used everyone,' he said, 'but the teacher didn't know that. He believed in Jake, thought he had a great future, and I think Jake respected him. He went to his funeral at least.'

'He died in a car accident,' Mike reminded himself.

'That's right. Not long after Jake won the prize for making the film. Jake actually cried at the funeral.' He shook his head, disbelieving. 'The family were so impressed by that. It meant so much that their father and husband had made a difference. It was all sham, of course, but they didn't know that.'

'The film,' Mike said, 'tell me about it.'

'I can't tell you much more than the paper did,' he said, referring to the article that accompanied the photograph. 'There was a strike, a big, long-term strike at one of the local factories. We're talking the time of the recession and the three-day week. You remember that?'

Mike nodded.

'Like having the Victorian times back again. Oil lamps in the blackouts and candles selling out in all the shops. I remember the kids running about the streets with flashlights and all the parents yelling at them not to waste the batteries.'

Mike smiled. He'd been only a kid at the time too. For him it had meant missing school because the heating didn't work and half the time there was no power.

'The strike?' he reminded Alastair.

'Ah, yes. It was at a local pit. When we still had such things as coal mines back home. They'd been on the three-day week, like all the rest of us, short of cash, and, believe me, where we lived everyone was short enough without adding to it. It was a crazy time to call everyone out, but they did it. I forget the reasons behind it. Showing solidarity or some such, as I recall, but it fascinated Jake. He went round interviewing management, strikers, pickets, anyone that would talk to him. Went into their houses, showing how hard up they were and how much they must have believed in what they were doing if they were putting their whole livelihood at risk by acting like this. Saw himself as a proper documentary filmmaker.'

'And Max, what was his part in this?'

'Max just tagged along so far as I could see. Carried stuff. I think he helped with the editing, but I don't know much more than that really. Max idolized Jake. I don't think he needed to do much to be happy, it was enough just to be there.'

'And yet Jake allowed him to take equal credit.'

Alastair shrugged. 'Who knows?' he said. 'Who knows why Jake does anything? Maybe the teacher made him give Max credit. I don't remember, Inspector. It was a long time ago.'

Mike nodded and was about to speak again when someone called him from across the room. He excused himself and left Alastair to his thoughts.

That had been a strange, eventful period. Alastair himself had been on short time. By then he was working in a hardware store and the pay was average at best. He was looking forward to Jake leaving school that summer so he could at least contribute to household expenses, but the teachers wanted him to stay on. Alastair had not been happy. The idea of another two years supporting his son was not something he relished. Already Jake worked four nights a week in the local chip shop, keeping late hours as they stayed open to catch workers coming off the closing shift, though even they had been affected by the three-day week. But Alastair couldn't see the point in him staying on at school any longer. Just what did Jake plan on doing with his life anyway?

Jake had loved that winter. No streetlights, walking home in the pitch black or through streets lit on one side while the other showed only candlelight through the curtains. Alastair had never been able to work out the way the power zones worked. Why, for example, their neighbours three doors down had power when they did not or vice versa. It had been a fine time for Jake, the streets around their home almost deserted and no one to watch what he did or where he went.

Alastair frowned. He needed to talk to Max again.

* * *

Peterson had arrived at his daughter's house accompanied by two local officers.

'As you can see, sir, the back door's been forced, but it was only when it blew open that anyone noticed. Your daughter asked the postman to give her letters to a neighbour but didn't leave the keys with anyone to switch lights on or anything.'

'She had a lot on her mind,' Peterson commented.

The officer nodded. 'If you'd take a look around, sir, but nothing's been disturbed as far as we can tell and there's nothing obvious missing.'

Peterson walked slowly through his daughter's house. The children's rooms, filled with their toys, the youngest's bed still unmade. The room his daughter and her husband shared, bed made, everything tidy but for a shirt sticking out of the laundry bin in the en suite shower room.

Downstairs, everything looked normal. As tidy as a house could be with three children in it. TV and VCR still in their place. Stack system and CDs on the shelf in the comer. Nothing missing as far as he could see.

In the kitchen, an unwashed mug sat in the sink, traces of lipstick on the rim. Other breakfast pots, washed and in the drainer. His daughter, Peterson remembered, had always been very organized. It was no real surprise that she would have everything done before she had to take the children to school. The post had arrived, she'd said, just before she'd been about to leave. She'd opened the mail, seen the pictures and left for his house.

Everything done, except for that unmade bed . . .

Peterson turned to one of the officers. 'When's SOCO due to arrive?'

'Probably not until tomorrow, otherwise it'll be Monday.'

Peterson nodded. Like many scenes of crime units, this one was now civilian-run. They'd have to come out from Bristol and, with there being nothing missing and his daughter not being here, this would not have been graded as priority.

'I just want to look at something again.'

He beckoned to the officer and led him back upstairs to the room shared by the youngest children. The smallest one had her bed under the window. It was stacked with teddies, all neatly arranged at the end and the bed covered with a Barbie quilt and pillow. The quilt was pulled back, whereas all the other beds were neatly made.

Peterson eased the quilt back a little further. In the middle of the bed, decorated with blue and yellow beads, lay one of Essie's braids.

CHAPTER SEVENTEEN

Macey was ecstatic. He sat with the stack of nationals in front of him, explaining to Liz and anyone else who would listen that this was definitely 'it.' Macey had finally made it big. Liz, having pored over the copy he'd pushed under her nose and done her best to congratulate him effusively enough, wanted to move on, but Macey, despite his worldly wise, done-it-all air, was like a sponge, in need of constant praise.

'How's Charlie getting along, anyway?' Liz asked him.

'We'll find out later on today,' Macey said. 'I tried to call him this morning but he was having his physio or something. Those hands.' Macey shuddered elaborately.

Liz cast him an amused glance. 'I like him,' she said.

Macey nodded agreement before looking up sharply. 'Knew it would only be a matter of time,' he said, then more loudly, 'Inspector Croft, nice to see you again this morning.'

Mike didn't bother replying. He grabbed a chair from a nearby desk and sat down, leaning forward to study Macey's newspapers.

'How did you know?' he asked.

'Saw your lady on the TV appeal and recognized her,' Macey said. He reached into his desk and pulled out a folder of clippings, found the one he wanted and gave it to Mike.

A local journalist had caught them both on camera during an earlier case Mike had worked on in Norwich. Maria had been professionally involved with a woman suspect. Mike had forgotten that this particular picture even existed.

'There are others,' Macey said. 'Things your lady's been involved in and dragged you along to. Some sort of charity ball, I think one of them is. You look nice in a dinner jacket. Want me to find it?'

Mike shook his head. 'I'll pass' he said. 'And you didn't think of the consequences, that we might not want this information released?'

'Oh, you're asking me so nicely, Inspector. It makes me nervous. Is the bad cop waiting round the corner?'

Liz glared at Macey, before asking Mike anxiously, 'You think it will make things worse?'

Mike shook his head slowly. 'I doubt it will make much difference' he said. 'Not to Essie or to Jake. To the family, though, now that it's publicly confirmed Jake Bowen has their child, I don't imagine it's going to be easy for them.'

'Or for you' Macey said. 'How does it feel to know she was taken because of you, Inspector Croft? That this little girl has been kidnapped by a psychopath because you're dating her auntie?'

'Macey!' Liz was outraged, but Mike was wearied beyond retaliating. It was something he'd been charging himself with every hour since Essie disappeared.

'How do you think it feels, Mr Macey?' Mike said softly. 'If I could trade places with her, then you can be certain that I would.'

He got up then and walked slowly back towards the door.

'He didn't deserve that, Ed,' Liz told him angrily.

Macey threw her an apologetic look. It lasted all of a second and she almost missed it.

'Can I quote you on that, Inspector Croft?' he shouted at Mike's retreating back.

* * *

Peterson was back at Honiton by the time Mike got there. Mike had driven slowly along the Dorchester road, allowing cars to rush past him on the dual carriageway and vaguely aware of impatient drivers behind him when the road narrowed for the villages.

He didn't care. Macey's words had bitten all the harder for being true. He should have come back at him, Mike thought, told him what he really thought of someone who could expose his guilt so openly, but Mike knew he'd only have regretted it. He'd done his best to stay professional and calm, knowing Macey was merely being Macey, riding high upon the moment and made brave by success.

He would, though, do anything to know that Essie was safe once more. Would, as he had told Macey, willingly have traded places with her. He wondered if Macey would print his parting comment and how he himself would have to respond if Macey did; and if, in some half-conscious way, he had been hoping to use Macey to deliver a message to Bowen.

His despairing mood was not lifted as he drove back into Honiton.

Police were still doing the last of the house-to-house calls, with extra officers drafted in from wherever they could be spared. The incident room was full to overflowing, desks crammed in wherever they could be fitted. Notice boards and stacks of paper vied for space with empty cans and sandwich bags.

Peterson waved him over as soon as he came through the door.

'I need a couple of hours, Mike. If anyone asks, you can't raise me. My battery's flat in the mobile or something.'

'What's wrong?'

'I'm getting my family out, Mike. I just need a couple of hours to make arrangements.'

'Certainly, but out where?'

Peterson shook his head. 'I'm sorry, Mike, I'm not telling even you. I'll be leaving something with my bank, saying where they can be reached should anything happen to me, but I'm telling no one else.'

Mike had never seen Peterson so rattled. 'What did you find at the house?' he said.

Peterson led him over to where the evidence was being filed and pulled from the box the bag containing Essie's hair.

'This was on my granddaughter's bed.'

* * *

Charlie Morrow had come back from the morning's physio and logged on again. He'd spent several hours so far sitting on the side and monitoring various of the user groups that Macey had directed him to. The thing that had struck him most was the banality of it all. The 'public rooms', to which he had easiest access, were places to exchange gossip; to shock the unwary and enjoy the mild frisson of discussing sexual practices, both regular and somewhat dubious, with the illusion of complete freedom.

Talk had turned to Jake from time to time. The filmmaker was something of a legend, even though, on closer inquiry, it turned out that no one in the public rooms could honestly say they had seen one of his films. They were, in the main, collectors' items, expensive and exclusive.

Jake Bowen had started out in soft porn and his early work was being re-released now that he'd hit the headlines. 'He's an artist,' someone said, implying that artists were allowed to cross the line between good and bad taste; explore the difference between life and death and the full range of sexual experience.

Charlie doubted any of them really knew what they were talking about. Jake was not some esoteric filmmaker; exploring the links between a good fuck and a fear of dying. He realized quickly that of all those he encountered in the user groups, he was likely to be the only one who had actually seen one of Jake Bowen's special editions.

The beautifully shot and cruelly erotic images still lived in his mind and haunted his dreams.

He wondered if Jake would contact him; if Jake would be as curious about Charlie Morrow as Charlie was about Jake and, if he was, how he would choose to make contact. He decided to make another opening for Jake, just in case.

He picked at random a half-dozen of the sites and left a message on each, varying the suggested meeting time by five minutes.

The message read: 'Meet me at eleven p.m. Regards, Charlie.'

* * *

Maria phoned Mike just after two o'clock. She was using a public phone and he called her back.

'How are you?' he asked.

'Pleased to be out. Someone had to shop.'

'You've seen the papers today?'

'I've seen the journalists. Most of them are camped outside Jo's front door. I went out over the wall and through a neighbour's garden. I think Jo's about to cave in and agree to move out for a few days.'

'Where will she go? Will you go with her?'

'We've relatives in Kent, that seems favourite at the moment, but no, I don't think I'll be going. I have to get back to Oaklands.'

'Not to work, surely?'

'Not with patients, no. I've off-loaded my urgent cases as best I can but there's always something to do. I've a backlog of paperwork like you wouldn't believe.'

'At least I'll be able to talk to you there.'

'There is that.' She paused. She'd been giving things a lot of thought, particularly Alastair Bowen. 'How are you getting along with the father?'

Alastair was across the other side of the room, talking to another officer. 'Slowly,' Mike said. 'He's got a lot to tell, but it's hard work.'

Maria took a deep breath. 'You think he'll talk to me?'

'To you? I don't know. I don't know if Peterson would even agree.'

'Suppose he did, would Alastair?'

'He hates shrinks, won't have anything to do with ours. We were hoping he'd work with the forensic psychologists, but he won't even entertain the idea.'

'Can't you force him?'

'How? Torture went out with the Inquisition.'

'Very funny. Look, can't you at least ask him? Not as a shrink but because of Essie. You say he came forward because he heard about Essie?'

'So he claims. Look, frankly I take everything he says with a large pinch of salt.'

He thought about it for a moment, watching Alastair from across the room. Maria might be able to get through in a way that he could not.

'I'll talk to him,' he said. 'That's all I can promise.'

* * *

Alastair Bowen was not at first amenable to Mike's request.

'She's not asking as a psychiatrist,' Mike said, 'but simply because of Essie.'

'I didn't think personal involvement was allowed.'

Mike sighed. 'You're involved,' he pointed out.

'Hardly the same thing though, is it?'

He fell silent then and Mike decided to wait him out. He went to fetch coffee for them both from the machine in the front office. On his return Alastair began to speak.

'I took Jake to see a counsellor,' he said. 'We paid for it. I thought I should at least give him a chance.'

'What made you think he needed help?' he asked.

Alastair frowned. 'His mother thought there was something wrong,' he said. He sipped his coffee slowly, pausing to stare into the polystyrene cup as though it might give him inspiration. 'Jake was always a bit of a loner, I suppose. Didn't play with other kids unless you forced him to. He was always different. I knew it would only be a matter of time before his mother realized something wasn't right, but I couldn't tell her what it was. Not what it really was.'

Mike made no comment, not certain he wanted to provoke another of Alastair's statements that Jake had been born the way he was.

Alastair was not to be put off by a little silence.

'I know you don't believe me, Inspector Croft,' he said, 'but you had to be there to understand. See what Jake did to people, to . . . animals. To his toys even. You had to be there to understand, and in the end it was obvious to me. I hadn't been imagining things. That look *was* there right from the time that Jake was born. That look of pure evil, wrapped up in charm.'

'Perhaps,' Mike ventured, 'hearing you say it so often . . .'

'Made him that way? No, I've told you before. I did my best for the boy, tried all I knew to save him, but none of it would work. Then he kept getting into fights at school and the teachers started poking around about how he was at home — was he happy? Was he having problems? — and his mother decided maybe they were right. The loving little boy she'd always convinced herself he was, was showing his true colours and she didn't know what to do.'

'How old was Jake?' Mike asked.

'Just turned thirteen,' Alastair said.

Mike waited, to see if Alastair was about to find significance in the age, but he made no comment on it. Instead, he went on, 'You can imagine, we kept it pretty quiet. I mean, the background we came from, no one "went into therapy" or whatever the jargon is today. They'd have laughed themselves stupid, those neighbours of ours. But I did it for my wife and she did it for Jake. It was this young woman, the therapist. Fresh out of college from the look of her. Green as grass. She was no match for Jake. He refused to cooperate for weeks, and I was all set to give up, but his mother reckoned he was getting in less trouble at school and it must be working. So we carried on. He didn't talk to her, not for all that time, then, suddenly, he poured out his soul to the stupid woman. Talking about all the abuse and cruelty he'd suffered. Blamed me for everything.'

'You admitted to having beaten him,' Mike said quietly.

Alastair's eyes flashed with a sudden anger. 'And I make no apology for it,' he said.

'She called in the social worker. Got the police involved. We managed to keep it quiet, but it almost got to the courts. Then two days before we were due to appear, he laughed in her face and told her it was all lies. Told her how much of a fool she was.'

'And she believed him?' Mike asked.

Alastair shrugged. 'The police carried on poking around for a while, but then the case was dropped. It was only his word and he'd gone back on that.'

'But there was some truth in what he'd said,' Mike persisted. 'Did you make him retract his statement?' Alastair Bowen refused to reply, fixing Mike with an icy stare.

Mike leaned across the table towards him. 'Talk to Maria,' he said, hating the desperation he could not keep out of his voice. 'Talk to her about Jake. How it all began. Anything you might know that will help us to save Essie.' Memories of the time he'd spent with them, at Lyme and on other family occasions, flooded back. Mike pushed himself away from the table, got up and walked over to the window, staring blindly at the bright, sunlit world outside.

'She's probably already dead,' Alastair said softly, 'you know that, don't you?'

Mike turned angrily and crossed back to where Alastair was still seated, all pretence at professional calm gone.

'And that's what I'm supposed to tell the family?' he said. 'Is that all you have to say? I'm not going to give up, none of us are. You want us to write this off and wait around till there are other Essies? Other Julia Normans? Other children? I know what it is to lose a child, Alastair.'

'So do I, Inspector Croft,' Alastair said heavily. He sat forward with his head in his hands. 'So do I.'

* * *

Jake had decided that the focus of his attention from now on should be Mike Croft, as he was the one most in contact with Alastair. He needed to find a way of getting Alastair alone and Inspector Croft looked most likely to be the one to show him how.

He went down to the basement, gave Essie milk and washed her, changing the wet towels she was lying on. He sat for a while watching the child. She moved restlessly in her sleep, her flickering eyes telling him that she dreamed.

Jake pulled the child to him and held her in his arms, cradling her gently. Her skin was so very, very soft and he had washed her with perfumed soap, the scent clinging to her as he brought his head close.

'Does your mummy love you, little girl? Does she play with you and cuddle you and tell you how special you are?' He smiled suddenly. 'I know your auntie does,' he told her. 'And your Uncle Mike.'

CHAPTER EIGHTEEN

29 June

Saturday arrived with unexpected rain. It was just over a week since Julia's body had been found and a week exactly since Mike had met with Maria and Essie at Lyme. He'd returned to the woods above Colwell Barton, the murder site still cordoned off and the entrance to that part of the woods barred.

The trees grew thickly enough to shelter him from the worst of the rain and the rhythmic beating of it falling on the canopy of leaves was soothing.

He'd gone into the office early to catch up with some of the reports he'd not had time to read and would not have time to look at later. Most of his day about to be taken up with the return match between Max Harriman and Alastair Bowen.

They'd had a more complete set of toxicology results on Julia Norman's body. They confirmed the high level of amphetamine that early results had suggested and also a residual amount of barbiturates. The guess was that Julia had been kept sedated for quite some time, then pumped full of uppers, enough to compensate for the weakness brought on by blood loss. She'd have been high enough to fly when Jake brought her to the woods, then at some point she'd been hit from behind, just beside the left ear, hard enough to put her down. Then Jake had finished the killing of Julia Norman.

The blood loss had been a difficult thing to account for. Had she lost too much at once, the experts said, the body would have gone into shock and she might well have died sooner. Jake must have taken things slowly, Mike thought; watched Julia dying over many days before bringing her here. It was that element of calculation that he found so sickening.

He stood just outside the inner cordon surrounding the small altar on which Julia had lain. The flowers were completely withered and many had gone. Despite the officer on guard on the main path, souvenir hunters had been here, finding their way into the woods from across the fields, taking the flowers.

Yet other people had come into the woods to lay wreathes or light candles, as Jake himself had done.

There was no stopping them, short of increasing the guard, and with manpower stretched to breaking point on the rest of the inquiry that was impossible.

Mike glanced at his watch. He would have to collect Alastair soon. It was so still and silent here in this part of the woods: only the sound of falling rain and the occasional fizz as heavier drops forced their way through and hit the dust on the forest floor. It was not a comfortable place to be.

Mike glanced around. The creeping feeling between his shoulder blades, as though someone was watching him from the shadows, refused to go away. Jake had observed Macey in the woods that day; watched him and captured his reaction on film. Mike wondered how many times he himself had been the subject of similar Jake Bowen attention.

He turned away and scrambled over the fallen trees, climbing back towards the path.

After his talk with Alastair the day before, he'd sent for whatever records had been kept from when Jake had been thirteen and ready to accuse his father. Mike was not sure what to make of all that. Alastair was clearly convinced that his son was evil incarnate, but what had come first? Had Jake given Alastair cause for doubt right from babyhood — something Mike, remembering the adoration he had felt for his own baby son, found hard to believe. Or was it that Jake's actions had so impressed themselves upon his father's memories that Alastair could simply not remember the time before.

He must speak to Charlie Morrow later, he reminded himself. The *Crimewatch* special on the Jake Bowen case was scheduled for Tuesday and, following the recent media publicity, Charlie had agreed to participate.

Mike tried to visualize the manpower tied up with this investigation all over the country: hundreds of officers expending thousands of hours chasing one man whose imagination and sheer audacity had so far left everyone standing.

Reaching the path, Mike looked back down into the gully where Julia Norman had died.

Mike remembered Essie, her small body in his arms and plump little arms around his neck. He stood on the path, staring back at nothing, and wept.

* * *

This time Alastair Bowen had made a big effort to get through to Max. He'd sat opposite the other man, his hands idly playing with the cuttings books that lay on the table, and he'd begun to talk.

At first, Max had made a big show of not listening, but slowly Mike had seen him drawn into Alastair's tale. It seemed to Mike that Jake's father had gone to great lengths to dredge from his memory one of the few stories he could remember about Jake that had pleasure in it. And there had been a part for Max.

'I can remember,' Alastair said, 'the winter fair when you and Jake were both about seven years old. Jake was just coming up for eight in the New Year, but you were that little bit younger; weren't you, Max? A spring baby, where Jake was a winter child. I always thought that the winter fair marked the start of Christmas. Still almost a month to go, but there would be the smell of chestnuts in the air and the chill of that cold northerly that always seemed to blow across the valley. You both loved the fair, you and Jake. The noise and lights and all the fuss of unloading. You'd be out there, the pair of you, from the moment the first lorries arrived, getting in the way and hoping for a free ride when the men were setting up. You always reckoned you were going to run away one time when the fair came. One day, you'd say, the winter fair would leave town and take you with it.'

'I did one time,' Max said.

Alastair switched his gaze, focusing on Max. 'I remember;' he said. 'Your mam was going frantic, blaming me, blaming Jake. It was three days till the police fetched you back.'

'Should have let me be,' Max said. 'I'd have been all right.'

Slowly Alastair nodded. 'I guess you would,' he said. 'You'd have been away from Jake.'

A look of anger crossed Max's face and for a moment it seemed as though the rapport slowly being built up would fall apart, but Alastair pressed on.

'We didn't have a lot to spend. You'd both saved what bit of pocket money you'd got, saved for weeks, and I'd given you both a bit extra, I remember, but it was the deciding what to spend it on that took the time. Round that fair we went a dozen times, just taking it all in, till you and Jake decided which rides and which sideshows you'd go on.' He shook his head, a smile curving the comers of his mouth and a softness in his eyes. 'I don't know why you took so long, though. It would always be the same thing, year after year, from the first time I took you and you were old enough for anything other than the baby rides.'

Max returned the smile, both men now locked into the memory. 'The waltzers first,' Max said. 'Then the big wheel and the shooting gallery.' He grinned at Alastair, 'That was because you were good at it and Jake always wanted to go one better.'

'It took him another five years even to come close,' Alastair said, and there was pride in his voice, 'but he never gave it up, even though I always told him it was fixed. That you had to compensate for bad setup and sights that weren't aligned and all you stood to win anyway was some stupid soft toy.'

'Jake never gave up on anything he started,' Max said. 'He always won in the end.'

'The funny thing, though,' Alastair said slowly, 'whatever else happened, you always finished up with the same ride. Even when I'd have thought you'd grown too big.'

'The carousel.' Max laughed aloud. 'It was magic, that thing. When we were little kids we'd sit up there on those painted horses and pretend that we could ride away for ever. I don't think Jake ever stopped thinking like that. We always wanted to ride real horses, but you never had the money for lessons and neither did my mam.' He laughed briefly. 'Closest we got were the seaside ponies. Old nags that never did anything but walk up and down between the breakwaters. The carousel was better all round.'

From his corner of the visitors' room Mike watched these two men, engrossed in their shared memories, with a kind of fascination. He didn't know how much of this was truth or how much a deliberately rose-coloured fabrication, but it was encouraging to see the developing rapport. Was this the breakthrough they had hoped for? He was unprepared for Alastair's sudden change of tack.

'What happened to that other film, Max? The other one you made with Jake?'

Max stared at him. 'I don't know what you mean,' he said.

'Oh, yes, I think you do. The one with the girl from the carousel. The pretty little thing that helped her brother take the money.'

Max stood up and turned towards the door. He's pushed him too far, Mike thought. Fuck it, I thought we were getting somewhere.

Then, abruptly, Max sat down again. 'It was Jake's first experiment,' he said. 'It wasn't easy getting more film, but Jake had a bit of a job by then and so did I, so we managed. Got this girl to meet us after she'd finished. It wasn't hard, she liked Jake — everyone liked Jake. She was, you know, flattered like, that Jake was that bit older. She must have been thirteen, fourteen at most, but she had great little tits and we weren't the first she'd gone with.'

'You made the film in Jake's bedroom,' Alastair said.

'Yeah. Lighting was a big problem, but we improvised. Jake used the darkroom at school and he borrowed a photoflood bulb. Over the weekend, no one noticed it was missing. That helped a lot, and we brought up every lamp you'd got in the house and a big flashlight he'd got from somewhere. It worked OK. We got the girl drunk on cheap cider. She wasn't used to the stuff and it didn't take that much. She did pretty much anything we wanted after that. I filmed Jake and he filmed me. Jake had all these magazines he used to pinch. I mean, they were nothing special, not like the stuff Jake produced later on, but, you know teenage boys — all hormones and no sense of responsibility. It was a laugh.'

'Not for the girl,' Alastair said with a cold gentleness that took Mike by surprise. Alastair's anger at what Max was saying was as palpable as his own. 'And I don't think many teenage boys, even after reading mucky books, would tie an underage girl to the bed and rape her repeatedly, just for a good laugh.'

Max stood up again, his face stony, closed down once more. This time he called for the guard, demanding to be taken away.

'Why didn't you tell me about that other film?' Mike demanded when he had gone. 'You saw it and you didn't report Jake then?'

Alastair shook his head. 'I never saw it,' he said. 'I guessed from the rumours that were flying around and the accusations that Sally Wilson made. But no one believed her, even though the evidence was all there. Sally and her sister, they were known for it all over town and no one gave a damn.'

'That was why Max got equal credit on the other film,' Mike said quietly.

Alastair nodded. 'Yes,' he said. 'I believe it was.'

CHAPTER NINETEEN

1 July

Little of use had happened over the weekend after Alastair's meeting with Max. They had talked on the return journey, Mike driving Alastair back to where he was staying, but Alastair had added only one thing to Mike's small fund of knowledge. Mostly, he seemed to want to be alone with his thoughts and resented Mike's intrusion.

'You realize that we could charge you?' Mike asked him at one point. The rain had begun again, falling in heavy drops against the windscreen. Alastair stared at it, an expression of concentration on his face.

'You could,' he conceded. 'I would not oppose you if you did.'

'You've obstructed a police investigation,' Mike persisted. 'Kept back evidence that could have saved lives. Protected Jake when you knew he had committed murder.'

'When I *suspected* he might have done, Inspector. I knew nothing for certain. I still know nothing for certain.'

'You're playing games, Alastair. This isn't a question of semantics, it's about people dying. About a child that might still be alive. It's about why the hell you kept quiet.'

He braked sharply, not having seen the car in front signal to pull out. His hand poised above the horn until he realized it had been his own fault.

'I suggest you concentrate on your driving, Inspector,' Alastair told him with his infuriating calm. 'And watch your speed. You don't want to be seen breaking the law.' Mike seethed but said nothing. He eased back on the accelerator, back from the eighty-five he'd been doing — far too fast for the driving rain.

'Why *did* you protect him, Alastair? I can understand any parent wanting to think the best of their son, but you despised Jake. You had no illusions about him.'

'Despise him? No, it wasn't that. I . . . pitied him.'

'I don't buy that, Alastair. I don't buy that at all.' There was silence while Mike thought it through. Nothing Alastair had said so far explained his protection of his son. The key seemed to be Alastair's decision to wait until his wife had died before coming forward.

'What were you protecting your wife from?' Mike asked suddenly. 'What was it Jake knew about you that you were afraid she might find out?'

It was a long time before Alastair gave any response. 'There were things,' he said. 'Just things I had done.'

* * *

Mike had spent the Monday morning reviewing his notes and sitting in on the briefing Peterson had been giving to those still on house-to-house or following up the previous year's holiday traffic. It seemed an impossible task. Mike was bitterly aware, as was every officer from the most inexperienced probationer up, that the sheer quantity of information they had gathered could be working against them. Their man might already have been questioned, made a statement, even come forward with information. He might be on a dozen lists and, until the information was cross-referenced, the significance not be seen. Computers helped, but the information still had to be put onto the system and that took time. Other serial killers had fallen through the gaps just because of this kind of confusion: the problem of referencing and cross-referencing; of collating and making sense.

And there would be the *Crimewatch* programme the following night, with all the extra statements and witnesses and people who were trying to be helpful. They needed the exposure and they needed the support the programme would generate, but Mike and everyone else on the team dreaded the extra paperwork.

* * *

At midday Mike left Honiton to see Charlie Morrow. The road was choked with holiday traffic and Jake, parked in a side road and reading the morning paper, had little worry about being seen. He'd changed his location three times that morning, checking that Mike's car was still parked but risking being away for upwards of fifteen minutes at a time.

In Jake's mind this was giving the policeman the illusion of a sporting chance.

He kept a good distance behind on roads that offered little opportunity for turning off or overtaking, driving with the windows wide open, enjoying the summer sun.

Jake followed right up to the gates of the nursing home and watched Mike go inside. Then he passed on by.

* * *

'I'd got used to seeing my face in the mirror,' Charlie said, 'but to go public like that, it was another thing entirely.'

Mike put the newspaper down and sat back in the easy chair. 'Are you sure you can cope with this television thing?' he asked. 'It's even more public than the newspapers. No one would blame you if you couldn't.'

'Wouldn't they? Maybe not, Mike, but I'd blame myself. This is no time for pissing about. That bastard's out there and

I want to play my part in catching him.' He hesitated, then asked, 'There's been nothing more, I suppose?'

'On Essie? No, nothing. I spoke to Maria a few times over the weekend and we're in close contact with everyone on the case in Norwich, but so far there's been no word. We're into the second week now.' He shrugged helplessly. 'They've interviewed everyone who was in the area over and over again. Jake must have been convincing to get Essie even to talk to him. There's an alleyway running at the back of the school. We guess he must have taken her out that way.'

'And no one noticed anything wrong?'

'Essie was seen standing by the gate talking to a man. She was still on school premises at the time and the woman swears she saw her turn away as though she was about to cross the playground towards the other entrance. She was busy with her own kids and noticed nothing more. We've a couple of other similar sightings, but . . . well, I've been with Maria once or twice to pick up Essie. Kids and parents everywhere. Cars double-parked. It's pure chaos. It's not as hard to imagine as you might think. If Jake looked confident, and we know he would, then he might well go unnoticed.'

'And the man Essie was talking to?'

'Tall, sandy-haired, clean-shaven. Wearing jeans and a light-coloured shirt. Possibly blue, but that's about all we have. Another witness is convinced she saw the man bending down to tie Essie's shoe. She was wearing these little canvas lace-up things. She's still not that good at bows . . .' He trailed off, distracted, finding it hard to think that clearly about the little girl.

'Is Maria still with her sister?'

'No, she's gone back to Oaklands, Jo and her mother are staying with relatives. It seemed best to get her away from the media fuss.'

Charlie nodded. 'This *Crimewatch* thing, the whole programme's devoted to Jake Bowen, or so they tell me.'

'That's right. God knows, there's more than enough to fill it.'

'I'm sure he'll be well flattered,' Charlie said.

It was late afternoon by the time Mike got back to Honiton. He found Peterson and Alastair with others in the briefing room, making final reviews of the footage to be shown on *Crimewatch* the following day. Much of it could have been library film from any big case, showing officers on house-to-house, others in slow-moving lines, searching the fields around Colwell Barton.

He got water from the cooler and sat down, watching the screen. Peterson came over.

'That stuff's come in from up north,' he said. 'It's on your desk.'

'Anything useful?'

Peterson shrugged. 'All a bit vague. There's the counsellor's statement and a social worker's assessment based on a home visit. Plus Alastair's and Jake's statements to the police and another from his mother. Not a hell of a lot more. Alastair called the local vicar in as a character witness, that sort of thing.'

'You've shown Alastair?'

'Not yet. Thought I'd give you the pleasure. At least he talks to you.'

Mike smiled wryly. 'And you're telling me that's a good thing?' He sipped some water and tried to relax in the uncomfortable plastic chair. 'I still think we should charge him.' he said. 'Stop treating him with kid gloves and see what facing an obstruction charge would do for his recall.'

'I'm tempted to agree, Mike, but so far I've been vetoed. We're to see what we can get out of him this way, see what he can pull out of Max too. I mean, having Max in custody hasn't got us a whole lot further and, frankly, I don't think Alastair gives a damn about it either way. It strikes me that, now his wife's gone, nothing matters to him very much.'

Mike shrugged. 'I don't know,' he admitted. 'It's funny, you'd think he'd want to talk about his wife, dying so recently. But he seems to have put her right out of his mind. Never mentions her unless I do.'

‘I think he sees that as a personal matter,’ Peterson suggested. ‘Not something he would appreciate us trampling over.’

Mike thought about it, wondering again what Alastair had been keeping from his wife. Did she have her suspicions about Jake too? Or, as Alastair had insisted, did she continue to view Jake as a precious and innocent son?

‘Charlie’s all set for tomorrow,’ he said. ‘I thought maybe he’d have second thoughts, but he’s going ahead with it.’

‘That’s good. I suggest we break early tonight, Mike. Sleep’s been in short supply lately and we’ll get none tomorrow night.’

‘I won’t argue,’ Mike said. ‘Look, I’ll arrange for Alastair to be taken home, then try and get something to eat. I don’t remember having lunch. Are your family holding up OK?’

Peterson nodded. ‘As well as any of us are,’ he said.

* * *

Jake had been waiting, parked in the side road he had used earlier. He’d been prepared to give them fifteen minutes more, then finish for the night. If they came out after that, well, then it was the luck of the game and a score for them.

He’d changed cars, swapping the red Sierra for a small green hatchback that he kept in a lock-up garage ready for occasional use, one of several he had scattered up and down the country.

Suddenly Peterson, Mike Croft and Alastair Bowen came out together and stood for a moment talking in the bright evening sunshine. Jake watched, seeing his father up close for the first time in almost eighteen years.

Mike left, alone, a few minutes later and it was a young officer in uniform who opened his car door for Alastair to get inside.

Jake watched them pull away, then waited for a slow count of ten before following, the anonymous little hatchback tailing a couple of cars behind on the Dorchester road.

CHAPTER TWENTY

The house was at the end of a narrow lane, single-track with banks on either side, topped by an unclipped hedge. Jake had driven about a quarter of a mile past the entrance to the lane and parked the car on the verge at the side of the road, then walked back to find the best way of approaching the house unseen. By skirting back towards the main road, he found a gate and climbed over it into a field, then followed the hedge back the way he had come towards the house. It took over an hour and several detours — finding gaps in hedges, having to cut back into neighbouring fields, before Jake finally had the house in sight.

It was not the best of positions. He was quite exposed, crouched beside the hedge and at the top of the slight rise, and visibility was restricted. Jake could see only one side of the house and the path immediately in front of the door.

The house had a small garden in front and a larger one behind. A low fence separated it from the field. It was run down and overgrown, the once cultivated shrubs and brambles promising to provide much better cover when it finally grew dark.

The evening was warm and Jake lay in the sun barely moving, watching the house. Once a man who was not his father came out into the garden and walked down the path, casually glancing around. Once a face appeared at an upstairs window. But that was all.

At eight o'clock, Jake turned over on his back and closed his eyes. There was still sufficient heat in the sun and in the baked earth to satisfy him. Stretching out like a basking cat, he slept.

He woke after dark. Lights had gone on in the house and his watch told him that it was five past twelve. He could still see with little difficulty, his eyes accustomed to the summer dark that was still merely a velvet blue at this time of night and helped by a thin moon. Keeping to the shadows, Jake began to move towards the house. His trousers were a light grey and his shirt was pale. Anyone glancing from the house would probably have seen him despite his caution, but Jake paid no heed to that. It was a chance he'd have to take for now.

He got close enough to see through the unblinded windows and into the living room. His father and a second man sat watching the television. A single table-lamp was lit close to Alastair's chair. As Jake watched, the first man, the one he'd seen in the garden, came through the door with tea things on a tray. Jake ducked down as he came to pull the curtains closed, then moved around to the other side of the house.

The kitchen was in darkness, but the windows had neither curtains nor blinds and Jake could see inside. He moved to the back door, tried it. It was locked, but a cautious push at top and bottom moved it slightly against the frame. Not bolted then, just the single fastening. He completed his circuit of the house and stood for a brief time in the shadows beside the front door, listening to the night-time silence. Any noise he made forcing the back door would sound like a rifle crack in the still air.

Jake took the more direct route back to his car, following the narrow track to the road. Once there he put on the light summer jacket he'd had lying on the back seat. He kept a basic toolkit in his car. He took out a penknife and the wrench from his socket set, together with a flat-blade screwdriver and a roll of ducting tape. The screwdriver was nowhere near as long as he would have liked, but it would have to do. Then he made his way back towards the house, moving cautiously but quickly along the track.

Two lights burned in the house, one in an upstairs room and one in the living room that Jake had peered into earlier. Jake went around to the rear of the house and tried the back door again. Still locked but not bolted. He pushed against it, seeing how far he could ease it from the frame, and tried the screwdriver, forcing it into the gap. It was an easy fit.

He circled the house again, looking for open windows. The night was still warm and surely no one would be sleeping with them closed.

On the ground floor there was nothing, but upstairs the windows in the lighted room were open wide and the small window that probably led onto the landing was a little ajar. There was still the problem of getting up there, though.

Jake stepped back into deeper shadow and studied the situation. There was nothing to climb and his previous reconnaissance had shown no outbuildings that could hold a ladder.

Slowly, he retraced his steps. His watch told him that it was one fifteen, and the blue of evening had given way to a deeper night. He slid the screwdriver blade into the crack in the door and levered hard, trying to compensate for the shortness of the blade. He needn't have been concerned. The door gave easily with a loud crack as the wood splintered from the frame.

Jake stepped back into the deeper shade at the side of the part-open door, keeping his gaze focused on the ground so as not to be blinded as the light in the kitchen suddenly snapped on and poured through the window. The first man into the room saw the broken door. Jake heard him shout something to his colleague. Heard the footsteps on lino and then the door was wrenched wide. Jake's arm came down as the man ran outside. The blow landed badly, the wrench catching the man's shoulder on the downward stroke, enough to make him stumble but then begin to turn. But Jake's backhand caught his chin as he swung around and the man went down, his half cry not loud, but echoing in the silence. Jake hit him again just to be sure and then again, even though he lay still. He could see the blood darkening the metal of the wrench and feel its slickness on his hand. Jake paused, to wipe his blood-marked palm on the other man's clothes, then moved on into the house.

The second officer had run upstairs to Alastair. He came down again, calling to his colleague as Jake stepped into the hall. The officer was trying to be calm, advancing slowly down the stairs, his hands a little outstretched and his voice as steady as he could make it, telling Jake to put his weapon down.

Jake took a step back towards the kitchen door, keeping his exit clear, and the officer seemed to take this move as uncertainty. But Jake was only repositioning for attack. This man was older, more experienced than the one he'd dealt with outside. Jake let the man come on, to give him the feeling that he might be getting somewhere, bring him close enough to strike and wait to see what opportunity offered him.

He lowered the wrench slightly, let his shoulders relax and took another step towards the door, the move bringing him around so he faced the bottom of the stairs. The officer took another step down, still talking to Jake, the tone calm and measured, more and more certain that he was in control.

Even when Alastair appeared on the landing, the man neither faltered nor turned, just raised his voice a little to tell Alastair not to move, then turned his attention back to Jake.

Jake allowed him one more step, then moved forward with a speed that had the man reeling even before the blow was struck. He fell forward, almost taking Jake with him, one hand clutching at what was left of the right eye, where Jake's blow had landed.

Jake did not wait to see what damage he had done. Alastair had taken a moment to respond, but now he was running. Jake took the stairs two at a time, catching up with him at the bedroom door, reaching forward to slam it just as his father's hand touched the handle.

'I think you should come with me,' Jake said.

* * *

Below him, in the hall, Jake could hear the policeman's voice. He must have a radio or a mobile. He obviously hadn't hit him hard enough.

He reached out and grabbed Alastair by the arm, swinging him around and twisting the wrist against the older man's back. Alastair gasped with pain, his knees buckling as his arm was taken further up his back. Jake kicked at Alastair's legs, dropping the wrench and grabbing at the other arm, pulling back so that his father hit the floor face-first. He bound Alastair's hands tightly with the ducting tape, opened the knife and picked up the wrench, which he shoved through the belt of his trousers. Then he pulled up on Alastair's bound hands and forced him to his feet, turning him around so that he could see the knife. Then, with the knife blade pressed against Alastair's back, Jake forced him down the stairs. The officer he had injured still lay on the floor, blood pouring from his face, the eye closed and the surrounding skin already turning blue. Jake kicked the radio from the man's hand, then kicked the officer in the head, the blood spurting from the growing wound. He left him screaming on the hall floor as he forced Alastair out through the kitchen door and into the night.

CHAPTER TWENTY-ONE

Tuesday, July 2

Mike was woken at two p.m. with the news that Alastair had gone and two officers were down. He was dressed and at the house only twenty minutes later.

First reports were confused. One officer; though wounded, had managed to call in. He didn't yet know about the other one. Road-blocks were being set up — Mike encountered one, hastily arranged, a police car pulled up across the road and an officer with a torch stopping what traffic there was — but they had little hope of tracking Jake. Fast as the response had been, he still had the jump on them.

An ambulance and two police cars, blue beacons creating artificial daylight, stood in front of the house. Peterson was on his way, Mike was told. One officer was still conscious, about to be taken away in the ambulance. The other had not been so lucky and had been declared dead at the scene.

'What happened here?' Mike asked one of the uniformed officers who'd been first on the scene.

'A bloody fuck-up,' the man said. 'We don't know for sure. Jenkins, the man who died, he was coming out of the back door when he was attacked. Bowen must have hit him about a half-dozen times. Moran, he's likely to lose an eye, but he's lucky to be alive. And he's still conscious, sir, just. Claims he got a good look at our man.'

Mike glanced towards the ambulance. It was about to depart and he had no wish to delay it. 'You've someone going with him?'

'Yes, sir, and there's an ARV unit been actioned. If Bowen knows there's a witness, he might have a second go.'

Mike nodded, wondering what the hospital would make of an armed response unit in its emergency room. He was surprised that the man had been allowed to live. Did Jake think he was more seriously injured than he was, or had he been in too much of a hurry to finish the job?

He walked round to the back of the house. The body still lay on the floor, waiting for the duty surgeon and the pathologist to arrive. Some officers stood beside the fallen man, while others were still putting up a cordon, separating the house and gardens from the fields beyond. Light from the kitchen showed the way the lock had been forced, giving Jake access to those inside. It was, as the uniformed man had said, an almighty cock-up, Mike thought.

Peterson had arrived by the time Mike returned to the front of the house. He was talking to the uniformed police.

His face was grave as he came over to Mike. 'We're going to look even bigger bloody fools,' he said. 'And we've a dead officer into the bargain.'

'They should have been armed,' Mike said. 'It was madness to think Jake would pass this one by. I want protection for Charlie at least until the *Crimewatch* thing is over. And for Maria too, now she's no longer with her sister.'

Peterson nodded. 'Lot of good it did here,' he said.

CHAPTER TWENTY-TWO

Mike did not want Maria to hear about Alastair on the morning news, so he called her himself when he returned to Honiton at seven that morning. She was shocked, devastated. Mike had not realized that, emotionally, she had so much riding on being able to talk to Alastair Bowen; so much hope that he might lead them to Essie.

'I'm coming down to you,' Maria told him abruptly. 'I can't stand it, just sitting here, trying to work when there's nothing I can do to help.'

'Stay there, Maria. It's too dangerous here, you must see that.'

'Nowhere's safe, Mike, and no one, not until he's put away. Wherever I am he could come for me.'

'We'll arrange protection for you.'

'And much good that will do. Look, Mike, I won't be argued with.'

She hung up then and when Mike tried to call her back she'd switched to the answerphone.

Sighing, he put the receiver down, not bothering to leave a message she'd refuse to hear.

* * *

'Why don't you put an ad in some of the nationals?' Liz asked Charlie, 'or in the *Dorchester Herald*. We know he reads that. He knew all about Macey.'

They'd been listening to Charlie telling them about the message he'd left on the news groups. So far, there'd been no response from Jake Bowen.

'It's an idea,' Charlie agreed, 'though there's no guarantee he reads the small ads.'

Macey nodded thoughtfully. He'd come here to get Charlie's reaction to Alastair's kidnapping and to talk about the *Crimewatch* programme. Charlie's responses would make it into the late edition.

'How about the Lonely Hearts column?' Liz asked.

'Maybe,' Charlie agreed thoughtfully. Jake had been known to pick up potential models that way. 'I could give it a go, what is there to lose?'

Macey laughed harshly. 'Mark my words, advert or no advert, all you have to do is wait for long enough and Jakey boy will come to you.'

Liz ignored Macey's almost gleeful attitude. 'It should go in as a small display ad,' she said. 'We do them in bold type surrounded by little black hearts or flowers. Really makes them stand out.'

'Did it work for you, then?' Macey asked her. 'Or are you still looking, darling?'

Liz paid him no attention. 'What do you think?' she asked Charlie.

'That it's a good idea.' He pulled a pad and paper towards him. 'How many words can I have?'

'Best keep it short. I think you can have up to thirty words, but make it snappy.'

Charlie was deep in thought, doodling on the comer of the pad. 'It's got to be something he would know at once,' he said. 'What do people usually put in these things?'

'Oh, things in common, the sort of person you're looking for, that kind of thing.'

Charlie thought about it. 'Vincenza's place,' he said. Referring to the house where Jake had stored some of his more spectacular work. It was where Charlie had received his injuries, Jake having booby-trapped the safe he'd used for storage.

This was something Jake could hardly miss.

Charlie scribbled a sentence on the paper, amended it, scribbled again, then read out the result.

'J,' he said. 'Remember Vincent's place? We should meet again. Regards, Charlie.'

* * *

Jake watched his father wander through the basement rooms. He'd left the doors wide open and the camera running so that he could observe the old man passing from room to room on the CCTV screens, study his reaction to the different settings Jake used as backdrops for some of his more unusual films.

Alastair sat down briefly on the single bed in a room full of bondage equipment and decorated by a full-length mirror that covered most of one wall. Jake saw him studying himself in the mirror, a look of pain in his eyes and confusion, as though he wondered how he had found himself in such a place.

Then his father went back into the largest of the basement rooms. Essie lay on her pile of towels in one corner, sleeping restlessly. She'd had a fever this last day or two and Jake knew, as he watched his father go to her and touch her face with his fingertips, how dry and hot the skin would feel. He could sense it as though he felt it with his own hands.

She was quite seriously unwell. No real food, probably not enough fluids and the effects of such long periods of sedation had taken their toll.

Jake left his room with its bank of television screens and, with a sawn-off shotgun resting easily across his arm, went down to the basement, checking his father's position through a peephole in the door before going through.

'She's sick,' Alastair said as Jake entered.

'I know.'

'Why take the child, Jake? What do you plan to do with her?'

Jake sat down on the basement steps and pondered the question as though he'd given it no previous thought. 'I've not decided yet,' he said. 'I thought I'd leave that up to you.'

Alastair winced. 'What have I to do with it? I don't even know this child.'

'You need to know a child to care for her?' Jake asked. He sounded surprised. 'What do you think to my workplace, Alastair?'

'Your workplace. This is where you make that filth.'

'Some of it. The rest I make on location.' Jake smiled. 'Some real stars have lived here for a time. Julia Norman, for instance. Beautiful girl, and so versatile.'

'And does anyone survive this place?' Alastair asked him. He was looking at the child, but, Jake guessed, thinking of himself.

'Not so far,' Jake admitted.

'And you plan to kill me too?'

Jake nodded slowly. 'I expect so,' he said. 'But not today. At least, not so long as you behave. They're doing a real Jake Bowen *This is Your Life* show on the television later on tonight, I thought you might like to watch it with me.'

Alastair shuddered, suddenly cold. 'And the child?' he asked again.

'Oh, she can watch too,' Jake said.

CHAPTER TWENTY-THREE

Late Tuesday evening Jake brought Alastair upstairs. He kept him covered with the shotgun and guided him into the living room, where the television was already on.

'Sit there,' he told him, directing Alastair to an old-fashioned dining carver, with wooden arms and a high back. He kept the gun pressed against Alastair's throat while he secured his hands to the chair with plastic cable-ties and his ankles to the front legs with tape. 'Behave yourself,' Jake told him, 'and I'll free one hand later to let you have a beer while we watch the programme.'

Alastair struggled against his bonds when Jake left the room, but it was of little use. The heavy plastic of the ties bit into his wrists and his efforts to move threatened only to overturn the chair. When Jake returned only moments later with Essie in his arms, Alastair had already given up. In his mind he had begun to prepare himself to die and he was amazed at how little it mattered any more.

Jake had put fresh towels on the sofa and he lay Essie down, propping her head with cushions. He'd given her no more of the sedative since midday and she was semiconscious, restless and confused. She had started crying for her mother in the brief moments of lucidity that came and went, and watching them both on camera, Jake knew that her whimpering had begun to irritate Alastair.

'Quite a little family,' Jake commented, glancing at his father, He leaned over the child and whispered to her with a show of tenderness and deep concern, 'Be quiet, Essie baby. The film about your Uncle Jake's about to start and Uncle Mike might well be in it too.' He straightened up and turned back to his father. 'Now, about that beer.'

True to his word, he freed one of Alastair's hands, opened a can for him and let him hold it. He'd made popcorn too. Alastair watched as he gave a small piece to Essie, placing it in her mouth, but she couldn't chew, didn't even seem to realize that it was there. He shook his head as Jake waved the bowl in his direction, a chill running through him at the sight of his son's slight smile.

'Well, all the more for me then,' Jake said.

They sat together in the comfortable room, the large blue sofa piled high with cushions, the lights softly shaded and the curtains closed against the threat of a summer storm announced by a rising wind. Jake smiled and relaxed as his life story unfolded on the flickering screen. Alastair watched his son, unable to take his eyes from Jake's calm face.

On screen, the presenter said, 'We pick up the story of Jake Bowen when he was just fifteen years old and well known in his local community for a film of quite another kind.'

Jake had talked about himself as the next John Pilger, Alastair remembered, told local journalists that he had high hopes of a career as a documentary filmmaker, righting wrongs and telling the world the truth. He'd been convincing too, almost persuaded Alastair on occasions.

'Ah, that was a great year,' Jake commented. 'You know the funny thing? I thought for a brief time that was where I wanted to be. Front line, changing the world.'

'Was that why you made the other film? Raped that girl?'

Jake raised an eyebrow. 'Oh, so you *do* know about that. I was never sure. Max tell you, did he?'

Alastair said nothing.

'It was the power thing,' Jake volunteered. 'That was it with both those films. A power thing. Pretty heady stuff when you're just fifteen, not that you'd understand that.'

'Understand what? I understand that you abused the trust we all put in you. Abused that girl too, you and Max.'

'What trust?' Jake asked mildly. 'Now, be quiet, I want to hear what they have to say.'

They sat in silence as Jake drank his beer and watched the TV; the slow procession of his life. Alastair in turn watched his son. They made little mention of the early films, the ones that built his reputation in the industry. Jake had still been living with his parents then, and Alastair remembered the shock he had felt when he had realized what kind of films his son made. Jake had been proud of what he did, though, talked about it like an art form, always pushing the envelope of acceptability, always fighting for the best production values he could get with the equipment he could afford. Alastair knew it would annoy his son, though he gave no outward sign, when the presenter merely skipped through a brief commentary of Jake's early career in film, noting only that he first came to police attention after a raid on a sex shop in a Leeds back street. They missed out too on what Jake had described as his constant search for authenticity, mentioning only that he sometimes intercut his images with library footage and seemed to have an obsession with the links between sex and death.

Charlie Morrow described the day he had been injured in the blast that Bowen had prepared, his burns showing in every detail in the studio lights, every ridge and furrow that mapped his face, the way the dead skin pulled at the comer of his mouth and half closed one eye. Alastair watched as Jake leaned forward to get a closer look.

'Wonderful,' Jake whispered softly to himself. 'A wonderful effect.' He glanced across at Alastair. 'Do you know,' he asked him, 'just how much it would cost to produce something like that? You'd need a top effects artist to get it any other way.'

Alastair had no reply.

They moved on then to Jake's more recent crimes. The killing of a woman called Marion O'Donnel, whose body was found in a burning car. The murders of Caldwell and the others and finally the death of Julia Norman only two weeks before.

Jake sat forward, watching intently as Peterson talked about the latest outrage.

'This young woman was a gifted artist with a stunning future ahead of her. The death of a young person is always tragic, but this, this needless, wasteful death, seems to me especially sad. As if this is not difficult enough to deal with, we have reason to believe that Jake Bowen is implicated in the kidnapping of a young child, Essie Holmes, snatched from outside her school.'

'You take a good picture,' Jake remarked to the child as an image of Essie dressed in her school clothes filled the screen. He listened with the most rapt attention as they talked of witness statements and repeated the appeal made earlier by Essie's grandmother and Maria. They finished the account with an excerpt from the video of Julia, with Jake's voice enhanced and the sound cleaned up, giving instruction about how to move, how to pose, what to do to turn the punters on, and finishing with Jake's laughter as the girl told him some silly joke that even the enhanced tape couldn't catch.

Alastair heard the laughter and felt despair. 'Let the child go. She's no earthly use to you.'

Jake frowned. 'No imagination if you think that,' he said.

'The child will die, Jake. Let her go, or finish this whole thing now.'

Jake looked at his father in mild surprise. 'You'd like me to kill you both now?' he asked. 'Didn't think you were so ready for it, Alastair.'

The programme had reached the description of Alastair's abduction the night before. Jake laughed when he heard about the officer killed in the 'vicious attack', his laughter louder and less restrained at the mention of the bravery of the other officer, who, despite his wounds, had managed to call for help.

'We came very close to Jake Bowen last night,' Peterson was saying, 'and we know he's getting overconfident, that he will get careless. We would appeal to him to give himself up. We accept that he probably needs help as much as he deserves blame, and he has nothing to fear in coming forward. Someone somewhere knows who Jake Bowen is and where he is. They must know that they're protecting a killer or at least suspect that something is amiss. Someone has suspicions — has doubts about a loved one or worries that a neighbour might not be all he seems.'

Jake was shouting quite uproariously now. 'Do you have doubts about a loved one, Father, or suspect I might be something not quite pleasant? Oh, come on, Alastair, you must see the joke.'

Alastair just stared at him. 'Why do this, Jake? Why cause all this suffering?'

Jake shook his head, bringing his laughter slowly under control.

'You don't get it, do you?' he said. 'You really don't.' He gestured with his beer in Essie's direction. 'You see it never was a question of *why,* Alastair. It was just a question of, well, *why not?'*

CHAPTER TWENTY-FOUR

3 July

Wednesday morning at five o'clock Mike arrived back at Honiton. They had been manning the phones for most of the night, taking calls, finally closing the lines at three in the morning.

Driving back on empty roads, watching the sun come up, Mike was filled with a sense of unreality. The TV studio and Jake Bowen seemed to belong to another world. He wanted nothing more than to grab a few hours' sleep and forget everything for a while.

He was surprised to see Maria's car parked outside the pub where he was staying. He'd tried several times the day before to speak to her again, only getting the answerphone. When she hadn't appeared that afternoon or early evening, he had assumed that she had changed her mind and was just giving them both time to cool down.

Maria was asleep in the front of the car, the seat reclining as far as it would go and an old travel rug thrown over her legs. He tapped gently on the window. She woke and smiled, then opened the door and slipped into his arms.

Mike forgot he was supposed to be angry. 'God, I've missed you,' he said. 'When did you arrive?'

'Late last night. Well, early this morning really. The hotel was all shut up so I slept here.'

Mike had a pass key for the front door. He let them both in and took Maria up to his room.

'It's not a massive bed,' he told her.

She smiled. 'I'm sure we can manage. Anyway, I think we're both so tired we could sleep anywhere just now.'

'Sleep?' he questioned. 'I haven't seen you in so long.'

'If you're serious about that in half an hour, let me know. That's if you're still awake.'

He sat on the side of the bed and watched her undress, too tired even to remove his shoes. He finally shed his clothes and lay beside her, too much aware that he needed a shower and that he couldn't remember the last time he had shaved. Her body felt so wonderful curved against his own and the rhythm of her breathing so soothing as she drifted into sleep. Half an hour later, Mike was not awake to tell her anything at all.

* * *

Jake had locked both Alastair and Essie in one of the smaller rooms so that when he brought their breakfast down he could carry the tray without having to trouble with the gun.

He went to the top of the basement stairs to retrieve it before letting Alastair back into the outer room, locking the main door and slipping the key into his pocket.

Urging Alastair into the outer room at gunpoint, Jake returned to the smaller room to check on Essie, aware that his father still hovered near the door, watching him.

As Jake bent over the child, Alastair made his move. He had in his hands one of the leather straps taken from the bondage room and leapt at Jake as he knelt beside Essie's makeshift bed, the strap between his hands as though he planned to strangle Jake from behind.

Jake was ready for him, rising to his feet and striking backwards with the stock of the gun, hitting Alastair hard enough on the temple to send him, dazed and reeling, across the room.

'Just what did you plan to do?' he asked him. 'Strangle me? Do you even know how, Daddy dearest? And were you planning on taking the child with you? Or did you just think about your own skin? You'll have to try a damned sight harder than that, Alastair. A bloody sight harder.'

He left his father lying there and returned upstairs to watch them from his viewing room. Jake felt pleasantly surprised at his father's actions. He hadn't really thought the old man had it in him to try and fight.

* * *

Max Harriman had already heard the news about Alastair's kidnapping when Mike arrived to see him. Max was excited, unable to sit still. The one thing on his mind was how much they'd need him now the competition had been removed.

'He'll kill him, you know,' Max told Mike gleefully. 'Jake hates his father. Really, really loathes that man.'

'Why?' Mike asked him. 'What did Alastair do to make Jake hate him so much, and why wait all this time? He could have got rid of Alastair long ago.'

Max stopped his pacing and stood still, shaking his head. 'I told you, Jake hates his father. The way Alastair treated him all his life. He robbed him of his childhood, you know. Beat him, denied him all trace of affection. He was never a father to him. Never.'

'No, I don't buy that, Max. When I brought Alastair here you were talking about what must have been good times. When Alastair took you to the fair, those times you all shared together.'

He leaned forward across the table. 'I need you, Max,' he said, sensing that flattery was going to get him further just now than any other means. 'Explain it to me, what went on between the pair of them that grew so much hate?'

Max hesitated for a moment, then sat down facing Mike.

'It isn't easy to explain,' he said. 'I mean, both parts of it were true. They were locked into this . . . this circle, like they were playing games with one another. One minute Alastair would be all over Jake, spoiling him, buying him new toys, taking him out. Then you'd look round and he'd have got mad with Jake about something and he'd be beating seven shades out of his backside. Or throwing all the stuff he'd bought him on the bonfire. Jake said to me once he had to learn fast not to cry out when his dad hit him. I could never understand that, because if he didn't yell, Alastair would hit him even harder. If it'd been me, I'd have yelled the place down and begged for mercy on the first hit.'

'But Jake saw it as a challenge?'

'Must have done. He saw it as a kind of test, I suppose. Like, how much stronger than his dad could he be? It was like I said, they were locked into this kind of game. Jake never played with any of the stuff his dad bought. He said he never knew how long he'd have it, so what was the point? What his mam bought, though, that was different. One Christmas, we both had an Action Man. We used to take them up to the old allotments at the back of the school and have mock battles and stuff.'

'And Jake's mother bought that for him?'

Max nodded.

'And did Alastair never try to destroy those toys, the ones his mother had bought for him?'

Max laughed. 'You've got to be joking, Inspector Croft. The woman had forearms the size of hams and a left hook like you'd see from Mike Tyson. Alastair wouldn't dare to cross that woman.'

This was a new element. Was it true? Mike asked himself. 'And yet,' he said, 'she stood by and let her husband beat Jake? Beat him so badly that at one time it almost got to court?'

'Oh, you heard about that, did you? That was a laugh and a half.'

'I don't understand.'

Max sighed patiently. 'Jake thought it was a big joke,' he said. 'He was, what, thirteen, fourteen, and already he could have the average female doing back-flips. That woman, she would have done anything for Jake. It was such a joke, when he said he'd been stringing her along all the time. There was a right stink. He'd had the police involved and all sorts. Alastair ranting and demanding an apology, and this woman, her career was fucked up before she'd even begun.'

'But it was the truth, wasn't it, Max? Alastair was guilty of cruelty.'

Max shrugged. 'That's not the point, Inspector he would never have seen his dad go down for it.'

'Why not?' Mike pressed him. 'What linked those two? They hated each other and yet Alastair constantly protected his son and Jake seems to have done the same. And I don't understand what Jake's mother did about it all. She allowed this to go on and yet I get the impression that Jake loved her and that Alastair did too. And you say that they were afraid of her?'

Max Harriman was silent for a while, as though thinking it over. 'They were scared of her,' he said at last. 'Alastair knew what Jake was, what he did. But she wouldn't have it.'

'But she backed the idea that Jake get counselling.'

'Why not? She blamed Alastair, she blamed the school, she blamed everyone bar Jake when she thought he was going off the rails, playing truant and that. I don't know what it was, Inspector Croft. Maybe, well, she'd lost two or three babies before Jake came along. It must have been hard to accept that your kid was a problem child.'

Max grinned. 'There wasn't a thing that frightened Jake. Nothing he couldn't or wouldn't do, even from being a kid.

He always said that the biggest kick you could get out of life was doing all the things that people were afraid of doing and watching their faces while you did them. That was power to Jake. He used to say that you had to teach yourself not to be afraid. That anyone could do it, it just meant challenging yourself a little bit more each time until one day you realized you weren't scared of anything any more. You could do whatever you wanted. He said people were always asking themselves "Why?" whenever stuff went wrong. Jake always said they should be asking themselves why not.'

'But you said that he was afraid of his mother.'

Max nodded. 'But not later on. I think he respected her, kind of. She was tough, you see, as tough as Jake. She kept that family going by working all hours, more than Alastair ever did. He was in work, then out of it again. He was a lay preacher at the local church and that was what really mattered in his life.'

'But he left that, suddenly, and went to live in York.'

Max shrugged. 'Caught with his hand in the collection plate, wasn't he?'

'Alastair?'

'Yes, Alastair. Oh, it wasn't the first time, but this time he couldn't cover it up. He had a drink problem, and every now and then he fell off the wagon. This was one time.'

Mike absorbed that slowly. 'And was that why he beat Jake, when he was drunk?'

'No, no. You take things so literally. Look, the only one Alastair hurt when he was blitzed was himself. He'd fall over things, run into things, whatever. Someone would find him in the street and take him home. Anyone got knocked about then, it was Alastair. She'd lay into him with whatever came handy.' Max laughed, the memory obviously amusing him.

Mike tried to take all of this on board. 'I still don't understand,' he said. 'Why did Jake's mother allow the physical abuse to go on?'

'She didn't know about a lot of it,' he said, shrugging. 'Anyway, she wasn't one to spare the rod and spoil the child herself. When Jake cheeked her she'd backhand him and not think twice.'

'But is that the same thing? What we're talking about with Alastair is a systematic pattern of abuse.'

Max sighed and stared down at his hands, laying them flat upon the table. 'Alastair thought he was doing right,' he said. 'Thought Jake had the devil in him, and maybe he was right. Jake could outfox the devil, if you ask me. And his mam, well, I don't know. Maybe she didn't know the half of it. Maybe she thought it was up to his dad to punish him. And she always knew how sorry he'd be afterwards. Alastair would always be so terribly sorry. He'd go out and work all the overtime he could, bring in more money than usual, spend time doing stuff around the house. I don't know, maybe it was just the way things were.'

Mike looked thoughtfully at Max, uncertain of how much he really understood about Jake's family and how much truth there was in what Max said. So much seemed contradictory. He wondered how much further he could push things that day.

'Did Jake kill your mother?' he asked.

Max blinked in surprise. 'He didn't need to,' he said cryptically, 'she was already dead. All Jake did was stop the breathing.'

* * *

Maria should probably not have been in the incident room, Peterson thought, but she was a difficult lady to keep out of anything, and anyway he had no inclination to try.

'We've got a team of forensic psychologists and behavioural experts working on this, but if you ask me they can't agree on a damn thing.'

Maria grinned. 'That's the problem with shrinks,' she said. 'Have you heard the light-bulb joke?'

Peterson shook his head.

'How many shrinks does it take to change a light bulb?'

'I couldn't tell you.'

'One to change the light bulb, at least two to counsel the light bulb on the experience of coming out and half a dozen students to write up the research papers.'

Peterson laughed. 'You missed out the pop psychologist to write the coffee-table book,' he said, 'and a couple of tabloids to plaster it all over the front page.'

'And someone to propose the conspiracy theory,' Maria added. 'You said I could see those pictures?' Peterson had the file in his hand. He laid on the table the photographs that had been sent to his daughter.

'She's still in shock,' he said. 'Won't let the kids out of her sight, though I can't say I blame her. I don't mind admitting, Maria, this has about finished me with the force. I got shifted into this, so they said, because of my experience. Head the investigations, they said, and I've got to admit that at first it was good to be hands-on again. Superintendents are desk jockeys these days. Glorified bloody administrators, hassling the troops into getting an optimum clear-up rate or whatever the current jargon is. But I have to tell you, I'd as soon be back behind my desk again. I sometimes wonder if I'm losing it.'

Maria shook her head. 'You know you're not,' she said. 'You're just under incredible stress . . . we all are.'

Maria looked more closely at the images Peterson had spread upon the table, the young children playing in the garden, with the mocking injuries marked upon their bodies. She fought hard to hold on to her professional calm.

'He's subtle,' she said quietly. 'And he knows exactly how much all this is going to hurt.'

The phone on Peterson's desk began to ring. He picked up the receiver, listened for several minutes, then scribbled something on the notepad on his desk.

'That was Mike,' he said, looking excited, animated. 'Max came through with something, a London address. He claims that Jake rented a flat and uses it as a letter drop.'

CHAPTER TWENTY-FIVE

It was a beautiful evening after a perfect summer day. Jake stood on the clifftop looking out to sea, watching a lone cormorant skimming the waves, its prehistoric shape black against the grey-blue waters.

Alastair stood a few feet away, his hands unbound, the short-barrelled shotgun Jake held cradled across his body enough to keep him from running.

'I love this place,' Jake told him. 'It took me nearly two years to find it and another two to restore, but it's been worth every penny.'

Alastair turned his head slightly to regard his son. 'It's pleasant enough,' he said, 'but I wouldn't like to be this close to the cliff edge. Another year or two and this whole thing could be washed away.'

'I doubt that,' Jake said. 'This place will see us both dead and gone.'

Alastair said nothing but followed Jake's gaze, looking far out to the horizon. It seemed such a barren, lonely vista. Would anyone hear him if he called out? Or was everything as empty as this damned view of open ocean?

'What are you going to do with me?' he asked.

'Talk to you, for a while anyway. There are things I want to know, Alastair. This seems like it could be a good time.'

'As good as any,' Alastair said slowly. 'What is it I can tell you?'

Jake glanced at him. 'Did you ever love me?' he asked.

'Love you? Of course I did, you were my son.'

'Is that an answer? I don't think so.'

'It's the only one I can give. I did my best for you, Jake. Gave you all I could.'

'You gave me all you could,' Jake repeated thoughtfully. 'And what was that, Alastair? You gave me your hatred and a taste of the belt at least once a week just in case I'd done something you didn't catch me at. You told me I was bad even when I tried to do my best to be good. You made your own story up in your head and, by God, you lived by it, and I never understood why you hated me so much. What it was that I had done to you that forced you to write me off practically before I was born and never, ever revise that view whatever I said. Whatever I did. I want to know it, Alastair, what it was that made you feel that way?'

Alastair shifted restlessly under his son's relentless gaze. Jake's voice was calm, as though he'd asked about the weather or some odd item of the news. Alastair wanted to deny his words, to tell him that he'd misunderstood, but he could not bring himself to lie.

'Even when you were a little child,' he said, 'you had that way with you, of doing things or saying things that only caused us pain. You were always evil, Jake, killing and maiming and telling lies. Creating hurt and pain where there'd been none before. I had to hurt you, Jake, show you what the pain meant. That you couldn't go on with your vile games and your lies and your . . . your deceits.'

'Ah, but they weren't deceits, were they, father? Not all of them, not in the beginning, and I know where all of this began, Alastair. Thinking about it, I really do, and it's so simple that it's almost laughable. That day I caught you with that woman in my mother's room. You on top of her, pounding away, with your white arse showing and your trousers down around your ankles. You'd not even taken time to get undressed before you started poking her. And she was squealing like some stuck pig. That's when it all began between us, your resentment of me. And all your lies about me won't change any of that.'

'It wasn't like that,' Alastair began to protest. 'You were far too young to understand. After you were born, I never went near your mother again. She wouldn't have me even touch her, scared she'd get pregnant again and lose another one. Or maybe have another like you, I don't know.'

'You're right, I wasn't old enough to understand,' Jake said, 'but you decided I was old enough to take your belt to. I was beaten raw, and all the time you were lying and screaming what an evil little bastard I'd turned out to be, and I can remember the pain of it. And the worst pain of all was not knowing what I was being punished for.'

'I was desperate,' Alastair protested. 'I loved your mother and I knew she'd never forgive me.'

'Not again, you mean. Not after all the other women.'

'I know that I was wrong,' Alastair said slowly, spacing out his words as though to give them weight. 'And I regret all that, Jake, I really do. But you were never easy . . .'

'And when she came home and the neighbours told her what you'd been about. The lies you told her, about me killing her blasted cat. And you hitting it with that broken line prop until you broke its bloody back. I watched you bury it, and I heard her crying because she thought I was turning out like you and couldn't bear the thought of that. And you know what, Alastair? I could still taste the blood in my mouth where I'd bitten my tongue when you'd knocked me down. You'd given me a real gift that day, you'd taught me that you were weak and stupid and helpless and that I didn't have to be like you.'

Alastair stared out towards the darkening horizon, his jaw clenched and his body tight and rigid.

'I didn't make you the way you are,' he said. 'Nothing I did or didn't do taught you to be what you became, Jake, and you know that. If I lied about the details, I didn't lie about the rest. You were evil as a child, even more evil as an adult, and you had more scope to play your games. I never had a part in that.'

'You created me,' Jake told him mildly. 'Sowed the seed in my mother's belly. I'm sad for you that you didn't like the results.'

He turned his face away from his father, gazing once more out to sea. 'No, but you're right, of course. You had nothing to do with what I became. You wouldn't have begun to know how to do that. You never had that much about you, anything like the skill or the imagination to create someone like me.' He paused reflectively. 'It's sad, don't you think, that a father should despise his son so much or a son so hate the father?'

'If you hated me so much,' Alastair questioned harshly, 'why didn't you finish me off? Get rid of me earlier?'

'Why should I waste my time? It was much more fun to know that you were waiting, every day of your life, you were waiting for me to come back and you were living your life in fear. I enjoyed that, Alastair. Enjoyed that so much.' He sighed, as though suddenly weary of the game. 'Move closer to the edge, Alastair, and then look down. Go on.'

Reluctantly, the older man moved forward.

When Jake spoke to him, his voice was soft. 'Have you ever thought what it would be like to go on walking? To look down at that rush of white water scouring away at the cliff and just become a part of it all. To let go and leave all of this behind. Look down. Spread your arms and fall into the wind. Ask yourself just what it is you have to lose, what you have left. It's all finished for you, Alastair, this life. Why not let it go?'

Jake had moved closer to him, picking up from the grass the palm-sized digital camera he had left lying there. He lifted it to his eye, gun in one hand and the camera in the other, watching his father's face.

'It would be so easy,' Jake told him gently. 'You could make your peace with the world and then just let it all go.'

Alastair stood at the very edge of the cliff, his eyes fixed on the boiling rush of water foaming on the rocks, then he jerked around to face Jake.

'I won't do it!' he shouted at his son. 'If you want me dead, you'll have to be the one to kill me.'

Jake fired then, hitting Alastair with both barrels full in the face, then trained the camera on his father's body as it spiralled down, arms stretched upon the wind, the splash tiny as it hit the sea.

CHAPTER TWENTY-SIX

Honiton had become the focus for something of a media circus following the *Crimewatch* programme, although with the coming of evening things had quietened down a little, journalists and photographers wandering off to pick up some local colour in the pubs.

Mike, Peterson and Maria had driven a dozen miles to find a quiet place to eat. They'd found a little restaurant in Lyme Regis, the relative anonymity of the seaside town promising them the chance of a quieter evening.

The raid had taken place on Jake's London flat and they were still waiting for reports to come in. A quantity of letters and what appeared to be house agents' details had been found, some of them going back four or five years. Mike had arranged for everything to be faxed through to him in Honiton, together with the first of the witness statements from neighbours. It would take time to arrive and everyone needed a break, so Peterson had suggested they all go and eat.

It had not been an easy day, Maria thought. She'd stayed inside avoiding the media crush, wanting to be useful yet so much aware that she had no real business being there. She'd prowled around the incident room, making tea, washing mugs and emptying bins, anything to keep busy, until Peterson had taken pity on her and given her the psychological reports to read.

'The problem is,' she said, picking up on an earlier conversation, 'there's so much pressure now to get it right. The public expect that anyone with half a degree in any of the mind sciences can get inside the killer's head and anticipate exactly what he's going to do.'

'There've been some spectacular successes,' Mike argued. 'The Jamie Bulger case, for instance, and early stuff on that London rapist working the railway stations.'

'John Duffy,' Peterson provided. 'That was a first. Then the floodgates opened.'

'And the level of expectation sky-rocketed.'

Maria paused as the waitress arrived, aware of the look the woman gave her and wondering if she'd been recognized. She carried on.

'The problem is the notion that you can be right all the time, and with Jake Bowen that's not easy. The man is ordered and intelligent. He doesn't seem to act from fear or impulse, he plans. And my guess is he's read all the same books we have.'

'Would you class him as a psychopath?' Peterson asked her. 'There seems to be some debate even about that.'

Maria prodded at the food on her plate. She was hungry but found it hard to eat, guilty about even that simple act of normality. 'It's a more complex question than you might think,' she said. 'For what it's worth, I don't believe I would. Neither do I think Jake Bowen is insane. My guess, and that's all it is, is that Jake knows exactly what he's doing and exactly what effect it's going to have. That he's even capable of becoming emotionally involved with those he hurts and kills. I think Jake Bowen understands what we would call right and wrong, can even empathize with it. I just don't think he cares.' She lay her fork down and poured water with a hand that trembled only slightly. 'That's what scares me so much.'

* * *

Macey had been out all day and Charlie only reached him at his home number late that evening.

'There's been no joy,' Charlie said. 'No replies to the ad as yet. I've been sitting by the phone, staring at it like a lovesick teenager. Anything your end?'

'Little things here and there, nothing conclusive. Your friend Peterson's had road-blocks all over the place, disrupting the holiday traffic, and the national press and TV've been out in force. It's been all right from my point of view. They've all been so bloody bored, I've been the most interesting thing around today. If I'd taken up all the offers of drink I'd had I'd have been comatose by now.'

Charlie laughed. 'So it's the move to London next, is it?'

'Living in hope, Charlie. Look, how long do you want this ad to run? Some bright spark on the force is going to see it and then the shit's really going to hit the fan. Depends whether you're bothered about that, of course?'

'Give it another day,' Charlie said. 'If he makes contact we're going to have to bring Mike in on it anyway, but if it comes to nothing I'd as soon not have him, well . . . bothered. We'll cross that bridge if and when we have to.'

'I can just see the headline, Charlie, "Injured Cop and Maverick Reporter Snare Woodland Killer". You know, it's a funny thing, but no one's come up with a tag for this one. He's not the something ripper or the what's-it strangler or the wherever poisoner.'

'Problem is, Macey, there's too much variety in what he does and he's too mobile. You know how folk like to pigeon-hole. Jake's problem is he wants everything.'

'Yeah, right. But he ought to have a tag line.'

'If he phones I'll recommend he gets a publicist,' Charlie promised.

He put the phone down and stared at it, willing it to ring. For all his attempt at humour, Charlie was finding this harder and harder to cope with. He knew that everyone involved in the Bowen investigation must feel the same. It was the not knowing, the feeling that Jake could be anywhere, that made it so hard to be rational. Charlie Morrow was no coward, but he wondered what he was going to do if Jake really did make that call.

* * *

When they arrived back at Honiton a pile of faxes awaited them. Half a dozen officers sat at their desks, working the late shift, still sifting through the phone calls that had come in the night before. *Crimewatch* had generated over 700 calls and a list of 270 names. Most would turn out to be entirely innocent; a few would be vindictive. Three or four names had come up more than once, and that might or might not be promising. All needed feeding into the database and cross-referencing with what information they'd already got.

Maria had gone in with them, her presence accepted but not mentioned. She had the feeling that as long as she kept her mouth shut, so would everyone else, and when Mike picked up a stack of papers from the newly faxed pile, so did she.

'What am I looking for?' she said.

Peterson raised an eyebrow. 'Try and establish some kind of order,' he said at last. 'Sort the documents by type and then by date. Then we'll list them, see if we can establish a pattern and if it fits with what else we've got.'

Mike was reading another fax. 'They talked to the cleaning lady,' he said. 'They got lucky, she lives only a few doors away. It's one of those converted houses,' he explained, 'and the other tenants knew who she was.'

'Was she helpful?' Peterson asked.

'Well, it sheds some light in one way but complicates it in others. She met the tenant only once, but apparently there are a number of people who stay there on an irregular basis. She thinks they're actors of some kind, which fits with what we know, but she said she didn't ask too many questions.'

'How does she get paid?' Maria asked.

'By post, once a month, in cash. It arrives on the twenty-eighth of every month in a padded envelope. When there are people staying there, she doesn't have to clean, but she gets paid the same anyway. If she has to do extra cleaning when they've gone, she gets paid an extra three hours, so obviously Jake must know who's in residence and approximately when.'

'It also means that quite a few people have keys, presumably.'

'Apparently.' Mike referred back to the fax. 'There are regulars who don't stay there but just pick up their mail. She's got instructions to leave the mail on the table in the hall until the Sunday. Any uncollected mail gets put in the sideboard cupboard in the living room. She thinks someone goes through it from time to time, and presumably those using it as a mail drop know where to look for stray letters.'

'The rest just gets left there,' Peterson commented, looking at the pile of faxes on the table. 'How long has she been doing the cleaning?'

Mike scanned the fax again. 'Three years, I think. Yes, that's right. She was recommended by the previous woman, a Mrs Lee, who's moved to Bangor apparently. They were neighbours. That was the only time she met the real tenant. The flat's rented under the name of Matthews. They're trying to find the landlord now, see how Jake pays his rent.'

'My guess is cash in a padded envelope,' Maria said. 'I don't suppose the landlord cares as long as Jake pays his rent and doesn't wreck the place.'

'They must have a way of contacting Bowen,' Peterson said. 'I mean, when the cleaning lady left, how did she let him know?'

Mike put the fax back on the table and sat down. 'He calls once a month,' he said. 'Her home address, since there's no direct line to the flat, only a communal phone in the hall. Just checks that she's got the money, asks if anything's needed and that's it. Apparently he asked this Mrs Lee if she knew of anyone who could help and gave her a bonus for finding someone.'

'And no one got curious or suspicious, because they were well paid and not being asked to do anything illegal,'

Peterson concluded. 'Do we know when Jake's due to phone her again?'

'Last Tuesday,' Mike told him. 'We're a month adrift on that one. They're keeping a twenty-four-hour surveillance on the flat for the next few days, but the raid was hardly unobtrusive. I'd guess the most we can hope for is one of the regulars picking up their mail.'

'Could lead us somewhere. It's the best we've got so far.'

Maria was sorting through the lists of house agents' notes. Some were two or three pages long and had become separated during faxing, so she began putting them in order and stapling them back together, the simple task soothing, taking just enough of her concentration.

'He's looking for a place to restore, by the looks of these,' she said. 'Or at least, he was five years ago.' Peterson pulled the small stack of collated sheets towards him and skimmed through. 'Older properties, detached, and with large gardens.'

'Hmm, and all of them with outbuildings or basements or both,' Maria added. 'Only one problem.'

'What's that?'

'If these are the ones Jake left in London, then they're obviously the ones he didn't want.'

CHAPTER TWENTY-SEVEN

4 July

Thursday morning emerged out of a light drizzle that looked like nothing and soaked everything it touched. Jake had decided it was time to go back to work. The new samples he had ordered had come in and he was eager for a change of scene.

He felt an enormous sense of relief now that Alastair had left him. It was something he had waited a long time for and now that it had happened the euphoria was such that Jake wanted to share it.

The pity was that he had no one to tell. That was the good thing about film, knowing that it could be shared, that somewhere along the line there would be feedback from delighted fans.

The film of Alastair's demise was not enough on its own, but sooner or later Jake knew he'd find a way to work it into something special.

He liked driving in the rain. He enjoyed the sense of isolation, of separateness, being in the shelter of his car and watching the world around him disintegrate into millions upon millions of fragmented pieces. He liked the way the windscreen wipers, sweeping across the screen, restored his world for a merest instant before the rain shattered it once more. Deliberately, he set the wipers on single stroke rather than repeat, to make the most of the effect. It was a very visual, very Jake Bowen thing.

There was still the problem of what to do with Essie. Now Alastair had gone, he'd increased the sedation, hoping the dose was right, so she'd be certain not to wake before his return. The truth was, Jake had no real interest in the child.

He could film Essie — dead or alive or dying, she had financial potential — but was that what he really wanted to do? He guessed that everyone had written her off for dead by now; that they were hunting for a corpse and not a living child. Jake wondered if it would be more fun to let them know that Essie was still alive and then stand back and watch the response.

Whatever, he thought, he would have to take action soon, the child was definitely sick and he wasn't sure how much longer she would last.

* * *

Jake could not have anticipated Alastair's body being found so soon, but he had taken no account of the strong current that whipped around the headland and struck the foot of the cliffs, only to be turned back out to sea. The body, its shattered face battered by the ocean currents, fetched up on a stony beach only miles from where it had entered the water. Mike was sent to identify it.

'It isn't pretty,' the pathologist told him. 'I'll try and fit the post-mortem in some time today, but I can't promise anything.'

'Cause of death was gunshot wounds?' Mike asked.

'To that, a provisional yes,' the pathologist told him. 'Unless the shotgun was used to hide something else, of course. But whether or not he was dead at the precise moment he hit the water, well, I think that's pretty academic, don't you, considering half his face was blown away?'

Mike didn't feel qualified to comment. He had a sudden vision of Jake Bowen standing in a courtroom arguing it out with the prosecution, but he let it be.

'We've had dental records sent for,' he said. 'Will they be of any use?'

'Oh, yes. There are still plenty of teeth left. Most of the injury is to the upper portion of the head.'

They entered the small room at the side of the mortuary that was usually set aside for relatives identifying their dead.

'I put him in here,' the pathologist said. 'We're a bit full right now. Car crash last night on the M5. Maybe you heard about it?'

Mike nodded. 'Seven dead.'

'Yes, nasty. Anyway, here's your man.'

Mike had seen bodies pulled out of the water before, some of them so bloated and discoloured they looked scarcely human. Alastair had not been immersed that long, but the rocks and tide had done their own damage and the shotgun wounds had been further scraped and beaten by the tides, turning Alastair's face into a bloody pulp.

'I'd like to see his hands,' Mike said.

'Certainly. There's a ring still on the left, looks as if it's been there for a long time. A wedding band probably. They always get tight as we get older and the body gets, well, that little bit bigger.'

Mike looked closely at the dead man's hands and at the ring that he'd seen so many times, a broad band of light yellow gold.

'Until we've got the dental records nothing's positive,' he said, 'but I believe that this is Alastair Bowen.'

'Well, if I meet up with another six-foot middle-aged male I'll let you know,' the pathologist announced with satisfaction. 'Until then we'll assume this is your man. I'll get the reports to you as soon as I can.'

Mike phoned Peterson from the mobile in his car. 'I'm pretty certain,' he told him. 'Gunshot wounds to the face, but I'm in little doubt.'

'Right,' Peterson said quietly. 'Well, that's that then. Another one chalked up.'

'Anything on the house-hunting?'

'I've people doing the rounds, and we've contacted the other agencies. You remember, there were a couple from up north and others from further along the south coast, but it's going to be pure luck if we come up with anything. Agents vary in how long they keep their records, so we're pulling the property guides from the local papers for that period as well.'

'Sounds like a long shot.'

'The man's got to live somewhere, Mike.'

* * *

Jake had taken a break for lunch. He was sitting in a roadside cafe finishing his tea and reading the paper when he saw Charlie's advert in the Lonely Hearts section.

He read it twice, just to be sure, then a slow smile spread across his face. So, Charlie Morrow had a sense of humour.

He tried the number from the pay phone in the cafe, only to have Charlie's direct line intercepted by the reception switchboard.

'I'm sorry,' the woman told him, 'he's not in his room right now, he's having his physio.'

Jake declined to leave a message. He felt somewhat put out by the delay. A call to the *Dorchester Herald* came next. 'Sorry,' he was told, 'but it's too late to place an advert for tomorrow. We usually need at least two days.'

He put the receiver down, thinking quickly. Then called the *Herald* again and asked to be put through to Ed Macey.

Macey was not at his desk and it was Liz who took the call.

'Hello, Ed Macey's desk.'

'My but your voice has changed. Are you taking anything for it?'

Liz giggled. 'Macey's not here right now,' she said. 'He'll be about ten minutes. Can I get him to call you back?'

'No, thank you, love. I won't be here by then. I'm calling to leave a message for a man called Charlie Morrow. He's got a small ad in your Lonely Hearts.'

He felt the change in Liz's attitude even before he next heard her voice and was amused as she began to stall.

'A message, you say, for Charlie Morrow. OK. Right. If you'll tell me what it is, I'll pass it on. Of course, I will.'

Jake leaned back against the wall, looking out across the cafe. He heard a couple of clicks on the line and guessed Liz would now be recording the call. The slight echo when he next spoke made him wonder if she'd switched to speaker phone.

'I take it you're recording this for posterity. Well, that's all right. No doubt your experts will have a lot of fun pinpointing the accent and getting it all wrong.'

'I wouldn't know,' Liz told him. 'I mean, I don't know much about those things.'

'No? Well, never mind, give yourself another year or two and I'm sure you'll be the expert Macey is. Now listen close and tell this to Charlie Morrow. I'll meet him where Marion O'Donnel died. He'll know the place I mean. And tell him if he comes alone, I'll consider giving him the child.'

'When?' Liz asked him. 'I've got to tell him when.'

'It's a sacred place, love. He'll know what time.'

'No! Wait!' Liz shouted. 'Wait, don't hang up yet. Charlie can't drive. His hands—'

'Of course. I hadn't thought of that. Well, tell . . . Ah, yes, tell Maria Lucas that she has to drive him. She'll do that for the sake of the child, I'm sure.'

He paused, enjoying the panic in Liz's voice, but also the fact that her nerve had held enough to remind him about Charlie.

'We should get together some time,' he said. 'Have a little chat, maybe take in a film, or have dinner. My place maybe? Or should it be yours?'

* * *

Macey was mortified that he'd not been the one to take the call, but listening to the tape he had to admit that Liz had done well.

'You OK?' he asked her. She was smoking again, he noted. Probably not a good sign.

'Sure I am. Sure. I just got off the phone from talking to a murderer. He invited me to dinner. How the hell am I supposed to feel?'

'Make him take you somewhere special,' Macey advised, realizing even as he said it that he'd gone too far. He patted Liz's shoulder in his usual parody of comfort and dug a packet of cigarettes from the bottom of his drawer. 'Here, love, I'm sorry,' he said. 'And there aren't many people hear me say that in one lifetime.'

* * *

Charlie was as excited as Macey, but worried too.

'He won't keep the appointment,' he said. 'It's all just one big joke to him, seeing us running round in circles. I've got to get on to Mike. He'll never agree to Maria driving me.'

'Don't see he'll have much choice,' Macey said. 'She's a lady with a mind of her own and she'd do anything to get that little girl back. Charlie, what's this place he's talking about?'

'It's a place called West Kennet. Other side of Devizes.'

'And presumably he means midnight as the meeting time. Do we have to bring them in on this . . . Sorry, stupid question. OK, you get on to Peterson. But, Charlie, you cut me out of this and I'll never let you rest, you know that, don't you?'

CHAPTER TWENTY-EIGHT

It was something like a two-hour drive from Honiton to Devizes they had estimated and West Kennet was just a little further on. There was no village there, only a cottage, a gate leading to a path between ploughed fields and, at the top of a steep hill, the long barrow itself silhouetted against the skyline.

'I've not seen the place since last winter,' Charlie told Maria as they drove. 'It's a bleak spot at the best of times and I won't forget that night in a hurry. Tipping it down with rain, visibility a few feet and this red-hot shell of a burnt-out car that just wouldn't cool, no matter what Mother Nature chucked at it.'

'He won't be there, will he?' Maria said. 'And what he said about letting Essie go, that's not true either, is it?'

Charlie looked at her. She was staring straight ahead, trying to concentrate on the road, but her hands gripped the wheel so tightly he could see the bones of her knuckles through the skin.

'He knew what he was about when he said you had to drive, didn't he? I wish I didn't have to put you through this, love.'

'I know, Charlie. It's just we're none of us fooled by this, we know it's just another Jake Bowen line, and yet—'

'We can't afford not to go, just in case he plays it straight with us this time.'

Charlie shifted uncomfortably in his seat. He didn't find it easy to be anywhere for long. There was so much of him that rubbed and chafed where the new skin was growing or the scarring pulled at the surrounding skin. He took pills at night and hated doing it, but the few hours of oblivion were precious and it was the only way that he could sleep.

It had been chaos since Peterson had been told about Jake's call. He'd been furious with Macey and with Charlie himself, but his rant had been cut short by the need to act on the information. And Macey would have to wait for his exclusive.

'When we're done with this, you can write the bloody book,' Peterson had told the journalist. 'I'll give you rights to my frigging memoirs, but you've got to hold off on this one. If the public knows he's making fools of us yet again then all the cooperation we're beginning to get will come to nothing. And we'll still be no nearer finding that child.'

Macey had agreed to back off, albeit reluctantly. 'But anyone else gets so much as a whiff of this,' he promised, 'and I'll publish the whole damn thing, with or without your cooperation. You mark my words on that.'

Kennet was way outside Peterson's jurisdiction. Charlie had been a serving officer on the local force when he'd been injured and the help they had received had been unstinting. An ARV had been in place since before Maria had collected Charlie. There were officers in the cottage beside the gate that led to the barrow and still others at the monument itself. An unmarked car with a young couple in plain clothes sat in the lay-by fifty yards up the road and officers equipped with night sights were stationed at vantage points all around the area.

Peterson and his opposite number from Devizes had taken up position in the shadows of Silbury Hill, the giant earthworks that faced the West Kennet long barrow across the Devizes road.

Mike was following Maria's car with two armed officers.

It was a massive operation. Charlie wondered how much it was costing and what must be going through Jake's mind when he set it up. He wondered too what Maria was thinking just then, but he found he couldn't ask. Probably the same hopeless thoughts that were going through his own mind.

'We're almost there,' he commented as they reached the traffic island a little over a mile from their destination. The Wagon and Horses pub was in darkness and the unlit road curved ahead and out of sight. 'Just take it slow,' he said, 'or you'll miss the pull-in. It's not well marked.'

Maria dropped her speed. In the mirror she could see Mike's car a good way behind. He had orders to go past her when she parked up, then stop further along the road. She saw Silbury looming out of nowhere on the left, just before Charlie told her they'd arrived and pointed to the lay-by on the right-hand side.

'Well, now we're here,' she said, her voice unsteady for all that she tried to remain in control, 'what do we do?'

'It's ten to twelve,' Charlie said. 'We get out and walk to the place where Marion O'Donnel died and then we wait.' And when it's plain the bastard isn't here, he thought, I suppose we turn ourselves around and go back the way we came.

Miles away, Jake had the windows open and if he listened hard he could hear the sea. He'd been watching the late film, an old B-movie horror flick, the sort he'd grown up with and still loved, where the heroines scream so prettily and threaten to fall out of their clothes and evil can be destroyed by a cross and a sharp stick.

He sipped his beer and thought about Charlie Morrow and all his entourage waiting for him in the dark in the middle of nowhere.

'Next time, Charlie,' he whispered to himself, highly amused by his little escapade. Anyway, he thought, it wouldn't be so bad. At least this time the rain had stayed away.

CHAPTER TWENTY-NINE

5 July

It was eight o'clock on the Friday morning. Mike figured he'd had less than an hour's sleep, but somehow rest would not come. His mind was running in all directions, refusing to either make sense or be still. He felt more deeply depressed than he could ever remember, except perhaps when Stevie had died. Nothing had as yet quite matched that, but the way he felt now came very close.

Beside him Maria slept. She'd cried herself to sleep, having kept a hold on her emotions until they'd been alone. She had driven back with Peterson in stony silence, then finally broken down. It was a revelation to him. Maria never cried, was always in control, always the one to give comfort. It was the final confirmation of just how hopeless their situation seemed.

The only compensation he could find was gratitude, that she trusted him enough to let him see how utterly bereft she felt.

'I dreamed of calling Jo,' she'd told him, 'and telling her that Essie was safe and it was all over. I knew I was just kidding myself, Mike, but it was something to hang on to, you know.'

'You'll still get to do that,' he told her. 'It will be all right.'

And she'd been kind enough not to tell him to his face that he was a liar.

It was almost two weeks since Essie had disappeared from her school and they were no further on.

He must have dozed again despite himself, because the next time he looked at the clock it was almost nine. The bedroom window was open and sounds from the street filtered in: traffic noise and people's voices as they went about their day. He lay still, nagging at the random thoughts still plaguing him, then he turned over and woke Maria.

'We're going to talk to Max,' he told her. '*You're* going to talk to Max. We have to know where Jake bought his house.'

* * *

It was early afternoon by the time they got to the prison and Max was in flirtatious mood. Maria was a beautiful woman and Max liked attractive females, though he was fickle when it came to type. His last preference had been for blondes, but he was quite prepared to change his mind.

'Nice of you to brighten my day, Inspector Croft,' he said. 'But you'll excuse me if I ask what the lady sees in you. She could take her choice, if you ask me.'

Maria raised an eyebrow at Mike but she returned Max's smile. 'I suppose I don't always like the obvious,' she said.

'Nice answer, yes, nice answer. It's good to look at the unusual. Jake always said you should try and view the familiar from an unfamiliar angle. That way you learn to see things as they really are.'

'And does that work for you, Mr Harriman?'

'Oh, call me Max. It's not often that I get the choice. But to answer your question, yes, I find it works for me. People are so hidebound, don't you think?'

Maria nodded. 'Probably,' she said. 'Sometimes people have big ambitions, big ideas, but reality gets in the way of achieving them. I think, for most of us, our families and the need to earn a living end up taking priority over the rest.'

Max shook his head. 'I never wanted that,' he said. 'Family, it just ties you down. It's better to be free of all of that.'

Maria nodded slowly. 'I used to think that way,' she said, 'but it can get lonely sometimes. You never wanted someone special in your life, Max? Someone who thought you were the most important thing in the world?' Max grinned at her. 'He thinks that way about you, does he? I'm not surprised. You're quite a catch for a humble copper.'

Maria laughed. 'I'll keep reminding him of that. But did you never want that for yourself?'

Max narrowed his eyes and contemplated the question. 'Just what is it you want from me?' he asked Maria. 'I mean, this is very nice and I'm quite happy to waltz around the question all the day, but I'm curious just the same.'

'What do you think I've come for?'

'The same thing all of them ask for. Tell me about Jake, they say. What did Jake do? What did Jake say? And I understand the fascination, I really do. My whole life has been spent looking at what Jake has done with his and trying to get close, even within touching distance, of half that he's achieved.'

'But sometimes you'd like to be valued for yourself,' Maria stated. 'I think that's natural, Max. Everyone would want that.'

Max scratched his head, then got up and began to pace around the room. From the corner Mike observed, content to let things take their course for a while. He watched Maria shifting into her professional role, the change in her almost physical as she moved back mentally into her working clothes, and she said nothing as Max paced the room, gathering his thoughts. It seemed like a long time before he sat down and began to talk again.

'Has he got rid of that father of his yet?'

'I wouldn't know,' Maria lied smoothly. Confirmation of Alastair's death had not yet hit the news. 'Do you think he might?'

'Oh, yes,' Max told her. 'Why else would he take Alastair away?'

'It's your story, you tell me.'

'No, if Jake's got him, then it's a dead story now. It doesn't matter any more.'

'What does matter?' Maria asked him. 'What would matter now?'

Max thought about it for a while, then said, 'Perfection. Getting things the best they possibly could be. Nothing else was good enough for Jake. Pushing the envelope, was how he put it. Always pushing the envelope.'

He glanced over at Mike, then, turning his attention back to Maria, said, 'Jake, now, he never went for that family thing. He'd seen his own lot, where that got them. Jake wanted more than that. He wanted a place of his own, away from the back streets, somewhere he could breathe. And a studio. Somewhere bright and airy he could work. He wanted to retire at forty-five and live in luxury the rest of his days. Somewhere warm, with open skies and blue seas. And he wanted to be famous. To be admired for his work. For what he had achieved.'

Maria held her breath. The mention of a house seemed almost too perfect. 'Did he get all of those things?' she asked him. 'We know about the flat in London of course, you told us that, but does that fit with Jake's dreams?'

'Oh, that. That was just convenient. That wasn't what Jake wanted, only somewhere to send post and for people to stay. Jake had his own place and his own life quite apart from that.'

'Did you ever go there? To Jake's other place?'

Max awarded her a pitying look. 'Do you think I'd tell you even if I had?' he asked. 'Honestly, you really think I'm thick or what?'

She was losing it, Maria realized. She'd tried to push him far too fast. In an attempt to salvage things, she asked, 'And you, Max, did you ever dream of a place like that? A place in the sun with blue seas all around?' But Max just laughed at her. 'You think you're oh so clever, don't you, love? But you're not. None of you are. You just go on your blinkered way, hoping for the best, and Jake runs rings around you all.'

He would say nothing after that. Maria tried once more to draw him out but he just sat in silence, listening to her with a slight half-smile hovering around his mouth. Maria wanted to claw it off his face, to rant and scream and demand that he helped them, but she knew that it would do no good. Finally she stood up and Mike did the same. 'We're going now,' she said. 'Goodbye, Max.'

She gave him a moment when she reached the door, time to change his mind, but Max didn't so much as move.

When they got out to Mike's car she sat in the front seat and cried, tears of anger and of pain for Essie.

'Do you think he really knows?' Mike asked her when she'd calmed a little.

Maria shook her head. 'We were stupid even to imagine he would,' she said. 'Think about it, Mike. If you wanted to keep something hidden, would you tell a blabbermouth like Max? Someone who worshipped your shadow? No, he'd know Max would only want to boast about it — Jake having got his dream. Max Harriman doesn't know where Jake is. He doesn't know a damn thing.'

* * *

Back at Honiton, Mike found his desk piled high with house agents' details and back issues of property pages covering the relevant years. Two officers were already working their way through the stack, marking with highlighter anything that looked as though it matched their brief.

Most of the notices in the London flat were for the south coast, in the main not much further west than Dorset and to the east as far as Kent. There were a few for the Yorkshire coast and Moors, but as Jake's most recent activity was all more southerly-based, they were giving priority to these and leaving the northern cottages aside.

Peterson was not in sight. Mike knew that he had to come clean about their trip to see Max. Maria was a civilian, personally involved, and the whole trip an impulse that had come to nothing. Peterson was not likely to be impressed.

But the Chief Superintendent had other things on his mind. 'I've got the pathology reports on Alastair,' he said. 'It's definitely him, dental records are a match. He died of the gunshot wounds, no sign of drugs or other injury. And he'd eaten a meal three or four hours before he died. Last meal for the condemned man? Or was Jake planning on keeping him alive and then changed his mind?'

Mike shrugged, not really caring either way any more. 'We're not likely to find out,' he said, 'unless we find Jake.'

They went back into the incident room. Several dozen people, sorting information, inputting data, generating more and more facts and figures and suppositions. Maria was sitting at Mike's desk, leafing through the London faxes once again. 'He's got to be close to the sea,' she said. 'Just from the way Alastair was found.'

'Or he might easily have taken the body and dumped it over a cliff. We've got the coastguard trying to estimate a point of entry, looking at the currents and tides,' Mike commented.

'But about a third of the house details are for coastal properties. Lots of them have "ocean view" or "sea view" or "clifftop location" as part of their selling blurb.'

'But it leaves about two-thirds of them that did not,' Peterson pointed out. 'Look, I admit it would be nice to narrow it down, but right now I'm not sure we can risk doing that.'

Maria was not going to be put off. 'Max talked about Jake loving the ocean,' she said. 'About his dreams of an open view and a clear sky.'

'He was talking about a retirement place,' Mike argued. 'Somewhere warm, he said.'

'There's something we haven't taken account of yet,' Peterson noted.

'What's that?'

'A private sale. Jake might have seen the house in the small ads. My daughter bought hers that way. In fact, I'm not even sure they even advertised it. The previous owner just put a board up outside the house with a phone number on it. She spotted it when she was out one day and the whole thing was done without an agent.'

'Well, we can pull in all the small ads that appeared in the local papers,' Mike said. 'Though it just adds to the mountain of stuff to plough through. And we'll just have to hope that Jake wasn't as observant as your daughter.'

* * *

The late afternoon sun turned the sea to fire on the horizon. Mike and Peterson had called a briefing — 'assembling the troops', as Peterson called it — to see what the day had achieved. Maria left them to it, needing to get away from the hothouse atmosphere of the incident room. She drove down to the coast road, in places not much more than a narrow trackway, and finally pulled her car to the side of the road on the top of a grassy cliff.

It was another magnificent day. She loved weather like this, bright days at the beginning of summer, when the land was still green and the dustiness of August seemed a long way off.

She sat on the grass beside her car, gazing far out to sea, the lazy crash of waves sounding below her as she tried to imagine Jake Bowen and where he was. How different was his view from hers? Did he see the same ships far out on the horizon, the same waves, the same sunlight burning on the water?

Peterson had been talking to the coastguard. An aerial survey had been proposed using a police helicopter and the coastguard flight. In the course of the afternoon, he had come round to Maria's way of thinking about Jake. That he must be right on the coast in view of the sea. Somewhere he could have pitched Alastair's body into the ocean without the risk of being overlooked.

'Do you know how many miles of coast that is?' Peterson had asked Maria.

She didn't, and for that matter neither did he. She worried now that she might be wrong; that Peterson would put the time and effort into this and waste it all when he could be looking somewhere else.

But it was no good feeling guilty, Maria told herself.

They had to begin somewhere and, deep down, her instincts told her she was right.

* * *

A few miles along the coast, Jake stepped through the gate with Essie in his arms. She was half awake and crying, confused and frightened by this strange man who, for most of the time, seemed to be part of her bad dreams.

Jake carried the child easily. She weighed little and was still too doped to struggle very much, though she blinked in the sudden light and tried to turn her face away.

It was a wonderful day, Jake thought. The bright blue sky and silver-painted sea below, almost too bright to look at, like a mirror reflecting the sunlight. He laid the child upon the soft grass at the edge of the cliff and looked down at her, fascinated by the way the sunlight was absorbed by the darkness of her skin: the odd lights and colours, and a tonal quality white skin did not have. He turned his head this way and that, an artist assessing his subject, and what treatment he should use to give it life.

Then he bent abruptly, seizing the child by one arm and one small ankle, and lifted her high into the air, swinging her out over the surging water.

Essie was aware enough to scream, her body twisting in his hands as she reached frantically, grabbing at the empty air.

CHAPTER THIRTY

It was close to midnight. The sky an inky blue, flecked with silver stars. Mike stood, gazing out of the window as behind him Maria put the telephone receiver down. She had been talking to Jo in spite of the late hour. Jo never slept anyway these days.

Two hours north, Max Harriman lay dozing on his bed, his thoughts and dreams filled with Jake and the high places he had loved even as a child. His dreams remembered Jake standing at the very edge of a barren granite cliff: grey clouds, grey sea, grey headland beneath Jake's feet; his arms spread wide as though he could lay himself upon the wind and fly.

Macey and Liz sat by his office desk, neither of them inclined to go home, the whisky bottle set between them slowly diminishing as the night passed.

'You ever been married, Macey?' Liz had asked.

'No, never have.'

'You ever wanted to?'

'You offering?'

Liz giggled. 'I don't think I'm right for you,' she said.

* * *

Sitting on the edge of his bed in a darkened room, Charlie Morrow tried to think of ways to sleep without the pills he was holding in his hand. He had just poured water into the glass and tipped out the little white pills when the telephone rang.

'We should talk, Charlie,' Jake Bowen said, and in the background Charlie heard a small child crying.

* * *

Macey stared accusingly at the telephone on his desk when it began to ring. 'Who the hell at this time of night?'

It was Charlie, excited and confused, as close to panic as Macey could imagine he would ever get.

'He's called again, Macey.'

'Then phone the bloody police.' He reached and switched on the speaker phone so Liz could hear.

'I can't. He says he'll kill Essie if I do and I believe him.'

'The kid's already dead, Charlie, we both know that.'

'No. No, she's not. Listen, he had her talk to me. Poor little bugger sobbing for her mum. He says he'll trade, me for the child, and I've got to go along with it. You must see that.'

'Charlie, Charlie, you're not thinking straight. Hold on to yourself. It's a recording he's got. The kid's dead and that's how you'll end up if you chase this.'

'I've got to take that chance.' The sound of Essie's crying had affected him as nothing else could.

'Think, Charlie,' Macey demanded again. 'You're a bloody copper, for fuck's sake. This isn't the way to go.'

He paused, waiting for Charlie's response, sensing that his initial panic was now starting to subside. 'Look, I can be with you in less than an hour. Don't do anything till I get there. Promise me that.'

'I don't know if I can. He said he'd be back in touch and I can't predict what he's going to do.'

'Just hold on. I'll be there.'

Macey put the phone down before Charlie could say another word. He turned to Liz.

'Get hold of Mike Croft, his mobile number's in the book. If you can't reach them that way, call the pub and keep it ringing till someone answers. I'm going to Charlie.'

'Are you legal?' Liz asked him, pointing at the whisky bottle.

'God knows,' Macey told her, then he was gone.

* * *

Charlie Morrow waited in his room staring at the telephone until he could no longer bear the sight of it. He switched on the computer and began to write a note addressed to Macey and to Mike, recording everything he could remember from Jake's telephone call. All that had been said or that he had heard in the background or gained an impression of.

There was a tapping on his bedroom window, French doors opening onto the garden. Charlie opened the door. Jake stood outside.

'Coming, Charlie?' he asked.

'I'll get my coat.'

'Be quick then.'

Jake watched him as he crossed the room and took his raincoat from the wardrobe. Charlie took a second while his hands were out of sight to remove his watch and press the button to set the timer, then he dropped it on the desk as he passed by. Macey would at least know how long he'd been gone. Some kind of lifeline for a drowning man.

* * *

By the time Macey arrived, Liz had done her job and the local police were already there expecting him.

'DI Croft said you might show up,' the sergeant in charge told him. 'You'd better come and look at this, but don't touch anything.'

Macey thought he was well beyond the need to be told that, but he let it pass and followed the officer down the hall.

'He went out through the French windows,' the sergeant told him, 'and someone heard a car engine start up about the time we think he left.'

'Charlie couldn't drive,' Macey said, 'he could barely close his hands to pick up a cup.'

'He could use the keyboard on the computer.'

'Well, yes, he could pick away at it with two fingers if that's what you mean, but that's a lot less control than it would take to drive a car. Jake came for him, that's obvious, isn't it?'

Macey crossed to the computer and read the brief message Charlie had typed on screen. It was full of spelling mistakes and typos and had obviously been done at speed. It recounted what Macey already knew. Jake's phone call, and the crying child and then Charlie's guess that Jake's next contact might be in person and too soon for anyone to help.

'I'll set the timer on my watch,' the message said. 'You can draw some conclusion from how long I have been gone and work out how long it took for him to get here since he called me. I listened as closely as I could and there was no car engine, no sound at all in fact, except I think I heard a clock chiming in the background. The line was clear, no breaking up, and you know what mobiles can be like around here, so he must have called from somewhere the reception was good. I think for certain he must have called from home. I know it isn't much, but anything might help.'

'The watch?' Macey asked, then saw it on the desk. Macey compared it to his own.

'I took his call at ten to midnight,' Macey said, and he looked expectantly at the officer.

'It was twenty past by the time it had been relayed to us. Another ten before we made it here.'

'Which gives a forty-minute window for Jake to get here and take Charlie away.'

He looked at the message on the screen, remembering that he'd watched Charlie type. His hands were becoming more useful all the time but even so it was a slow process. He held his hands above the keyboard and pretended to input the words, Charlie-style, two fingers at a time and having to look to see each letter. It would have taken quite some time, Macey calculated. Just how long?

'The *car,* you say, was heard, it left here around twenty past the hour?'

The sergeant nodded, somewhat reluctantly, Macey thought.

'Looks like you just bloody missed him,' he said.

CHAPTER THIRTY-ONE

6 July

Jake had bound Charlie's wrists with ducting tape and used more tape to wrap around both Charlie and the seat to keep him from moving.

Essie lay in the rear of the car, dressed only in the pink T-shirt she had been wearing for the past two weeks. Her hands and ankles were tied and a piece of tape covered her mouth. Charlie had seen her face as he'd been pushed into the car, frightened brown eyes begging him to help.

'What are you going to do with her?' he asked Jake. 'You said you'd let her go. Gave me your word.'

'And you trusted me. Now that is touching.'

'Yes,' Charlie told him. 'I did.'

Jake drove in silence for a few minutes more, clearing the side road that led from the nursing home and turning back onto the main dual carriageway. At this time of the morning it was all but empty. Charlie waited, not certain what was safe to say. Jake drove another mile before pulling the car to an abrupt halt at the side of the road.

'What are you doing?' Charlie asked him, his mouth suddenly dry.

'Letting her go,' Jake replied. 'Here looks as good a place as any.'

He was out of the car before Charlie could say a word and had lifted the child from the back seat.

'I'll untie her hands and feet,' he told Charlie, 'wouldn't want her to roll into a ditch and not get out.'

'You can't just leave her there. She's only a child.'

'Oh, I thought you wanted me to let her go?'

'Of course I do, but not here. It's a major road.'

'Well, she's more likely to be seen then, isn't she?' Jake said. 'Or I could change my mind?'

Charlie dared say nothing more. At least, he thought, the child was free. He had to hope she'd have the sense to stay off the road.

He could see her in the wing mirror as Jake moved off, sitting by the roadside, the tape still across her mouth and the look of terror in her eyes.

'You see, I always keep my promises,' Jake told him as they drove away.

When Jake next stopped the car Charlie could hear the ocean through the open door. Jake left him for a brief while and returned with a sawn-off shotgun in his hands. He took a knife from his pocket and cut the tape that bound Charlie to the seat, then stood back and let him struggle free.

'This way.'

The gun directed Charlie along a narrow crazy-paved path between borders filled with flowers. The air was cool and sweet. Charlie could just make out a whitewashed house. The door was open and a soft light burned inside.

They entered through the kitchen, a large square room with windows on two sides and another door leading through to a narrow hall. There were stairs going up and other stairs going down through yet another door of painted wood that could have passed for an under stairs cupboard. Charlie had to duck his head to go through, but then the passage ceiling grew to more than normal height as it passed below the stairs. He counted fourteen steps, then another open door. The gun was tight against his back now as Jake reached around and switched on the light. Fluorescent beams blinded Charlie for a moment and he almost fell down the two steps just inside the door. He blinked rapidly, trying to adjust, and Jake prodded him with the gun to move him forward, then closed the door and sat down on the higher of the two steps.

The room was empty but for a mattress on the floor. Through another door, Charlie could glimpse a toilet and wash bowl and he noted that the room was warm. A vent overhead was feeding in heated air from the rooms above.

'Finished looking?' Jake asked him, smiling at Charlie.

'There isn't much to see.'

'Oh, I don't know.' From the pocket of his jacket Jake produced the digital camera he so loved to use and raised it to his eye, the gun resting across his lap but one hand still in contact with the trigger. 'Now strip,' Jake ordered.

* * *

Frank Bennet and his wife were not used to being out so late, but they were going to a family wedding and Frank's shift pattern meant they'd had to start out late in order to get there for the Saturday morning. Em had managed to sleep a little while Frank was out at work, so she drove while Frank dozed in the partly reclined seat beside her.

She didn't like night-driving very much but it did have the advantage, she thought, that there was no one else around and she was so looking forward to her niece's wedding.

Music played quietly on the radio, something soft and classical that Em recognized from an advert on TV. She was in a relaxed mood, paying little attention to the road ahead. When the tiny apparition appeared in its little pink T-shirt her first reaction was to scream and swerve the car onto the grass verge, missing the hedge and ditch by inches.

Frank woke from his doze in equal shock.

'What the hell, woman? What did you do?'

He thought she must have fallen asleep at the wheel and blundered off the road.

'A child, Frank, a little girl. She's on the road.'

* * *

Jake was fascinated by the scars on Charlie's body. He'd made him remove his clothes and even the pressure bandages that wrapped his upper body and his arms until finally Charlie stood naked in the centre of the room.

And Jake had filmed him, recorded every inch of Charlie's frame, like a sculptor admiring his handiwork.

'Did it hurt you, Charlie? Does it hurt you now?' he asked. 'Can you tell me how it feels to let so much of you burn and shrivel. What is it like when people stare at you, wondering what happened to you and if it's catching? Tell me about it. I want to know.'

For a brief time, Charlie put up with this humiliation, fear of the gun keeping him in his place. Then he grew sick of it, decided that Jake was going to kill him anyway and, if he was going to die, then he was going to do it with his clothes on and his dignity intact. He bent, picked up his shirt and began to put it on.

Jake lowered the camera. 'What are you doing, Charlie?'

'Getting dressed. You've had your money's worth, the side-show's closing.'

'I don't think I've finished.'

'Don't you? Well, I have. You've got me here because of that baby and you've freed her now. God willing, she'll be all right. You want to kill me for putting my clothes on, then go right ahead. I'm not playing your stupid games any more.'

Jake smiled at him, a slow grin spreading across his face, then raised the gun level with Charlie's head.

CHAPTER THIRTY-TWO

6 July

By seven on the Saturday morning, Essie was in hospital in Swindon and Maria was with her.

She had spoken to Jo and the Kent police were driving Essie's parents down with a full escort. They should have arrived by mid-morning and Essie's ordeal, everyone hoped, would be coming to an end.

Peterson watched Maria as she sat beside Essie, stroking her hair and talking softly to her. Coming close, he crouched down beside the bed. 'I know it's a lot to ask,' he said, 'but anything she can tell you now that might give us some clue?' Peterson knew all too well that once the parents arrived it would be impossible. They'd just want to get away from it all and it might be weeks before they allowed the police to talk to the child again.

'I'm doing what I can,' Maria reassured him. 'I want to get Charlie back as much or more than anyone. He saved Essie's life, I'm sure of that.'

* * *

Macey was already in his office. Looking at Liz, he wondered if she'd even left since last night. She looked as exhausted as he felt. He was desperately trying to knock the story into shape, ready for the early afternoon edition, and it would be passed to the news agencies, maybe even direct to one or other of the nationals after news of Essie's release and Charlie's trade broke on the breakfast shows.

Peterson had authorized Macey to release the entire story, hoping that it would capture the public imagination and shake something loose.

Liz was deeply upset about it all. She was relieved for Essie and her family, but had been crying for Charlie most of the night and her eyes were red and sore.

At eight fifteen Mike arrived. He'd already spoken to Maria and had something to add to Macey's story.

'Essie told us they were near the sea,' he said. 'We want that released, so we're passing it straight to the media across the board, but Peterson said you were to have the full version now and play it for all it's worth. Jake took her out of the house and onto the clifftop. She remembers him carrying her and thinks it was only a short way, through a garden. He held her over the water and she saw the sea below her, a long way down. He had hold of her only by an arm and a leg and she thought he was going to let her fall. She thought she was going to die.'

'Oh, God,' Liz said.

Macey was silent for a moment. 'I'm assuming you want me to quote that in full,' he said.

* * *

By ten Mike was conducting the morning briefing. A grid-pattern search by helicopter had been assigned, shadowed by those on the ground. The search was concentrating on the miles of coastline, each unit taking a number of properties gleaned from the guides and estate agents' details Jake might have used five years before.

'You're probably looking for a lone male,' Mike reminded them. 'Though we can't rely on that. You have basic descriptions in the written brief, but you must remember that Jake Bowen changes his appearance to suit. The properties on your lists are all well off the main roads, some very isolated, so the slightest sign of trouble and you call for back-up. We want no heroics and no more dead officers.'

He waited, letting his gaze travel around the room and hoping that his words were sinking in.

'Questions?'

There were a few, but everyone was eager just to be getting on.

'Remember' Mike emphasized as the meeting broke up and he was worried by the slightly gung-ho attitude he sensed in the room, 'you call in every location as you get there and the result immediately you've got one. I want to know where each and every officer is at all times. We've got armed units standing by all along the coast road. Don't hesitate to call on them.' He gestured to the stack of strike-proof vests on a nearby table. 'They're to be worn,' he said. 'I know it's hot and I know they impede you, but we've got enough dead to bury without adding to their number.'

He watched the men and women assigned to him file out of the incident room, knowing that this scene was being repeated all along the coast. Road-blocks had been set up. Jake Bowen had to be somewhere close by. They just had to find him.

Please God, he thought, let's finish this today.

* * *

Jake watched as the helicopter flew overhead for the second time that morning, then he walked back, barefoot, through his garden.

He stood in his kitchen waiting for the kettle to boil and watched the mid-morning news on the portable TV. The news was full of him: Essie being found and Charlie Morrow being lost; the mobilization of every available officer up and down the coast; all leave cancelled on his behalf.

He made instant coffee — strong and black, very sweet and scalding hot. He sipped it slowly as he watched the bulletin, then took his coffee with him upstairs to his viewing room.

Charlie Morrow seemed to be asleep. Jake switched the camera angles, examining Charlie as he lay on the single bed. He pulled in to focus on the big man's face, studying the network of scars and patchily growing beard, the rough, stubbled areas between a network of red polished skin.

His breathing slow and even as he slept.

Charlie was not asleep, not deeply. He had dozed a little from time to time, but the dead silence of the soundproofed room was not conducive to his brand of relaxation. Anyway, he found it hard to sleep at all without his pills.

Lying on the narrow bed, sensing that Jake was watching him, Charlie forced himself to keep very still, to pretend a lack of concern he could not feel. He tried not to imagine what Jake had planned for him and concentrated his thoughts on what might lie ahead should he finally get out of here.

He listened to the faint noises carried by the heating pipes, straining his ears for the slightest clue to Jake's movements above his head. He tried to imagine what the day must be like outside. Hot and dry, close enough to the sea to hear the roar of the tide, taste the tang of salt on the air and hear the cry of birds.

Lying there, fooling Jake into thinking he was still asleep, Charlie made up his mind that whatever Jake might have in mind, he wasn't going down easy.

* * *

Peterson and Maria had arrived back at the incident room in Honiton. Calls from the operational units were already coming in, each report being plotted on the maps pinned to the office walls. Mike snatched a moment to greet Maria before being called away and Peterson too was immediately swallowed up in the organized confusion.

Maria perched herself on the edge of one of the desks, suddenly surplus to requirements. The effects of the last days were beginning to catch up on her in full measure.

She wanted to crawl away somewhere and get some sleep. She wanted news to come in saying that Charlie had been found, Jake arrested and all of this was over and done with.

Staring at the red and blue pins scattered over the maps, she tried to second-guess the pattern of the search, to imagine Jake's reaction as he felt the net closing in on him. Maria wondered what would happen if they reached the end of this intensive search, the close of this incredibly expensive day, and Jake had not been found.

* * *

Jake had spent a little time watching Charlie on the CCTV screens. He was not the most cooperative guest he'd ever had. He refused to beg, refused to panic, even declined to shout, and for the last two hours had remained on the mattress fast asleep.

Jake began to gather his things together: his passport in the name of John Phillips, sales rep, and a spare in another name; his credit cards and, again, a couple of others he had acquired along the way. It always amazed him how helpful and un-nosy the banks could be, provided you kept money flowing through their accounts.

He also packed a bag and stowed it ready in the boot of his car. It left one question: what to do with Charlie Morrow?

* * *

In Dorchester, Macey watched the latest bulletin on a portable television someone had brought into the office. He was booked for an interview later on that day, together with

Peterson and Essie's mum. It was likely to be an emotional affair. And Macey's exclusive coverage of the story had been sold in reworked forms to no less than three of the national dailies and one of the major Sunday broadsheets. Macey had hit pay-dirt.

Liz sat down beside him, staring at the screen.

'You should be pleased,' she said. 'You could cut any deal you wanted right now. Any story you wanted to write.'

'Not any deal,' Macey said slowly. 'And not any story. The only one I want to write just now, love, would say that Charlie's safe and well.'

Liz turned to stare at him, for a moment not certain whether to believe him or not.

'You really mean that, don't you?'

'Yes,' he said. 'I really do.'

CHAPTER THIRTY-THREE

By lunchtime, Charlie had grown tired of his own silence. He lay on his back on the single bed and recited poetry, dredging from his memory the fragments of verse inflicted on him from primary school on.

He had begun, he estimated, about half an hour before, with nursery rhymes, and amazed himself with just how many he could remember. Exhausting those, he'd graduated to passages of Shakespeare he'd been forced to learn, line by line, comma by comma, in his early years at grammar school.

'Tomorrow and tomorrow and tomorrow . . . You hear me, Jake? Quite an actor I could have been, given half the chance. Fancied myself as Hamlet, but I didn't fit the tights. You listening to me, Jake? I'll bet you are.' He paused a moment, waited for a response. 'You going to get your arse down here and talk to me, or what? You're a lousy host, you know that? You don't come down here, Jake, it won't be just the poetry. I might be forced to sing.'

* * *

Mike was at the road-block on the Dorchester road when Macey finally caught up with him.

'Rumour is you've had a couple of false alarms?'

'I won't ask where the rumour came from. There's been nothing concrete, Macey.'

'Mind if I tag along when you leave here.'

'You'd follow me if I said no.'

'Damn right I would. I'm going nuts back there.' He hesitated for a moment before asking, 'You think he's dead?'

'I don't know, Macey. Depends what Jake had in mind.'

'I keep thinking, you know, if I'd got there sooner—'

'There's nothing you could have done.'

'I'm not certain I believe that.'

'What you believe, Macey, quite frankly doesn't matter. We got Essie back and we'll find Charlie Morrow. Jake's been calling the shots long enough.'

Macey watched him walk back to his car, shoulders set square against argument. 'You really believe that, do you, Inspector Croft?' he asked. 'Or doesn't what you think matter any more either?'

* * *

By one p.m. Jake had decided it was time to leave. He listened in to Charlie's monologue one last time — the microphones he'd rigged up fed the sound through to the viewing room.

Charlie was singing a very unmusical rendition of something from Gilbert and Sullivan. He seemed to know only about half the words, making up the rest as he went along. Jake listened for a short while, amused at Charlie's version of the sorrow of a policeman's lot, wondering how long Charlie's change of mood would last and slightly regretful that he would not be hanging around long enough to find out. He switched off the basement sound and left his prisoner totally alone. The appeal of killing Charlie was just not there if there wasn't time to set it up properly and film the action. In Jake's philosophy, if you couldn't do things right, they were often better left undone. He put the rest of his essential gear into the car and left the house, he thought, for ever.

CHAPTER THIRTY-FOUR

Jake got all of half a mile, driving down the single-track lane towards the main road, before being met by a police car on its way up. He was forced to back up the way he'd come, the police car following closely and finally parking across the exit from Jake's yard.

'Can I help you, officers,' Jake asked. 'I hope it won't take long. I was about to go out.'

'Anything special, sir? Maybe you could phone if you're going to be late for an appointment?'

'No, nothing special.'

'Well, then, if we could just step inside?'

Jake gave in as gracefully as he could, relieved he'd stowed his luggage in the boot and not on the back seat of his car. One officer followed him inside. Jake glanced back, curious as to what the other might be doing. He was speaking into his pocket phone, consulting a map and a list which he'd taken from the car.

* * *

The call came in to Honiton that a double-crewed unit had another possible. The third so far.

'Lone male, fits the general description, sir; and he seems a bit edgy.'

'Who wouldn't be?' Peterson questioned. 'OK, give me the location and I'll put the nearest back-up on standby.'

Peterson listened, matching the details to the grid reference. The property was right slap-bang on the coast. He signed off, prepared to call the other units in.

* * *

'What's this all about?' Jake asked the officer who'd followed him inside.

'Have you seen the news today?'

'About the policeman and the little girl? Yes. Yes, I have.'

The other officer joined them now, moving to the other side of the small kitchen as though wanting to keep Jake in full view. Jake realized that he was being far too stiff, that they were not at ease with him. He tried to compensate.

'Can I offer you some tea?'

'That would be nice, but what we'd really like to do, if it's not too much bother is to check your basement.'

Jake filled the kettle from the kitchen tap, his back to both the men. It was on the tip of his tongue to ask them where their warrant was. Instead he lied as smoothly as he could. 'I'm sorry, officer, but I don't have a basement here.'

He plugged the kettle into the socket and began to turn, then saw that what he'd taken for a list in the policeman's hand were house agents' details — a photocopy of the write-up he'd seen when first he'd come looking at the house.

'It says here, sir, that this house has a full-sized basement. Have you had it sealed or filled in?'

The lunchtime washing up was still stacked on the draining board, including the sharp knife Jake had used. It was more impulse than thought that made him snatch it and he lunged forward, then slashed across the body of the nearest man, the blade catching the man's sleeve and deflecting upward, opening his cheek. Then he was out of the kitchen door and into the narrow hall.

* * *

Mike took Peterson's call just after leaving the road-block.

'It could be nothing, Mike. We've had two false ones already and brought them in, but it's not going to amount to much.'

Mike took the reference and checked it against his own map. He was about five miles away. 'On my way,' he said.

He ran to his car, shouting at Macey to join him.

'It might be nothing,' he said, 'but it's the best fit we've had so far.'

He'd slammed into gear and taken off before Macey had time to fasten his seatbelt.

'You think this is it?' Macey asked him. 'God Almighty, do you always drive like this?'

Mike didn't trouble to answer, too intent on taking a thirty-mile bend at twice that speed. Macey too fell silent, thinking about Charlie Morrow and visualizing his next by-line.

* * *

It took Jake only seconds to descend the basement steps and unlock the cellar door. The gun he'd used earlier had been propped beside it, left loaded but broken. Jake snapped it closed and then he was inside, with Charlie at gunpoint, and heading back towards the stairs.

The uninjured officer met him three steps from the top, and then he saw the gun.

'Back off,' Jake ordered him. 'I can kill this one and still have another barrel left for you.'

They moved slowly to the top of the steps, the gun pressed close against Charlie's spine. The other officer, his hands raised, was trying to talk Jake down.

'This is no good, sir. Lower the weapon. I've called for reinforcements.'

'And they've a bloody long way to come, haven't they, officer?'

They were going to die, Charlie thought, and Jake was going to get away again.

The idea that Jake should escape free and clear suddenly enraged Charlie Morrow. That he could go on killing and maiming and destroying people's lives. He had to take a chance.

They were almost at the kitchen door now, the hallway cramped and overfull with the three of them. One police officer had backed up and gone through the kitchen door when Charlie made his move. He dropped and turned, came up with his hands reaching for the gun, deflecting the shot at the moment Jake fired. The two men fell, Charlie on top of Jake, struggling for control, but the younger man was stronger and he still had possession of the gun. He hit out with the rifle stock, catching Charlie's shoulder a glancing blow, and forcing him aside. Jake rolled forward, twisting his body as Charlie struggled once more to gain control. Then Jake had pinned him down, was sitting astride his legs with the gun raised and pointing straight between Charlie's eyes. Charlie thrust upward with both hands, praying to deflect the shot before he fired, but the expected explosion of sound and pain never arrived.

A look of shock spread across Jake's face and he fell forward, the knife he had used to slash the policeman's face wedged deeply in his back.

CHAPTER THIRTY-FIVE

It seemed a long time before anyone arrived and when they did it was all at once. Patrol cars screaming down the lane, a helicopter hovering above them. Armed police emerging from ploughed fields, sprung from some lunatic effect-artist's dream.

Charlie had led the other officer outside, after helping him to get his injured colleague from the house and fetching the first aid kit from the police car. They sat in the garden, Charlie doing his best to clean the face wound and stop the bleeding.

'It's not as bad as it looks,' he said hopefully. 'A bit of a scar, maybe, but that's all.'

He saw the other man studying his face and then pulling his gaze away, embarrassed. 'I'll be all right,' he said. A macho man, trying not to cry.

The sun was hot on their backs but the young man who had killed Jake Bowen shivered as though freezing cold.

'What's your name?' Charlie asked him.

'George, George Mitchell. What will happen next?'

He was still a child, Charlie thought, and, now it was all over, very scared.

'You did what you had to do,' Charlie told him. 'No one can tell you anything else, believe that.'

'I feel sick, and look at me, I'm shaking like a bloody leaf.'

'You and me both,' Charlie said. 'You been in the force long?'

George Mitchell managed a weak half-smile. 'Six months out of my probationary year,' he said. 'God, what a start.'

Charlie laughed. Yeah, what a start, he thought, and it was far from over yet. There'd be the inquiry, the immediate suspension from duty, the debriefing and the counselling, and George's slow realization that he had killed a man.

'We'll get through it,' Charlie told him. 'Don't you worry, we'll get through.'

The first of the police cars arrived then, their sirens screaming through the still air. There was an ambulance, with its flashing blue light, and people everywhere, shouting instructions and running across Jake's close-clipped lawn. They broke around Charlie and the others like a flood. The injured officer was led away. Someone was trying to organize the chaos of parked and now wedged cars, and the armed officers were being stood down and lounging in the garden, waiting for someone to tell them what to do.

A senior officer came and took George Mitchell aside, quietly encouraging him to tell his story, easing him back into a system that had its own rules and its own closed door.

Charlie didn't feel a part of that any more. He ignored their questions and their anxious looks, and the ambulance man who said he was in shock and needed medical attention. It was all suddenly so alien to Charlie Morrow. Now Jake was dead, he didn't feel a part of anything.

He was standing on the cliff, looking out to sea, when Mike Croft arrived. He had Macey with him and Charlie took a moment to wonder how Macey had wangled that.

'Charlie! You OK?'

'Yeah, I'm fine. Just fine.'

As he watched, a cormorant skimmed lazily above the ocean, the same one that Jake had watched so many times. It was, Charlie thought, an inspiring sight, something unchanged for generations and still going on.

'You ever thought about what it would be like to stand here with the wind in your face and the sun on your back and then just let it go? Step over the line?'

'Charlie?' Macey's voice was scared and Charlie felt a hand gripping his arm.

'It's all right, Macey, I'm not going to jump.'

He turned away, let Macey lead him back from the edge.

'Too earthbound, Macey,' Charlie said. 'I never learned to fly.'

AFTERWORD

Three weeks to the day after Jake Bowen's death Julia's body was finally released to her parents, and that same morning Alastair Bowen was accepted back by the community of St Bartolph's Church. He was to be cremated that afternoon, but Mike had decided not to remain for that.

He had attended the brief funeral service as the police representative, selected because he had most contact with the man during those last few days.

There were few people there, the media being kept outside and only a handful of folk wanting to be openly acknowledged as Alastair's friends sitting with him in the church. Alastair had left instructions in his will. No flowers and no hymns, just a few words spoken by a cleric who had never known him and whose eulogy could have been for anyone.

It was a sad end, Mike thought, and he was glad when it was over and he could slip away.

Outside, the press was there in force, but Mike was not the main focus of their interest. That was reserved for those who had known Alastair in life and were less able to brush the questions aside with official words. Mike was soon back in his car and ready to go.

He sat back in the driver's seat and reached for his mobile phone. Maria's number was first in the memory.

'It's all finished then?' she asked him.

Alastair's funeral, yes, but there was so much yet that wasn't over. There'd be the inquest, and the internal inquiries into what could have been managed better and what lessons had been learned. And then there was Essie. She was healing well, the memories hazed by the sedative Jake had given her, but Mike knew it was likely to be months before Jo would so much as speak to him again. She was depressed and paranoid, unable to let either of her children out of her sight. The nightmares were a torture when she slept and the waking memory pervaded every conscious hour. Jake Bowen had left a terrible legacy.

'Are you still there?' Maria asked him, he had been silent for so long.

'Yes, I'm still here. I was thinking, that's all.'

'There's a lot to think about.'

'Can I see you tonight? There's something I want to ask and I can't say it over the phone.'

She sounded surprised. 'Pick me up, seven thirty. We'll go and eat somewhere.'

They finalized arrangements and Mike switched off his phone, smiling to himself. In his pocket was a ring, an emerald, because Maria liked them, and as he started the car to drive home Mike was hoping she would say yes.

THE END

MIKE CROFT SERIES

Book 1: The Greenway
Book 2: The Secrets
Book 3: Their Final Moments

Thank you for reading this book. If you enjoyed it please leave feedback on Amazon, and if there is anything we missed or you have a question about then please get in touch. The author and publishing team appreciate your feedback and time reading this book.

Please join our mailing list for free kindle crime thriller, detective, mystery, and romance books and new releases.
http://www.joffebooks.com/contact/

Our email is office@joffebooks.com

http://joffebooks.com

We hate typos but sometimes they slip through. Please send any errors you find to corrections@joffebooks.com We'll get them fixed ASAP. We're very grateful to eagle-eyed readers who take the time to contact us.

Printed in Great
Britain
by Amazon

32122859R00248